Caro Fraser was educated in Glasgow and the Isle of Man, before attending Watford School of Art and London University, King's College, where she studied law. She was called to the Bar of Middle Temple in 1979. After leaving Art School, Caro Fraser worked for three years as an advertising copywriter. She then studied law, and read for the Bar, after which she spent six months in pupillage. Before turning to writing, Caro Fraser worked as a shipping lawyer. She is married to a solicitor and has four children.

The Pupil

CARO FRASER

PHŒNIX

A PHOENIX PAPERBACK

First published in Great Britain by Orion in 1993
This paperback edition published in 1994 by Phoenix,
a division of Orion Books Ltd,
Orion House, 5 Upper St Martin's Lane,
London WC2H 9EA

Reissued 1997

Typeset by Deltatype Limited, Ellesmere Port, Cheshire

Printed in England by Clays Ltd, St Ives plc

For Michael Fitzgerald

Chapter one

Sir Basil Bunting, QC, was the head of chambers at 5 Caper Court, London, one of the most prestigious and successful sets of private and commercial litigation chambers in London. He was an elegant old man, with a serene countenance and a dignified manner. His white hair was crisp and thick, brushed well back from his high forehead; his shoes were well polished, his suits immaculately cut; his fountain pen, its old gold beautifully faded with the use of years, was always full of ink; his pocket handkerchief, thrust with careless arrogance into his breast pocket, was thick and white and large; his eye, as it rested with satisfaction upon the things in his life, was calm and majestic. To shake Sir Basil's hand, its skin silkily translucent with age, was a dry and pleasant affair – but brisk, very brisk.

For Sir Basil, QC, was a great man. The very sight of him inspired confidence in his clients, those powerful businessmen and multinational corporations whose own reputations and substance echoed Sir Basil's respectable worth. When Sir Basil rose to address a court on behalf of those clients, the calm assurance of his manner and grave modulation of his voice encouraged everyone, including the judge, to believe that truth and justice were on his side. The fees he commanded were legendary.

Part of Sir Basil's greatness lay in the fact that he seemed a remote, solitary figure. Not reclusive by any means – quite the opposite; a debonair and sparkling conversationalist at cocktail and dinner parties, a popular speaker with a fund of fresh legal anecdote, much in demand at the Annual Convention of the Shipping Bar and at Arbitrators' dinners. But he was unmarried and seemed, therefore, to the outside world to be a man without a personal life.

He had been born shortly after the First World War, the eldest of three children. Law had been his calling from a very early age, as, indeed, his father had intended it should be; for Basil was destined, in his father's ambitions at least, to succeed him as head of chambers at 5 Caper Court. There had been a brief flirtation with an army career, but ill-health had put paid to this, and he had reluctantly laid down his arms and resumed his practice at the Bar shortly before the outbreak of the Second World War. This proved to be a fortunate occurrence, from Basil's point of view, for while the war carried off most of Basil's contemporaries at the Bar to fight for King and Country, Basil remained snugly ensconced in the Temple, performing a little fire-watching from time to time, with the field clear for him to establish a practice which put him far ahead of those contemporaries when they returned from active service.

And so, his reputation already golden before he had reached his thirtieth birthday, the path to the top had seemed open and without obstacle. The dignified contemporaries of his father were already tottering into dotage and disuse – those, that is, who had not taken their seat upon the Bench to live out a useful old age in the years of their declining faculties – and when Basil's father, Sir Hector 'Bunny' Bunting, announced his retirement, the vote of chambers had gone unanimously in favour of adopting Basil as their head at the tender age of forty-four.

But, despite so much rapid success at so young an age, Basil had not found happiness beyond the long and absorbing hours spent in chambers. Perhaps the fact that he had not served during the war lent a strangeness to his contact with other men of his age, for he was aloof and uneasy in their company. He had grown accustomed to the somewhat ponderous and proper manners of the assortment of relics and oddballs that had remained at the Bar during the war years, and had himself assumed an arrogant and unsettled air that rendered him unattractive to men and women alike. As a young man, he was lonely and unsought, and spent most of his time pursuing his flourishing practice and nurturing the talents of new tenants in chambers.

Among his family, however, Basil was cherished and respected. Many of his happiest days were spent with his two sisters and their children, and if he harboured any regret concerning his single condition, it was that he had no son to succeed him at 5 Caper Court. He had, however, a nephew, Edward, the son of his sister, Cora, and her husband, Frederick Choke, and on him Sir Basil's hopes were pinned.

Frederick Choke was a wealthy businessman whose success had enabled him, at a relatively early age, to retire to the countryside of Surrey and to the peace and seclusion of sixty thousand acres of farmland, whose management absorbed and delighted him as business never had. His wife, Cora, ran her social life with an industry and vigour that consumed all her energies and resources, and no one paid great heed to Edward, their son and heir, until, emerging at the end of a public school career of startling mediocrity, he presented them with the problem of his future. What Edward Should Do became a family topic, debated by parents, aunts, uncles and godparents regularly at mealtimes. It was not long, however, until it occurred to Frederick Choke that his brother-in-law, Basil, undoubtedly owed him a debt of gratitude. It had, after all, been Frederick who secured for Basil that opportune appointment as head of the Government Board of Enquiry into the Thanet Nuclear Disaster, whereby Basil had earned his knighthood. Sir Basil should find a place for Edward at 5 Caper Court.

Sir Basil had accepted the suggestion with alacrity. His dynastic sense was fired by the notion that, although he had no son, his own nephew might one day don the mantle of responsibility at 5 Caper Court. Cora Choke was both invigorated and relieved by the prospect of her son adopting a sufficiently noteworthy profession to enable her to brag about it at bridge, and Frederick regarded the matter as entirely settled as soon as the idea first entered his head. There was, of course, the problem of whether or not Edward would take kindly to the idea, but the bucolic Edward seemed both surprised and grateful that anyone should take the trouble to think of him, and acceded graciously. He had heard chaps vaguely talking about going to the Bar, and as it seemed to be one of those places where one might reasonably go, he didn't mind if he went.

And so Edward secured a place, on the strength of his A-levels in history, economics and English (these had struck his careers master, who regarded Edward as 'difficult to place', as a good, broad career base) at Cambridge, where he did not distinguish himself in any way, and emerged with a dubious lower second in law at the end of three years. The first steps on the road to Caper Court had been taken.

So it was that, at the end of the long vacation in the year in which Edward had taken his final Bar examinations (passing them at the second attempt), he was about to take up his pupillage, that arduous, year-long apprenticeship of research-ing and book-carrying, under the tutelary authority of Jeremy Vine, one of the fast-ascending stars in the legal galaxy.

In the fortnight before Edward's arrival, Sir Basil was sitting in his room in chambers contemplating a variety of letters spread out before him on the polished surface of his desk. After consideration, he drew several into a pile and placed them dismissively on one side of the desk. The remaining three he arranged in a row before him, cleared his throat lightly, and fell to their re-perusal. As he read, a gentle knock sounded at his door and a tall, gaunt man of forty or so, dark and slender to the point of painful thinness, came in.

'Michael,' said Sir Basil, casting a cold but courteous glance over the top of his spectacles, 'thank you for sparing these few minutes. How is your case before the Lord Chancellor coming along?'

'Slowly,' replied the thin man with a smile, settling himself in one of the various handsome chairs that stood around Sir Basil's desk, vacant reminders of the important persons who generally sat there in conference. Michael Gibbon was a quiet, thoughtful man with a mild sense of humour; as a lawyer, he was painstaking and exacting. He was not altogether fond of his head of chambers, but tried to treat him with respect and cordiality. For his own part, Sir Basil found Michael's abstracted manner and slightly ill-kempt appearance pro-foundly irritating. However, since Michael achieved regular, quiet success in his practice, Sir Basil treated him with forbearance and only occasional impatience.

Sir Basil sat back in his chair.

'Now,' he said, 'we must discuss the tiresome matter of the pupil quota. Quite why the Bar Council thinks it necessary to tell us how many pupils we are to take in a year, I cannot think. Still, there it is. Apart from my nephew, Edward, whom you know, we must select another. I suppose they have their uses, fetching and carrying, that sort of thing.'

'They do also serve a function eventually – as members of chambers, I mean,' said Michael, the faintest of smiles lighting his face.

'Naturally,' replied Sir Basil testily. 'But we do not take more than one tenant every two or three years, and it is my hope that Edward will be joining us at the end of his pupillage. Any other young man that we take will have to look for a place elsewhere, once his year as a pupil is up. His value to us is necessarily limited. As he is to be your pupil, whoever he may be, you may feel it something of a waste of your time. Were it up to me, we should take on no more pupils than we can usefully employ.'

'I imagine I'll find a pupil rather an asset,' said Michael. 'And might it not be better to take the view that he stands at least as good a chance as Edward of getting a tenancy here? After all, accusations of nepotism, that sort of thing . . . ?'

Michael knew that he was treading on thin ice with this last remark, but somehow he could not resist needling his head of chambers. On this occasion, Sir Basil had to bite back a reproving remark to the effect that the choice of the next tenant lay with him. It was, after all, technically a matter which concerned everyone in chambers.

'Let us not concern ourselves with that at this stage.' He drew the three letters towards him. 'Now, of the six that you have interviewed, only the letters of three strike me as being in any way suitable. I feel we should choose from among these – Cross, Letchworth and Peters.'

'What about Mr Ramisamola? I thought him most promising.'

Sir Basil sighed. Michael seemed determined to make this a

trying afternoon. 'I hardly think,' he said, 'that chambers is quite ready for a coloured – ah – element. Do you?'

Michael said he supposed not. Still, one didn't want to appear racially prejudiced, even if one was, he observed, by now thoroughly enjoying himself.

'No one beyond these four walls is likely to hear of our decision in that regard,' replied Sir Basil waspishly, realising too late that this made him sound both bigoted and under-hand. 'I have not included Mr Ramisamola, in any event, because his background is not quite suitable.'

'Well,' said Michael, 'of those three you mentioned, I rather liked Cross and Peters. Letchworth was a bit stodgy, as I recall. Cross is the one with the scholarship, I think – maybe it would be rather a waste of his year if he's not likely to get a tenancy here.'

'A year spent at 5 Caper Court could hardly be called a waste of any young man's time. Don't you think?' Sir Basil's eyebrows rose a shade.

'No, but – ' Michael began, sensing the contradiction.

'Cross seems to be an exceptional scholar – a first from Bristol, I see; Pembury Prize for Jurisprudence; Jeffers Memorial Scholarship.'

'I liked him,' observed Michael. 'I suspect there's not much money at home, hence all the scholarships. It's a difficult year to get through, without support.'

'What about Peters?' Sir Basil scanned the letters again and glanced up.

'Oh, very able. On the whole, I think I preferred Cross.'

'Well, as he is to be your pupil, your preference is what counts. Perhaps you could see to answering all these?' He swept the letters towards Michael. 'Now,' he said, glancing at his wristwatch, 'I think it may be time for a little sherry.'

Michael would far rather have been on his way to El Vino's, but it was one of the penalties of a late afternoon conference with the old man that one had to partake of his sherry. Not so much the sherry that anyone minded, but the business of making friendly conversation with Sir Basil sometimes seemed a bit of a strain.

It was with a light heart and a sense of relief, therefore, that

Michael clattered downstairs at six o'clock, just in time to catch one of the typists before she left.

'Joyce, would you mind . . . ? Just a very short letter. I want to get it out tonight, if I can.' Joyce, with one sleeve of her coat already pulled on, gave a wry smile, took her coat off, and switched on her typewriter.

'Seeing as it's you,' she said, and sat poised over the keyboard, waiting for Michael to start.

'To Anthony Cross, 24 Croft Road, East Dulwich. Dear Mr Cross, I am pleased to inform you that, after careful considera-tion, we have decided to accept your application for pupillage at 5 Caper Court. Perhaps you would be kind enough to telephone me at chambers to discuss a suitable date for you to start, although I would hope that next Monday would not be too early. I look forward to hearing from you, et cetera.'

'New blood, eh, Mr Gibbon?' Joyce rattled out the envelope and handed the letter to Michael.

'New blood, indeed, Joyce. I hope you will be kind to him as only you and Violet know how.' Joyce laughed with all the conceit and vigour of the worldly-wise twenty-four-year-old.

'Long as he's not too cocky, we'll be just lovely to him.' She pulled on her coat. 'Just like we are to you.'

'Ha,' said Michael, fiddling with the franking machine. 'Goodnight, Joyce.'

At six-fifteen, Michael stepped out into the lovely late summer air and headed through Caper Court and up King's Bench Walk towards El Vino's. He was looking forward to having a pupil; it would take some of the weight off his shoulders, even if it did mean explaining everything as they went along and checking all his work. It might be amusing, too. Michael thought, with a faint conceit, that he would make rather a good sort of pupilmaster. As for Sir Basil's nephew, God help him with Jeremy Vine. A most unattractive prospect, being the pupil of one of the Bar's most arrogant personalities. Small chance of the boy learning anything. But the evening and life generally were far too good to worry about Edward Choke.

Coming through the back door of El Vino's from Clifford Court, Michael found it already thronged, the air thick with cigar and cigarette smoke. In those days, Fleet Street was still alive with newspapers, and the clientele was a rumbustious mixture of journalist and lawyer. David Liphook and William Cooper, the youngest of the nine members of chambers at 5 Caper Court, were at a small table in the far corner, halfway through their first bottle, David's face slightly flushed and his thick hair a trifle disordered.

'. . . the most incredibly tight dress,' he was saying, while William listened, wolfing down the remains of the basket of table water biscuits. 'Hullo, Michael!' David acknowledged Michael's arrival briefly, then carried on. 'But by the time I'd gone to order a cab and got back to the table, she'd gone off with that moron Swales. So that was a promising night of romance nipped in the bud.' William made a sympathetic noise through his biscuits, then swallowed.

'Michael, you made it. We thought you might never wrest yourself away from Sir Basil's sherry clutches. 'Scuse me,' to a passing barmaid, 'can we have another glass here?'

'And another bottle,' added David. 'I was just telling Will about this most fantastic girl I met at Annabel's. God, she was gorgeous.'

'The one that got away, eh?' said Michael, winking at William. David Liphook, a diminutive, stocky man, was a legendary womaniser, lusting after most of the skirt in the Temple, and famous for his indiscriminate worship of the fairer sex. He was especially renowned for his astonishing number of failures. Just when the most fabulous creature in the world seemed to be about to fall prey to his ruthless charm, fate or some other fellow would rob him of her. But even throughout his regular accounts of these near-misses, he remained bright-eyed with optimism, patiently scanning the crowd in every bar and at every party for The Face, the one with whom it would all end and with whom he would find eternal joy and peace. William Cooper, a patient, faded young man with pale, long features and a yearning eye, had been listening to David's outpourings with apparent sympathy and interest. Now he gave a deep sigh and leaned back in his chair.

'Let's have some smoked salmon sandwiches,' he said. As

he was ordering them, David quizzed Michael about his session with Sir Basil.

'Oh, we were discussing who I'm to have as my pupil. Amazing, really – we must have had over forty applications.'

'We're such a bloody good set, that's why,' said David, taking a satisfied slug of his wine. The fresh bottle came and he filled the glasses up almost to their brims. David believed neither in modesty nor moderation. Michael lowered his face and sipped from the overfull glass without lifting it from the table.

'It was a bit strange, though,' he continued, 'making the choice in that arbitrary way. I can't say I really cared, mind you. The three we'd narrowed it down to were all perfectly adequate, in their way.'

'It's a somewhat random way of determining someone's fate, I suppose,' said William, casting his poet's gaze mournfully towards the plate of smoked salmon sandwiches that was weaving its way towards them, balanced in the middle of the arm of the waitress, who was also expertly wielding two bottles and a number of glasses.

'Well, any choice is random, come to that,' said David.

'Renshaw only chose me because I was the only applicant who'd been to the same college at Oxford as he had,' said Michael, squeezing a wedge of lemon over the interior of a sandwich. 'I picked this chap – Cross, his name is – because he seems extremely bright. Anyway,' he added with a sigh, 'it doesn't really matter in the end, because Basil has apparently decided that his nephew is to be our next tenant.'

'Bloody cheek,' said David mildly. 'It's not up to him – it's up to the whole of chambers. And on point of principle, I certainly wouldn't pick any nephew of Sir Basil Bunting's. Mind you,' he added, chewing on a sandwich, 'he's a nice bloke, Edward Choke. I've met him a couple of times.'

'As for it being a chambers decision,' said Michael, 'you'll discover that Sir Basil's wishes count for a good deal. Look at that business over the coffee-makers.'

'I still think chambers should pay for them,' muttered David.

'It all comes to the same thing,' said William, 'except that those who didn't *want* a coffee machine in their room – '

'Yes, well, without breaking open that particular debate again,' interrupted Michael, 'the point I was trying to make is that, as you have yet to discover, when it comes to a major question of chambers policy or make-up, the old man is very influential when it comes to the final decision. Anyway, everyone always agrees on these things in the end.'

David looked darkly at his wine.

'I have to go,' said Michael, draining his glass and standing up to leave. 'See you tomorrow. Off for a spot of serious night-clubbing, David?'

'Good God, no. Not after last night. Will and I are going to Mario and Franco's for a bite. Won't you come?'

'I don't think Elizabeth would like it, somehow,' replied Michael with a smile and some regret. 'Anyhow, I have some letters to write to the disappointed hordes who failed to become my pupil.'

Chapter two

Wednesday was not going well for Anthony Cross. His day had begun at 4 a.m., and it was now nearly nine. It had been drizzling steadily since the first grey shadows of dawn had crept over the City, and the lanes and alleyways around Spitalfields market were glistening with rain and vegetable refuse. The great steel barn of the fruit market echoed with the shouts of porters, the whinings of fork-lift trucks, the crashings of crates and the tramp of feet. Things were only just beginning to slacken off.

Anthony had a holiday job in the market as a porter. He worked for an importer called Amos Oxford, and was subject to the brute tyranny of Mr Mant, a lowly clerk in the employ of Mr Oxford. What Mr Mant did was not very clear, but it seemed that he had been doing it at Spitalfields, man and boy, for forty years. While Anthony hauled crates and tallied sacks of onions, Mr Mant would emerge regularly from the cracked wooden den that he called his office, and where he spent murmuring hours thumbing through dirty lists of produce, and shuffle across to the cafe with his little stainless steel teapot. There it would be filled, and Mr Mant, small and dark and bent and unwashed, would make his way back to his office with his tea and a doughnut. He never offered to share his tea with Anthony. His communication with the outside world during working hours was limited to shouting 'You effin' little bastard!' at Anthony and to offering gratuitously unpleasant, if sincere, compliments to the passing office girls. At nine o'clock each morning, after four trips to the cafe and back, Mr Mant would betake himself to the Gun, the public house that opened at four in the morning for the benefit of the market traders, and there soliloquise over a pint of Guinness and a roll-up.

It was the mere fact of the steady rain that made Anthony's life so miserable. Wheeling the heavy handcart, with its iron-rimmed wheels, in and out of the market, he had become drenched. There was nothing waterproof he could wear without sweating horribly, and now he could feel the damp seeping in under his jersey, through his shirt and into his skin, blotting and chilling him. The rain made the cobbles slippery, and a treacherous film of muck and rotten vegetable matter lay everywhere. Anthony's working gloves had become sodden and unmanageably heavy, forcing him to discard them, and now his hands were chafed from tiny splinters on the sides of the raw wooden pallets. Dodging the roaring fork-lifts, he made his way to the cafe and bought his first cup of tea of the day. He leaned against a pillar of the market and gazed vacantly as he drank it, a tall, good-looking boy, with a soft, girlish mouth, deep, thoughtful eyes, and dark hair matted with the rain. He stared unseeingly at the mountains of produce, at the piles of fat melons and bloom-covered purple grapes, at the light wooden boxes afloat with parsley, the gleaming green peppers, box upon box. The overhead lights gave everything an unreal lustre, like a great, bountiful harvest in a stone and iron setting.

Through the cockney clamour of the porters and traders, the sharp bubble of Indian and foreign voices rose and fell. Buyers of every race and description crowded the refuse-strewn lanes around the market with their vans and carts: Bengalis in small, sombre knots, silent families of dispossession and alarm; tall, swaggering Pakistanis with full faces and lazy eyes; lone Hasidic Jews with their old plastic carrier-bags and doleful demeanour, skirting the crates while the rain pattered on their high-crowned hats; Soho Chinese (sensitively referred to by Mr Mant as 'bleedin' slopes') darting watchfully from lorry to fork-lift, their high voices jabbing the air with orders; and the calm, cynical cockneys, battered faces as old as the centuries, milling slowly and cheerfully back and forth, whistling, occasionally breaking into an unlikely rapture of song, lighting up, stubbing out, bantering and bullying.

As Anthony watched it all, he saw out of the corner of his eye Mr Mant returning from the pub. With a sigh, he tossed his plastic cup among the rest of the rubbish and turned to his final, distasteful task of the morning, the disposal of five rotten bags of potatoes. Through the fibre of the sacking oozed liquefying potato, and the stench choked Anthony as he hauled at the slimy sacks, dragging them across to the other piles of refuse near the car park, where the scavengers were already congregating. Lone West Indian women with plastic carrier-bags fished among the rotting mangoes and blackened cabbages, the rain soaking their sandals and squelching between their bare toes. More organised gangs, Indian families from Brick Lane, with vans and hatchback saloons, were loading crates of discarded lemons and piles of shrivelled chilli peppers into their vehicles. God knows what restaurant those would end up in, thought Anthony.

As he pondered the dreadful possibility of spending one's entire life as a market porter, with the echoing sheds of Spitalfields forming the boundaries of one's vision, the very epitome of his musings suddenly turned the corner from a side street and came lurching towards him in a fork-lift truck driven at full speed. Len and he were friends, if only by reason of their proximity in age, but the differing scopes of their separate ambitions and dreams often formed part of Anthony's private meditations. Apart from a burning, but unrealised longing to play striker for Millwall, Len's great ambition in life, ever since he had first come to work in the market at the age of sixteen, had been to drive a fork-lift truck. It struck him as the height of sophistication to career around in a battered Toyota at speeds far greater than were strictly desirable or necessary, exchanging banter and obscenities with other drivers, forking up sheaves of pallets with utter disregard for the safety of their contents, and, of course, chain-smoking throughout the entire operation without ever seeming to move one's hands from the controls. Len had eventually achieved his ambition at the age of twenty. Someone had once foolishly remarked in Len's hearing that it was particularly difficult to overturn a fork-lift truck; snatching up this gauntlet, Len had proceeded to overturn two Nissans and a Toyota within the space of three months, before receiving a severe warning from the supervisor. He had then stopped reversing around corners at top

13

speed and settled down to comparatively sober driving, making only occasional forays against innocent motorists who happened to cut through the market, and only now and again demolishing entire loads of produce through carelessness.

That Wednesday, Anthony watched him as he sped through the rain, dropped down a gear, braked, and came to rest in a crate of lemons.

' 'Allo, Tone,' he said nonchalantly, flicking his fag end into a puddle and jumping down from his cab. 'Bloody hell,' he remarked, surveying the spilt lemons with pride. 'That's a bit of a waste. Better tell your old lady to make some pancakes, eh? Fancy some grub?'

Anthony's mouth watered at the thought of a mushroom omelette and fried bread, washed down by a large cup of hot, sweet coffee. He glanced round. Mr Mant had apparently gone back to converse with his circle of acquaintance in the Gun. He nodded, and they set off through the rain to the cafe.

Len was a tall, well-made youth of twenty-two, cheerful of disposition and, it must be said, fairly simple. He regarded Anthony with a mixture of admiration (for his obvious intelligence) and pity (for his inability to appreciate the finer things of life, such as Millwall and Worthington Best Bitter). Their discussions were normally limited to cars and television programmes, but now and then Len's imagination would be fired by a leader in the *Sun*, and he would seek out Anthony to discuss current affairs with him, feeling that Anthony's views lent breadth to his own, and that he could safely re-rehearse those views to his own credit later in the pub.

Len had finished his mixed grill and was watching Anthony speculatively as he mopped up the last of his mushroom omelette.

' 'Ow long are you working 'ere, then, Tone?' He lit a cigarette, leaned his face on his hand, and stared deeply at Anthony. Anthony looked up.

'I don't know. Not much longer. Until I get a pupillage, I suppose.'

'What's one of them, then?'

'It's like a – a sort of apprenticeship for becoming a barrister.'

'That's not the same as a solicitor?' Len had gleaned this

14

from one of their more searching discussions concerning the law as a profession.

'No, that's right. Barristers are the ones who wear wigs and stand up and talk in court.' Anthony was careful to explain things to Len in terms of reference to television drama.

'So how long does it last, this apprenticeship?' Len blew out a long plume of smoke.

'A year. That is, you can't earn anything for the first six months. I mean, you're actually not allowed to until the second six months.'

'Bloody 'ell,' said Len in disgust. 'You wouldn't catch me going in for that caper.' Anthony admitted that it was not, perhaps, quite Len's cup of tea.

'But it's worth it, eventually. At least, it's supposed to be. Once you become established in a tenancy, you can earn quite a lot.'

'Yeah?' Len's interest was faintly aroused.

'But I don't think you'd like it,' added Anthony quickly.

'No. You need O-levels an' that, don't you?' recalled Len wistfully. His memories of the remedial unit at Litt Park Comprehensive were stirred. O-levels had been bright, unattainable, shining things. His attention slipped away from Anthony and his career, a life that might have been, and moved on to more immediate interests.

'You fancy coming to a disco in Hackney tonight?'

Anthony shook his head; he had never yet accepted one of Len's invitations, but he was touched that Len continued to issue them.

'I can't. I've got to go and see my father,' he said. And then he sighed, thinking of his father and wishing that he could go to Hackney, after all.

Anthony's mother and father had met in the early sixties, when she had been plain, seventeen-year-old Judith Hewitt. Coming as she did from a background of solid respectability, with no aspirations beyond having a home and a family of much the same pattern as her mother's, Charles Cross had seemed to her an anarchic, daring spirit, a revolutionary nineteen-year-old. He had long hair at a time when Beatle haircuts were considered outrageous, he smoked marijuana (and persuaded Judith without difficulty to do likewise), he read American underground magazines and admired Allen Ginsberg and Robert Crumb, and he had recently been expelled from his public school. Who could resist his eccentric charms? It appeared, unfortunately, that his own immediate family could, particularly when, without advance notice and at a time when he had no job nor any prospect of one, he married the then-pregnant Judith and asked them for money to assist matters.

They had refused, becoming particularly unpleasant about the whole thing, and said that they would have nothing further to do with him unless he divorced Judith, and started a new life by going to university, still regarded in those days as something of a talisman by the aspiring middle class. Since he was already rather bored with Judith, and not especially interested in their future child, he agreed with unseemly promptitude, and Judith was left without even the where-withal to salvage the semi-detached lifestyle to which she had formerly aspired, and which she had so recently rejected (on Charles Cross' recommendation) as bourgeois and contempt-ible. No sweet daily routine for her of 'Housewives' Choice', trips to the shops with the Silver Cross pram, ironing, hoovering, baking and darning, making and mending. While her husband was disporting himself on an East Anglian campus (from which he dropped out after three terms), she was left in a pair of rented rooms with a new baby and only the scantest of support from her own unsympathetic family.

Some months after the baby was born, its father, in a fit of sentimentality, visited Judith in her two-room flat, bringing with him as a present five ounces of Lebanese Gold, which they smoked together. He persuaded Judith to name the baby Anthony, and not Kevin. He visited regularly after that, bringing money now and then, and three years later, Judith found herself pregnant once again.

When Charles Cross (or Chay, as he had taken to calling himself) subsequently heard that his ex-wife had begun proceedings against him to obtain maintenance payments for baby Anthony (and, presumably, for the new baby), he refused to have anything to do with the new child, let alone interfere in the choice of name for it. As a result, the unfortunate child was christened Barry.

Judith stumbled on through life. After a few years she resumed her studies and eventually obtained, with the help of her relenting but ever-grumbling mother, who looked after the children while she studied, a teaching qualification. Bewilderment still lived in her eyes, but she had not entirely abandoned the dreams and hopes of her youth. She invested much ambition in her two sons, and watched with surprise and delight Anthony's careful, brilliant academic progress. It seemed to her that he was destined to travel on roads where she could not possibly follow; she was immensely proud of him.

Barry – Barry was not the kind of child in whom one could absorb one's lost hopes. At eighteen, with none of his brother's dark charm and intellectual ability, he was a laconic, large youth with an irrepressible sense of humour, quite devoid of any ambitions or cares. He attended a local sixth-form college, where he supposedly studied for A-levels. No one, least of all Barry, seriously hoped he would obtain any. He and Anthony regarded one another with an affectionate tolerance.

When Anthony returned that morning with his carrier-bagful of lemons, the house was empty, his mother at work and Barry at college. The silence and the rainy morning light filling the kitchen gave Anthony a dreary sense of futility. The day stretched ahead of him, life stretched ahead of him, both unfilled. He made himself a cup of tea and went through to the sitting room to fetch his book. It was then he saw the letter lying on the hall table, addressed to himself. He picked it up. It was postmarked EC4. It was probably, he knew, a polite rejection from any one of the sets of chambers to which he had applied for pupillage. But still his heart raced as he tore open the envelope. He read and re-read Michael Gibbon's letter, as though unable to comprehend its contents. Excited beyond words, he paced round the empty house, longing for someone to return so that he could tell them. Caper Court! The best, the very best! Why had they chosen him? Well, they had, there it was. The man Gibbon and he had got on well, but he had never dared to hope . . . Suddenly the unfilled day was possessed of brilliance, life seemed full and promising. With a pupillage like that, he told himself, one could do anything. If one worked hard enough – and hadn't he always worked hard? – then the pupillage might turn into a tenancy, and there was the future, clear and assured. To fly with the gods and angels of 5 Caper Court. The arduous slog at school, at university, at Bar School – it had all been worthwhile. Never mind the work ahead, it would be proper work, in the real world. This was one pinnacle of achievement, with greater and better things to come. He forgot his tea, picked up the letter again and took it with him from room to room, reading it over and over.

Next Monday! Only five days away. A surge of fear and excitement rose in him at the thought of next Monday. Oh, God, how blessed he was. The urge to tell someone was now too great. He rang his friend Simon, but he was out. Who could he ring?

Bridget immediately came to mind, but he found himself vaguely reluctant. She had been his girlfriend at university, a relationship formed at a time when the young and lonely cleave to one another – the first term. Absorbed in work and too emotionally apathetic to take any positive step, he had allowed it to drift on. In ways it was convenient, financially, particularly when it came to finding rooms and flatshares. But of late, Anthony had become aware that Bridget was seeking anxiously in the relationship some form of security, and the promise of a conventional future. For although she was a mediocre creature – moderately pretty, marginally intelligent, and only minimally demanding – she did love Anthony with the habitual affection that often passes for love in those who yearn only for safety. She had recently begun her articles with a firm of Holborn solicitors and, anxious to consolidate matters and move into the grown-up world of mortgages, joint accounts, engagements, and similar absorbing projects, had begun to nag Anthony about his ambitions at the Bar.

'Why don't you switch and become a solicitor instead?' she had said. 'It's much more secure, and you'd always have a regular income. The way things are going, I can't see you ever getting a pupillage.'

Anthony had been stung by the notion that he should suddenly abandon his cherished project and slide into the murky half-life, as he saw it, of a City solicitor. How second-rate. She seemed to have no idea of how much it meant to him, how hallowed a place the Temple was and how blessed all those who lived and worked there, even unto the lowliest criminal hack. She understood nothing. But then, for Bridget, law was a means to a financial end, to a decent job, car, house, nanny. It might as well have been computer programming, for all the intellectual pleasure it gave her.

The nagging had only fixed Anthony more deeply in his ambitions, and also aroused in him a sense of resentment that Bridget should presume so much. True, he had let the relationship develop into a much more serious pattern than he had ever wished or intended, mainly through a mixture of apathy and a genuine desire not to be unkind. Recently, however, he had begun to realise that, unless steps were taken to end it, things would become tiresome and very difficult. Bridget seemed to attach considerable significance to the last four years, as a portent for the future.

Nonetheless, his elation and happiness that day naturally overcame his misgivings, and so he rang her office. Bridget, of course, was pleased, and when she suggested going out the following evening to celebrate, his prudence deserted him and he agreed. It was only later that it occurred to him that the conversation the next night would have to be carefully engineered, if their mutual pleasure at his brightening prospects were not to develop into a fatal case, on Bridget's part, of 'making plans'.

By the time his mother came home from school, Anthony's euphoria had flattened out a little. He had rung Michael Gibbon, been told he was in conference, and had left a message to say that he would be there at nine-thirty next Monday. To have spoken to someone, even a secretary, had relieved him. The matter was settled; if they'd written to him by mistake, they would have said so. They hadn't.

His mother, when he told her, was delighted but not in the least surprised. She had unwavering faith in her son's abilities, fully expecting him to achieve anything he wanted.

'That's wonderful. Is it a good firm?'

'It's called a set, Mum. A set of chambers.'

'Oh. Is it a good set?'

'Brilliant. The best there is.' Anthony remembered to show the letter to his mother. She liked the tangible evidence of his successes, and kept all his prizes, diplomas and certificates, piling them up against the day of his absence, so that she could trace and recall him. She read Michael Gibbon's letter now as though it told her something of the deep, mysterious future.

'This is what you wanted, isn't it?'

'Isn't it? God, yes. If this goes well, I mean, if they like me and I do well, then they might take me on as a tenant.'

Anthony and his mother had discussed this often enough for her to know what such a thing would mean. A chance for success, to turn the academic intangible into a prosperous reality. Money, an escape from the smaller, drearier end of suburbia. As for doing well and being liked, neither she nor Anthony had the remotest doubt that he would do both. But then, neither of them knew anything, as yet, of the existence of Edward Choke.

When she had fully digested the wondrous news, and stowed away Michael Gibbon's letter with Anthony's other trophies, which started with a jigsaw won at the mixed infants sports day and ended, so far, here, Judith turned her attention to the evening meal. She saw the carrier-bag of lemons standing by the sink.

'Anthony, what on earth am I meant to do with these?' she demanded. She was vexed at the prospect of throwing them out, helpless in the face of her upbringing. Waste not, want not.

'Len suggested pancakes.'

'Oh. Len.' Len's wit did not amuse her.

'I tell you what. I'll take half of them round to Dad's tonight.' Anthony could never bring himself, in spite of his father's requests, to call him Chay.

'Oh, I'm glad you reminded me. I'll just make something for myself. Put the news on, will you?'

'Don't get your hopes up,' called Anthony, going through to switch the television on. 'I've told Barry that we're both supposed to be going round, but he'll probably back out at the last minute.'

But Barry, when he returned home with the fruits of his academic labours stuffed in a dilapidated sports bag and a Hawkwind album under his arm, responded to Anthony's reminder of their father's invitation with enthusiasm.

'Oh, yeah, that's right! Good. I want to see this new girlfriend of his. Hope she's better than the last one.'

Judith said nothing. Although she absorbed all the information that her sons brought home concerning their father, she never asked any questions. She lent Anthony the car keys, ate a solitary omelette, and after watching the news for the second time that day, went to bed with some marking and lay, pondering the hope, the brilliance, that was to be Anthony's future.

It was quite a long way to the Chay Cross Islington squat, and by the time they got there, even Anthony's high spirits had begun to flag. They had stopped at Unwin's to buy a bottle of white wine, which was warming well in Barry's grasp as they mounted the wide, echoing staircase to Chay's flat.

Strictly speaking, the flat was not Chay's. As a squat, it had originally housed a commune of five people, all dedicated to the arts and vegetarianism. One by one, they had succumbed to Chay's oppressive influence, and left. Quite how someone who smiled so benevolently and constantly, whose voice was never raised in anger or complaint, and who never imposed his views or his music on others except in moderation – quite how this model of self-effacement had managed to wear down four like-minded individuals was a mystery even to themselves. But there he remained, smiling and alone (except for the ever-present, ever-changing girlfriend), quite unperturbed by the disdain and resentment of his law-abiding, rent-paying neighbours. For his was a noble squat, set in a handsome, if decaying terrace, populated largely by people of his own age and background, the only difference being that Chay lived there free.

Anthony and Barry's views regarding their father had varied over the years, and it was only in the past seven or so that they had begun to realise that he was somewhat out of the norm for ordinary fathers. Chay was still very much a child of the sixties, the kind of relic that Anthony and Barry recognised from historic television footage of the black-and-white era. Barry rather admired his father's bohemian lifestyle as one to which he, too, aspired, but which he knew he could never brave. The tree-lined streets of suburbia, which he could denigrate in the cosy comfort of the canteen at the sixth-form college, offered too much of a warm, known haven.

Anthony viewed him somewhat differently. He had never taken his father very seriously, had never much liked him, and stayed out of his way as much as possible. During his vulnerable years at university he had referred to his father as 'an artist', when asked. That was all very well, so far as it went. But only that day, and in the light of the prospects which he imagined were opening up before him, Anthony realised that Chay could become something of a serious social handicap.

Chay Cross was a thin, spindly man of forty-one, with the eager, faded countenance of the ageing hippy, rootless and feckless. He smiled a lot, a serene, knowing smile. His history was one of hedonistic self-justification. He had inherited and squandered money; borrowed from his family until they were weary; indulged in every lunatic experiment conceivable – physical, spiritual and chemical; embraced several religions, from Christianity through Buddhism to Baha'i and back again; dabbled with all known drugs, and several less well known, from mescalin to cocaine. He had used, cheated and discarded friends, lovers and family. He had embarked upon various artistic careers with neither the desire nor the ability to succeed, it seemed, in any of them – painting, sculpture, weaving, writing, poetry, metalwork. He satisfied his vanity by achieving smatterings of knowledge and endless terms of reference, catchphrases, the breathed names of the successful, their cast-off canvases and clay, their ex-lovers. He was a man of immense superficiality, anxious for the approval of the supposed arbiters of taste and intellectual and artistic fashion, seeking always to tap the vein of the present trend. At the same time, he managed to cultivate an image of eccentric naivety, purporting to disdain material wants and cares. He was, in trufh, a complete fabrication of a man, a fact of which Anthony was all too readily aware.

The first shock that greeted his sons that evening was their father's newly shaven head. For as long as they could remember, he had worn his hair, which had of late become grey and thinning, to his shoulders, occasionally tying it back with pony-tail bands bought at the women's hair-care counter at Boot's. But tonight they saw his rather pointed, knobbly skull gleaming unpleasantly through grey, bristly, day-old growth. It gave Chay's neck a strangely elongated look, and somehow aggravated the irritating quality of his bland smile.

'Oh, very cool, Dad,' said Barry, giving him a glance and then heading for the kitchen with the wine. He was hunting out Chay's new woman. Anthony was too startled to say anything. He was aware from his grandmother that he was supposed to look like his father, and had spent anxious, furtive half-hours at his grandmother's house, scrutinising old photographs of his father to see if it were true, and if there was any frightful possibility that he might, in middle age, look the way Chay did. The shaven head expanded the possibility alarmingly.

He followed his father into the long attic room that served as living-room, dining-room and bedroom, and tried to pay attention while his father showed him some of his recent efforts in his new field of creative endeavour, drawing cartoons. To Anthony, there was something faintly repellent in Chay's enthusiasm for his own work and its display to others; perhaps his own innate habit of self-deprecation was to blame. Still, he had to acknowledge that his father never admitted artistic defeat.

'Have you sold any?' he asked, ever seeking some evidence that someone might find something of substance in his father.

'One or two. Not to mainstream publications, of course. This stuff's far too way out for them.' His father continued to use the antiquated slang of the sixties; in some ways it was rather endearing, but it never failed to offend the delicate, modish sensibilities of Barry.

'Who's that meant to be?' asked Barry, reappearing from the kitchen.

'Denis Healey.'

'Looks more like Sue Lawley. Here, cop a glass of this, Dad.' He handed his father a tumbler full of wine. 'I've just been meeting Jocasta,' he said with a grin, stuffing crisps into his mouth.

A young woman came through from the kitchen and smiled at them.

'Hi,' she said nervously, and held out her hand. Anthony shook it and introduced himself. She could have been no older than himself, he thought, rather lovely in an inane way, with long, straight, black hair and bright, anxious blue eyes. They get younger and younger, thought Anthony. Anyone Chay's own age would laugh their head off, he supposed. Jocasta. Yes, well, that figured.

'I hope you'll like what I'm cooking for supper,' she said, and then proceeded to describe something which Anthony could not visualise, consisting of ingredients of which he had largely never heard.

'What's that? Soul food?' said Barry.

'We're vegans now,' said Chay, by way of explanation.

'Well, we're not,' said Barry, following Jocasta into the kitchen.

Over dinner, which Anthony suspected was mainly aubergines, cabbage and pine kernels, with ginger in it somewhere (although he could not specifically visually identify any of those things, except the pine kernels), Chay expanded on his veganism. Jocasta beamed at him worshipfully from behind the casserole.

'It's part of a whole purification system. For your body to operate your brain, it needs good, pure fuel. Red meat just makes you sluggish and excitable.'

'How can you be sluggish and excitable at the same time?' asked Anthony.

'That's what I mean,' said Chay, running a leathery hand over his bristles. 'A mass of contradictions. A body that's incapable of functioning properly with gross and unnatural

24

food intake. Hence the head is full of hate, the heart full of poison. For humans to use animal products is unnatural.'

'Even leather for shoes and belts,' put in Jocasta, glancing at Chay for approval. He nodded.

'That's right. Jocasta has made us both moccasins from hessian and velvet, so that animal products don't come into contact with our flesh.' He stuck out a bony foot from under the table; from the end of it dangled something that looked like an ill-fitting velveteen boot.

'That won't take you far on a nasty night,' observed Barry, abstractedly trying to mash the remains of his food into as small a lump as possible. Jocasta was staring at his plate.

Anthony changed the subject by telling his father about his new pupillage. Chay looked laid-back and amused. His contempt for the world of commerce, and for lawyers, bankers and stockbrokers, was well known.

'A web of corruption, greed and deceit. Still, if that's what you want, I wish you well of it.'

Anthony would have liked to point out to his father that he, Chay, had never seriously contemplated any real form of work in his life, simply squandering other people's money to stay alive, but he didn't. He knew too well the pointlessness of such an exercise.

'What about you, Barry?' said Chay, turning to his younger son. 'You going to become one of Thatcher's children?'

'No,' said Barry, pouring more wine into everyone's glass, 'I'm hoping for a sixties revival, so that I can fart about in a pair of flared jeans with some joss sticks, doing nothing.' Anthony laughed. Chay got up to fetch his tobacco tin.

'What about you, Dad?' asked Barry. 'What's the latest craze? What's next in the line-up of loony doings?'

'Well, since you ask,' replied Chay tolerantly, lighting an after-dinner joint, 'I'm undertaking fire-walking. At the moment, I'm involved in mental and physical preparation for the experience.'

'How d'you prepare yourself – drop lighted matches down your socks?'

Chay ignored him, taking a deep drag on the joint and passing it to Jocasta, who took it reverently. 'It's a process of cleansing the mind and body,' he continued, 'hence the veganism.' Hence the drugs, thought Anthony. 'Over a period of weeks one elevates the spirit to a condition where pain can be transcended. Then one is ready.' Jocasta's eyes glowed as she listened to him, a sweet, holy smile on her lips. 'All physical sensation can be sublimated if the spirit is in harmony with the elements that surround us. Earth, fire, water.'

'Are you going to try it?' Anthony asked Jocasta, shaking his head as she offered him the joint. She looked worried and rather shocked at the question.

'No. I don't think so, anyhow.' She looked over at Chay.

'Why not? Don't you believe you can transcend pain?' asked Barry. 'No thanks,' he added, refusing the joint.

'Jocasta's very young,' said Chay, with a condescending smile. 'She hasn't undergone the years of intellectual discipline and physical tempering required to undertake such a test of the spirit, and of one's faith.' He took the joint from Jocasta and inhaled; the tobacco glowed redly. The gesture suddenly swept Anthony with irritation. They bored him; their drugs bored him; his father's posing bored him. None of this was real – their food, their attitudes, their absurd posturing.

'I've got to be going,' he said, and got up. Barry joined him. They thanked Jocasta for the meal and Chay promised Barry he would let him know when the fire-walking was to take place.

Out in the street, Barry counted his change. 'Good. Enough for a quick pint and a McDonald's. She was a bit of all right, wasn't she?' They walked on for a bit. 'Can you imagine him in bed with her?'

'Don't,' pleaded Anthony. He thought of Chay's shaven skull, and wished Barry hadn't said that.

Chapter three

On Monday the 14th of September, a day shimmering with the promise of an Indian summer, Anthony set off in his Marks & Spencer suit to join the world of commerce and litigation. He left plenty of time for his journey and arrived early, then spent half an hour or so idling around the Temple, watching the barristers arriving at their chambers, envying them their sure place in the world.

When he eventually mounted the few steps to the entrance to 5 Caper Court, scanning with brief reverence the illustrious names listed on the hand-painted board, sharp with envy at the name of the youngest tenant at the bottom, his mouth was dry and his heart was in his throat. He had no idea why he was so nervous. He entered through a door marked CLERKS' ROOM – ENQUIRIES and found himself standing at a low wooden counter, behind which buzzed an array of computers and telex machines. A burly man in shirt-sleeves approached him.

'Can I help you, sir?'

'My name's Anthony Cross. I'm Mr Gibbon's new pupil.'

'Oh, Mr Cross. Yes, sir. We *are* expecting you today. It's rather unfortunate, though, because it seems that Mr Gibbon's gone up to an arbitration in the City. Won't be back till this evening, I'm afraid.'

'Oh.' Anthony's heart sank. He was uncertain what to do next. Should he go home? Walk around the Temple? Sit in the library until evening? The clerk waited the requisite thirty seconds or so while Anthony's discomfiture registered, and then smiled the bland, supercilious smile of the gifted barrister's clerk.

'Not to worry, sir. I'm sure Mr Gibbon would want you to go up and make yourself at home. We've a desk set up in there for you. Maybe you could help yourself to a few briefs while you're waiting.' The clerk lifted his chin slightly and smiled, as though giving a signal. Anthony recognised the little pleasantry and laughed.

'That's very kind of you.'

'Not at all, sir,' replied the clerk, lifting up a wooden flap in the counter and walking past Anthony to show him up to his new quarters. Anthony wished the man would stop calling him 'sir'. Its slightly mocking deference made him feel clumsy and ill at ease.

'By the way, my name's Mr Slee, sir. I'm the head clerk.' Following him up the narrow wooden staircase, Anthony fumbled around for a suitable response, and finally murmured something inaudible in the direction of Mr Slee's broad posterior. Mr Slee unlocked the door of Michael's room.

'Everything you want is there, sir. Make yourself comfortable. That's your desk – ' He pointed to a small, worn desk with a faded green leather top and a pretty patina. ' – and if you don't mind closing the door *firmly* behind you, sir, when you go out for lunch, and I'll unlock it for you when you come back in. I expect you'll be getting your own key in a couple of days or so, only Mr Gibbon hasn't said anything yet.'

Anthony murmured his thanks, and the door then closed, leaving him alone to survey his new surroundings.

The first thing he did was to open the window; although it was only nine-forty, the September sun made the air in the room warm and close. He began by examining Michael's desk, his bottle of ink, his blotter; he looked long and silently at the few pictures on the walls, which were mainly of ships of the last century; and then he considered with growing boredom the familiar array of law reports on the shelves of the bookcase that occupied one wall of the room. He grew mildly interested in the two cases of wine which stood just behind the door, and then flung himself into his chair in exasperation and ennui. It was ten-fifteen. He picked up the latest of the unbound law reports and read listlessly for a while, until the chatter of the autumn birds and the occasional sound of voices in the courtyard below drew him to the window.

The forlorn light that belongs to a warm September day gilded the courtyard. He leaned out and watched the figures

28

come and go, some sauntering in the dappled light of the plane trees near the car park, farther off; some stepping out briskly from the cloisters, their arms laden with documents, deep in conversation, voices rising and then dying on the soft air; some clattering noisily down the wooden stairs of chambers and running off through the archway into the Temple; then silence for a spell. There was an archaic sundial set into the brickwork of the building directly opposite, and for a while Anthony watched it, trying to catch the imperceptible movement of the shadow across the intricate metal dial. A bluebottle buzzed in briefly, enlivening the room with its sound, then buzzed out again, leaving an even more melancholy silence behind it.

Eventually Anthony drew in his head, having watched a shirt-sleeved figure through a window over the way as it perused a brief, answered the telephone, moved around the room, and generally behaved with the ease and remoteness of the distant and envied. Everyone in the world seemed to be occupied and useful, while he felt forgotten and alone. Deciding to try out the amusement value of Mr Slee's little joke, Anthony dared to pick up one of the briefs from a shelf and settled himself into his chair with a sense of purpose. After all, as he was Michael's pupil he would have to work on some of these cases, so he might as well make a start.

The brief seemed very complicated. It involved the purchase of a fleet of helicopters and the financial collapse of a subsidiary company which had, it seemed, been financing the purchase. All kinds of indemnities and back-to-back credit arrangements came into it, none of which Anthony felt he could possibly understand. Still, he ploughed relentlessly on, and by setting out the identities of the various protagonists on a piece of paper, with little arrows and legends to show their relationships to each other, he felt by the time lunchtime came that he had made some progress.

On into the afternoon he worked on the problem, endeavouring to unravel the tangled skein, and when he heard the sound of a key in the door he was surprised to see by his watch that it was nearly six o'clock.

Michael looked rather startled to see Anthony, who rose and smiled.

'Anthony Cross.' There was a pause. 'Your new pupil. We met a few weeks ago.'

Michael struck his forehead with the palm of his hand.

'Of course! I completely forgot. I'm so wretchedly stupid about my diary. Please forgive me. The clerks must have known you were coming today. If they'd mentioned it to me this morning, I could have left the address and you could have joined us at lunchtime. Still, I was in a hurry.' Michael was heaping a bundle of files and documents on to his desk and reaching into the cupboard with one spider-like arm for the sherry bottle and some glasses. He dragged them out, and then came over to see what Anthony was doing.

'What's this? You haven't been working on that helicopter thing, have you? I finished it last week. Still, it's quite interesting, isn't it?' Michael sounded so sincere that Anthony could only politely agree. 'Well, that kept you off the streets, at any rate. Let's see what you made of it.' He scanned the piece of paper while Anthony grew red and uncomfortable next to him. 'Mmm. That's about the gist of it. But what's the answer, eh?' Anthony felt ashamed to admit that he didn't know, but said as much.

'Well, that makes two of us,' said Michael, turning to the sherry bottle. 'Three, if you count the instructing solicitor. You can tell from the brief that he hasn't got a clue. If they ever *do* think they know anything, they stick it into the brief, no matter how glaringly obvious or redundant the information . . .'

Michael was staring dispiritedly at the sherry bottle when a light tap sounded on the door. A handsome, lean-faced man, with grey hair, came in. He glanced at Anthony, then smiled at Michael.

'Leo!' said Michael, looking up. 'Thank God. You've saved our lives. I was just about to inflict some of this fino sherry on my young friend here. Anthony Cross, my new pupil. Anthony, this is Leo Davies, one of litigation's legends.'

Leo shook Anthony's hand. Anthony saw that, despite the silver-grey hair, the man was no more than a few years older than Michael. His smile, although cool, lit up his blue eyes.

'Welcome to Caper Court,' he said. 'Come on, man,' turning to Michael, 'let's take the lad up the road for a proper drink. I need it. I've had a filthy day.' Anthony could detect a faint Welsh accent.

They set off together, Anthony in proud silence in the wake of Leo and Michael. They stood in the bar at El Vino's with their glasses of wine, Anthony listening and watching, glancing round from time to time to take in the atmosphere. He glanced at the two men as they talked, happy to be in their company. Leo Davies he found both charismatic and intimidating. He was an elegant man, his clothes expensively cut, in contrast to Michael's somewhat unkempt appearance, and his manner was indolent and cool, as though to temper the natural aggression and impatience betrayed by his quick gestures and arresting voice. Anthony could see why Michael had been so glad to see Leo; he was a quick-witted and amusing man. He gave, however, the curious impression of keeping himself slightly in check, so that when his natural good humour began to shine through with too much warmth, his cold demeanour would return to close upon it like a steel trap, as though at some reminder. He glanced at Anthony from time to time with his appraising blue gaze, as though to invite him into the conversation, but Anthony felt that there was nothing he could contribute. He was a very new boy indeed.

By the time he found the fresh air of Fleet Street, three glasses of wine and an hour later, Anthony felt elated, uplifted. Although he had contributed scarcely more than ten words to the conversation, the company, to say nothing of the wine, had filled him with a sense of glorious purpose. As he stood at the bus stop, gazing unseeingly at the traffic, he imagined a future when he, too, would talk with the brilliance and ease of Leo Davies.

At exactly the same moment, in a taverna in Naxos, Edward Choke was attempting, for a bet, to drink three more glasses of ouzo. The clamour from the table where he was dining with three college friends rose and filled the soft Greek night air.

'And I,' Edward was saying, as he slopped a little water into his ouzo, watching it turn milky, 'am going to be an absolutely brilliant barrister. Ab-so-lute-ly bloody brilliant.' He leaned

31

forward solemnly, his blond hair falling over his flushed, tanned face. 'And then I'm going to be a High Court judge.' He took a swig of his ouzo, then tipped his head back and finished it. One of his friends banged on the table with his fist and someone filled Edward's glass again. 'And *then*,' he continued, 'I'm going to be a Court of Appeal judge.' He swallowed the second glass and contemplated his friends sternly. His glass was filled again. 'And then – I'll become a Law Lord.' He drank the third glass off. 'Lord Choke of Chiswick.' He belched unexpectedly, and his companions laughed long and loud at this provocative wit.

The rest of Anthony's first week was a sobering experience. It was spent sitting in the arbitration rooms of the Baltic Exchange in the company of Michael, two other lawyers, and the appeal tribunal of the Livestock and Animal Feeds Trade Association. This body consisted of nine elderly, irascible men, two of whom appeared, to Anthony, to be certifiable, none of whom was possessed of one iota of legal understanding, and all of whom were convened to decide upon issues of blinding legal complexity. All in all, Michael explained to Anthony, it was probably just as well that it happened this way; they would come to a decision based upon common sense, how bored they were getting, and what time they wanted to get away for the weekend.

The most enlivening interludes occurred when the tea lady came round. It seemed to Anthony that teatime in a geriatric ward must be like this. By the time the clinking cups had been passed around, and everyone had settled back down with the right amounts of milk and sugar and Rich Tea fingers, the entire tribunal would have forgotten what had been discussed in the previous fifteen minutes, and counsel would have to begin all over again. No one ever had the right number of pages in their bundle, documents constantly had to be re-photocopied (one of Anthony's tasks), and squabbles would break out over charts and diagrams.

Anthony was dismayed. Was this to be his brilliant career; sitting in dusty arbitration rooms, mulling through endless documents relating to guano shipments of a decade ago? Over an early evening drink, Michael assured him that a barrister's time was not always spent thus, and indeed, once the arbitration was finished, life brightened considerably. Michael gave him one or two straightforward briefs to work on, and as he toiled away in Middle Temple library, flanked by the rows of silent, ever-present Far Eastern students, Anthony felt that he was getting somewhere.

On the Tuesday morning of that second week, as he clattered cheerfully down the chambers' stairs, Anthony bumped into the stocky, suntanned figure of Edward Choke. They had been friendly at Bar School, and Anthony greeted him with some surprise.

'Hello! What are you up to these days?'

'Just got back from Greece. Brilliant holiday. Have you been there? No? Really excellent – got to watch out for the ouzo, though. I'm starting my pupillage today.'

'I've been at it for a week now,' replied Anthony. 'We'll have to have a drink one evening. Where are you doing your pupillage?'

'Here, of course. Sir Basil Bunting's my uncle, which is a bit useful.' Edward had a cheerful awareness of his own probable merits, and was quick to acknowledge the fortuitous connection which had brought him to 5 Caper Court.

Anthony was momentarily taken aback. He had already formed some idea in the past of Edward's intellectual capabilities, and was frankly surprised to find him as his fellow-pupil. He managed to prevent himself from betraying his surprise, reflecting that anyone with such a useful connection would naturally put it to good use. The chances were that Edward didn't seriously aspire to a permanent place at 5 Caper Court. They chatted for a few moments, arranged to meet for a drink, and then Anthony hurried off. A small seed of doubt had been planted in his mind, and the imagined brilliance of his future career had lost a little of its lustre.

That afternoon did little to dispel his doubts. It was the custom of chambers to convene in the common room at Inner Temple for tea in the afternoon. Anthony, still somewhat reticent, rarely made any contribution to the conversation, except in response to a question or remark from Michael or

David Liphook who, as the youngest member of chambers, enjoyed exercising his benevolence to those his junior. Edward, however, seemed quite at his ease. Sir Basil was, after all, his dear and familiar uncle, and he already knew Roderick Hayter, the senior tenant, and a couple of others socially. Darkly, Anthony watched Edward making easy, amiable conversation, wondering what his real ambitions in chambers were.

Edward understood dimly that it was felt that at some time in the far future he should become the brilliant successor in chambers to his uncle. On this he had no real views. He was perfectly happy to be disposed of as others saw fit, provided life was tolerably comfortable and money and good times plentiful, and provided that no undue exertions were required of him. So far, his experience that day as Jeremy Vine's pupil had not been particularly taxing. He had been given a desk to sit at and some stuff to read. He didn't understand much of it, but then, that was Jeremy's business, not his.

To Anthony, however, Edward had suddenly appeared as a rival, someone capable of blighting his precious hopes. How could he possibly hope to compete with the favoured nephew of Sir Basil Bunting? Nursing these fears, he went unhappily that evening from chambers to his meeting with Bridget at a wine bar in the City.

His gathering gloom deepened when he caught sight of Bridget sitting on her own in a corner of the wine bar. It was never a light, social event, having a drink with Bridget; it always had the air of a serious assignation.

'Hullo,' he said, sitting down opposite her. She was wearing her invariable blue two-piece suit, with a high-necked Laura Ashley blouse, pearl earrings, and the small string of pearls that her father had given her for her eighteenth birthday. This, plus a pair of low-heeled Bally shoes, seemed to Anthony to be the uniform of every female articled clerk in London. She had an earnest expression on her face, and a glass of Perrier in front of her. Anthony wished that, just sometimes, since she was actually earning something, she would buy him a drink. She never did. She thought it was one of those things that men did for girls, never the other way round. He grubbed around in his small change, found he had enough for a half-pint of bitter, and then remembered that this was a wine bar.

'God,' he groaned, 'I wish we could meet somewhere where I could get a decent pint.'

'I like this place,' said Bridget, glancing around. 'Anyway, you know I don't like pubs. They're too smoky and it's bad for my asthma.' Anthony stared at her.

'Can you lend me a quid?' he asked. 'For a drink?' Surely, *surely*, she would offer to buy him one. She fished in her handbag and handed him a pound. He knew there was no question that this was anything but a loan.

'I've got something to tell you,' she announced, as he got up to go to the bar. When he came back with his glass of wine and sat down, she looked at him expectantly, as though it were he who had some news.

'Well?' he said dutifully.

'Claire's moving out of the flat soon. She's got a job in Cambridge with a community law project.' Claire was Bridget's flatmate, a large feminist who didn't like Anthony and, so far as Anthony could see, didn't much like Bridget either. Anthony took a sip of wine and winced; he thought he could see where this was leading.

'Are you going to advertise for someone to share?' he enquired innocently. Bridget looked at him for a moment.

'I thought that – that maybe this would be a good opportunity for us to . . .' She hesitated. 'Well, since it's bound to happen sooner or later –' Anthony saw that this was becoming difficult for her. She fortified herself with a sip of mineral water, and tried again. 'You always said that we never had the chance to spend much time alone together.' Anthony recollected saying something to this effect three years ago, when they were sharing a squalid three-bedroom flat with five other students; what he had actually meant was that he, Anthony, rarely got any peace. Bridget went on. 'So I wondered if you thought it would be a good idea if *you* moved in.' She looked trustingly, hopefully at him, which inclined him to be brutal.

'No way,' he replied quickly, taking a drink of his wine. 'For a start, I can't afford to, and for another thing, your mother would go berserk.' Bridget leaned forward intently, and Anthony realised his error in making it sound as though there were no other objections beyond these.

'Look,' said Bridget with a smile; her calm, managing smile. 'I can afford to help you out until you start earning.' You could buy me a drink for a start, thought Anthony. 'And as for Mummy . . .' Bridget looked down and smiled even more. Anthony began to feel uneasy. 'If we were – engaged – ' She glanced up at Anthony and then looked quickly away again. He wondered what expression was on his face. ' – then I know she would be all right about it. Daddy would probably even help out with a mortgage on a house. I've told them all about your pupillage and everything, and that you're bound to be successful very soon.'

So here we are, thought Anthony. He looked at Bridget for a moment. He looked at her face, pretty and blank, at her thin mouth and her anxious brown eyes, at her straight, mousy hair pulled back under its tight velvet band. He had looked at her face for so many years, he thought, that he didn't see it any more. He had no desire to kiss her, or touch her – the whole thing wearied him. The prospect of living with her, of *marrying* her, was awful, deadly. She must know that, too, he thought. Surely she must. He couldn't give out so many wrong signals, could he? How could two people sit and talk regularly with each other and fail constantly to make themselves understood? Well, that wasn't quite it – Bridget had made herself understood perfectly. For a second, Anthony considered the possibility of articulating his thoughts. He had to say something. She looked at him questioningly.

'Bridget, I don't want to get married,' he heard himself say. He knew that wasn't the right reply.

'Oh, we don't have to get married right away,' she said brightly. No, no, he thought – she must be more perceptive than this. Try again.

'And you don't want to marry me. Honestly.' This was a poser for her. Any reply in the affirmative would sound a trifle desperate. He went on, seizing his chance. 'It would be awful. We're just not right for each other. I mean, I love you as a friend . . . But I don't think getting married is a very good idea. Really.'

There was a silence. Bridget looked at her Perrier water. 'I thought the four years we've been together meant something to you,' she said, faintly accusingly.

'They do,' Anthony reassured her. No they don't, he thought.

'No they don't,' said Bridget, beginning to look a little damp around the eyes. 'I simply don't see where it's all meant to be going, Anthony.' Any minute now, he thought, and there would be serious tears.

'Look,' he said brightly, 'Let's go and get something to eat – no, on second thoughts, let's not. Let's just sit here and talk about something else. We don't have to make any decisions right now.' No, no, no. That was the wrong thing to say. Christ, what was the right thing?

'But Claire's moving out in two months,' moaned Bridget.

'Well,' said Anthony, striving to find some words that would simply stop this conversation, knock the whole subject on the head. 'Well – let's think about it, shall we? There's plenty of time. We'll forget about it for the moment.'

'You promise you'll think about it?' she asked in a small voice. Anthony promised, wretched with the knowledge that they were destined to have this awful conversation – no, in fact a much worse one – again in the near future. Mollified, Bridget dabbed her eyes and, to Anthony's amazement, offered to buy them both a pizza.

The evening improved, and over supper Anthony confided in Bridget his fears about Edward Choke. Bridget, in her best womanly way, reassured her man, massaged his ego, and brought him round to the sincere belief that he probably didn't have anything to worry about. The glow of her affection warmed him. At the end of the evening, Anthony kissed her quite kindly at the bus stop and went home thinking well of himself.

Chapter four

In many ways, given the manner in which he regarded his pupillage, Edward was very lucky to have Jeremy Vine as his pupilmaster. In Vine's world there was room for very little else besides Vine's ego and Vine's affairs. These affairs were of towering importance, naturally enough. He was a man in his mid-forties, a formidable, if somewhat bullying advocate, dark, heavy-faced, loud-voiced, a man who managed to convey the impression that he was under constant pressure. With the arrogance of the hard-working and meticulously thorough barrister, he believed that no one could attend properly to his affairs except Jeremy Vine himself. He detested holidays, and if obliged by his family to take one, would ring chambers daily to make sure that his practice was not collapsing, as he was convinced it must without his guiding hand.

As a result, he regarded Edward as little more than a mild physical inconvenience, taking up valuable space in his room. He had long forgotten his own apprenticeship, his only perception of himself being that which he presently held – of an extremely important and highly regarded barrister, shortly, no doubt, to be made a Queen's Counsel, with a flourishing practice and little time for those of weaker talents or fewer abilities. He found Edward useful for carrying books to and from court, or for running messages, but he took little time to set him work and oversee it, or to explain the dizzying machinations of the commercial court as he moved majestically from one important case to another, with Edward in tow.

Edward, although vaguely aware that he wasn't picking up quite as much as he perhaps ought to, was not unduly disturbed by any of this. David Liphook and William Cooper, who shared a room on the same floor as Jeremy, treated him kindly, for he was an eminently likeable, cheerful and amusing young person. When they thought he was insufficiently occupied, they would send him off to look up cases and make notes on them, and when Edward was doing this he felt that he was getting along fairly well. In fact, he was doing little more, and on many days a great deal less, than he had done at university.

Still, life pleased him. He was doing what a young man of his age was supposed to be doing. He shared a flat in a square just off the Brompton Road with three other young men. They gave rowdy dinner parties attended by other young ex-public schoolchildren, all largely indistinguishable in conversation one from the other, except that the girls squealed and the men roared; he played the occasional game of rugby, swam at the RAC Club (generally regarded as more amusing than the Oxford and Cambridge) and went to long and boisterous parties at the weekends. He had several girlfriends, enough money, and went home to his family every third or fourth weekend, where he would shout authoritatively at the dogs and delight his parents with his young, masculine presence. He was supremely content.

One day in early December, Edward and his pupilmaster were sitting in their room at 5 Caper Court. All was still. Outside the air was foggy and the gas lamps were being lit around the Temple, although it was only four o'clock in the afternoon. Jeremy was employed in researching some procedural points of law, which any moderately competent pupil should have been able to do for him, had they been allowed, while Edward, ostensibly reading a textbook, was making impressively little headway with the *Telegraph* crossword. There was a knock at the door, Jeremy called 'Come!', as men of his type will, and Leo Davies came in.

Leo and Jeremy did not get on especially well with one another, although they managed to conceal this fact. Leo found Jeremy humourless and pedantic, while Jeremy mistrusted Leo's glib elegance and charm. He disliked hearing Leo's laughter echoing round the building, as it so often did, suspecting, without foundation, that some of it might be directed at him. What irked him most was that Leo had an informality of manner that made Jeremy feel stuffy and constrained. In the blustering uncertainty of his twenties, Jeremy had found it useful, especially in court, to assume an air of unbecoming pomposity, which he now found impossible to discard.

'Jeremy, I was wondering if I might borrow Edward for a while. I'm fairly snowed under and I thought he might be able to help me with some pleadings. Good practice for him, eh?' he added, a little questioning Welsh lift to his voice.

Edward's heart sank a little. This sounded suspiciously like work. Pleadings – yes, they'd done a bit of that at Bar School and in the exams. That was a long time ago, though. Months. Jeremy sighed impatiently and leaned back in his chair, as though reluctant to lose his valuable assistant.

'Of course, of course.' Then he carried on with his work as if to suggest that he did not wish to be interrupted by any more trivia.

'Right,' said Leo lightly. 'Pop along in about ten minutes, then,' he said to Edward, and left.

Edward tidied his books away, went for a pee, and set off for Leo's room with a quaking heart. On the stairs he met Anthony. He had noticed over the weeks that Anthony's manner had seemed a little distant, but his present nervousness obliterated the recollection and he collared Anthony confidingly.

'God, Anthony, Leo Davies has just asked Jeremy if he could borrow me. He wants me to do some work for him!' Edward practically squeaked.

'Well, is that such a problem?' asked Anthony, on a note of genuine enquiry.

'It could be! It could be bloody awful. He mentioned something about pleadings. I haven't done any of those for yonks, and I wasn't much good when I did them. Jeremy never asks me to do anything like that.'

Anthony couldn't help smiling at the frantic concern on Edward's normally cheerful face.

'It won't be so bad,' he said sympathetically, wondering why on earth Edward was getting so worked up. 'He's a decent bloke. Tell you what. It's half-past four now. Whatever he gives you, he won't expect you do it this afternoon. Bring it to the bar at six and we'll have a look at it together.' Even though he ranked as a possible rival, Anthony genuinely liked Edward – one couldn't help it – and was naturally ready to help him with things that Edward found difficult and Anthony found so easy.

'Brilliant! I'll buy you a pint!' called Edward as he legged it up the stairs two at a time to Leo's room.

Leo explained the salient facts of the case briskly and lucidly to Edward, to whom it all sounded far too brisk and not at all lucid. He kept nodding attentively, hoping this would pass for understanding. I can always read it up later, he thought. It was something to do with a steel cable snapping on a ship and hitting someone, and the someone's family suing the ship – or, hold on, was it the ship or some insurance company? Leo was rattling on about something else now. Or maybe it was the chaps who made the cable that they were suing? He'd mentioned them at some point. Anyway, yes, it was a negligence claim against someone. Good, he remembered a bit about negligence pleadings. You just had to say things like, they were negligent in that they failed properly to tie up the cable, or provide a safe system of work, or –

'So d'you think you can manage that?' Leo was saying.

'I'll certainly give it my best shot,' replied Edward, with confident affability. 'I'll take the papers away and just go through them myself, shall I?'

'Sure. Here, you can take this . . . and this,' muttered Leo, thumbing through the documents. 'Let's see something on paper, say, tomorrow afternoon. Okay?' Leo knew little or nothing of Edward's abilities, save that he was a relation of Sir Basil's. Since he was a pupil at 5 Caper Court, no doubt he could handle the work. He gave Edward a smile and bade him goodnight.

Edward gulped as he glanced at the papers on the way back to Jeremy's room. It looked fairly formidable. Still, Anthony would give him a hand. No point in reading these till he saw Anthony. He went back to his room to fetch his briefcase.

'I'll just take these papers that Leo's given me to the library and – ah – look up a few cases,' he said to Jeremy. Jeremy frowned.

'I thought he wanted you to do some pleadings?'

'Well, yes . . . but there's a bit more to it than that.'

'Hmmph. Monumentally busy, is he?' Jeremy couldn't help asking. Edward could think of no reply, smiled brightly, and headed off to the common room for a game of bridge before his drink with Anthony.

It was nearly a quarter to seven by the time Anthony got to the bar; his father had rung him (an unprecedented event) and asked him to call round later that evening, which didn't leave much time for Edward.

By half-past six, Edward had already consumed three large Scotches and was becoming quite hilarious with several of his friends. When he saw Anthony, he rose to greet him with outstretched arms.

'Here he is, my saviour!' he announced. 'What'll you have? I've got the papers here,' he added, fumbling in his briefcase. 'Oh, now, Tony, these are some people. This is Hugh, and Alex – ' Anthony nodded and smiled; he already knew their faces from one of the rowdier coteries. ' – and Julia.' Anthony said hello to Julia. He had not met her before; he knew that if he had, he would not have forgotten. Curled up in one of the bar's capacious old armchairs, she appeared quite diminutive, but it seemed to Anthony that she had the longest legs he had ever seen. Perhaps they just seemed that way because of the length of her skirt. Or perhaps because, whereas most of the female members of the Bar wore black stockings, she wore stockings of some very sheer, dark mauve stuff. Her hair was short and soft and blonde, and her smile, Anthony thought, was devastating. He sat down beside her.

'I'll have a pint of bitter, thanks,' he replied to Edward, and then turned back to look at Julia. Hugh and Alex were engaged in some form of horseplay which involved one of them striking the other over the head with a rolled-up newspaper.

'I'm Anthony, by the way. I don't think Edward said.'

'No, he didn't. Hello, Anthony. So, why are you his

42

saviour? You haven't agreed to buy that clapped-out Metro of his, have you?'

'No,' he laughed, 'I said I'd look at some papers for him.' Now she laughed; it seemed to Anthony to be one of the prettiest laughs he had heard.

'Don't be a mug. Eddie's always asking other people to do his work for him. I know, I was at university with him. He hardly did a stroke of work. Don't be a mug.' Anthony realised that she, too, was a little drunk. He was somewhat lost for a reply. At that moment, Edward returned with his drink.

'Here we go!' he said heartily, setting down Anthony's pint. 'Now, where's this stuff of Leo's? Aha!' He passed the papers to Anthony, who took a sip of his pint.

'The thing is, Edward, I'm a bit pushed for time. I've got to go and see my father tonight – '

'Oh, it won't take you five minutes to have a look at them. Anthony's a genius,' he confided to Julia, who sipped her drink and tucked her legs up beneath her. They both looked expectantly at Anthony.

With a sigh, he picked up the papers and read through them in silence. When he had finished, he explained their contents to Edward in largely the same fashion as Leo had done.

'Yes, yes, I know all *that*,' said Edward impatiently. 'It's just – well, what do I *do*?'

'Well,' said Anthony slowly, 'that's a bit difficult to explain without actually setting it down on paper for you.'

Edward nodded; this seemed like the sort of thing he was after. Good man. There was a long pause. Eventually Edward broke it.

'D'you think you could? I mean, just a rough sketch, something for me to work on? I'm utterly hopeless at this kind of thing. Just something very rough, an outline. You're so good at this kind of thing, Tony.' He turned to Julia. 'He got a first. He's a genius.'

'Eddie, you're such a sponger,' remarked Julia, who rose from her chair, kissed him kindly on the top of his head, and left. Anthony watched her go. She wasn't very tall, but her legs were very long and she was quite lovely.

'I've never seen her here before,' he said to Edward.

'That's 'cause you're never *in* here, Tony. You work too hard. You want to get about a bit. Anyway, about this thing . . .'

'Whose chambers is she in?'

'I don't know. Some Chancery lot. God, what a thought. Now, they *really* work hard. God. But, look, what do you say? Just this once. Help me out. If you just put the drift of what I'm meant to be doing down on paper, I can flesh it out. He wants something by tomorrow afternoon.' Edward beseeched Anthony.

'All right, just a rough outline.'

'You're a prince. Fancy another?'

'No, thanks. I've got to go.' Anthony tied up the papers and put them in his briefcase.

'All right. Listen, thanks a million. See you tomorrow.' And as Anthony was going, he added, 'Nice girl, Julia, isn't she?'

By the time he got to Islington it was eight o'clock. The door to the squat was open. He found his father packing clothing into a large duffel bag. Two battered and overfull suitcases stood in the hallway.

'Off somewhere?' he enquired. Chay straightened up. He was wearing a long, feminine batik robe and his feet were bare. Anthony was startled to see that, although his father's head was still shaved, a wispy sprout of grey hair, some three inches long, was growing from the point of his head. It gave him the appearance of a radish.

'I'm going into a spiritual retreat,' replied Chay, smiling his holy smile.

'A retreat? Where?'

'The West Coast.'

'Which West Coast? Wales? Can I have a cup of tea?' Anthony headed towards the kitchen. After rummaging around, he could find only a box of ginseng and a packet of peppermint tea. He sighed, looked in the fridge, found a bottle of Aqua Libra and poured some into a cup. There were no glasses.

'California,' explained Chay. 'It's called the San Fernando Holistic Outreach Center. It's a spiritual community of individuals seeking tranquillity and oneness with their own

44

creativity and with God, whatever and wherever he may be. It's a concaulescence of souls. People concentrate on art, and on prayer.' Chay smiled kindly at Anthony.

'Sounds like a good holiday,' said Anthony. 'How much is it costing you?' Chay's smile shortened a little.

'Two thousand dollars for six weeks. But it's an investment. I look upon it as a means of getting in touch with my other self. I need to relate to myself, my feelings, to find out where I'm coming from in my art.'

'That's great, Dad,' interrupted Anthony, fearful that his father could go on indefinitely in this vein, unless stopped. 'But what's all the bit about God? I thought you were an atheist these days?'

Chay seated himself uneasily in the lotus position on a large bean-bag; his ankles were thin and unpleasantly pale.

'It's a mistake for anyone to commit themselves to such a state of certainty,' he replied. 'Which of us knows anything? What do you know, Anthony? What can you honestly and truly, searching in your heart, say that you *know*?'

'What I know is that you're off on an expensive jaunt in the Californian sunshine. Anyway, if you're so uncertain about God, you should become an agnostic.'

'I'm seeking for a means to legitimise myself, my existence,' replied Chay blandly.

'Well,' said Anthony, not knowing how to counter this, 'what do you want me for?'

'All this,' replied Chay, gesturing in the direction of his futon, his paintings, and the few other articles of furniture in the room, 'needs to be stored somewhere. This flat is very vulnerable, and there's no knowing how long I may be gone.'

'I thought you said it only lasted six weeks? Anyway, where do you expect me to put it? Mum's got no room.'

'You must be able to find somewhere. You've got friends.'

Why do I get lumbered? Anthony wondered. Why can't I just say no? I'll have to. There's nowhere – Then he remembered Bridget. Her flatmate was leaving any day now. She'd have a bit of space. He looked at his father and wondered how his new and lunatic ventures were spawned. He also wondered where Chay had got two thousand dollars from.

'Where's Jocasta?' he asked.

'She's gone ahead. I'm sending some things to her.'

So that's who's paying, thought Anthony. Silly woman. He sighed.

'I'll see what I can do. When are you going?'

'In a couple of weeks, or so. Plenty of time for you to find somewhere. It's only my few humble bits and pieces – you know how I believe that the spirit becomes encumbered by too many earthly possessions.'

'Don't I just,' murmured Anthony, and went through to the kitchen to pour the remains of his Aqua Libra into the sink. He came back through. 'Look, I can't promise anything, but I'll be in touch. See you, Dad.'

'Don't call me that,' Chay called after him.

At home, Anthony made himself a cheese and tomato sandwich and some coffee and sat down at the kitchen table to go through Edward's papers. It took him only half an hour to rough out the work that Leo had asked Edward to do. Surely Edward wasn't so thick that he couldn't polish it up a bit and set it out properly? He remembered what Julia had said, and remembered Julia. He hadn't thought about her since he left the Temple, and now the recollection surged pleasurably back. He thought about her for a while, and then he thought about Bridget. There could be no question of his going to live with her. But what about his father's furniture? Maybe she'd agree to store it for him, anyway. Not very likely. Oh, God, he would have to see her this weekend and they would have to talk about – about 'things', as Bridget called them. Things. Well, no good putting off the inevitable. He put Bridget out of his mind and began to think about Julia again as he cleared the papers up and headed for bed.

Edward spent all of the following morning in the library with Anthony's rough notes, trying to put the work into a finished state. At lunchtime he caught up with Anthony just outside chambers.

'Look, thanks a million for doing that stuff. I've worked it up a bit and I wondered if you'd just cast your eye over it. I mean, see that it's – '

'No,' said Anthony firmly. 'I didn't mind helping you out this once, but it's your pigeon now. I can't do it twice.'

'No, well, I suppose not. Anyway, thanks.'

When Edward showed the work to Leo, he was gratified by its reception; so much so that he quite forgot that he hadn't done it on his own.

'That's really very good,' said Leo. 'You've quite got the grasp of it. I didn't think you'd pick up on joining the insurance company as third defendant.'

'Oh, well,' shrugged Edward, 'it only occurred to me later on, actually.'

'Yes, I suppose it was only when you really grasped the point about the indemnity.'

'Quite,' replied Edward easily, wondering what on earth Leo was talking about. Still, it was good that it was going down so well.

Later that day, Leo mentioned Edward's work in conversation with Michael and Cameron Renshaw, one of the older tenants and a man fiercely keen to ensure that the good reputation of 5 Caper Court remained untarnished. He had initially been against Edward joining them as a pupil (a view expressed privately, of course), partly because he disliked the idea of someone being taken on just because he was Sir Basil's nephew, and partly because of his bias against anyone who didn't have a first-class honours degree.

'Your doubts about the old man's protégé may have been misplaced,' said Leo. 'I gave him some pleadings to do yesterday and he acquitted himself quite well. Very well, in fact. A bit ragged round the edges, but he'd grasped all the essentials. So maybe we won't have to worry about a great chambers debate over him. I imagine he'd do very well.'

'There's always Cross,' said Michael. 'He's really very good, too, you know.' Michael was fond of Anthony and, although the subject had not been discussed between them as yet, he knew that Anthony was hopeful of a tenancy at the end of the year.

'And he's got a first from Bristol, hasn't he?' remarked Renshaw.

'Well, of course, I don't know,' said Leo. 'Seems a nice lad.

But when pitch comes to toss, you wouldn't seriously want to set someone up against a perfectly competent pupil, who just happens to be Sir Basil's nephew, just on a point of principle, would you?'

'The principle being that nepotism isn't a good thing,' responded Michael dryly.

'On the other hand,' said Cameron Renshaw, lifting his large frame from one of Leo's chairs and hitching his braces, 'Edward Choke's a Cambridge man. Good thing, that. We're all Oxbridge men. Don't want too many new influences.'

'What rubbish!' burst out Michael with a laugh. 'I wouldn't call Bristol University a "new influence". We're not a club, you know.'

'That's not what I meant at all,' rejoined Renshaw, somewhat irked by the conversation. 'Nothing against your lad Cross, Michael, but is he – is he exactly our sort of people?'

'Well, I'm not exactly your sort of people, now, am I, Cameron?' asked Leo gently, with an amused smile. Renshaw looked nonplussed. He liked Leo; Leo amused him. He didn't care whether he came from a mining village or not. What he had meant was . . .

'Oh, bugger it all!' he roared. 'Who cares about these schoolboys? I'm off to do some work!' And he lumbered from the room. When he had left, Michael and Leo smiled at one another in silence.

'A tenner says young Master Choke is still with us a year from now,' said Leo. Michael hesitated for a second.

'You're on,' he replied.

Chapter five

In the third week of December each year, it was customary for Sir Basil to fret about the chambers party. The party was a tradition that went back to Sir Basil's father's time. In those days, Sir Basil seemed to recall, it had been a fairly civilised affair, with a few bottles of excellent champagne and some canapés, and was attended only by members of chambers and a couple of outside guests of sufficiently high rank, like the Master of the Rolls. (Mind you, reflected Sir Basil, the Master of the Rolls hadn't always behaved with the kind of decorum that one might have expected.) These days, however, the thing seemed to Sir Basil to be getting quite out of hand. The several bottles of champagne had grown to a couple of cases; there had to be a bottle of Glenmorangie for Cameron Renshaw, who absolutely refused to drink champagne; soft drinks and mineral water were laid on for those driving or bicycling home; a few cans of beer had to be provided, ostensibly for the postboy and the inhabitants of the clerks' room, although last year the postboy seemed to have mixed a good deal of Glenmorangie with several glasses of champagne and had to be carried to a taxi.

In addition to this, it seemed that a formidable amount of food had to be provided. Not just little biscuits with scraps of smoked salmon on them, but entire sandwiches, chicken legs, crudités, dips, vol-au-vents, sausage rolls, nuts, twiglets, crisps, cheese biscuits.

But what most exasperated Sir Basil were the numbers who attended. Far from being the intimate, serene event of former years, the dead hand of democracy had descended, and now the clerks, the typists, the postboy and, it seemed, their assorted relatives, also came. Last year a temp called Debbie had been sick on the stairs. Sir Basil was not looking forward to this year's party. It was no consolation to him to know that, all over the City of London, the heads of multinationals, the leaders of great conglomerates, and the chairmen of mighty banking institutions were all forking out so that their staff could get drunk and offensive.

He had suggested mildly to Mr Slee that perhaps the chambers party should be restored to its status quo, in return for which he would happily pay for the rest of the staff to disport themselves at some suitable restaurant. Mr Slee had drawn in a slow, whistling breath.

'Ooh, no, sir. Can't see that going down very well. Not with the girls, at any rate. Bit "them and us", if you get my meaning. If they thought you were getting snobbish about it, they wouldn't be best pleased. Bad as if you forgot their Christmas bonus.' This was a timely reminder. Sir Basil had gazed at his head clerk. As always, it was with some reverence. He had no idea how much Mr Slee earned exactly, but he knew that it must be in the region of some fifty thousand a year, if not more. Mr Slee had a five-bedroomed detatched house in High Wycombe and drove a BMW. Like all head clerks, his origins were lowly and his power absolute. Mr Slee and his kind could make or break a barrister's career. They negotiated fees and arranged conferences and hearings. They wheeled, they dealt, and they kept their ear close to the ground. Rub your clerk up the wrong way, and you could lose your footing. Mr Slee's word – though the word was always faintly humble and always discreetly spoken – was law.

So Sir Basil resigned himself to yet another invasion of his rooms by the lower orders. The best he could do would be to retire gracefully after an hour or so and hope that not too many cheese footballs were ground into the Axminster.

David Liphook, on the other hand, became quite school-boyish in his anticipation. He loved parties and general conviviality, and he loved free champagne. There was something particularly delightful about the prospect of getting legless at Sir Basil's expense, he reflected, as he watched Mr Slee take delivery of two cases of Moët one Thursday afternoon. Only marginally less delightful was the champagne for which one paid oneself, and he was looking forward to consuming considerable quantities of that at the cocktail party in Middle Temple Hall the following Friday night. He mentioned this to Anthony as they watched the van driver bring in the second case of champagne.

'It's always a spectacularly good time, the run-up to Christmas,' he observed with satisfaction. 'The Middle Temple cocktail party should be fun. Are you and Edward going?'

'I suppose so,' said Anthony. 'What's it like?'

'Oh, excellent! Always completely brilliant,' replied David confidently, although close cross-examination would have elicited the fact that David had very little recollection of last year's affair, save that of trying to heave his bicycle over the locked gates of Devereux Court at well past midnight.

Anthony, however, as he stood at the back of a sparsely populated Middle Temple Hall on the following evening, was not sure that the night promised to be especially brilliant. The ticket had set him back ten pounds, which he couldn't really afford, and so far he had spent half an hour in desultory conversation with two or three fellow pupils and had drunk two glasses of warm champagne. Bridget had phoned him that afternoon, nagging at him to make a decision about the flat, and he thought he had the beginnings of a headache. Just as he was considering leaving, David Liphook and Edward made their boisterous way into the hall. They both looked flushed and riotous.

'Tony!' exclaimed Edward, ambling up to him. 'Thought we'd find you here! Told you we'd find him here,' he added over his shoulder to David. 'Where's the champagne? Where's that woman?' He found a waitress and relieved her of six glasses of champagne. The hall was beginning to fill up now.

'We've been in the Devereux,' confided Edward to Anthony, quite unnecessarily, and launched into an account of the improbable events that had occurred in the pub. Anthony listened, amused, and drank another two glasses of champagne; he was beginning to enjoy himself now that Edward had arrived. When the crowd in the hall had grown more dense, Edward scanned the room.

'Wait here,' he said, and set off towards the other end of the hall. He reappeared a few moments later with two unopened bottles of champagne.

'Here we go!' he announced, and popped a cork. David gave a hoot of laughter. Heads turned at the sound. Anthony had often observed the rowdier element at functions before, but it was a novel experience to find himself part of it. Edward filled his glass; it foamed over and splashed on to his shoes. He licked some off the back of his hand and drained his glass in one gulp. Before he had noticed, Edward had poured him another. David was telling a story about a man in a bar and a piece of string, and at its conclusion Anthony found himself exploding with laughter. I must remember to tell Barry that, he thought. Someone else began to tell another joke, and Anthony glanced down at the floor as he listened. The polished wooden boards seemed to slope away from him at a strange angle, dizzyingly. He looked up quickly, alarmed, and leaned gently against Edward.

The flow of conversation was ceaseless, and after a while Anthony discovered that he was talking animatedly to some girl about the iniquities of the judicial system, and that the girl was Julia. She was dressed in scarlet and was gazing at him with sympathy and interest. Or so it seemed.

In fact, Julia was thinking that Anthony probably didn't get drunk very often, and looked rather sweet doing it. He was very attractive, in a dark, serious sort of way. He had soft, messed-up hair and a nice mouth. She wondered what it would be like to kiss him. She tried to say something to him, but the noise in the hall had grown and he had to lean over to hear.

'What?' Whatever it was, she tried to repeat it, but Edward was braying at them about going on to a restaurant, and a few moments later Anthony found himself in the dark, crisp December air, walking up Middle Temple Lane rather unsteadily, flanked by Edward and someone called Piers. Piers seemed to be a very good bloke. Very funny. Anthony wondered where Julia was.

She reappeared sitting next to him in the restaurant. They were in some rowdy Italian place in Piccadilly Circus, all sitting round a large table. There were ten or twelve people, it seemed to Anthony, all as drunk as he was; he didn't know a lot of them, but Edward seemed to. Edward always did. Good bloke, Edward. Very funny.

Although he was sitting next to her, Anthony didn't really talk much to Julia. She always seemed to be talking to people in the other direction from him, laughing a lot and leaning over. Her bare shoulders glowed in the light from candles stuck in bottles, and he noticed, glancing rather often, how her blonde hair curled in softly at the nape of her neck. How nice it would be to touch it. I'm drunk, he thought. It was just as well he wasn't getting much chance to talk to her. She'd think he was a complete idiot. God, this menu was long. Where were the rolls? He was starving.

It took everyone a long time to order, and then the food took a long time to arrive. Someone put a plate of avocado and bacon salad in front of Anthony. He ate it. Edward ordered a lot of wine. It was red. Not as good as the champagne, but Anthony drank it, anyway. It wasn't so bad once you'd had a glass or two. Someone put a plate of veal in a strange, sticky sauce in front of him. He wasn't really feeling hungry any more, he decided. Then he drank three glasses of mineral water in quick succession and felt better. Edward ordered more wine. Anthony decided not to have any more. But then he had some profiteroles and a lot of Cointreau in a large tumbler, which didn't help. Cointreau, he reflected, was really better in tumblers than those little glasses it usually came in. He should remember that – always have your Cointreau in big glasses. Better still, mugs. Big mugs. Julia was speaking to him.

'Here's a present. Merry Christmas.' She pushed a cigarette packet across the table to him.

'Oh, thanks. I don't smoke.'

'It's empty.'

'That's all right, then.'

'Put it in your pocket, like a good boy.' And she leaned against him, searching the inside of his jacket for the pocket. He could smell the soft skin of her arm as she moved; not perfume. Just skin. And softness. She laughed and looked at him for a moment. He looked back, wondering what he should say. But at that moment the bill arrived; and it was given to Edward to divide up. This process, conducted with the aid of a propelling pencil (whose point kept breaking) and a pocket calculator (which Edward was well beyond using efficiently), took some fifteen minutes, and spiralled into a series of rows over who had had what and whether Piers, who hadn't had a starter but had had cheese and biscuits, should pay extra or less. Those who hadn't had any liqueurs then demanded a discount, and then someone pointed out that service wasn't included, and the whole thing began all over again. Anthony eventually found himself, after complex negotiations which no one could follow, writing a cheque to David Liphook for twenty-three pounds (which he probably didn't have in the bank) and being given five pounds eighty in change by Edward.

At last they trooped out into the night and the sobering cold of the December air. Anthony caught up with Julia.

'Where do you live?' he asked her. She told him; it was the opposite direction from the way in which his own home lay. But he found himself continuing to walk beside her, and as they got further and further on their way, people began to peel off towards buses and taxis and underground stations, and at last they were walking by themselves.

They were talking – inconsequential stuff about people and work. Anthony still felt rather drunk.

'I'm very glad I met you tonight,' he said, after a silence. He wished he knew where the hell they were going.

'Are you? Why?' asked Julia.

'Because,' said Anthony foolishly. 'Because, because.' He stopped on the pavement. 'I'm drunk.'

'I know.' She gave a shiver of anticipation. 'Will you kiss me?' she asked him. Anthony looked up and down the empty street.

'Here?'

She took a step towards him and pushed him gently into a darkened shop doorway and raised her mouth to his. Kissing her was the softest, warmest thing Anthony had ever known. He had kissed numerous girls, mainly Bridget, but never had

54

he felt such extraordinary pleasure as this. He pulled her closer, sliding his hands beneath her coat and caressing the skin of her back; he wanted to go on kissing her forever. He wanted to stop kissing her just so that he could start it all over again. As he kissed her, he found himself thinking about all the other girls he had kissed and, absurdly, about the first girl he had ever taken out. Her name had been Lorraine. They had been fourteen, and they had gone to the pictures together to see *True Grit*. It had been raining outside the cinema, and when they got into their seats, Anthony remembered, Lorraine had sat there with her anorak hood up, the toggles tied under her chin. Every time he had thought about holding her hand, he had looked sideways at her and the whole thing had seemed impossible. The recollection of this suddenly made Anthony laugh in mid-kiss.

'What's so funny?' asked Julia, laughing at him laughing. Anthony told her. Then he kissed her again, and this time it seemed even better than before. He was aware that she had somehow wrapped one of her legs round the back of one of his, as though to bring him even closer, and he slid his thigh between hers and gathered her against him, as though to absorb her, to melt her into him with kissing.

It stopped eventually, as even drunken kissing must, and Julia tried to look at her watch. She stepped back into the street and squinted at her wrist.

'My God, it's half-past two! The last tube went ages ago,' she moaned. They walked on further, growing chillier and less light-headed with each step. They didn't talk much this time, and to make the silence comforting, Anthony took her hand; its warmth filled his. At last they found a cruising taxi, and Anthony put Julia into it. She gave him the briefest of kisses before closing the door, but it was enough to remind Anthony of their moments in the doorway of the shop. He wished he could find that doorway; it would be sacred forever. He watched her cab speed off into the night, leaving him in a deserted street somewhere in the West End. He had a vague idea of the direction in which they had been walking, and he headed off east. He knew it was probably four or five miles to his home, and he had no money for a cab, but in his exhilaration he felt as though he could walk tirelessly forever.

I'm in love, thought Anthony. This is what it's like.

The next morning, Anthony didn't so much wake up as regain consciousness. The walk home and two Anadin Extra and four glasses of tap water had helped, but things were still looking bad. He didn't lift his head from the pillow; it seemed better to leave it there. He discovered he was thinking solicitously of his head as though it were an object detached from his body. He rolled his eyes experimentally; they seemed to be attached to little fiery strings that reached into the back of his brain, and his eyelids felt as though they had dried out into some kind of thin sandpaper. His tongue filled his mouth entirely and, disgustingly, still tasted vaguely of Cointreau. The thought of Cointreau made him feel ill. Maybe he could be sick, he thought hopefully. But the very notion of climbing out of bed and making the effort inclined him against the idea. He would just lie there for a bit and maybe things would get better.

He wondered what time it was and tried to squint at his clock radio without moving his head; the fiery cords behind his eyeballs tugged painfully at the back of his skull. Twenty-five past eleven. Downstairs, his mother began to hoover. Please God, don't let her come and hoover in my room, he thought.

He closed his eyes and suddenly remembered Julia. His heart jolted painfully in his chest. He groaned and rolled on to his back, thrusting the pillow over his face. No, it was all right. He hadn't done anything irretrievably awful, he discovered, as he pieced together his scattered recollections. He took the pillow off his face and found that breathing helped. They'd just talked. And kissed. That had been fantastic. He tried to relive the kiss, but the bumping of the vacuum cleaner on the stairs told him that his mother was heading towards his room to hoover at him in protest at his late arrival home the night before. Whenever his mother wished to register her disapproval of any of his social activities, she would come and hoover round his bed the following morning. It seemed to Anthony to be quite the most vindictive thing a person could do.

He rolled out of bed and headed for the bathroom with gentle, careful steps, bent over like an old man.

It wasn't until the following Monday morning that he found the cigarette packet in his inside jacket pocket. On it, Julia had written her telephone number.

David had been right about the run-up to the Christmas vacation, Anthony discovered. Although people continued to work as hard as ever during the day, there was a general air of hilarity around the Temple and in the City.

On the day of the chambers party, however, Anthony silently reminded himself of his resolution, made in the wake of the previous Friday night's proceedings, never to drink champagne again and never even to *look* at a Cointreau bottle. But as the party grew closer, he felt his resolve weaken. And when he was actually standing in Sir Basil's room with Edward and the other members of chambers, it vanished altogether. It would not look good, he decided, if he were to refuse the glass of champagne which Sir Basil proffered with a benevolent festive smile.

The conversation was desultory and somewhat slow; only the members of chambers and two High Court judges, themselves former members, were present. It was understood that the hoi polloi were not to show up at the party until six o'clock. It was five-thirty and all the typists were crowded into the Ladies', applying fresh make-up and squirting perfume hopefully over themselves.

After a while, Anthony was approached by Sir Basil.

'Well, Anthony,' he said, shaking Anthony's hand. 'I don't really think we've had the chance of a proper conversation since you joined us, have we?' Sir Basil had heard, to his agreeable surprise, that Edward had acquitted himself well in a piece of work performed for Leo Davies, whom Sir Basil regarded as one of the more demanding members of chambers. He felt, therefore, that he could afford to be gracious to Anthony, who would now necessarily be leaving them at the end of his pupillage.

'Do you feel you're profiting from being with us?' he asked. The word 'us' sounded rare and exclusive when uttered by Sir

Basil. Anthony sensed very strongly his position as an outsider.

'Yes,' he replied hastily, 'Michael's a very good pupilmaster. I'm very lucky.'

'And where do you think you will be looking once you leave us?' The baldness of the question startled Anthony. He knew that Edward, as Sir Basil's nephew, must be something of a favourite, but he had not realised that the matter was already so completely decided. It took him some seconds to recover. In the intervening silence, Sir Basil murmured something about 'excellent vol-au-vents' and then said, before Anthony could speak, 'I have some very good friends in 3 Dover Court – lots of civil litigation. Perhaps that would suit you, mm? We'll have a little talk next term. Merry Christmas.' And he sailed off to join another little knot of people.

Anthony felt wretched. He realised that his dismay must have shown on his face, because Michael stepped over and said lightly, 'What's up?'

Anthony recounted his conversation with Sir Basil. 'It was just a bit of a surprise,' he added. 'I mean, there's another three terms to go, and I wasn't sure that Edward was all that keen . . .' He realised that this must all sound rather self-pitying. Michael sighed and squinted sadly at his champagne glass. The old man really picked his moments, he thought.

'Look,' he said, 'this isn't really the time or place, but we'll have a talk about it soon. I know he's the big chief, but technically it's not his decision. We all have a say, you know.'

Anthony nodded, unconvinced. He felt that his hopes had been utterly dashed. If Sir Basil wanted Edward as the next tenant, and if Edward wanted to stay – well, that seemed to be that. Michael, for his part, was angry with Sir Basil. He knew that Anthony had exceptional ability and that if he were given the chance, he would make the most of it. He knew a little of Anthony's background and circumstances and he wanted, for reasons that he himself could not fathom, to see him free of those beginnings. Anthony was his protégé, just as Edward was Sir Basil's. He hadn't doubted Leo's word when he had praised Edward's work, and so far Jeremy had voiced no complaints about his pupil, but what he had seen and heard of

Edward did not convince him that he merited the tenancy, and all its possibilities, as much as Anthony. Things would always be easy for Edward, but Anthony's ambition was solitary, and Michael wanted to help him achieve it.

There was not, however, a great deal to be done that evening. It didn't help Anthony's frame of mind to have to watch Edward, whom he sincerely liked, at his jovial ease amongst the rest of the guests. After a decent interval, Anthony decided to take his leave and go home.

As he made his way downstairs, Mr Slee put his head round the door of the clerks' room and uttered words that made Anthony's blood run cold.

'Oh, Mr Cross, your father's here. Just on my way to tell you.' Unfortunately for Anthony, he and Sir Basil had decided to leave the party at the same time, and Anthony heard Sir Basil's voice on the stairs behind him.

'Your father, Anthony? Why, you must take him upstairs to meet a few people. It is a party, after all.' To give him his due, Sir Basil spoke purely out of kindness. He knew that his few words with Anthony earlier must have indicated that he regarded the matter of the next junior tenancy as one which was now closed, even though he assumed that Anthony could never seriously have been under any illusions on the matter.

To Anthony, the words sounded almost malicious. But he knew that Sir Basil's preconception of his father must be of an ordinary professional man. Sir Basil tended to assume that most people's fathers were of that kind; that men should follow any other bent seemed to him to be beyond understanding. Like Michael's sloppiness of dress, he suspected that it was done from anti-authoritarian motives.

Anthony smiled in a vague way in Sir Basil's direction and then went into the clerks' room. His father was standing beside the wooden counter. He was wearing an old pair of jeans, boots, a T-shirt and a combat jacket. His head had not been shaved for some three or four days – nor, for that matter, had his face – and the strange tuft of hair sprang up from the centre of his head like a piece of chewed string. Normally his father's appearance would not have struck Anthony as being particularly out of the ordinary, but in the austere, civilised setting of barristers' chambers he looked incongruous, dreadful. Anthony felt mortified. His eyes met those of Mr Slee, but Mr Slee's face was blandly devoid of any expression. Mr Slee knew what he knew and he saw what he saw.

Anthony greeted his father unenthusiastically, noticing that Chay was not wearing his usual saintly, supercilious smile. He was not smiling at all. His face looked even thinner than usual and his expression was one of mingled anger and humility, slightly watered down – the expression that one glimpses fleetingly on the faces of vagrants in the street. Anthony was aware that Sir Basil had entered the clerks' room behind him and was now exchanging a few words – rather loudly it seemed – with Mr Slee before leaving.

Sir Basil had seen and digested Anthony's father in a matter of seconds. He had come into the clerks' room out of mild curiosity, and with every intention of meeting Mr Cross as a matter of civility. He did not now think that such civility was required. Sir Basil put on his overcoat and left, without addressing Anthony or his father. As he made his brisk, businesslike way across King's Bench Walk to his car, he reflected that it would have been utterly impossible, even if the circumstances had been different, to have countenanced giving a tenancy at 5 Caper Court to a young man with a father such as that. Most extraordinary, he thought. Young Cross seemed really quite a decent young man; but then, one never knew.

Back in chambers, Anthony was exchanging words with his father.

'You've been *what*?' said Anthony.

'Busted,' repeated Chay in low tones. 'It was at a club last week. It was only two ounces,' he mumbled apologetically.

'Oh, my God,' said Anthony quietly. Mr Slee reappeared from the inner sanctum where he had been discreetly busying himself.

'I'm just shutting up shop now, Mr Cross. I'm a bit late for the party.' And he smiled his knowing, deferential smile.

'Right,' said Anthony with a sigh. Taking his father by the arm, he escorted him out into the night. Behind them, Mr Slee turned the lights off in the clerks' room and locked the door.

They walked in silence through Caper Court and up Middle Temple Lane.

'We'd better find a pub,' said Anthony.

When they were sitting down with their drinks, Anthony looked across at his father, who glanced guiltily up at him as he sipped his pint. Anthony felt as though their roles were reversed; he felt like a troubled parent with an exasperating child, and Chay had assumed an air of superficial guilt, which would vanish just as soon as some solution were found to the problems he had created.

'Why didn't you ring me?' said Anthony at last. 'Why did you just turn up like that?'

'Sorry if I don't meet the high standards of your acquaintances,' responded Chay, sulkily. 'The phone's been cut off.'

'Oh, great. How did that happen?'

'No more bread. I really hoped I'd have got to the States before the last of it ran out. I've only got my Giro now.'

'What about Grandpa?' Chay's father was still known to make the occasional hand-out to the son he despised.

'No chance. Not after last time.' There was a silence.

'Well, what do you want me to do? I can't put up bail for you, you know.'

Chay shook his head. 'No – Graham did that. No, I need somewhere to stay for the night. The electricity's been turned off, too. It's freezing in the flat.'

'What about Graham? Can't he put you up?'

Chay shrugged. 'He's gone to France for Christmas.'

And no one else in their right minds will have you, thought Anthony. What the hell was he going to do with him? There seemed to be only one solution.

'I'm just going to ring Mum and tell her I won't be home tonight,' said Anthony, rising from the table. 'Then we'll go round to Bridget's.'

Chapter six

The business with Bridget was not easy. Anthony knew it wasn't going to be.

'Well, how long's he going to be staying for?' hissed Bridget in the gloom of her hallway. She was huddled into a blue candlewick dressing-gown, and the sound of the television came from her living-room.

'Not long, I promise,' hissed back Anthony.

'I'm not staying here on my own with him!'

'I know, I know,' said Anthony placatingly. 'I'll be here.'

'You're moving in?' Anthony gazed into her pleased brown eyes; she smelt faintly of Oil of Ulay and Horlicks. Julia had smelt of champagne and cigarettes.

'Yes,' he heard himself say. 'I've been meaning to ring you.'

'Oh, Anthony, that's wonderful.' He gave her a perfunctory kiss as the lavatory flushed and Chay emerged. He was quite himself. Bridget had known Chay since she had first known Anthony and had tended, since their first acquaintance, to treat him like a tiresome teenager.

'Come on,' she said crossly to him, 'I'll find some sheets and you can make up the spare bed.' He followed her meekly down the hallway to Claire's old room.

That night Anthony lay in Bridget's bed, unable to sleep. He had no notion of what he was going to do with his father. Tomorrow he would have to go and get some of his belongings from home and make a show of moving in with Bridget. She wouldn't put up with his father otherwise. He would smooth over any difficulty with his mother by explaining this to her. He wouldn't mention Chay's arrest. He would make it appear as though the whole thing were purely a temporary arrangement. It was going to have to be. He glanced at Bridget sleeping tidily next to him, then thought of Julia. He hadn't seen her since that Friday night, and he hadn't rung her because he couldn't see the point. He had no money. He couldn't even take her out for a drink. God, he wanted to see her. Maybe he should just ring her, just to talk, to make sure that she hadn't forgotten him. No, no point in that. He sighed deeply in the darkness. The next instalment of his scholarship money wouldn't come through until next term, and he had very little left of the earnings from his holiday job. All he could do was think about her, her silken blonde head, her long legs, the special smell of her skin. Her mouth. He tried to summon back what he could recall of their long, drunken kiss, but the sound of snoring came from Chay's room down the hallway, and reality blotted out the memory.

The following evening, Anthony went home to collect his other suit, a bundle of shirts, and some underwear.

'You're not taking very much,' remarked Judith, as she rolled up pairs of socks for him. It was part of her 'good-parenting' policy not to interfere too much in her sons' affairs, but she could not help making this remark to gain some extra reassurance.

'I told you, Mum – I'm not staying long. Just until Dad goes abroad.' Not that there was much chance of that now, with a court case coming up. He hadn't told Judith about that. Quite what was to happen over the next few weeks, Anthony could not imagine.

The next difficulty that arose was the question of what to do with Chay over Christmas. Bridget wanted to go home to her parents in Gloucestershire, and Judith wanted Anthony to be at home for Christmas.

'I'm not having your father staying in my flat on his own!' said Bridget heatedly, when the matter came up for discussion. In fairness to Chay, he had been self-effacement itself. He had padded about in his hessian and velvet boots, had cooked bland, inoffensive little vegetarian messes, done his washing at the launderette, and been quiet and unobtrusive. So much so, that he had managed to become a most irritating presence in the flat.

'Why not?' said Anthony. 'He can look after the place for you, see that you don't get burgled.'

'What? He'll probably invite a load of his hippie friends over, and I'll come back to find syringes and the furniture all broken.'

'Well, that's hardly likely,' said Anthony. 'He hasn't got any friends. Not any with enough money for drugs, at least.'

Chay chose that moment to make his entrance. He came in looking gentle and Jesus-like, and carrying two Safeway's bags full of groceries and wine, bought with his dole money. He had thought that regular small offerings of this kind might obviate the need to pay Bridget any rent.

'Thought I'd make us some supper,' he said, taking his bags into the kitchen, giving them his kindest, wisest smile.

'He can't do any harm,' said Anthony in a low voice. 'And it really will be safer if someone's staying here while you're away.' There was something in this.

'Oh, I suppose so,' grumbled Bridget.

That night Anthony made love to Bridget out of some strange sense of duty. It was what people who lived together did, and he couldn't stay there on false pretences. But weren't these utterly false pretences? He stroked Bridget's hair absently and wished she were Julia. God, this was awful – this was probably the worst, the most duplicitous thing he had ever done in his life. He'd just made love to Bridget, without wanting to, knowing that she expected it, and because he felt he had to say some sort of 'thank you' for letting Chay stay in the flat over Christmas. And all he could think about was some girl he'd kissed once and who probably wouldn't even remember his name if she saw him again.

Anthony was quite wrong about Julia, but far too in-experienced in the ways of the world to realise the beneficial effects of his apparent lack of interest.

Julia was a young woman who was intensely aware of her own worth. She came from a wealthy family, she was clever and beautiful and charming, and she led much the same sort of life as Edward Choke, expecting pleasure as her due. Unlike Edward, however, she was intelligent and single-minded, and was prepared to work hard to achieve her pleasures. But she was also very vain, as beautiful, intelligent young women invariably are, and her vanity had been wounded by the fact that Anthony had not taken the trouble to call her. At first, she had not really cared very much whether or not he did – he had been exceptionally pleasant to kiss, but then so were a lot of men, all just as attractive as Anthony. But as the days went by, and he didn't ring, the thing began to nag at her. Her irritation was compounded by the fact that she saw him once or twice round the Temple, although he failed to see her; the sight of the back of his unheeding head added to the impression that he had not thought of her since that Friday night, and was not likely to do so in the future.

This idea was more than Julia could bear. She was not accustomed to indifference. Men paid attention to her, sought her out; now she was being ignored. She had anticipated that she would see him from time to time in the bar, and intended on any such occasion to act coolly and distantly by way of retribution. But the opportunity never came; she found herself going there in the evening in the hope that he might appear, turning to glance at each tall, dark-haired figure that came in. It was never Anthony. Once or twice she had been about to ask Edward about him, but she succeeded in maintaining the appearance of rigid indifference that was her code. Julia found herself, uniquely, wounded and confused.

Anthony, unaware of any of this, spent the larger part of Christmas worrying about Chay, and what to do with him. He went round to Bridget's flat every other day over the holiday to make sure that he hadn't sold her furniture, and would find Chay drifting around in his preoccupied way, eating muesli, meditating, or rubbing ointment into the fading scorch marks on the soles of his feet. He seemed happily unperturbed by the prospect of the court case coming up in a few weeks' time. It perturbed Anthony, however. Things couldn't go on like this indefinitely. He couldn't go on living with Bridget, that much was certain.

But three days after the start of the Hilary term, Chay resolved matters by disappearing. It was Anthony who noticed that his father's few belongings had vanished from the spare room. And it was Bridget who discovered that the seventy pounds that she had tucked away in her tights drawer had vanished, too.

'Your bloody father!' she stormed.

'He must have done a bunk,' said Anthony lamely. 'I'll pay you back.' Bridget was not impressed by this unlikely offer.

The couple of days following Chay's disappearance were passed in stony rage on Bridget's part and perplexity on Anthony's. Then Anthony received a telephone call from Chay in chambers. He was in the States, he said, with Jocasta.

'We're preparing to go into retreat,' he told Anthony in holy tones.

'But you're on bail!' exclaimed Anthony. 'Graham's going to have to pay out if you don't show up in court!'

'Look,' said transatlantic Chay calmly, 'he's a friend. It's cool. I'll be with him in spirit. Don't tell him where I am,' he added quickly. 'He might accidentally tell the police. I'll square it with him when I see him.'

'What about Bridget's seventy pounds?'

Either Chay didn't hear him or decided to ignore the question. 'Got to go. Peace.' And he hung up.

As he put the receiver down, Anthony discovered that he felt quite relieved. Thank God he was gone. At least he was off Anthony's hands. He could stay in America, for all he cared, although that, unfortunately, seemed unlikely. The police could extradite him if they wanted to, although that was even unlikelier. After the last few weeks, Anthony felt he'd had enough of his father. He was no longer interested. Now he could concentrate on his work. And, oh, joy of joys, it came to him suddenly that he wouldn't have to go on living with Bridget. In a week's time his scholarship money would come through, and he could ring Julia. If she still remembered him.

Anthony's phone call to Julia could not have been more perfectly timed. After four weeks of wounded pride and faint nervous tension, Julia's original idle supposition that he would certainly ring had been replaced by an avid wish that he would. The obscure object of desire had become clouded by longing itself.

She felt her heart tighten as she recognised his voice. 'Oh, Anthony,' she said as casually as she could, 'how have you been? Good Christmas?'

'Not bad. A bit – busy. What about you?'

He'd been busy, had he? With whom, she wondered.

'Oh, so-so. Lots of parties.'

'Great.' There was a pause. 'Listen, I wondered if you were doing anything on Saturday. Whether you'd like to go out, or something.' He found himself wishing that he could sound less clumsy, less off-hand.

'Saturday,' she said thoughtfully. She had already been invited to a dinner party, but now she dismissed it from her mind. 'No, I don't think I'm doing anything.'

'Fine,' he said, 'I'll pick you up around seven-thirty. Where do you live?' She gave him her address in Kensington. 'I thought we might go out to dinner,' he said, 'but I don't really know any restaurants in your area. Why don't you think of somewhere and book it?' God, he shouldn't be asking her to do that; it sounded as though he really didn't care where they went.

'All right, if you like,' she said, thinking that he might at least show a little less indifference about the whole thing.

'Right.' Anthony wished he could think of something else sensible to say. 'I'll see you on Saturday, then. Bye.' He hung up. Julia sat looking at the phone. He'd been abrupt, almost casual; but at least he'd called.

The problem with Bridget was one he kept putting off. Nothing had been said since his father had left, but it was clear that Anthony hadn't moved into the flat quite as whole-heartedly as Bridget had imagined he would. Now, as he told his first downright lie, Anthony resolved that he would tell her the next day that he would not be staying.

'Why on earth is your pupilmaster taking you out to dinner?' asked Bridget, as Anthony shaved on Saturday evening.

'He's not. I said, invited me *round* to dinner.'

'Oh. Does he know you live with me?' Anthony met her eye in the mirror.

'I haven't mentioned it.' He rinsed his razor and pulled out the plug, wiping round the basin with a cloth.

'That's my facecloth! Don't use that!' She made an exasperated little noise as she snatched it from him. Anthony thought with dread, and not for the first time, what it would be like to be married to her. 'Don't you think you should? It would be nice to go to things together.'

In view of what he intended to tell her next day, this made Anthony feel like a complete heel. And since, buried beneath what he admitted was a veneer of guilt was an irrepressible, surging joy at the thought of seeing Julia that evening, he felt that he was behaving as badly as it was possible to behave. But he hadn't *wanted* to get himself into this situation. It had been forced on him. In response to Bridget's remark, Anthony made a noncommittal noise into the towel as he dried his face.

With a mounting sense of guilt, Anthony changed into the new red silk shirt that his mother had given him for Christmas, and a tolerably new pair of brown corduroys.

'You look very nice,' said Bridget in a small voice, as she watched him from the bedroom doorway. He felt he could say nothing, and gave her a fleeting kiss as he brushed past her to fetch his jacket from the hall. I'm a brute, he thought, as he checked his pockets for keys and change, and rummaged in his mind for something conciliatory and kind to say. He turned and smiled at her.

'Don't wait up,' he said, and left.

It took him the better part of an hour to get to Kensington, and he arrived at Julia's fifteen minutes late. The flat stood in a large, quiet, tree-lined street, whose houses, all now converted into expensive flats, were imposing Victorian buildings set back from the road. The air was cold and sharply still, and the solitary sound of his footsteps on the pavement made Anthony's throat tighten with nervousness. He pressed the doorbell and a buzzer buzzed; he let himself into the cavernous hallway and mounted the stairs to the second landing.

The girl who opened the door was not Julia, but her flatmate, another blonde, but tall, and with ragged hair and a chilly smile.

'Hi, I'm Lizzie,' she said in a lazy voice. 'Come in. Julia's busy fixing herself.' She sauntered into the living-room and Anthony followed her, introducing himself as he went.

'Drink?' she asked.

'Please. D'you have a beer?' Lizzie said she would go and look in the fridge. She came back with a can of low-alcohol lager, which Anthony accepted, not wishing to appear rude. Girls' flats were like that, he thought. He sat down at the end of a long, enormously plump sofa and gazed round the room. It was the kind of room that Anthony associated with other people's parents, not the kind of place that twenty-two-year-olds lived in. Lizzie followed his glance.

'Nice flat, isn't it?' she said, with her slow smile. 'It's my mother's. She and my stepfather have gone to Brazil, so she's let me have it for a year.' Anthony murmured that it was very nice indeed, gazing at the bookshelves that stretched from floor to ceiling, and the long, expensive curtains and deep carpets. They talked in a hesitant fashion, with long silences, of their respective jobs, and then Lizzie excused herself and wandered out to the kitchen.

Although Anthony thought that he remembered Julia quite well from the last time he had seen her, the reality of her when she entered the room stopped his heart. Everything about her, the blonde hair, the grey eyes and slender body, seemed suddenly intensely vivid and fresh. She was wearing grey jeans and some sort of blue top, low cut and in a soft, silken material; and some jewellery – Anthony was too dazzled to notice what.

'Let's have a drink before we go,' she was saying to him. 'What on earth has Lizzie given you?' She picked up the can of Kaliber and made a disgusted little face. 'Have a proper drink,' she said, pouring him a gin and tonic. Anthony didn't really like gin and tonic either. Julia's voice sounded casual, but she, too, was nervous. She, too, had forgotten quite what Anthony looked like, and how attractive his dark, clear-cut features and deep eyes were. She handed him his drink and they sat down.

The imposing surroundings, the altogether grown-up nature of the flat and its furnishings, put a constraint upon them that they would not have felt in a more cheerful, untidy setting. This room called for low voices and discreet movements. Their conversation was almost as stilted as Anthony's and Lizzie's had been.

Julia glanced at her watch and drained the contents of her glass. 'We'd better go,' she said, rising. 'I booked the table for eight-thirty.' Anthony had scarcely touched his drink; he looked around and set it down gingerly on a small, polished table. His spirits were somewhat dampened. He felt quite remote from this lovely creature; he couldn't believe that they had ever kissed, that his body had ever been pressed close to hers. The idea of such intimacy was almost embarrassing. She was probably regretting the whole evening, he thought.

They made their way downstairs and out into the bitter January air.

'Where's your car?' asked Julia.

'I haven't got one,' replied Anthony, startled. Each looked at the other in surprise.

'How did you get here?' she asked.

'Well, I got the train and the tube,' said Anthony. How did she think he'd got here?

'How awful for you,' said Julia, and they walked on. 'Well, it's not too far, so I suppose we can walk. Unless we see a taxi. It's a new French place, La Poubelle. Lizzie's boss says it's really good.'

Anthony hoped they wouldn't find a taxi, and reflected that if it was the kind of place Lizzie's boss went to, it would probably cost an arm and a leg. When they got there, Anthony saw, with a sinking heart, that his surmise had been correct. The restaurant was small and smart, decorated in pastel green with dark wooden chairs and tables, and was very full. When they were seated and Anthony looked at the menu, he saw a few figures in the region of four or five pounds. Maybe it wasn't going to be too bad, after all. Then he realised that those were the starters. He looked up and his eyes met Julia's. She smiled at him, her gentlest, most private smile, and suddenly he didn't care. He didn't care how much it cost or whether he had to starve for the rest of term. He was having dinner with Julia, and she looked glad to be there.

With the wine and the cheerful surroundings, they became more relaxed. The conversation was easy, general, and then, as the evening lengthened, grew more personal. Anthony told her about his father, which she seemed to find far more amusing than he did.

'He sounds much more fun than my father,' mused Julia, twisting the stem of her wine glass. 'Fun' wasn't exactly the word he would have used about Chay, reflected Anthony.

'My father's deadly dull,' she went on. 'An old sweetie, but quite deadly. He's the chairman of a pharmaceuticals company. Can you imagine anything more stultifying than that?'

Anthony, at that moment, was studying the bill with care. 'Did we have salads? I mean, did we both have salads?'

'God, I don't know. Does it matter? Let's just pay it and go,' replied Julia cheerfully. She stretched across the small table to peer at the bill in Anthony's hand; the movement pressed her small breasts together as she leaned forward, and Anthony was shot with a sudden longing to slip his hand into the top of her blouse and caress her breast.

'You're right,' he said, with difficulty. 'Let's pay it and go.'

Outside, they had walked no more than ten yards down the street when Anthony found himself kissing her. He wasn't quite sure whose idea it had been, but he supposed that it had been on both their minds for some time. Someone walking past bumped against them, and they parted regretfully and walked on.

'Would you like to come back for coffee? Or there's some brandy that Lizzie's brother brought back from Greece. Metaxa. Just the thing for a January night.'

They walked back in silence.

In the flat, the dignified, grown-up hush intimidated Anthony once again. Julia brought the brandy in crystal glasses, and he wished that they were paper cups. But when she switched all the lights off in the room except one small lamp, and came and curled up in his lap on the sofa, the imposing shades retreated, and all that existed for him were Julia's warmth and loveliness.

After a long time, Julia opened her eyes and looked at him. 'Would you like to see my etchings?' she whispered.

'What?' he whispered back. She laughed and pulled him to his feet. He followed her down the corridor to her room; he could hear the sound of Lizzie's radio, and Lizzie moving about in her bedroom.

'Fortunately, she's miles away from my room,' said Julia. Certainly the flat seemed to Anthony to be very large and the passage very long. Julia turned the handle of her door and Anthony went in with her. He wasn't quite sure what he felt; terrified, slightly drunk, completely in love.

'Julia,' he said quietly. He couldn't see her in the darkness. 'What?'

'Where are you?' They both giggled stupidly. She put her arms around his neck.

'Here.'

His eyes grew accustomed to the gloom. She stopped kissing him and moved across the room. He stood uncertainly, and then a glimpse of the long, pale loveliness of her legs told him that she was undressing. The white glow of her skin in the darkness seemed to be the most tantalising, sexy thing he had ever seen. With shaking fingers he undressed, found the bed, and slid beneath the sheets to encounter her soft, slim nakedness.

'God, you are the loveliest thing I ever saw,' he breathed, pulling her towards him. 'Ever, ever.'

'You can't see me,' she said softly, shivering, and laughed.

'Oh, yes, I can,' he said fiercely, and began to kiss her.

In the flat in Leytonstone, Bridget put down her copy of *Riders* and glanced at the alarm clock. Two-thirty. It must be an awfully good dinner party, she thought.

When Anthony got back to Bridget's the next morning, it was ten o'clock, and she was standing in the kitchen in her candlewick dressing-gown, waiting for the kettle to boil. He came into the kitchen and sat down, feeling oddly detached, his mind frayed by tiredness and guilt.

Bridget said nothing, did not even turn round. He watched her pour boiling water on to a teabag in a mug. The atmosphere was unexpectedly restrained; he had anticipated anger, perhaps tears, but instead all she said was, 'Would you like a cup?'

'No,' he replied shortly. 'No, thank you.' He felt suddenly irritated by the quiet dignity of her voice, by her evident intention neither to rebuke nor accuse. He wished she would.

He stared vacantly at Bridget's collection of little porcelain pigs standing in a row on the window sill. She brought her tea over to the table and sat down.

He realised that he must say something now, immediately, and rubbed his hands over his face in weariness and apprehension. Then he looked at her, at her compressed, unhappy mouth, at her brown eyes staring at her tea, at her unbrushed hair. The sense of elation, of bubbling happiness at his new-found love, which he had carried with him ever since leaving Julia's, seemed far away, belonging to some other world.

'Bridget, listen – ' he began, then paused. She looked up at him, dumb appeal in her eyes, the expression of a trapped animal. She knows what I'm going to say, he thought. 'I really can't stay here any longer, you know.' He looked down at his hands. 'For a start, I can't afford to pay you anything by way of rent. And you need the money. You need someone who can pay you properly.'

'And?'

'And what?' He looked at her, momentarily thrown.

'You said, "for a start". What's the rest? What's the real reason?'

'Oh.'

'You didn't have dinner with your pupilmaster last night, did you?'

He looked down again, not wishing to see the tears whose beginnings trembled in her voice. 'No,' he said, with gentle finality. 'No, I didn't.' He had to look up at her then, and wished there was some kinder, less honest way of saying it. 'I've met someone else.'

There was silence for a moment as he waited for her to speak. But she said nothing, merely stared at the table. He hesitated, then got up and went through to start putting his things together, while she sat mutely, her hands round her mug of untasted tea, wishing it was any day but Sunday.

Chapter seven

Sir Basil gazed sternly at the papers spread on his desk before him. This was not good, not good at all. For the first time since Edward had joined 5 Caper Court, Sir Basil felt faint misgivings. The work that he had given Edward to do had not been particularly complex, but it had to be admitted that the results which he saw before him were not up to standard. He uncapped his fountain pen, deleted a line of Edward's untidy writing, and began to write above it in his own meticulous hand. After a moment he sighed, and put down his pen. There was no point. The thing was too bad to be repaired. He would simply have to start all over again.

He gathered the papers together and descended to Jeremy Vine's room. Jeremy was bent over his work.

'Edward not here?' said Sir Basil darkly, his glance directed at Edward's empty chair. Jeremy looked blank, still lost in the fog of his own concentration.

'No.' He thought for a moment. 'No, I think he's gone to the common room to have some coffee.'

'At ten in the morning?'

Jeremy wondered for a moment what all this was about. Sir Basil closed the door and approached Jeremy's desk.

'I gave this work to Edward to do, and the thing he has produced is useless. Useless,' repeated Sir Basil crossly. 'Boy doesn't know the difference between waiver and estoppel.' He frowned at the carpet before speaking again. 'How do you find him?' he asked Jeremy.

'Oh, well,' began Jeremy uncertainly, 'he seems quite bright.' Jeremy had scarcely any idea of Edward's ability, since he had hardly taxed it himself. 'One's always a bit rusty to start with.'

'Hmm. True, I suppose.' Sir Basil sighed. 'Tell Edward to come and see me when he gets back, would you?'

Edward received the summons with a quaking heart. He had had those papers of his uncle's for five days, and he'd only got round to them yesterday afternoon. He knew the results were dreadful, but he rather hoped that Sir Basil would be too busy with the rest of the case to care. Even though Sir Basil was his uncle, Edward was not looking forward to this interview. In business, Sir Basil was all business.

It felt exactly like being back in the headmaster's study, thought Edward, as he entered his uncle's room. The air was heavy and foreboding, and the distance from the door to his uncle's desk seemed very great. Sir Basil looked at Edward over the tops of his spectacles as he came in.

'Sit down, Edward.' He smiled – only a small, not very encouraging smile, but a smile nonetheless. Edward sat down and, as he did so, decided to take the initiative.

'I've been meaning to come and see you about that work I did for you, Uncle Basil,' he said, with a sheepish smile.

'Oh?' Sir Basil was taken slightly off guard. 'Yes, well.' He looked sternly at Edward. 'I have to say that it is not what I would have expected, Edward.'

'The truth of it is, I didn't manage to get round to the papers until yesterday – Jeremy's kept me pretty busy, you know – and I admit I rather rushed them. There are one or two points I've been thinking about that I'd really like to go over again. I don't think I got them quite straight, you know.'

'Mmm. Like the difference between waiver and estoppel, I suppose.'

Edward laughed lightly. 'Well, quite,' he said. 'I feel perfectly stupid about that.'

'As well you might,' retorted Sir Basil. 'It's a fundamental point.' But he was relenting. Obviously the boy had just gone slapdash at this. If he'd taken his time and tackled it properly, it probably would have been perfectly respectable. He handed the papers back to Edward.

'Here – you can give it another try. But don't bring me second-rate work again. If Jeremy's keeping you too busy for you to apply yourself properly to other work, then for heaven's sake say so.'

'Righto!' said Edward, getting up to go.

'Edward,' said Sir Basil, as his nephew reached the door.

'Yes?' Edward really hoped that his uncle wasn't going to discuss the finer points of those papers with him now.

'Edward, you know that your parents and I hope that you will be able to make a career for yourself at 5 Caper Court, in due course.' There was a pause. Edward, uncertain at first whether this was a question or an observation, saw that some sort of a reply was needed.

'Well, yes, of course – I hope so, too.' He hadn't really given the matter much thought, of late.

'Because,' continued Sir Basil, with thoughtful deliberation, 'you must remember that Anthony Cross is also a pupil here. No doubt he is as keen as you are to make a good start.' Sir Basil had not changed in his attitude towards Anthony since their conversation on the evening of the Christmas party. As far as he was concerned, Edward would be the next tenant. But perhaps a sense of rivalry with Cross might give Edward the impetus to work a little harder and so quell any doubts that other members of chambers might have.

'Anthony?' said Edward, with some surprise. It hadn't occurred to Edward that Anthony was a serious rival. Sir Basil gazed at Edward, wondering what effect his words were having.

'You see,' he went on, 'the matter does not rest entirely with me. So you must make sure that you take care to display your talents to their fullest advantage. I do not think I need say any more.'

Edward nodded. He knew that his uncle was only trying to needle him into doing a bit more work, and he didn't feel unduly concerned. Still, it was interesting to know that Anthony thought he might stand a chance at a tenancy.

'Right. Yes. I'll remember that,' said Edward, and hurried off.

That evening, Anthony was sitting waiting for Julia in the common room, gloomily reflecting on the state of his finances, when Edward accosted him.

'Listen,' he said, 'I had my uncle going on at me this morning. He says you're keen to get a tenancy at Caper Court.'

Anthony looked at him, startled; outspokenness had always been one of Edward's qualities. For a moment, Anthony was lost for words.

'Well,' he replied slowly, 'I suppose I'd always had hopes, but your uncle's given me the idea that you'll be staying on.' He glanced uncomfortably at Edward. 'I don't really feel like talking about this, you know,' he added.

'No, well,' sighed Edward, picking up a copy of the *Evening Standard* from a table. 'It's all a bit of a bore. I don't know. I don't know if I want to work that hard.' His eyes scanned the sports pages. He seemed to be prepared to let the subject drop. Anthony watched him for a few moments, wondering what was to be made of all this.

'On the other hand,' Edward suddenly said, brightening, 'you can earn a fortune, can't you? Look at Roderick Hayter – what a life.' He glanced at the paper again. 'I don't fancy England's chances against France, do you?'

'No, not really,' said Anthony blankly. He was perplexed. 'The thing is,' said Anthony at last, 'if you've really made up your mind that you do want to stay on, you might tell me, so that I can try and get fixed up somewhere else.' It had cost Anthony much to say this, to confront his own worst fears openly and bluntly.

'Oh, good Lord,' said Edward, folding up the paper and putting it back, 'I would if I were you. See what else is open, I mean. Everyone needs some sort of insurance.' And with that, he announced that he was off to the bar.

Anthony sat there, thinking. The only real hope he had had since his conversation with Sir Basil was that Edward might not really want to stay on after his pupillage. Now that hope seemed to have been dashed. He sighed. It was time, he thought, to have a talk with Michael. It wasn't the end of the world. There were other chambers; Sir Basil had mentioned 3 Dover Court – they were a decent enough set. But they weren't the best.

Anthony decided that he didn't want to think about it any more. Over the last two months since Christmas he had been trying to accustom himself to the idea of going to some other chambers. After what Edward had said, it simply wasn't worth brooding over. More worthy of his attention was Julia, and the recent drain on his expenses. At first, the delightful discovery of how much they enjoyed being in bed together had put matters on a fairly economical footing. They spent long, happy hours in Julia's flat. When they weren't in bed they cooked messy meals and drank cheap wine, and spent weekends talking and finding out about one another. In short, they were immersed in the peculiar delights of a love affair's early stages, and needed little beyond themselves to make life amusing.

But the realities of everyday life intruded further and further, and gradually matters fell back into proportion. Julia was naturally gregarious, and needed to enjoy the company of others besides Anthony. She wanted to see her friends more often, and when she looked through the pages of *Time Out* it struck her that there were quite a few good films and plays that it would be nice to see on Saturday nights before going to bed with Anthony.

So she had begun to take Anthony to dinner and drinks parties, and he slowly became established with Julia's crowd. They were friendly, silly, spoilt young people from well-to-do, middle-class families; most of them had been to public school, and all of them worked either in the City or in the media. They struck Anthony as immensely confident, careless creatures – but then, he supposed, if he had a decent income, or any income at all, maybe he would behave with their ease and arrogance. He watched Julia with them. She sparkled, she spoke their nonsense, she shared their blank disregard for anyone who wasn't of their class or kind. At such times Anthony felt that she was a million miles away from him, but he loved her, wanted her so passionately that he sought to become part of these people. To a large extent, he succeeded. He was naturally friendly, and he found it easy to adopt their manners and jokes, and to enjoy their company. But in his heart, he felt as though he belonged to another race. He was unsure of what he was, or where he fitted in. These people were utterly without doubts.

That which he had known from the outset became increasingly evident – that the gulf that separated him from

Julia's world was money, or rather, the lack of it. Not that Julia and her friends had limitless private incomes – most of them relied on what they earned, with a little back-up from home. But in small things, Anthony felt the distinction very deeply. They had, or shared, their own flats, while he still lived with his mother. Some of them had cars, and those that didn't thought nothing of taking taxis wherever they went. For Anthony, considerations such as the expense of a taxi compared to the cost of a bus fare weighed heavily with him, and he resented it.

A recent outing to a restaurant in Walton Street with several of Julia's friends had consumed the remainder of Anthony's scholarship money with three weeks to go until the end of term. Now he sat in the common room fingering the three pounds fifty that he had left in change.

Depressed as he was, the sight of Julia never failed to lift his spirits. That evening she swept into the common room, bringing gusts of cold March air, a great scarf wound round her neck, hiding her mouth. She pulled it down and smiled at Anthony.

'Guess what? We have tickets to the opera on Friday! Anthea's mother got six, and she doesn't want the other four. Only twenty pounds each, but they're really good seats. It'll be brilliant fun. Have you been before? We can order smoked salmon sandwiches and a bottle of wine in the bar beforehand. You've got to wear your swankiest gear. I don't really like opera, but it's a pretty flash night out. What do you think?'

Anthony groaned.

'Julia, I have exactly three pounds fifty left in the world. I'm going to have to borrow from my mother for the rest of term.'

'Rubbish,' said Julia, unwinding her scarf and unbuttoning her coat. She and her friends were accustomed to bemoaning their lack of money. It didn't mean a thing. There was always money to be found from somewhere. 'You can always borrow the twenty pounds from your mother, in that case. Or cash a cheque. Now, where are we going this evening?'

'Nowhere,' said Anthony shortly. Sometimes Julia's blithe disregard for money exasperated him. 'I told you. I'm skint.'

'Well, who isn't? But surely we can stretch to a steak and a bottle of wine?' Anthony sighed and gazed longingly at her lovely face.

'When I say skint, I mean it,' he replied patiently. 'Completely boracic. No money.'

Julia was annoyed. It wasn't Anthony's fault that he didn't have any money, but it was becoming tiresome.

'Does that mean that you can't come to the opera on Friday?'

'It certainly does,' said Anthony. She sulked for a moment.

'Well, look, I really want to go,' she said pleadingly. 'Would you mind if I gave the ticket to someone else? I can always see you on Saturday.'

'Of course I don't mind,' he said, minding like hell. It was the first time that his lack of money had prevented him from spending an evening with her; this was probably just the beginning. 'Who will you give it to?' he asked.

'Oh – I don't know. Anyone who can rustle up twenty pounds, I suppose. Piers, maybe. He loves Mozart.'

I'll bet he does, thought Anthony. They had seen a lot of Piers Hunt-Thompson lately, far too much for Anthony's liking. He was an extremely tall young man, with an ebullient, cynical sense of humour and a good deal of money. Although he did not possess Anthony's good looks, he had a certain arrogant charm, and Julia often found his amusing conversation a relief from Anthony's worries over money and his future. Piers had no such fears, being already two years into a promising criminal practice. He possessed one additional attraction – he was in love, extrovertly and good-humouredly, with Julia. This made him an almost irresistible companion, particularly since the acknowledged fact of having Anthony as her boyfriend prevented Julia from having to put up with any serious nonsense from Piers.

Anthony was stung with jealousy at the thought of Piers having Julia to himself for a whole evening. He was more Julia's type; she would probably start to prefer his company if she spent too much time with him. The thought of losing Julia was the bleakest prospect he could imagine; worse, even, than losing the tenancy at Caper Court. And there was that problem, too. For a moment he was about to unburden himself and tell Julia of his conversation with Edward. But he knew that she was not in the mood; much as she cared for him, Julia wanted mainly to have fun, not to be faced with other people's anxieties. And now she would be having fun with Piers on Friday night. He was determined not to let it happen. Twenty pounds wasn't a lot of money. He would think of some way of raising it. With this thought on his mind, he told Julia that he had work to do at home. Sulkily, she sloped off to the bar; Anthony hoped she wouldn't find Piers there.

Anthony was trying hard, in tribute to some fear that he could not himself have identified, to make himself as inconspicuous as possible as he searched the pub in the Old Kent Road for Len. He shouldered his way gingerly through the crowd and the smoke, hoping that this wasn't Len's night at the gym.

At last he caught sight of him, tucked away in a corner at a table near the Gents'. He was sitting with a crowd of five or six other young men, all smoking and laughing, a great raft of full and half-full pint glasses on the table. Len greeted Anthony without surprise, and pulled up a stool for him. A couple of the young men stopped talking for a moment and eyed him curiously, then carried on talking. Len made no introductions.

'What brings you 'ere, then, Tone? You're not often down my manor.' He took a long pull at his cigarette.

'There was something I wanted to see you about,' said Anthony, beginning to wonder if this was a good idea. He hadn't seen Len for several months, and although they had been friends in the market, Anthony did not feel at ease with him in these surroundings. 'Look,' he said, 'let me buy you a drink. Do you want to come with me to the bar, and we can talk?'

Len nodded. 'Be back in a tick, Baz. Watch me gear for us,' he said to one of his friends as he rose. Baz watched Len and Anthony as they walked to the bar, gazing after them with the peculiar, unblinking, animal stare that an Eastender gives to strangers.

'What's up?' asked Len, as he took a sip from his pint. Anthony paused. There had been no preliminary exchange of pleasantries, how's the job, how's your mum – Anthony felt that it would have been easier if there had. As it was, he had no alternative but to make his request cold.

'Well, the fact is, Len, I was wondering if you could lend me a few quid. Just for a month or two, until my scholarship money comes through, you know.' Len stared at Anthony for a second or two, and Anthony wondered if he'd committed some obscure breach of Old Kent Road etiquette.

'I'd like to help you, my son,' replied Len, 'but I don't know.' He eyed Anthony; Anthony was about to say that it didn't matter, when Len continued. 'Wait here a mo,' he said, and went back over to his friends. Anthony sipped his pint and watched as Len bent over to talk to one of them. Then he came back over.

' 'Ere you go,' he said easily, handing Anthony five twenty-pound notes. Anthony looked at them and across at Len's friends.

'Look, if this makes things difficult – ' he began. Len waved a dismissive hand.

'Don't worry, Tone. They're good mates. Anyway, you said a couple of months, and I know you're as good as your word. You barristers 'ave to be.' He laughed. 'Anyway, I know where to come looking for you if you're not, don't I?' He gave Anthony a slight, friendly punch on the shoulder, and Anthony managed to laugh with him. He hoped Len was joking.

'Look, that's really great of you, man,' said Anthony gratefully. 'You'll get it back very soon, I promise.'

For form's sake, they stood chatting as they finished their drinks, although Len wanted to get back to his mates and Anthony wanted to go and phone Julia. As they talked, Anthony was aware that each was eyeing the other curiously. They had grown up a bit, he supposed, since their days last summer in the market. Len seemed to have changed physically; he looked less of a boy now. His neck had thickened and his expression was slightly more purposeful, less amiably vacant. At last Anthony looked at his watch.

' 'Fraid I'll have to go. Look, thanks for the loan, Len.' Again, Len waved his hand dismissively as he swallowed the last of his drink.

'You look after yourself,' he said.

'I will. Cheers, then.' Anthony felt it difficult to make a

graceful exit. He inched his way through the crowd, praying that he didn't accidentally nudge someone and spill their drink. Over his shoulder he heard Len call out, 'Keep in touch, Tone!'

When he got home, Anthony rang Julia.

'I've decided I can manage Friday night, after all,' he told her. 'So don't give the ticket to Piers.'

'Oh, that's great,' said Julia, and yawned. 'He couldn't come, anyway.'

It was time, Anthony decided next day, to confront the problem of his future. It was becoming clear that he would have to start 'looking elsewhere', as Sir Basil had put it. He tackled Michael on their way back from court.

'Sir Basil mentioned that he knew some people in 3 Dover Court,' said Anthony, after he had expounded matters to Michael, 'and I was wondering if I should take him up on that. It seems a good option.' He said this with a heavy heart, knowing that not only was it an inferior set, with fewer prospects, but that there was no certainty of a tenancy there, either. And without a tenancy, once his scholarship money dried up, Anthony knew that his chances of a career at the Bar were finished. He simply couldn't survive.

'Well, they're all right,' admitted Michael. 'But it's not the same kind of work as we do here, and I thought that was what you really wanted to do?'

'Yes, but I don't honestly think I can afford to hang on at Caper Court.'

'Well, you never know. I suspect that Edward's not all that great shakes.'

'Maybe he's not. I'm not bragging, but I'm sure I can do a great deal better than he can. But that's not the point. He wants a tenancy at 5 Caper Court, Sir Basil wants him, and that's the end of the story, as far as I'm concerned.' They had reached the archway that led into Caper Court. Michael drew him away and led him under the trees that lined King's Bench Walk.

'You know,' said Michael, 'it's not just a carve-up between

Sir Basil and his nephew. Despite what you think, it is up to every member of chambers, you know.'

Anthony sighed. 'Yes, I know. But look, honestly, the other tenants hardly even know me. Why should any of them prefer me when Sir Basil's nephew is in the running? I'm quite sure my welfare is the last thing they're interested in.'

'But they *are* interested in the welfare of chambers. They don't want to have to carry someone just because of who his uncle happens to be. It's up to you to make yourself known to them. Start pushing a bit. Good Lord, I can handle a few of my cases without you, you know. Go and pester them for work. William's absolutely snowed under, and Roderick will almost certainly give you work, if you ask him.'

Anthony looked at him hopefully.

'I will. I would, but . . .' He kicked at the dead leaves littering the cobbles, and paused, searching for words.

'What you want to say to me is "Can you look me in the eye, Michael, and tell me that I have an odds-on chance of a tenancy if I stay?" That's what you want to ask, isn't it?'

Anthony smiled ruefully. 'Yes,' he said. 'Yes, I suppose it is. You see, the scholarship I won is for the year of my pupillage only. I could manage a third six months, with my mother's help, at Dover Court if I had to, and if I was sure of a tenancy at the end of it. But I'd have to go there now. If I leave it till next autumn, I won't be able to afford it. Then what?' There was a long silence, Michael gazed up at the stark branches of the plane trees against the March sky, while Anthony picked forlornly at the black paint on the railings with his thumbnail.

'Anthony,' said Michael heavily, 'I can't make the decision for you. I won't say that I don't see further in these things than you do, because as regards the decision in chambers, I do. But I can't promise anything. Nothing's certain. If you really think you haven't a chance, then look elsewhere. But you're very, very talented, believe me.' Anthony looked at him quickly and looked away again. 'I don't think you should ever say that you can't afford to back yourself. Especially not when you know you're the winning horse.'

They said nothing more, and walked back to chambers in silence. Once or twice on the way upstairs Anthony thought of saying something more. But he knew that Michael had said all there was to say on the subject. It was a gamble. Either he took it and won – everything. Or lost everything. Or else he decided not to take the risk. At the moment, that seemed to be the most sensible option.

'I'm just going to take these back to the library to look up that list of cases,' Anthony said to Michael.

Mounting the polished staircase to the gallery of the library, Anthony looked for an empty table to work at. He spotted Edward hunched over some papers, various textbooks scattered on the table around him, all open at the section on estoppel. He greeted him.

Edward glanced up. 'Hullo!' he groaned. 'Tell me you've come to take me away from this misery for a game of bridge and a drink.' Anthony laughed and sat down opposite.

'That bad, is it? Well, at five-thirty, I promise I will.' He thought briefly and cheerfully of the hundred pounds that Len had lent him. 'What are you working on?' he asked Edward, squinting across at the textbook headings.

'This,' replied Edward hollowly. 'This completely nightmare piece of work that my uncle gave me.' And he shoved the now rather grubby papers over to Anthony and laid his head down on his folded arms, sighing. Anthony picked them up with interest and scanned them. They seemed fairly straightforward. Why on earth did Edward have all these books open at the section on estoppel?

'Come on,' he said encouragingly, 'it's not too bad, for heaven's sake.' Edward rested his chin on his arms and looked at Anthony with his round, childlike blue eyes.

'It is if you spent all last night in the Devereux and then lost your wallet on the tube.' And he closed his eyes and groaned again.

'Well, I'd say it was probably a question of waiver, rather than estoppel, wouldn't you?' said Anthony, as kindly as he could. Edward opened his eyes.

'Is it? Oh, good. I'd been wondering about that. I was quite sure it was estoppel.' He paused and took back the papers from Anthony, scrutinising their mysteries. 'Yes, that helps a lot,' he said, unconvincingly.

Anthony smiled and pulled out his list of cases. As he went back and forth from the shelves, heaping up his books, he would glance at Edward from time to time. Edward laboured on, oblivious, breathing heavily and rumpling his blond hair with his left hand as he scribbled away. He now had all the textbooks open at the section on waiver. Anthony brought back the last book and stood over Edward, watching him. He looked like a schoolboy, Anthony thought. That was the quality that everyone liked in him. He had a puppyish innocence, a sort of uproarious, tail-wagging charm. He didn't mean any harm. He didn't mean anything, really.

Anthony sat down and began his work, making quick, concise notes and setting out the relevant points on the cases in his rapid, neat hand. He felt as though his own confidence and quiet capability were thrown into sudden sharp relief as he sat opposite Edward, who was now frowning in puzzle-ment over some passage of text that he was reading for the third time. Every nerve in Anthony's body quickened as he sensed the other man's laboured thinking. Edward was pondering a problem whose essence and solution Anthony had grasped in the few minutes in which he had read the papers. Edward was not up to it. The realisation crept over Anthony as he watched Edward; he felt a little surge of pity. Then Edward looked up suddenly and smiled, cheerful and confident.

'I think I've got the hang of it now,' he said. Then he looked back down and frowned, and started writing again. 'We can go for that drink in a bit.'

'Yes, okay,' replied Anthony. In that moment he made his decision. Michael was right. He must finish this race. He had never lost anything yet, and he would not lose this.

Chapter eight

In the light of his decision, Anthony did as Michael had suggested, and began to badger the other members of chambers for work. If his policy was to pay off, and Anthony was determined that it must, then he would have to bring his abilities to their attention, make himself the only obvious choice for the next tenant. Edward could sink or swim.

At first he confined himself somewhat shyly to David and William, a little apprehensive of approaching Roderick Hayter or Jeremy Vine. But his success with the younger tenants eventually prompted him to approach the more senior members of chambers. He soon discovered that Jeremy would trust no one with his work, except for the most trivial of chores, and he had Edward to do those for him. So Anthony turned his attentions to Roderick.

Hayter was a quiet, sallow individual with white, thinning hair and a prominent nose. He was reputed to be wealthy in his own right, and it was well known that he had one of the most successful and remunerative practices at the Bar. Edward was full of tales of the awesome splendour of his country estate, his cars, his racehorses and his paintings. He and Anthony had exchanged no more than one or two words since Anthony's arrival at Caper Court.

He knocked on Roderick's door. A faint 'yes?' came in response, and Anthony went in nervously. Roderick was sitting in his shirt-sleeves at the far end of an austere, rather dark room, writing at his desk. One of the secretaries was standing next to him with an assumed look of respectful attention. He finished writing, handed her a tape and some papers, and then glanced up at Anthony.

'What can I do for you?' he asked, without smiling.

'I wondered,' said Anthony, 'if I might be able to take

some work from you. Michael suggested that I should ask you.'

'I'm quite sure Michael gives you more than enough to keep you busy,' replied Roderick dismissively. 'I imagine, however, that you want to make a decent impression on us all, mm?' Anthony hadn't expected anything quite as blunt as this. 'Still, at least you've come to ask me for work, which is more than young Choke has. Nor do I expect he will.' Roderick smiled his cold smile. 'He probably thinks he doesn't have to. He's probably right. Don't you think?' Anthony was to discover that this addition of a small question at the end of observations, forcing one into a response, however fatuous, was one of Roderick Hayter's more unnerving habits.

'No, perhaps not,' replied Anthony, feeling like a fool, without exactly knowing why.

'Well, since you ask, I think I can make sure your weekend is kept extremely busy.' Anthony's heart sank as he thought of Julia. Roderick was out of his chair now, leaning across to the book-shelves, on which lay rows and rows of briefs, all neatly bound with pink tape, like so many spotless sheaves of starched legal linen.

'It just so happens that we're in the House of Lords in a week's time.' He brought back to his desk an enormous mound of papers and rifled through them. 'You've been following the *Lindos*, of course?' This was the name of a ship; the case concerning its mysterious disappearance in the middle of a voyage from Iraq to Rotterdam with a cargo of several hundreds of thousands of tons of oil had been the subject of a controversial Court of Appeal decision some months ago. Anthony thought feverishly.

'The scuttling case?' he ventured.

'Indeed, the scuttling case. Or rather, as we maintain, *not* the scuttling case. Now, you can take these away and read them over the weekend. These are the judgments at first instance – ' He handed Anthony one folder. ' – and in the Court of Appeal.' He handed him another. Then he picked up a third bundle. 'And these are the various sets of pleadings. That should keep you busy. By Monday you should be fairly well acquainted with the facts of the case.' Anthony stood with the documents piled up in his arms. 'Then next week you can begin to go through the evidence.' Roderick patted the remainder of the enormous pile of papers. 'Don't imagine that you will be of the least use to me,' said Roderick, returning the papers to the bookshelf. 'This is merely an exercise to acquaint you with the realities of the shipping world. And it may be interesting for you to see how the House of Lords works. Thank you.'

Realising that he had been dismissed, Anthony left with his heap of folders. He knew that Roderick had meant it when he said that he could not be of any use to him. This, then, was purely an onerous exercise which was going to screw his weekend up. He thought gloomily of Julia's party on Saturday night. She wasn't exactly going to be happy when he told her that he had to work instead. He would have to, if he was going to read all this and do his work for Michael, too. It crossed his mind that, since it was unlikely that Roderick would have time to grill him on the finer points of the pleadings, he might have been tempted, had he been Edward, just to give it the skimpiest read-through and trust to luck. But he knew that the thorough completion of any task, no matter how apparently unproductive, was a habit ingrained in him; he knew it was a habit that every good lawyer had to develop. You never knew when that small scrap of seemingly irrelevant information might suddenly become crucial, when that brief letter or idle telephone note might become a turning-point in a case. Everything had to be read and digested, just in case.

Anthony was right; Julia was extremely displeased when he told her.

'I can't believe you have to work *all* weekend!' She sat up angrily in bed and reached for a cigarette. Anthony took it gently from her fingers, running his other hand down the curve of her back as he did so.

'You're smoking too much.'

'So what if I am? It's not your business.' She took the cigarette back from him and lit it, pulling the sheet crossly up over her stomach. He caressed and kissed that, too, before Julia pushed his head away.

'I just can't believe you want to mess up my party like this,' she muttered. Anthony sighed and rolled on to his back.

'I don't. But, like a prat, I asked Roderick Hayter for this work and he gave it to me. If I come to the party, you know what'll happen. I'll have too much to drink and then . . .' He turned over again and pulled her down on to the pillow, gazing into her face and stroking her cheek. '. . . I'll want to take you to bed . . .' He kissed her gently, urgently. '. . . and make love to you all night, because you're so fucking gorgeous. And I'll get no work done on Sunday.'

Julia let him kiss her. 'Please come,' she whispered. Anthony shook his head. 'I can't,' he whispered back.

'God, you're so stubborn,' moaned Julia, staring up at the ceiling. 'I wouldn't let anybody else treat me this way.' She paused and turned to glance at him. 'Maybe I won't let you.'

Anthony laughed, sat up on the edge of the bed, and began to pull on his underpants, enjoying his moment of ascendancy.

'Oh, yes, you will,' he said lightly. 'Because you adore me. You can't live without me.' He leaned back over and kissed her again. 'Can you?'

'Don't be too sure about that,' she said, smiling.

When Saturday night came, however, Anthony's confidence in his own charm had somewhat evaporated. He had spent the day reading through pleadings and judgments until he was bored rigid and his head ached. He had suffered several jibes from Barry, on his way out to a Meatloaf concert at Wembley, and was now sitting wondering whether he was, as Barry had tactfully suggested, a boring fart. He leaned back and stretched his arms above his head. He bet Roderick Hayter wasn't poring over papers at this moment. Maybe, on second thoughts, he was. Anthony sighed and looked round the kitchen. He wished there was some beer in the fridge; he could just do with a drink right now. He got up and made himself a cup of tea, thinking, as he waited for the kettle to boil, of Julia and her party. It was only nine o'clock. It wouldn't really have got going yet, he reflected. Maybe he'd been a bit extreme, saying he would work all evening. He'd been at it since nine-thirty this morning; he was entitled to a bit of time off. If he left now, he calculated, he could be at Kensington by ten-fifteen.

He needn't stay the night – he still had sixty pounds of Len's money left upstairs, and could always get a taxi back around one or two o'clock. Then he'd still be fit to do some work the next day. At the back of his mind was the knowledge that he would be unable to leave Julia once he got there, but the idea that he could get back at a decent hour if he wanted to persuaded him that he should go to the party, even if just for a couple of hours.

Although he had made the walk to her flat from the tube station countless times now, his stomach still churned nervously as he mounted the steps and rang her bell. The noise of the party poured out into the night air from the half-open windows of the flat, and cars were parked all the way along the pavement to the end of the street. Lucky neighbours, thought Anthony. He should have brought a bottle, perhaps. Lizzie answered the door. She was wearing an extremely tight-fitting black dress with a halter neck and black fishnet stockings; her eyes were rimmed with kohl and she had sprayed glitter in her shaggy blonde hair. Anthony found her appearance somewhat startling.

'Very nice,' he said, kissing her cheek. Their acquaintance had improved, albeit on a shallow, social level, over the months.

'Julia said you weren't coming,' said Lizzie, taking him into the kitchen, where most available surfaces seemed to be covered with bottles, glasses and cans. 'Here, have a glass of whatever you want.'

'Where's Julia?' Anthony poured himself a glass of what seemed to be, judging from the label, the least offensive of the white wines on offer.

'Oh, she's around somewhere,' said Lizzie vaguely. 'Listen, I have to get back. See you in a minute. Have something to eat.'

Anthony finished his wine, poured himself another glass, and ate a couple of token hors-d'oeuvres that were lying on a tray on top of the cooker. He was taking his time, anticipating Julia's pleasure and surprise when she saw him. He had never enjoyed such confidence of possession. He loved walking across a room towards her, kissing her, putting an arm round her, claiming her. He was keenly aware of the envy, never betrayed, only faintly ghosting the air, of other men as they watched him. She was beautiful, and she was his. He stood, savouring the delay, eyeing the National Portrait Gallery calendar that hung next to the fridge, as he sipped his wine. His eye ran over the date boxes for March. Lizzie had scribbled in several indecipherable things, apparently with eyeliner pencil or the end of a burnt match. Under various dates, in Julia's small, curling fist, were written: 'hair – 2.30', 'coat for alterations' and 'cooker man'. And then, under next Friday's date, the 23rd, she had written: 'Piers – drinks – 6.30'.

Anthony pondered this, not liking it. She had told him, he was sure she had told him, she was having dinner that night with her parents and friends of theirs. He reflected, then went to look for her. He couldn't see her in the living-room; big as it was, it seemed to be packed with people. He stood and talked to a few of Julia's friends – he still did not think of them as his own friends – expecting at any moment to glimpse Julia's blonde head. After a while, he gave up and wandered out into the hallway. He glanced into the dining-room, equally crowded, the air full of UB40, then turned and looked down the long corridor. Someone was standing in the doorway of Julia's bedroom. He began to walk down the corridor, and realised, as he drew closer, that there were two people, standing close together. They seemed to be talking. The man was wearing a yellow jacket. Silk, thought Anthony, as he approached. He tried to thrust a cold certainty to the back of his mind. They weren't talking, but kissing. He stood and watched them, still faintly curious, without embarrassment. She was kissing this man exactly as she must have kissed him, Anthony, that first Friday night. He found it shocking, faintly exciting. They were oblivious of him, completely lost in one another.

It was Piers who first became aware that someone was standing there. He pulled away from Julia and looked around. Julia opened her eyes. They widened.

'Anthony!' she exclaimed. It was just like very bad acting in a film, thought Anthony. Piers smiled.

'Well, well,' he said easily, leaning back against the wall and fishing in his jacket pocket for some cigarettes, 'in flagrante delicto.' He looked imposingly tall and assured in his expensive clothes, but Anthony could see that he was nervous. Anthony looked questioningly at Julia, uncertain what to say.

'So you didn't think I was coming,' he said at last, trying to keep the pain out of his voice.

'Oh, my Lord!' groaned Piers, blowing out cigarette smoke. 'No dramatics, please.'

'Belt up,' said Anthony.

Piers was relieved to receive his cue to leave. 'Such a bore,' he murmured, leaving Julia and Anthony and walking back down the corridor.

'I suppose you were going to take him to see your etchings as well?' demanded Anthony. It was not what he wanted to say, but he found that he couldn't help himself. He felt as though his stomach had fallen away; his brain was whirling with despair, seeking answers, lies. Julia leaned back against the wall and closed her eyes.

'I was only kissing him, for God's sake, Anthony.' He realised that she was really rather drunk.

'That was more than kissing him! And what were you doing here, in your bedroom?'

Julia opened her eyes. 'We're not *in* my bedroom. We're in the hall. Anyway . . .' Her voice trailed off. Anthony turned as if to go. She did as he had hoped, and took his sleeve.

'Look, look, look,' she said tiredly, unargumentatively, 'we were just kissing, that's all. Poor thing, he's been like a begging dog, and I wondered . . .'

'Wondered what?'

She giggled. 'Bit pissed,' she explained, with her charming, sleepy smile. 'I *wondered*,' she repeated gravely, 'what it would be like to kiss him. Don't you wonder what other girls would be like to kiss, Anthony?' She almost pouted at him, pleadingly. Oh, God, thought Anthony, she *is* drunk. But he felt the ache of misery receding.

'No, I don't, he said kindly, despairingly. She snuggled at him tentatively.

'Don't go. I've said I'm sorry.'

'No, as a matter of fact, you haven't,' remarked Anthony,

relenting. He knew he would not go, not so long as Piers was around. Typical of Piers to take advantage of the fact that she wasn't entirely sober.

'Well, I am. It was nothing, really, just a sort of joke. I do, do love you.' And she pulled him into the darkness of her bedroom, closing the door behind them. Anthony wondered fleetingly, disturbingly, whether this would have been happening with Piers, if he hadn't turned up. He could smell Piers' expensive cologne on her hair.

'No,' he said in the darkness, leaning against the door. 'No, you're having a party, and you've got guests. Come on.' He opened the door and steered her out along the passageway to the living-room. Julia went obediently, relieved to be forgiven. He decided that the matter of the calendar and next Friday night was best left until some other time.

While Anthony worked away, trying to make a favourable impression on the other members of chambers, Michael had been doing his bit for the cause, in a quiet way.

'What do you think of Anthony?' he asked David and William one evening in El Vino's.

'Very good,' remarked David, raising his eyebrows and scratching the back of his neck. 'Reminds me of myself at his age.'

William let out a burst of laughter. 'That's a joke! You did next to nothing, half the time. You certainly never asked *me* for work.' David looked at William.

'You never had any, that's why.'

William laughed again.

'I really think he's remarkably good,' said Michael. 'He has a first-class mind. He'll do very well, if he gets the chance.'

'Aha! The chance! That's what this is all about, isn't it?' said David, smiling, leaning over the table. 'Someone tells me that you've got money riding on young Mr Cross.'

'Very bad form, Michael.' William shook his head reprovingly. Michael looked annoyed and embarrassed.

'Well, the fact is, I *do* think he should get his chance,' he continued, frowning. At that moment, Stephen Bishop joined them. He was a round, solid man, somewhat given to puffing

94

as he spoke, and to wearing old-fashioned suits with pin-striped trousers.

'Well, here's another vote,' remarked David, as William rose to fetch another glass.

'What's another vote? What are we voting for?' enquired Stephen, looking round at them, the light glinting on his spectacles. 'God, this Court of Appeal hearing has me finished! And it's still got another week to run. Thanks.' He sipped his wine.

'Michael's plugging his pupil for the great Junior Tenant Stakes,' said William. 'We're lining up the votes.'

'Oh, don't ask me. I hate all this decision business. You know me – anything for a quiet life. What does the old man want? That's the way I get my guidance. He is my spiritual mentor,' said Stephen loftily, smiling. 'I do whatever he wants. That's the easiest way out.'

'You're not serious!' exclaimed Michael.

'Of course I am!' said Stephen in surprise. 'What is this? Australian Chardonnay?' He leaned over to look at the label. 'It's really rather good. Didn't you get a couple of cases of this, David?' he asked, turning towards him. 'I thought I remembered having some at your place. Not bad at all. How much a case?' He was trying, Michael saw, to change the subject. He found this sort of thing a bore. But Michael was not to be deflected.

'You can't, as a matter of principle, just go along with Basil in everything,' he pursued. Stephen looked faintly annoyed, and put down his glass.

'Look, I don't know Cross. He may be very good. But I gather that Basil's nephew is perfectly competent, and I don't see why we can't all just go along with that. It's hardly worth wasting good drinking time over. I don't see why we should have a great chambers rumpus over it.'

'There's something in that,' said David languidly. 'Anyway, it's more than just a question of how good he is. I mean, we have to get on with the man on a social level. He has to be one of us. I think Edward's an excellent chap, very good company. He's rather amusing, and I often think this set could do with a bit more amusement.' He sighed.

'You're beginning to sound like Cameron,' said William.

'Ho ho,' said David in reply. 'Thanks for nothing. I hope I'm not an Oxbridge snob, at any rate.'

'You can't count on Cameron, Michael,' remarked William. 'There's someone who could go either way. The fact that Edward's a Cambridge man counts for a lot, but then he's a great one for academic merit.'

Michael sighed, gazing into the depths of his empty glass. Should he care? he wondered.

'You're right,' he said to Stephen. 'Not worth wasting good drinking time over. Let's have another bottle.'

As it turned out, Anthony was extremely glad that he had read the documents thoroughly over the weekend. He had managed by great effort of will, once Piers had roared safely off to Barnes, to leave Julia's at two-thirty and go back home, so that he had been able to work through Sunday. On Monday, just before lunch, he returned the folder to Roderick, who rattled off several questions concerning the judgment at first instance. Anthony was startled, but managed to answer them.

'Well, at least you've read that much,' Roderick remarked dryly, returning the folders to the shelf and hauling out the larger bundle of documents. 'I won't ask you about the Court of Appeal judgment, because it makes me furious even to discuss it. A complete travesty. But, of course, that fool Greenwood shouldn't even *be* in the Court of Appeal, certainly not sitting on shipping cases.' He pushed the bundle towards Anthony. 'They're far too heavy for you to carry, and anyway, I don't want you losing any, so you can work over there.' He indicated a small table in the corner of the room. 'I've told Michael, so you won't need to trail around after him and Mr Khan.'

This was a disappointment. Mr Khan was a litigious Indian merchant who had become enmeshed in a rather fascinating way with some Syrians over a cargo of steel piping. This unsuccessful venture was presently the subject of an extremely complex fraud case, whose machinations Anthony had been looking forward to following. Better still, Mr Khan was a generous man who liked to live well, and who insisted on hosting excellent lunches for his counsel and instructing solicitors while the case was in progress. Now Anthony was to be denied these pleasures, toiling away instead over unspeakably tedious documents in Roderick's gloomy room. Perhaps if he worked fast enough, he reflected, he'd be able to join Michael's case again by Friday.

But Roderick worked Anthony at a grinding pace. By Thursday evening Anthony had ploughed his way through the documents and felt that he was able to give Roderick a pretty concise exposition of all the salient points and the relative strengths and weaknesses of their case.

'Excellent,' said Roderick. 'But since all the evidential questions were disposed of at first instance and in the Court of Appeal, you may find that it's of little practical value next week. Still, it's always useful to have the fullest possible background to a case, wouldn't you say? What the House of Lords will be dealing with are the points of law upon which we base our appeal. There are four of these. Two of them utterly useless, as everybody involved is aware, but this is a belt and braces job.'

Roderick then gave Anthony more points to research and lists of cases upon which to make notes. By the time Friday evening came, Anthony was grateful to be excused by Roderick, and went back to Michael's room.

'Had a good week?' asked Michael with a grin, as Anthony dropped into his chair.

'Don't talk about it,' replied Anthony, groaning. 'That man never stops working! And he expects everyone else to keep up with him.'

'That's why he's as good as he is.'

'Well, yes – but he's a bit – ' Anthony hesitated.

'Arrogant? You could say. You may have noticed that there are certain members of the judiciary for whom he hasn't a great deal of time. He's usually right. But he does run a case for all it's worth.'

'Well, I'm just glad it's the weekend.' He sighed, rose, bade Michael goodnight, and went out. On his way downstairs, he put his head round the door of Jeremy Vine's room. He found Edward still there. Jeremy was in the City, and Edward was taking the opportunity to arrange his social life and do a bit of serious telephoning.

'Fancy a drink?' asked Anthony. 'I've just had the most appalling week with Roderick.'

'Yes, I heard you'd been putting it about a bit,' retorted Edward, a trifle coldly. Anthony felt a slight pang; he supposed his tactics must be glaringly obvious. He was somewhat at a loss.

'Yes, well, you know how it is,' he said. 'How about that drink?'

'Can't, I'm afraid. Piers Hunt-Thompson is having a drinks party. It's at his father's house in Upper Brook Street, the swank. Aren't you coming?'

'I haven't been invited,' replied Anthony, somewhat discomfited. Then he remembered Julia's entry on her calendar. He'd forgotten to ask her about it, but here was the answer.

'Well, look, I've got to dash,' said Edward, gathering his things together. 'Have a good weekend, Tony.'

'Thanks. Oh, if you see Julia, tell her to give me a ring later.' Anthony went home disconsolately.

Chapter nine

When Julia failed to ring that evening, Anthony called her the following morning and went over to see her. She had been rather short on the telephone, and Anthony was suppressing a faint dread as he sat morosely on the Piccadilly Line on the way to her flat.

It was midday when he arrived and she was alone in the flat, still wearing one of the large, crumpled men's shirts that she slept in, and that always seemed to Anthony to make her appear tiny and vulnerable. She looked cross and had mascara smudges under her eyes.

'Want a coffee?' she asked, as he followed her into the kitchen.

'Thanks.' He wondered what to say next, how to broach the subject of the previous night. 'You seem a bit the worse for wear,' he remarked, as she handed him his coffee.

'Do I? Thanks,' she said shortly, taking her coffee off to the living-room.

Anthony's sense of impotence grew and, without wanting to, he said, 'Have a good time with Piers last night?'

She gave him a cold glance and sat down at the far end of the sofa, tucking her legs up beneath her and pulling the shirt-tail down over her bare thighs.

'Don't start that again. You were bad enough last week.'

'Was I? Well, perhaps I had some cause to be.' He decided against pursuing the subject of the party. 'Why didn't you tell me that you were going to Piers' drinks party?' Anthony was still standing in the middle of the room, his coffee untasted. Julia raised her eyebrows and took a sip of hers.

'Why should I? Anyway, I did, didn't I?'

'If you recall, you said you wouldn't be seeing me last night because you were having dinner with your parents.'

'Good grief, this is like the Spanish Inquisition. So what if I did? I probably just said that because I thought you might be hurt that Piers didn't invite you.'

'Hurt? You wouldn't expect Piers to invite me, would you? Not when he's been sniffing after you for the last God knows how long. He'll jump at any opportunity to get me out of the way, and you'll jump right back, so far as I can see.'

Julia banged her coffee cup down on the table and stalked past him to the window, where she folded her arms and stood looking down at the street. Anthony went on, goaded by her silence.

'That's about right, isn't it? Look at the way you were behaving with him at your party, when you knew I wouldn't be there – God knows what would have happened if I hadn't shown up!'

'Thank you, Anthony,' she said in a low, hard voice, 'for showing such complete trust in me.' Still she did not turn round.

'What do you expect me to think? And where did you go after the drinks party last night? Or did you stay at Upper Brook Street?'

'Since you insist on cross-examining me, we went to dinner – six of us, if that will set your mind at rest.'

Anthony stood sullenly, not knowing what to say. He felt again that sense of exclusion that seemed to dog him in all his doings.

'I'd rather you didn't see so much of Piers,' he said at last. It sounded pompous and unnatural, but he could think of no other way of saying it, particularly when he was talking to her nightshirt-clad back.

'Piers is one of my oldest friends,' she replied tightly, and then turned round. He could see tears glinting in her eyes. Allowing for her natural tendency to emotional exaggeration, Julia felt persecuted. 'I've known him since school. He's funny and sweet, I like being with him . . .'

'And he's got plenty of money, hasn't he? Which is one thing you certainly like,' pursued Anthony.

'I can't help it if you never have any money!' she exclaimed. 'I *like* going out to nice restaurants, I *like* being with people who

100

don't have to keep counting their small change to see if they can afford the tube fare home – '

'Thanks,' said Anthony shortly. He chose his moment, knowing that tears were a sign that her defences were slipping. 'You won't have much further use for me, then.' And he put his coffee mug gently on the windowsill and turned to go.

'Oh, Anthony,' she said with a sob, pulling at his hand, 'I'm sorry. That was a rotten thing to say.' He turned round. 'It's just that . . . he is my friend, and he does care for me.' She put her face against his shoulder. 'I would hate not to see him. But I do love you,' she added softly.

Anthony found her irresistible when she wept, and now he put his arms round her and hushed her.

'Just don't go out with him on your own, if he asks you,' he said, kissing her hair. 'Please?'

'Oh, I won't. I don't want to! I couldn't help it if he didn't ask you to his stupid party last – ' He stopped her mouth with a kiss, then led her back to her bedroom and the unmade bed, and drew the curtains.

On Monday morning, Anthony arrived breathlessly at Roderick's room, where Roderick was busily sorting out papers with the help of his junior counsel, Lawrence Ross. Anthony was not particularly fond of Lawrence, who was a bright-eyed Scot with a rasping voice and eager manner. The kind, Anthony guessed, whose hand had always shot up first at school when a teacher asked a question.

'Anthony, you're late. Lawrence, this is Michael Gibbon's pupil. He's been working with me for the past week and will be following the case. Anthony, bring that red folder – no, the blue – and you'd better ask the boy to bring these. There's too much for you to carry.' He heaped books and documents into Anthony's arms and slung the red velvet bag containing his robes over his shoulder.

They met the instructing solicitors in the waiting-room downstairs, and Anthony was given his security pass for the House of Lords. The five of them were rather cramped in the taxi on their way from the Temple to Westminster. Anthony tried to follow the cursory conversation between Roderick and the solicitors, while Lawrence interjected what he hoped were serious-sounding, coherent remarks. When they arrived, Roderick set off at a tremendous pace, Anthony and Lawrence scuttling behind him through the long archway, past the security men, up the winding stone stairs and along the carpeted corridors to the robing room. The postboy had somehow mysteriously manifested himself and was handing books to an usher as they sped past.

Anthony found that he was unaccountably nervous as he put on his robes; he had trouble fastening his collar. He could do no more than briefly admire himself in the small, square mirror – the sight of himself in his snowy wig never failed to arouse in him a faint thrill of self-admiration.

Although he spoke very little, Roderick seemed to do everything at double-quick speed, largely to suppress his habitual nervousness, and Anthony was almost forced to run after him as he whisked out of the robing room. Anthony tried to take in his surroundings as he trotted along. They proceeded down a long corridor, on one side of which arched windows were set into the stone wall, with hard stone benches below; on the other was high wooden panelling punctuated by various portraits of long-dead peers, with doors to the various chambers. As they rounded a corner, Anthony was startled to see a small television screen jutting out above his head from the wall. It bore some sort of message in green letters, but they were walking too fast for him to read it.

Roderick slowed down as they approached a mob of people milling in small knots in the corridor. There were barristers, solicitors and clients, and among them, stately and to all appearances oblivious of the hum around him, stalked the usher, grey-haired, beautifully attired, watchful and majestic.

Roderick and Lawrence were studying the court list on the wall, and the solicitors went to sit on one of the benches under the high window. Anthony looked around uncertainly, then joined Lawrence and Roderick as they moved away from the list.

'That couldn't be worse,' Roderick was saying. Anthony looked enquiringly at Lawrence.

'Lord Allen is sitting in the Barker-Bentley case, so we won't have him,' he explained. Roderick bit his nails and said nothing. Anthony was aware that the composition of the court and the inclinations of the various Law Lords would affect the case radically. Roderick Hayter had been counting heavily on the influence of Lord Allen, who had often given judgment in cases of a similar nature and whose thinking was in line with Roderick's own argument in this case, to sway the rest of the court.

At a signal from the usher, the knot of people outside the chamber fell silent and stood back as an untidy little procession of old men trooped along the corridor and filed into the room. Anthony went in behind Roderick and Lawrence. He had no idea of what to expect. Perhaps the chamber of the House of Lords itself, with the rows of benches and the Woolsack at one end. Instead, he found himself in a large room, high ceilinged and panelled in dark wood, with high, arched windows looking out over the sluggish grey waters of the Thames. The old men had seated themselves behind a large, horseshoe-shaped table, on which were arranged bundles of paper and neat stacks of books, an identical stack and bundle for each Law Lord. Lawrence and Roderick sat down at a long table arranged on the left of the room, facing their Lordships, and opposing counsel sat at a similar table on the right-hand side of the room. There was a central lectern from which counsel would address the court. The solicitors sat at a table behind Roderick and his retinue, and at the back of the room was a row of chairs for the various assistants and hangers-on.

Anthony examined the Law Lords curiously, as everyone sat coughing and shuffling and waiting for the proceedings to begin. They looked remarkably unimpressive in their everyday suits, without wigs and robes, and a couple even looked a little frail. At the extreme left, Anthony recognised Lord Buckhurst, one of the better-liked and well-seasoned commercial judges, on whom Roderick was now pinning his hopes. Next to him sat Lord Seaton, who was fidgeting and glancing around in apparent annoyance, although after watching him for a few minutes, Anthony deduced that this was a nervous tic, a sort of angry blink. It gave him the appearance, together with his distracted habit of looking all about him, of being about to rise impatiently and leave. In the middle, fat and smiling and genial, was Lord Fenton. Anthony knew from Roderick's previous observations that, since he had little commercial experience, Lord Fenton's views would carry almost no weight, although his cheerful appearance lightened the atmosphere somewhat. Of the other two, Lords Cole and Ennersdale, Anthony could not tell which was which, and it took Lawrence's impatiently whispered assistance to identify Lord Ennersdale as the one with the grey face and thick, white hair, who looked gloomily out at the court through gold-rimmed glasses. It was generally understood that Lord Ennersdale was the least likely to be sympathetic to their case and Roderick, glancing at him that day, mistrusted the determined, malevolent look in his eye. On the far right sat Lord Cole, a very frail little man, almost completely bald, hunched over the table like a sad monkey.

Roderick rose to open the case for the appellants, standing square on to the lectern, twitching at the sides of his robe with thin, nervous fingers as he addressed their Lordships. The morning did not go well for him. He got no further than ten minutes into his carefully prepared exposition of their first ground of appeal, when Lord Ennersdale interrupted him.

'Do I take it, Mr Hayter, that we are dealing first with that point with which Lord Justice Greenwood dealt in the final part of his judgment?'

'That was my intention, my Lord.'

'Well, I find this – ' There was a long pause, and then an irascible sigh. 'Please go on, Mr Hayter.'

Roderick continued. Five minutes later, Lord Ennersdale interrupted him to take issue with him on his argument. A brief exchange took place, Roderick was about to resume, when Lord Fenton interposed an observation of no relevance whatsoever. Lord Fenton, however, made his remarks so genially and with such evident satisfaction that Roderick dealt with the interruption quite politely, and then endeavoured to carry on. But they were all bitten by the bug now. Lord Buckhurst came in with some questions that indicated that his views might not be running in quite the same direction as

Roderick's, and then Lord Ennersdale picked up the ball and ran with it, rather tetchily, for several minutes. Roderick, Anthony could see, was becoming impatient and vexed. He managed, however, to deal with the next two grounds of appeal without interruption, except for one sad enquiry from Lord Cole, and things settled down again for a while. The mood was not good.

Anthony watched the court, wondering what was in their minds. Lord Ennersdale was taking in every word, Anthony knew, though he rarely raised his eyes to Roderick, but sat staring at the papers on the table before him, running one leathery hand over and over his long jaw. Lord Seaton had sat from the outset with both elbows on the table and his hands shading his eyes. Anthony wondered if he was asleep. Lord Fenton seemed to be doing his best to appear imposing and benign, but he looked rather bored and probably wished he were somewhere else. Lord Buckhurst looked singularly grave, and interrupted Roderick with a deadening regularity. His interruptions always prompted Lord Fenton to throw in a word or two, just to show that he counted. As for Lord Cole, he seemed to have given up after his first intervention and was dozing quietly on the sidelines – or apparently so, for his eyes were closed.

Lunchtime came, and Roderick expressed himself not well pleased with the morning's proceedings.

'I can't understand Buckhurst. I cannot *think* why he is taking this line. Greenwood must have been speaking to him. Or else,' he sighed, 'we are doomed to be sacrificed to policy.'

In the afternoon Roderick resumed his argument. He droned on for some ten minutes or so, and though Anthony tried to concentrate, he found himself gazing through the far windows at the river cruisers on the Thames, plodding along under the leaden spring sky. Then he became aware that Roderick's voice had stopped. The pause became uncomfortable as Roderick thumbed through his papers.

'If your Lordships will bear with me for one moment . . .' Roderick leaned down and muttered something to Lawrence, who riffled hurriedly through the documents in front of him, then shook his head. Lawrence in turn hissed to Anthony,

'The red folder! Where's the red folder?' Anthony was startled. Their Lordships were attentively and politely pretending to look with interest through their documents. Lord Seaton began to blink and look round. Counsel on the other side tried to look preoccupied and nonchalant.

'I – he said the blue folder. He's *got* the blue folder,' said Anthony in a low voice.

'I know he's got the *blue* folder. It's the red folder he wants. Didn't you bring it?' Anthony felt his hands beginning to sweat.

'No!' he muttered, frantic. 'He said to bring the blue one!'

Lawrence rose in a half-crouch and gave Roderick the news in an undertone. Oh, Christ, oh, Christ, thought Anthony. He stared down at the table; the documents swam before him in a white blur. He felt the blood begin to pound beneath his wig, which became unbearably hot. He breathed steadily, trying to recollect. Then he fished hopelessly in his briefcase and among the documents. Roderick was straightening up.

'If it please your Lordships, I intend to proceed to that other matter – '

'But Mr Hayter,' said Lord Ennersdale snappishly, 'have you completed your remarks in this regard?'

'My Lord, no – But I think it appropriate to return to them at another . . . juncture. If your Lordships will be so good as to turn to – '

'But Mr Hayter,' persisted his Lordship, 'wishing no discourtesy, I believe we may find it rather inconvenient to have to pursue the argument in this circuitous fashion. If perhaps . . .'

Anthony was barely listening. His fingernails were pressed tight into the palms of his hands, and he was aware only that some awful blunder had been made. He had left some vital document behind. The whole case would founder because of it. He was living his worst nightmare.

In fact, the lack of the folder, while an inconvenience to Roderick, merely forced him to abandon his carefully prepared dissertation and take up another tack. It was clumsy and did not assist the smooth exposition of the argument but, in substance, it was of a minor nature. He was far too experienced to be unduly thrown by the mishap, but Anthony was sure, with the self-centred certainty of the young, that he had somehow upset the case. He did not know what was in the red folder – in fact, it contained merely a few sheets of paper setting out ancillary points which Roderick had intended to bring in should things not be going their way, and which he was now making in any event – but he was sure that it must be something vital.

Lawrence managed to compound Anthony's certainty by his very manner, as they packed up their belongings at the end of the afternoon. Anthony's morale sank lower and lower. Roderick, in fact, had forgotten the matter entirely, until Lawrence mentioned it as they walked back through Caper Court, Anthony trailing in their wake in the miserable silence which he had maintained all afternoon.

'The red folder? Oh, that wasn't in the least important – probably my fault that we left it behind, anyway.'

But Anthony was walking too far behind to hear.

The following day, Roderick's grim silence merely served to convince Anthony that the matter of the red folder had not been forgotten, and that it was at the forefront of Roderick's mind. But Roderick was habitually grim and silent during an important case, and what Anthony mistook for wordless wrath was purely concentration. Suffering under his own conceit, Anthony robed and took his place next to Lawrence. Their Lordships sat as before, giving the impression that they might have been sitting there all through the dark night and the slow break of day, like so many morose grey dolls.

Lawrence rose and spent twenty minutes dealing with subsidiary points, and then counsel for the respondents rose. Earnest Slattery was an imposing man of sixty or so, tall, of a rather rubbery thinness, whose naturally laconic self-confidence was improved by the indications given by the court the previous day that they might not be wholly sympathetic to the appellants' case. Slattery started off in an upright posture, but as his discourse gathered momentum and his eloquence rose to ever more satisfactory heights – to his own ear, at least – he began to lean on the lectern and gradually to drape himself over it, only now and then drawing his body back slowly so that he could glance down at his notes, then leaning forward again. He gave the impression, after a while, of a swaying eel. Slattery always smiled slightly as he spoke, which enhanced his air of confidence and imparted a sense of it to his audience.

Their Lordships reacted benevolently to Mr Slattery. From time to time, Lord Ennersdale would nod swiftly and approvingly at the polished surface of the table, and even Lord Buckhurst was seen to give a wry nod once or twice in the direction of his fountain pen. This became infectious, in that Lawrence took to giving occasional, furious little shakes of his head, as though appalled at the audacity of their opponents in putting forward such spurious and manifestly wrong-headed arguments. Roderick merely sat gazing at the table before him, occasionally glancing up at Slattery.

Eloquent though he was, Mr Slattery failed to rivet Anthony's attention. His glance wandered to the back of the room, where he saw, sitting amongst the clerks and assistants, a middle-aged woman, wearing a dress and a cardigan and rather good shoes, and knitting. She, like Earnest Slattery, was smiling faintly to herself. When she came to the end of a row she would look up, still smiling, turn her needles around, and continue knitting at a furious pace. When they rose for lunch, Roderick noticed her, too.

'Ah, is *she* here? That bodes ill for us. That's Earnest Slattery's wife. Whenever he's speaking in the House of Lords, if he thinks the case is going well for their side she comes along to listen to him. I think she's very proud of him. She can't understand a word of what's going on, mind you. It seems they share a mutual enjoyment of the sound of his voice.' It was perhaps the only time that Anthony saw him smile that day.

During the afternoon, Slattery continued. Mrs Slattery finished one ball of wool and started another. Just as the thing began to seem to Anthony to be interminable, Lord Buckhurst leaned forward to interrupt.

'I think, Mr Slattery, that I can safely say that we shall not need to hear from you on that point.' He glanced enquiringly at his fellow Law Lords. Lord Ennersdale looked up; the light fell on his glasses so that one could not see his eyes. He shook his head slightly, as did Lord Fenton, although Anthony guessed that he probably didn't know what he was shaking his head at, and could well have nodded if anyone else had done so. Lord Cole murmured something inaudible and stifled a yawn, and Lord Seaton merely clasped his hands and blinked crossly. This was bad, Anthony knew. It meant that they did not need to hear Earnest Slattery's arguments in opposition to Roderick's, since they had already made up their minds. Anthony glanced at Roderick, who merely dipped his head and pursed his lips. Lawrence was busy looking very grim.

Although disappointed that the flow of his eloquence was to be prematurely stemmed in this way, Mr Slattery graciously and rather wordily acceded to their Lordships' request and closed his argument. Mr Slattery's junior rose, opened his mouth, only to hear Lord Buckhurst say that they did not think they needed to trouble Mr Polson, thank you. This was galling to young Mr Polson, who had been working up his points for some days now, but a good omen for their case. He murmured his thanks and sat down.

It was over, and Anthony knew that, even although judgment would not be delivered for some weeks, possibly months, they had in all probability lost. He could not bear to contemplate the possibility that the red folder might have been in any way vital. While Roderick and Earnest Slattery moved off together down the corridor, talking and laughing in low voices, Anthony followed, ignored by the two self-important juniors, once again feeling shut out from the world to which he so wished to belong. He had blundered. Worse still, he had blundered on behalf of the most important person in chambers, next to Sir Basil. He felt that he could never redeem himself, and that he would almost certainly not receive any support from Roderick Hayter when it came to choosing the next tenant. So much for displaying his serious endeavour and hard-working abilities to the rest of chambers.

Mr Slee was standing behind the counter, opening the mail, when Anthony and Roderick returned to chambers. He looked up and glanced at Anthony's face, following him with his eyes as he made his way upstairs. The junior clerk, Henry, caught his glance.

'He never seems too happy these days,' Henry remarked.

'Who?' murmured Mr Slee, slicing into an envelope.

Henry jerked a thumb. 'Mr Gibbon's pupil.'

Mr Slee smiled, drawing out a letter, perusing its contents, and placing it in Sir Basil's tray. 'House of Lords can get you that way,' he said. 'Depressin' bunch of old buggers, by and large.'

'I reckon he's got the wind up because of Sir Basil's nephew,' said Henry.

'You never can tell,' murmured Mr Slee, 'you never can tell. And that's the truth.' He whistled briefly and softly as he slit open a large envelope. 'He's a perseverin' sort of chap, Mr Cross. Not something you could exactly say about Mr Choke.'

'Ah, but he's not the head of chambers' nephew, is he?' said Henry wisely, tossing into the bin the envelopes that Mr Slee was discarding.

'There again, Henry, family can be more of a hindrance than a help.' Some recollection of Anthony's father may have occurred to him then, for a censorious expression crossed his face as he gravely laid a set of papers in Cameron Renshaw's tray. 'But like I said, you never can tell.'

Later that week, Roderick was having a sherry with Michael Gibbon at the end of the day. Anthony had already left.

'I rather like your pupil, you know. He worked very hard on the *Lindos*. Seems extremely keen.' Roderick took a sip of his sherry. 'Miserable little sod, though. You'd have thought from his face that it was he who was losing the case, not I.'

Chapter ten

The year progressed, the clocks went forward, and spring's soft, green mantle fell over the legal world. The antiquated gas lamps around the Temple were no longer lit at four o'clock, barristers no longer scurried through the cloisters with their jacket collars up and scarves wound round their necks, and beneath the budding trees in Fountain Court the sparkling waters played. Bicycles reappeared in the bicycle rack in Brick Court, little breezes crept in through half-opened windows and ruffled the corners of weighty documents. Mr Slee began to work with his jacket off, and judgment was given in the *Lindos*.

They had lost, of course, and although Anthony had put the matter of the red folder behind him, he still felt that he had failed, through his carelessness, to acquit himself well with Roderick. He had, accordingly, given up looking for work from other members of chambers for the time being, and instead worked steadily away on Michael's cases. He had spent rather a jading morning listening to one of Michael's clients, a very tall, loquacious American businessman, talking of his case in terms of 'yes and no issues', referring to rival businessmen who 'headed up' companies, or were 'the moving minds' in various operations. It took the client, with his jargon, an hour longer to explain his position than it otherwise would have, and Anthony, meeting Edward on the staircase at lunchtime, felt relieved to rejoin the English-speaking world.

'You doing anything the weekend after next?' asked Edward as they crossed the lane to go into the hall.

'Easter weekend? No, I don't think so. Why?'

'Oh, my mother suggested I should have some people down. I thought you and Julia and Piers might want to come along. I might see if David Liphook is interested, too.' They lined up at the long tables in hall, each taking a plate.

'Yes, I'd like to. Thank you. I'll mention it to Julia.' Anthony was surprised; he hadn't imagined that Mrs Choke would be particularly anxious to extend hospitality to her son's rival in chambers. More probably, thought Anthony gloomily, the family regarded the question of the tenancy as settled and thought that Anthony was of no real significance, apart from being a colleague of Edward's.

'I've already asked her,' said Edward, watching the maid spoon some nameless casserole on to his plate. 'No peas, thanks. She's definitely coming – she and Piers have been down a few times.'

Uncertain as to whether he felt included or excluded by this piece of information, Anthony pondered the fact that Julia had already agreed to go. He had been careful not to mention Piers recently, but he knew that Piers still telephoned her and met her in the bar occasionally in the evenings. He made her laugh – and Julia loved to laugh. No doubt she relished rather more than Anthony the prospect of spending three whole days in his company.

On the Thursday evening before Good Friday, they had all planned to meet in the bar in Middle Temple and then take a taxi to Waterloo. David and Piers were in particularly hilarious spirits, which only served to deepen Anthony's sense of depression over the argument that he and Julia had had the previous evening. She had wanted to go with some friends for supper in Covent Garden, but Anthony had refused, saying that he couldn't afford it. He was determined to manage that term's finances carefully; he still didn't know how he was going to pay Len back. He had thought that he might be able to pay it in a lump out of his scholarship money, but that now looked impossible. In exasperation, Julia had offered to pay for him; he had refused.

'Oh, come on, Anthony!' she had exclaimed. 'I don't *mind* paying for you.'

'Well, I mind being paid for,' Anthony had replied. Some instinct told him that if she began to pay for things, it would somehow undermine him, that she would begin to feel sorry for him, or regard him as a bit of a nuisance.

'I honestly don't know why you make all this fuss.'

'It's not me that's making the fuss,' said Anthony.

'Well, I want to go. I haven't seen Louise since she came back from Italy.'

'I thought you were meant to be spending the evening with me?'

'And do what? Sit around the flat with a cup of coffee, or mope over a half-pint in the pub? No thanks. If you won't let me pay for one meal for you, you can sulk at home. I'm going.'

And she had gone. The atmosphere between them had not improved by the time they met in the bar. Anthony had determined that he would not appear to be short of money this weekend, and had set aside forty pounds, which was as much as he could spare. The train fare to Edward's would set him back almost half that amount.

As he bought a round of drinks he realised, with distaste, that he was making mental calculations of ways to eke out his money. Edward was insisting that everyone should drink doubles, which didn't help. He tried to raise his spirits by concentrating on Piers, who was being even more ridiculously funny than usual, but he was aware that Julia had said very little to him and was pointedly focusing all her attention on Edward.

In the taxi on the way to Waterloo, however, she sat next to him and responded with her soft, private smile when he surreptitiously ran his finger down her spine. After Piers had been extremely rude to the taxi driver and refused to tip him, so that he roared off into the night trailing a filthy stream of invective, they trooped to the ticket office. It seemed to Anthony that Piers' voice rang unnecessarily loudly in the cavernous air of the station. Several people turned to watch his tall, noisy figure making its confident way through the crowds of weekend commuters.

'Right,' said Edward, as they joined the queue, 'let's pool our funds and I'll get all the tickets. Five times thirty-six is . . . is . . . a hundred and sixty. Oh, is it? Well, all right, eighty. A hundred and eighty. Let's see – has anyone got change of a tenner?'

'Oh, don't start all that!' said Julia. 'Let's each pay for our own.'

'How do you make it thirty-six?' asked Anthony in surprise. 'I thought the fare was only nineteen pounds?'

'We're not going *second* class, laddie!' exclaimed Piers. 'Good heavens, they'll be drinking Tennent's Pilsner and being sweaty.'

Anthony had not banked on this. For a moment, he thought of saying that he hadn't enough money and was going to travel second class, but the thought of Julia and their argument the previous evening prevented him. He had a sudden vision of himself sitting in morose exclusion in second class while she and Piers hoorayed in their first-class privilege; it was unbearable. So he paid for the first-class ticket with his Barclaycard, thrusting aside the question of how it was eventually to be paid for. The very business of performing this, to him, reckless act served, however, to lighten his spirits, and he felt part of a very sociable, cheerful group as they boarded the train. Edward insisted on buying the drinks from the buffet, so that was all right, and Anthony felt himself to be really rather amusing as he described the near-death state of Lord Cole when he had attended the House of Lords to hear their judgment delivered. Piers laughed loudly and gratifyingly, and the sound of his approval, even although Anthony suspected he rather disliked the man, was sweet to Anthony's ears.

The journey continued in a very jolly fashion until, just after eight, the guard announced that dinner was being served in the restaurant car.

'Excellent!' said Piers. 'I didn't know we could eat properly on this train. Much better than the rubbish they serve in the buffet.'

A faint hope stirred in Anthony's heart as Edward said, 'Don't bother. We'll be there in an hour's time and we can get some supper at home.'

But Piers was determined to extract every ounce of amusement from his weekend, and to impose his personality upon as many people as possible. The restaurant car would provide him with a new audience.

'No, I'm travelling first class, and I'm bloody well going to have my dinner. Who's coming?'

Julia, laughing, said she would go. David said he was too hungry to wait until they got to Edward's, and Edward said oh, all right, since they were all going.

'What about you, Tony?' asked Edward, dropping a plastic cup upside down over an empty beer can. For a second, Anthony was about to refuse. Indeed, if he had been able to speak before either David or Edward, he would have done, and would have stuck to it. But now, being the last to speak, he felt that a refusal might seem too obvious an acknowledgment of his lack of money. So he said, casually, 'Why not?', knowing why not.

In the restaurant car, he picked up the menu. Even if he didn't have a starter, the cheapest main course, fish, was ten pounds. Even Edward was taken aback by the prices.

'Bloody hell! That's a bit steep for a lamb chop!' he exclaimed. He was a little drunk, and a couple of heads turned.

'Where's the wine list? We want a wine list. Waiter!' called Piers. 'Waiter!' Everyone said 'Ssh!' and when the waiter appeared Piers asked for the wine list in an ostentatious whisper. Edward ordered large gin and tonics for everyone.

'Not for me, thanks,' said Anthony quickly.

'Oh, balls,' said Edward. And balls it was. Anthony had a large gin and tonic.

'Right. Let's have two bottles of the Chablis,' said Piers, after consulting the very bad wine list in its leatherette binding. Anthony was about to say that he didn't want any wine, either, but he reckoned that it probably wouldn't make much difference.

Nothing made any difference, as it turned out. Anthony didn't have a starter, and ordered only the fish and, declining a pudding, some coffee. But when the bill came, Piers read out the total in a loud voice, divided it exactly by five, and announced, 'Twenty-one pounds thirteen each – call it twenty-two, with service.'

Anthony felt hollow; he was never going to be able to afford this weekend. He should never have agreed to come. And then that bastard Piers would have had a field day.

An unfortunate thing then happened. It was discovered that Anthony didn't have enough cash and didn't have a cheque book.

'Tell you what,' said Piers, 'you pay the whole bill with your Barclaycard, and we'll give you the cash.' There was no way that Anthony could refuse. As he signed the credit card slip for the seemingly astronomical figure of one hundred and ten pounds, he eyed the pile of coins and notes that the others had thrust across the tablecloth to him, and wished that it didn't exist. Perhaps he could just put it in the inside pocket of his jacket and pretend for the rest of the weekend that it wasn't there. He knew he was being unduly optimistic.

Fortunately, everyone managed to persuade the very tipsy Edward, when they got out of the train at Foxhampton, that they didn't need to call at the village pub for a quick one on the way home. Instead, they walked the mile or so along quiet, leafy lanes to Kepple House, where Edward's parents lived, Piers' loud voice and boisterous laughter filling the night. He never, in any circumstances, thought Anthony, moderated his voice. It seemed to be part and parcel of his manner, his class.

Instead of giving the noisy Piers the cautious reception that Anthony had anticipated, Edward's parents seemed more than delighted to see him. He was utterly at home, and greeted Frederick and Cora Choke with easy familiarity. He called to the dogs, two bounding, slobbering black labradors, and bent down to slap and scratch them, muttering 'Hello, girl! There's a girl!' in loving tones. Anthony felt uneasy, standing next to David in the hallway while Edward's parents greeted Julia and asked after her family. Anthony wished he could imitate David, who confidently stepped forward and shook Frederick Choke's hand, saying in his bright, enthusiastic voice, 'How do you do, sir? I'm David Liphook, in chambers with Edward.' Frederick and Cora Choke made much of their son's future fellow tenant. Then Edward introduced Anthony. They had less to say to him, but were polite and kind. Anthony felt awkward, and could think of little to say.

They had beer and cheese and biscuits in a kitchen that seemed to Anthony to be three times the size of his mother's living-room, Piers loudly encouraging the dogs, who stood trembling frantically by his thigh while he dropped chunks of cheese into their dripping jaws. One of the dogs mistakenly trotted round the table to Anthony's side, nudging at his knee with its moist nose, and he gave it a surreptitious kick, which he hoped went unobserved by his host and hostess.

Mrs Choke showed them their rooms. She led them upstairs to a long gallery which overlooked the hall on one side, and whose windows on the other side looked down on dark laurel bushes gleaming in the moonlight. Anthony's room was at the end of the corridor. He made a mental note of where Julia's was, two doors back. The house seemed to him to be very large.

'Piers, dear, you're in your usual room,' Mrs Choke said fondly to Piers. He would be, thought Anthony.

As he was busy thanking her and looking round the room, he heard Mrs Choke say in her bright voice, 'Don't be startled by any bumping and heavy breathing in the night – it'll just be one of the dogs. They love to sleep in this room, you know.'

'Great,' said Anthony. 'Thanks.'

The following morning, Anthony woke early. He stood at the window surveying the landscape. A cold mist hung over the lawn and gardens, and upon the fields and woods that stretched in the far distance. Gradually the creeping warmth of the sun broke through, pearling the air. The peculiar stillness of early day hung over everything. Anthony thought that he had never seen anything more tranquilly lovely than the graceful descent of the three oval lawns, separated from each other by flowerbeds and shrubberies, their grass filmed with dew, to the glittering water of the river. The slow call of moorhens drifted from the river bank, and through the mist up on the water he saw a swan slip from its reedy bed and glide soundlessly upriver. He opened the window and let the chilly air play around his face and naked chest.

He wondered, as he took deep breaths of the cold air, what it would be like to own such a place. When he had his tenancy, he thought, then his ambitions would have full rein. Perhaps one day he would have enough money to own such a house, to wake every morning to soul-healing loveliness. He closed the window, dressed, and went down to breakfast.

117

*

Friday and Saturday passed pleasantly. Piers and Edward went riding after lunch each day, and Julia and David and Anthony borrowed Cora Choke's sprightly new little Citroën –'just my old runabout' – and went off to investigate the surrounding countryside. They spent Saturday afternoon browsing round the junk shops of Napley, the nearest town, and Anthony bought Julia a cup and saucer, painted with green flowers. Then they went back to Kepple House for tea.

Edward's cousin, Anthea, had arrived in their absence, and Edward introduced her. Anthony thought her rather awesome. She was very tall, with slender hands and feet, and elegant, sinuous movements. She had straight, fine, blonde hair, which she would flick slowly back over her shoulders from time to time. She said very little, merely gazing with interested warmth at anyone who spoke, and smiling and rearranging her body by way of response. She rarely laughed, although one had the impression that she found most things mildly amusing. When Cora Choke informed her that David and Anthony were in the same set of chambers as Edward, she simply smiled serenely, glancing at all three politely, then shifted her gaze and attention elsewhere.

David was entranced. It seemed to be his fate to find himself attracted to the most incongruous women, all possessing physical and mental qualities which in no way corresponded to his own. When they all went to the village pub that evening, David, spellbound by her snaky charm, tried to engage her in earnest conversation. Her smiling silence was in marked contrast to his frank garrulousness, but he seemed quite happy to receive the occasional murmuring response, accompanied by a gentle toss of blonde hair.

Anthony watched David trying to teach Anthea bar billiards. She leaned casually, inexpertly over the table, her indolent slenderness out of keeping with David's stocky, proficient frame. She smiled always, muffing shots, pushing her hair back.

'I think he's totally smitten,' remarked Anthony, as the rest paused in their conversation to observe them. Julia agreed.

'She's not exactly talkative,' she said, having made a game effort at conversation on the way to the pub.

'She hasn't got a lot to say, that's why,' said Edward. 'She's a very dear thing, but totally dense. I sometimes wonder if her lift goes all the way to the top floor, as they say.'

'Really?' said Anthony. 'I thought all that enigmatic smiling masked a terrific intelligence. I've been feeling intimidated by her all evening.'

'That's because you're so self-deprecating,' remarked Julia. 'You always think other people are trying to put something over on you.' Piers laughed at this, although Julia had sounded quite serious.

'Well, she is a bit mysterious,' said Anthony.

'If she's as stupid as you say she is,' observed Piers tactfully, 'she'd make a very refreshing change for David. Have you noticed how he's always falling in love with really brainy women, and then working himself up into an agony because he thinks he's got to keep up some kind of intellectual façade? He actually turned down a ticket to the France–Scotland game to go and see some Russian film with subtitles at the NFT that his girlfriend wanted to see. Even he admitted later that it was bloody dreadful. Anyway, she didn't last long.'

'They never do,' said Edward. 'At least he's got nothing to fear in that direction from my dear cousin. She's supposed to be doing some secretarial work for my father at the farm office for the next few months. Poor old Dad.'

The truth of Edward's observations regarding his cousin's mental faculties became more evident as the evening progressed, and as Anthea became more talkative. But, however fatuous her remarks, David seemed highly appreciative, treating them as a superior form of wit. The fact that David laughed admiringly at her every remark surprised Anthea a little, but she didn't seem to mind. Piers seemed, to Anthony's acute discomfort, to enjoy engaging her in blindingly complex discussions about esoteric subjects. Piers always found other people's stupidity amusing. Anthony wondered how he could fail to be shamed by Anthea's innocent, smiling bafflement. He thought, and not for the first time, that Piers was really a bit of a shit.

This conviction grew. After their third drink, Edward announced that he was hungry and that they should all go and get something to eat.

119

'There's a fairly decent hamburger place,' he said, 'or there's a rather poncey little place called Arnold's that's just got into the *Good Food Guide*. That's your choice, chaps.'

Anthony had already determined that he would not be bull-dozed into spending more than he could afford, and said quickly, 'Well, I can't afford anything expensive, so I'd be happy to go for a hamburger.'

Julia, glancing at him, agreed. Piers eyed Anthony. 'Come on, Tony,' he said in his pleasantly lazy fashion, 'you've got that great stack of notes that we all gave you last night. So you can't plead poverty. Anyway, I loathe hamburgers. I thought you did, too, Julia.' Julia said nothing.

'I think we should all go for a decent meal,' said David, who thought the atmosphere of an expensive little restaurant might be more conducive to his suit with Anthea than a hamburger joint. 'Don't you?' he said to Anthea, who smiled and murmured something that sounded like an assent.

Edward yawned. 'Well, I don't frankly care. If you chaps all want to splash out, that's fine by me. It's supposed to be a very good place, or so Mummy says.'

Anthony saw that the matter had been disposed of; once again, Piers had had his way. He wondered how much of it was malice on Piers' part. He must know, he thought, that Anthony really had little or no money, but he knew that he couldn't argue against the observation that he did have enough cash on him. He felt he could hardly explain painstakingly to the company that he would need that money to pay off the Barclaycard bill that would eventually come.

But Julia saw how Piers was manipulating things and was determined that he should not have his way. She did not admit to a slight, rankling resentment of the fact that the lovely Anthea was being given the dazzle of Piers' attention, which she, Julia, was accustomed to receiving as of right.

'Well, you lot can go off to Arnold's if you like, but Anthony and I will go for a hamburger,' she said firmly. Anthony knew he should have been grateful to her for this, but he wasn't. He could not bear that she should pity him, that she should have to side with him in his poverty.

'No,' he said quickly, 'we might as well try this place. We can have a hamburger any day.'

Julia was relieved. She'd done her loyal duty, she thought, but she really didn't want to sit in a cafe with Anthony in a sort of social isolation. If she was at all troubled by the fact that she knew Anthony really could not afford all this, she managed to thrust it to the back of her mind. Anyway, she was accustomed to bathing in the warm glow of Piers' appreciation as well as Anthony's, and she was determined to put in a little hard work that evening to ensure that she diverted some of the attention from Anthea.

In the muted pink glow of Arnold's, each mused silently over the menu. Piers was wondering how long it would take Julia to become thoroughly fed up with the fact that Anthony hadn't a bean, and dump him. Anthony was wondering whether he could insist that they should each pay for what they had, and whether he could put Len off for while. Julia was considering Anthea's earrings and how much she'd paid for them, and wondering how good a judge Edward could possibly be of other people's stupidity. David was pondering the soft swell of Anthea's breasts beneath her angora sweater, and reflecting that he could probably see a good deal more of her if Edward stayed on at Caper Court. Anthea was wishing that that tall creep in the yellow jacket would stop talking at her in what he obviously thought was such a devastatingly clever way. And Edward was wondering whether to have the mustard-coated rack of lamb or the French duck. The lamb, he thought.

Chapter eleven

On Sunday, Edward's parents left for a ball in Yorkshire, where they were to stay overnight. Mrs Choke stood in the hallway of Kepple House, expensively attired in a red Versace suit that had probably cost twice Anthony's mother's salary for that term, and went through lists of reminders to Edward concerning the dogs, the central heating, the burglar alarm and the Aga.

'You're only going to be away for one night,' Edward pointed out patiently.

'That reminds me. Mrs Howell will be here tomorrow morning at nine, so make sure you're up in time to let her in.'

'Don't worry. The dogs'll wake me.'

'She'll make some lunch for you. Oh, I hope we're back before you go,' she said, glancing round at them as they stood in the hallway to see them off. 'But I doubt it. So lovely to see you all. Now,' she said to Edward, 'make sure that everyone has enough to eat and drink, won't you?'

'I'm cooking dinner tonight,' said Piers breezily. 'It will be absolutely excellent. Not quite as good as your cooking, of course,' he added gallantly.

'Piers, you are sweet,' she murmured, giving him a light goodbye kiss, a privilege bestowed only on himself, Julia and Edward. 'I'm sure it will be quite wonderful. Julia, dear, do give your mother my love. I shall be seeing her in London soon.'

They left amid a chorus of goodbyes, and Edward closed the door with a sigh of relief. Everyone sauntered back through the house, uncertain what to do with their day. The spring air was still and unseasonally warm. Piers took a dog and the *Sunday Times* out to a seat in the garden and lounged there, yawning and listlessly reading, occasionally scratching at the dog's floppy ear. What a very useful prop a dog was for the upper middle-class male, Anthony reflected. He sat on a low stone wall with the colour supplement and watched David and Anthea make their way down the long flight of stone steps that led down the side of the lawn to the river. David's voice, the only sound in the spring air, gradually faded as their figures vanished from sight behind the trees.

Edward reappeared with Julia.

'I'm taking Julia over to the stables at the farm to do a spot of riding. Either of you two want to come?' Piers shook his head without looking up, yawned tremendously, and turned another page. Anthony said no, he didn't ride, and then immediately wished he hadn't said that. Edward and Julia left.

After reading for a bit, Piers threw down the paper and stretched himself out on the long wooden bench, one arm flung over his eyes and his bare feet propped up on the end of the seat. Anthony could now study him more openly than he had been able to. He was fascinated by Piers' arrogance and self-possession and stared at him closely, as though, by some minute scrutiny, he could fathom the man. He looked at the long, ugly face, with its over-prominent jaw and nose that must have been broken at some time. Piers had not shaved that morning, and was wearing extremely baggy old cords and a tattered Aran sweater with holes in both elbows, yet he had still managed to look the perfect house guest that morning as he bade his easy farewell to Mr and Mrs Choke. Anthony considered his own clothing, his best jeans and the checked shirt that he had carefully ironed on Wednesday evening. He supposed that Piers didn't shop at C & A. Watching him, Anthony realised that it was the largeness of the man that he detested. The long legs, with their massive thighs, the broad chest, rising and falling in the April air, the large brutal hands, one of which was caressing the silky fur at the dog's neck. The thought of Piers' great naked limbs enfolding Julia's suddenly came into his mind, and stayed there like a bad taste in his mouth. He thought of how they had been kissing at Julia's party, and wondered whether Piers was good in bed. He continued to stare at the long, indolent body reclining on the bench.

He thought of Piers in privileged infancy, taught from his

earliest days of his own importance in the world. Of Piers at his expensive prep. school, a noisy and precocious eight-year-old. At Harrow, bullying and blossoming and basking in parental admiration, good at lessons, good at games. And all the while, thought Anthony, learning those careful little lessons of privilege. How to ride, how to shoot, how to compete and win, how to talk affably and winningly to women his mother's age, how to dance properly, the right way to refer to things, people, places. How to feel contempt for people such as Anthony, people without the right background.

And here he was, Piers Hunt-Thompson, lying in the sunshine, apparently oblivious of Anthony. Watching him, Anthony wondered, in a detached sort of way, what it would be like to take one of Mrs Choke's large Sabatier knives from the wooden block in the big, sunny kitchen, and slide it between Piers' ribs. The massive chest would shudder, and then cease, to rise and fall no more. The muscles of his great thighs, upon which he rose mechanically and majestically each day in court and which carried him so effortlessly and successfully through his world, would twitch their last. The large hands would caress no more dogs and women.

So dead had Piers become in his mind, that Anthony was rather surprised when he spoke. He spoke without moving his arm from over his eyes.

'Bit of a bore for you, isn't it, with Edward at Caper Court?'

'No, he's rather good fun,' replied Anthony, unthinkingly.

'No, no, I mean,' continued Piers, slowly lifting his arm and keeping it between the sun and his face, 'it's rotten luck to have to be in competition with the nephew of the head of chambers, I would have thought.'

Anthony was silent for a moment, apparently studying his magazine. But Piers persisted. 'After all,' he went on, this time looking across at Anthony, 'it's a bit of a shame that you won't get a tenancy. I understand Edward's thinking of staying on.' This last was said questioningly, and Anthony felt obliged to reply. He looked at Piers' smiling, insolent face. He had no inclination at all to discuss his affairs with him.

'Yes,' said Anthony, with an effort. He looked back at the magazine.

'Well,' drawled Piers, laying his head back down and closing his eyes, his arms folded over his chest, 'I think it's really rotten luck. You won't exactly be able to afford Julia for long, will you?' Anthony looked over at him. Perhaps the Sabatier idea was a good one, after all.

'I don't really want to discuss Julia with you,' he managed to say, wishing that this didn't sound so pompous, and also that he could manage to affect Piers' laconic, dismissive tone. Piers raised his eyebrows. His eyes were still closed and he couldn't know that Anthony was watching him, but somehow Anthony felt that he did.

'Well, face facts, Tony,' Piers went on. Anthony realised that he detested being called Tony by any man except Edward. 'She's a lovely girl, and expensive to keep. I regard her little fling with you as something of an aberration. She and I both had our eye on each other before you came along, you know.' Piers' tone was quite conversational. 'We'd been getting along very well. You're a nice boy, and I'm sure that you're an excellent tumble – ' His tone was openly offensive and mocking now. ' – but you're not quite our thing, are you? I mean, a bit of a comprehensive school novelty, really.' He opened one eye, delighted at the effect he was having. Before Anthony could find words to reply, Piers sat up suddenly, rose, smiled, and slapped Anthony unnecessarily hard twice on the thigh. 'But don't worry, laddie!' he exclaimed, with exaggerated heartiness, as though cheering up an old friend. 'I'll still carry on being nice to you. Talking to you, that kind of thing. After all, it's impolite not to be kind to people, I always think. A bit common.' And he smiled down at Anthony, picked up his newspaper, and sauntered off into the house.

Anthony sat in the warm morning air, watching an early bluebottle careering through the tulips. The dog that Piers had been caressing lifted its head, looked at Anthony, got up and walked away. Anthony tried hard not to feel humiliated, and failed. While he thought that Piers was possibly the biggest bastard he knew, it struck him that most of what he had said was probably true. If Edward got the tenancy – and the chances were that he would – he'd be in dire straits, finan- cially, certainly not able to keep up with Julia. They would drift apart gradually. Or probably not so gradually, if Piers made his move at a suitable moment. Even if he did get the tenancy, he wouldn't be earning anything like a decent regular income for a year or so. But the real truth, the one which Piers had more than hinted at, was that he didn't belong, that he was accepted by Piers and the others simply because he happened to be what Julia wanted at the time. Everyone treated him decently because, as Piers had said, it would be rude not to. Rude to Julia, that is, not to him. And when his time was up, as it surely would be, then he would drift back to the half-world of East Dulwich, and go on being a social misfit.

What Piers had said succeeded in robbing Anthony, briefly, of every ounce of self-confidence, and for the rest of the day had the effect of colouring every word uttered by the others with some nuance of slight or contempt. Even when Edward innocently said, that evening, 'You be wine waiter, Tony,' handing him two bottles and a corkscrew, he read some faint aspersion into the remark.

Although he had been determined that morning to ignore what Piers had said and not to let it trouble him, by the time evening came a deep gloom had settled upon Anthony. Julia was in high spirits, laughing and chattering as she helped Piers with the soup, and Anthony was both glad that she was too busy to observe that he was slightly withdrawn, and a trifle resentful that she hadn't noticed.

Piers, having commenced his assault that morning, set about finishing it off that evening. He cooked splendidly, loudly and ostentatiously, supplying everyone with an amusing running commentary based on his own culinary beginnings at his parents' summer homes in Italy and France, spattering his conversation with ludicrous bursts of French and Italian patois. Julia and Anthea loved it.

When they all sat down to eat at Cora Choke's round, black lacquered dining table – Anthea had managed, despite her intellectual failings, to arrange a large bowl of syringa with devastating good taste in the centre – Piers drew the conversation round to escapades of previous years. He began with Julia's eighteenth birthday party, bringing forth one hilarious reminiscence after another, prompting laughter and a flurry of

'Oh, *yes*!' and 'Do you remember after Edward's driving test how we . . . ?' Piers appeared to have been the star of every one of these doings. His large figure danced daringly at the centre of each narrated exploit, and he grew in brilliance in the minds of his listeners. Then the talk moved on, as Piers had known it would, to other parties, to hunt balls, to the names and reputations of people of whom Anthony had never heard, but whom all the others seemed to know intimately. Such were the ties of their bright, unassailable childhood and adolescence. Piers drew the thread even tighter. The others were so excited, so full of the enjoyment of their reflected selves in each memory and story, that they did not notice that Anthony was almost entirely silent. He tried to appear bright and interested, and to be largely preoccupied with his food, but from time to time he would catch Piers' eye, and could not ignore the expression on that large, ugly face.

Anthony drank as much as he could, which was a good deal, since Edward had ignored his father's adjuration not to make great inroads into the wine cellar. But, much as he drank, he could scarcely get drunk. It was a relief to him when the dinner party broke up. Piers and Edward rose and went out to toast the moonlight drunkenly and noisily on the lawn. Julia and Anthea joined them and sat on the low, stone wall. David still sat at the table with his coffee and port, in love and happy. Anthony watched Julia through the open terrace windows and listened to the sound of her voice and pretty laughter. Morose and full of wine, he went to bed.

Julia sat out in the chilly air, shivering slightly and laughing at the antics of Piers and Edward. Piers came over and gallantly whipped off his jacket, placing it over her shoulders. She slipped her shoulders thankfully into the warm, large sleeves, smelling the faint smell of Piers upon the cloth. She watched the moonlight on the river, only half-listening to the men's banter. Anthony hadn't bothered to come outside. Well, she didn't care if he wanted to sulk. She was having fun this weekend. She wondered vaguely if he would come to her room that night. The thought stirred in her a faint flush of desire. Stretching her arms languorously and thinking of this, she rose and went indoors, still wearing Piers' jacket. As she mounted the stairs slowly in the darkness, she suddenly felt a hand slide round her waist from behind. It was Piers.

'You forgot to give me my jacket back,' he said softly. She laughed and slipped it off, trying to turn away from his arm.

'Thank you, sir,' she said archly, handing it back to him, and pushing him not very forcefully away. But he pulled her back against him. This annoyed Julia and she stiffened.

'Let go, Piers!' she said. He pulled her against him and kissed her, breathing hard. This was not like the time at her party, when he had cajoled and seduced and said charming, absurd things. This was simply some large man in the darkness, much stronger than she was and smelling of brandy, kissing her when she did not want to be kissed. She struggled away from him.

'Get off!' she said more sharply. 'I don't like to be kissed like that!' He fell back slowly against the banisters, laughing, and groaned.

'All right, kiss me properly, then. I give in.' He sounded so idiotic that she did. She kissed him for a long time. When she went upstairs to her room, she thought, guiltily, briefly, of Anthony. She didn't think she was up to having him in her bed that night. Carefully she locked her door. Which was how Piers found it when he sauntered quietly along to her room an hour later, while Anthony slept restlessly two doors away.

It seemed to Anthony, when he awoke the following morning, that his brain had reached some hard-fought decision while he had slept. He knew, with a sudden certainty, that, given all the circumstances, he would have to tell Julia that for the time being at least he would not be able to go on seeing her. This realisation was largely the result of his acquired tendency – acquired through the years of adolescence and early manhood, when he began to perceive that only he, and no one else, would ever serve his interests – to detach himself from others in pursuit of his ambitions. He was aware that this affair of Julia, and the drain on both his finances and his reserves of pride, was distracting him from the attainment of his precious goal. He was conscious that the company of Julia and her friends – and now, blatantly, of Piers – was colouring his estimation of his own worth. He could not allow any notion of failure to taint him, no matter how bogus he might know it to be in reality.

He loved Julia. But Julia, like all people, wore many faces, and the one which he now saw most often – the public, socially agreeable face – was the one he liked least. The private, sweet, solitary face that he adored, he had seen little of recently. Perhaps, if he carried his resolve through, he might never see it again. For the moment, however, and in more than one sense, he could not afford Julia.

Lack of choice over the years had bred in him a sort of ruthlessness, the kind displayed by those who, in their paucity of options, know that once a decision is made, it is practicable only if put into effect without delay. And so he did not postpone the matter. After breakfast, he asked Julia to walk down to the river with him.

'All right. Let's get David – there's a rowing boat down there, so maybe we could do some exploring.'

'No, don't ask David. I want to talk to you.'

Slightly surprised, Julia left the house with him and they walked in silence down the lichen-covered steps.

'Well, what is it?' she asked, as they reached the little wooden jetty at the bottom. 'You look very grim, I must say.' Julia felt faintly nervous; she wondered if he had seen her kissing Piers last night. Once was unlucky, but twice might seem a bit much.

Anthony said nothing for a moment, but sat down on the warm wooden planking, his knees drawn up before him, and looked out over the water.

'Well,' he said at last, reluctantly, 'I've been thinking that maybe you and I should give things a rest for a while.'

'Oh, don't tell me you're in a huff because of last night! I know you felt a bit out of it, but – '

'No, I'm not in a huff about anything,' interrupted Anthony, speaking quite matter-of-factly. 'I just think that – well, things should stop.' There was a pause, during which she looked at him curiously and with concern. 'That's all.'

'That's all? We're just to stop seeing each other? Why?' Julia felt cold and a little panicky; not only did she love Anthony, as she thought, but she was unaccustomed to being put aside, no matter how gently. Such a thing had never happened to her before. Anthony picked at the wooden boards with his fingernail; his head was bowed in thought, and for a moment Julia, in her sudden frailty, wanted to reach out and stroke the dark, thick hair. He seemed very remote, and a little chill in her heart as she waited for him to speak told her that Anthony was not the kind of man who did something like this for effect.

Anthony sighed and looked up at the trees; he was careful not to look at Julia.

'You see, I don't have a great deal of money, as you know. That makes it difficult for me to do the kind of things you like to do.'

'But you know I don't care about that! I've told you I can pay for some things.'

Anthony allowed himself a slight smile.

'And I don't always like doing the things you like to do. Or seeing the people you like to see. Maybe they're an acquired taste.'

'Those are simply rotten reasons! The truth of it, if you had the courage to say it,' exclaimed Julia angrily, 'is that you're tired of me and you just want to finish it. Money's got nothing to do with it.'

He turned to look at her thoughtfully. 'Do you really think that?' He sounded genuinely curious. She could think of nothing to say. He looked back at the water. 'No,' he sighed, 'I sometimes wish I'd met you a year from now. As it is, I really think it's about time we called it a day.'

The finality in his voice was almost enough to make her embrace him and plead with him to change his mind, but an innate sense of pride prevented her.

'Maybe when circumstances have changed a bit,' he went on, 'when my finances are in better shape – '

She interrupted him coldly. 'Please don't imagine that you can just discard me and then pick me up again at your pleasure.' She felt thoroughly miserable and angry, and completely helpless.

'All right,' he said after a moment. Then he looked at her again, thinking how lovely she was; he felt utterly wretched, but at the same time determined to deflect any emotional thrusts she might make. Knowing that it wasn't a good idea, he leaned forward suddenly and kissed her tentatively. She kissed him back in a tired, hopeful way, and then he stood up.

'I think I'll apologise to Edward and tell him that I'm catching an early train,' he said. 'You can tell the others that all this was your decision,' he added, 'if it helps.'

No, she thought, it didn't help. She felt desolate, suddenly bereft. She did not speak.

'Well, goodbye.' Still she said nothing, did not look at him. 'I do love you, you know,' he added awkwardly. Oddly enough, as she watched him slowly mount the steps towards the house, she believed him.

Anthony told Edward that he had to go back early to finish some work for Michael, and this was accepted without remark. Piers watched Anthony with a curious smile as he got into the Citroën, Edward stuffing his bag in the boot in preparation to drive Anthony to the station. He had seen Anthony and Julia go down to the river together; that had been over an hour ago, and she still hadn't come back. And here was Anthony catching the early train.

But Julia, when she eventually reappeared, was cold and snappish and not interested in Piers' arch remarks. She vanished to her room.

In the train, Anthony felt about as numb with unhappiness as he'd ever been. He travelled second class this time. The bank holiday meant that the train was almost empty, and Waterloo station, when he arrived there, was depressingly quiet. He thought over his conversation with Julia as his train made its slow way towards East Dulwich, and wondered if he could have managed matters better – or even if he should have done it at all. But slight reflection told him that things simply could not have carried on as they had done. He had had no option. This knowledge did nothing to alleviate his misery, but as he realised that he need no longer worry about whether or not he was going to be able to afford each successive weekend, he felt an unmistakable sense of relief.

Chapter twelve

The next few days dragged barrenly along. Work seemed dry and repetitive, and the very aspect of the Temple itself, grey and austere, seemed as chilling as a prison. Anthony avoided Edward; he didn't want to have to answer any tactless, well-meant questions. He didn't even want to think about Julia. But, of course, he did. The same endless round of thoughts. Why had he done it? He knew the answer. The same answer that he gave himself each time he was tempted to call her. Where was the point? He had no money – worse, he had a debt that he couldn't repay. As he considered the wreckage of his finances, he hoped that Len would wait a couple of months. At any rate, Anthony was relieved that he had not been in touch. Perhaps he didn't need the money that urgently.

And then he reviewed his position in chambers. It was time to take serious stock, since he had gambled everything upon gaining this tenancy. The determined optimism that had filled him following his talk with Michael had faded. The business with Hayter had undermined his confidence, and he began to suspect that no amount of hard work was going to impress the other members of chambers if they had already assumed that their head of chambers' nephew would become the text tenant at 5 Caper Court. On whom could he count? It was almost impossible to assess his chances properly. Michael would support him, he knew. Possibly William and David – although David was a doubtful quantity, being so very much a friend of Edward's. Sir Basil and Roderick Hayter he presumed he could discount. And Jeremy Vine. That left Stephen Bishop, whom he counted as a possibility, Cameron Renshaw, who he knew thought well of his academic record, and Leo Davies.

Leo and Anthony had had little to do with one another. For

some reason that Anthony could not fathom, Leo treated him rather distantly. And for that reason, among others, he exercised something of a fascination for Anthony. He found him an attractive man, admired his reputation as a barrister, his wit and his elegance. He liked the musical Welsh accent that he seemed to hear constantly around him throughout the day, in the clerks' room, echoing down the stairwell, in the other members of chambers' rooms. Leo constantly visited other people, full of anecdote, restlessly seeking company in which to while away a few moments with his banter. Sometimes he exasperated Michael with his mercurial visitations, but the exasperation was usually displaced by amusement as he listened to Leo's latest piece of whimsy. He clearly annoyed Jeremy, not by his intrusions, for he avoided Jeremy mostly, but by his ability to coast cleverly through his work and still find time to idle away with the typists and the clerks. Jeremy thought it rather beneath one's dignity to chat to the more menial members of staff.

All this Anthony watched as though from the sidelines, for Leo rarely spoke to him and often passed him, apparently absentmindedly, without seeming to see him.

Still, thought Anthony, it was worth every effort to try and make some impression on him. So he went to Leo and asked if there was any work he could do for him.

'I don't know,' said Leo, after a moment's pause. He seemed taken aback by Anthony's visit. 'Sit down, at any rate.' His voice was neither friendly nor unfriendly. Anthony closed the door and sat uncomfortably while Leo examined the stack of briefs on his shelves. His room struck Anthony as being quite unlike those of the other members of chambers. It seemed to be in immaculate order. There was no trace of disorganisation; no books or papers littered tables and shelves. Everything was put neatly away behind the doors of some rather incongruously new cupboards which Leo had had installed. There were pictures on the walls, but not the conventional ones of ships or charcoal sketches of City and Temple scenes. These were steel-framed abstracts, their shapes and colours like a code, giving nothing away.

'No,' said Leo at last. 'There doesn't seem to be anything

133

suitable.' Anthony felt disappointed. Leo leaned back in his chair, a complicated, elegant affair of grey fabric and steel tubing, slowly smoothing his hands over his hair, looking at Anthony meditatively with his cool blue eyes.

'Right,' said Anthony. 'Thanks, anyway.' He got up to go.

'Why are you asking me for work?' asked Leo, still leaning back. 'Hasn't Michael got enough for you to do?'

No one had asked Anthony this question directly before. He had taken it as dimly understood that there was some sort of competition between himself and Edward, awkward though this unspoken acknowledgment had made him feel. He found it difficult to answer.

'I suppose I'm trying to get a broad experience of different kinds of work,' he said at last.

Leo smiled for the first time. 'Well, I gave young Mr Choke some work to do, and he did it fairly creditably, so far as I could see,' he remarked. Anthony hadn't known this. Or, at least, he did not associate what Leo said with the work with which he had helped Edward. 'So I can't see any reason why I shouldn't give you some – if the right thing comes along, that is.'

'Well, thank you.' Anthony wasn't quite sure what to make of this. He smiled and left. When he had gone, Leo sat looking after him, tapping his lower lip with his thumb. That really was a most attractive young man, he thought.

The news that Leo thought Edward's work quite good depressed Anthony. If that was the case, he thought, why should Leo bother rocking any boats by favouring someone who wasn't Sir Basil's nearest and dearest? It might have cheered him up a little to know that Edward was currently failing, in quite a considerable way, to make a favourable impression upon Roderick Hayter, and that Michael was discussing that very fact with Roderick and Stephen in Roderick's room.

'Yes, well, I never thought he was quite up to standard, despite what Leo said,' murmured Michael.

'Up to standard? He's so far below that he's practically invisible!'

'Oh, I wouldn't go quite so far as that,' interjected Stephen

Bishop. 'You set your standards far too high. He is only a pupil, after all. I've had him along on a couple of cases and he seems quite wide-awake.'

Roderick sighed. 'All right. I suppose he's not completely incompetent. But he won't do.'

'Why ever not?' asked Stephen, who was still of the view that everyone might as well fall into line with Sir Basil, if only for the sake of harmony. 'Even if he's not that good, we can always carry him. Other chambers do. This set of chambers might as well not exist if we're going to have to start disagreeing on a question like this. We should all be like- minded.'

'Well, I can't agree with you,' replied Roderick. 'As a silk, I rely on the work that comes to me from below. You know that. It may be fine for you at the moment, while you're still being briefed from the outset of cases. You can still put the hours in at your desk. My entire life is spent in court these days, and it's work from William and David that keeps me there. Ask Michael – he'll be taking silk in a year or two.'

Michael managed to look diffident and said nothing. He knew that everything Roderick said was true. He and Cameron Renshaw – and Sir Basil, come to that – relied, as silks, on work that emanated from the junior members of chambers. The implications of taking on someone like Edward were clear. If solicitors were reluctant to brief him, then little work would come their way from his direction.

'Well, that's a consideration,' conceded Stephen. 'But I still don't think he's that bad. Anyway, we can take a new tenant every year for the next three years, if it comes to it. That'll keep you busy.'

Roderick sighed and sat down. 'I don't know how it's come to this. In many ways, it doesn't really matter. It's largely a question of what David and William want. As the junior tenants, it's whether or not they can get on with him that counts. It's just . . .' He looked down in despair at Edward's work. '. . . rather depressing. Still,' he added, after a pause, 'I suppose if young Cross didn't exist, I wouldn't think twice about it.'

And that, Michael was forced to admit to himself, was perfectly true.

*

Ignorant of all this, Anthony toiled half-hopefully on. The following week, Leo Davies came to their room. He glanced briefly at Anthony, and then turned to Michael.

'Mind if I borrow Anthony?' Anthony's heart lifted. 'I've got something coming up that should be amusing, and I rather think I can use him. Remember that stevedore who was killed when a cable snapped? You won't believe it, but the shipping company is still refusing to accept liability.'

'They must be mad,' said Michael, sitting back in his chair.

Leo gave a chuckle. 'They're scared shitless. An American court is going to award that man's family a small fortune, if it comes to it. They're desperate not to give in. The hearing's in two weeks' time, and they're going to go down like lead. So,' he continued, turning and slapping his hand lightly on Anthony's desk, 'see you in my room tomorrow morning, bright and early, right? That okay with you, Michael?'

Michael nodded. 'Certainly. It should be very edifying for Anthony, the sight of Leo in the ascendant.'

When he began work with Leo the following day, Anthony discovered that he remembered most of the facts of the case from the time, many months ago, when he had helped Edward with it. He smiled as he found himself reading through his own pleadings.

Working for Leo was quite unlike working for any other member of chambers. Leo threw himself into a case with an enthusiasm that Anthony found wholly captivating. He was erratic and given to working in concentrated bursts of tireless energy, so that Anthony often found himself in chambers until late in the evening. He was glad of that, for it saved him from interminable evenings spent watching his mother watching television, while he tried not to wonder what Julia might be doing, and with whom. At first, he and Leo had gone their separate ways at the end of hard-working stints such as these, but on one particular evening their conversation regarding the case had become so absorbing that Leo prolonged it by taking Anthony for a drink. They repeated this on other evenings, sometimes going for supper to a wine bar, which Anthony found especially enjoyable. Leo was an expansive, brilliant talker, quite the best company that Anthony had enjoyed for a long time. Leo alleviated his loneliness. He felt suddenly, magnificently, befriended. Gone was Leo's formerly distant, cool manner. He treated Anthony wholly as an equal, making him feel as though he were making some genuine contribution to the case. Leo kept sounding him out, throwing his ideas at him, watching Anthony keenly as he waited for his response. There were days when Leo seemed chilled by the conviction that the hearing would go against them, days on which he snapped at and was short with Anthony. But the next day would find him buoyed up, possibly by some bungled tactic by the other side, possibly by the surprising credibility of the handful of witnesses that the instructing solicitors had now begun to bring along for a spot of coaching.

It was characteristic of Leo's temperament that he took each case very personally, investing a good deal of emotional currency in it. His optimism infected Anthony entirely, so that he felt a peculiar elation when the day of the hearing arrived.

As they walked through the cathedral-like hallway of the Law Courts, their footsteps echoing on the chequered marble flags, Anthony felt the first real excitement that he had experienced as a barrister. He had become, with Leo, so seamlessly involved in the case, so familiar with each argument and each unresolved possibility, that the external world seemed to exist merely as a backdrop to this minute drama. The death of a stevedore, two long years ago, had spawned a small legal industry, provided work for so many scurrying lawyers, pouring like maggots from his carcass. They bustled and sifted and collated, they telephoned, talked, argued and demurred, some left the case and others arrived, reading and re-reading, rehearsing and re-rehearsing, waiting and worrying. And here was the sum of it. They were there to force the hand of the dead man's employers, to set in motion the wheels that would grind out disproportionate hundreds of thousands of dollars into the lap of his family, serving the ends of justice. This was the sharp end of the drama. The rest was history, only to be brought to life by their actions that day.

Robed, he and Leo made their way along the stone corridors

until they came to the door of Number Five Court. Outside stood a little knot of people. Anthony recognised one of them, Jonathon, as the younger of their instructing solicitors, and greeted him. The older of the solicitors was conferring in a corner with the solicitor from the other side. Leo and counsel for the shipping company joined them.

'What's up?' Anthony asked Jonathon.

'Looks like we may not have our day in court, after all,' replied Jonathon.

'They're going to settle?' Anthony felt his excitement beginning to die away.

'It looks that way. Mind you, they've been on the brink of settling the thing for months. But I think they may have come up with an offer at last.'

Anthony watched Leo talking with counsel and the two solicitors. He noticed, absently, the way that Leo's hair at the back of his head looked silvery against the dull, brittle horsehair of his wig. Someone went to make a telephone call, and then came back. Leo turned to glance at Anthony and gave him a quick smile. The talking began again and went on for some minutes. Another two men and a woman joined the discussion, and then the two men left. Anthony watched anxiously. Suddenly the little group had broken up, and Leo was walking over to Anthony.

'That's that,' he said. 'Let's pack up and go home.' Everybody was moving away, talking in low voices. Bewildered, Anthony followed Leo back to the robing room, along the echoing corridors, past the doors of enviably busy courts, holding in his hands the useless bundles of documents, all neatly docketed and arranged. It had been for nothing, the past weeks and evenings of concentration, the hours spent immersing one's whole being in the case – all a waste of time. A handful of people had agreed at the last minute that they didn't have anything to argue about after all, and would everyone else please return to normal life. The courtroom doors had not even opened.

Leo said something to him as they walked back across the Strand, but Anthony couldn't hear him above the roar of traffic. In Middle Temple Lane, someone stopped Leo to talk to him, and Anthony felt constrained to go on ahead. He walked back up the wooden stairs of chambers. Michael's room was empty. He hadn't really much idea of what Michael had been doing the past week or so, and he had no idea where he might be. Suddenly life had returned to its former rather barren state. Anthony still felt dazed by the anti-climactic culmination of the past two weeks' effort. He tried to settle down to some work that he had begun a little while ago, but the thing seemed stale and lifeless. He felt suddenly and acutely friendless. His involvement with Leo during the case had become so complete that it was something of a shock to be thrown back into solitude. For a brief period he had felt part of things, and he wished intensely to have that feeling back again. He *must*, he thought, get this tenancy. Then he would be sure of himself. He would belong. But there was Edward, there was always Edward.

When the phone rang, Anthony was almost inclined to let it go on ringing. It would be for Michael. But at last he answered.

'Ah!' said Mr Slee's voice irascibly, 'I thought I seen you come in. There's a young lady to speak to you.'

For a painful few seconds, Anthony hoped it might be Julia, but he did not recognise the voice that spoke.

'Hello, Anthony?'

'Yes. Who is this?'

'It's Jocasta.' It took a moment for the name to register.

'Oh. Oh, yes! Hello. Where are you calling from?'

'We're still in the States.' Anthony thought her voice now carried a faint Californian lilt. 'Chay asked me to call and ask you to do something for him. He's *very* busy right now, or he'd have called you himself.' She made whatever Chay was doing sound improbably important.

'How's the meditating going?'

'Well, that's finished for the moment. We're really more into the creativity side of things just now. Chay's got something *very big* going down here. He's got an exhibition in one of the galleries.'

'An exhibition? What of?' Anthony was finding this a little difficult to take in.

'His paintings. His work. I can't tell you, Anthony, he's

139

been really inspired since we came to this retreat – I mean, he's been working non-stop, it's fantastic!'

'It must be. He can't paint to save his life. Anyway, he went through that phase about four years ago. What *kind* of exhibition?'

'The usual kind. Pictures on walls, that sort of thing. His opening was the most tremendous success, honestly! It's so exciting just being part of it. The critics all raved about his stuff. Anthony, your father's a genius.'

'No, he's not,' said Anthony reasonably. 'But people are remarkably gullible. It amounts to the same thing, I suppose. No, really, I'm very pleased. What kind of pictures is he painting?'

'Well, I read that someone called them minimalist abstract,' replied Jocasta doubtfully, 'but Chay calls it abstract primitive. It's fairly two-dimensional, anyway,' she added confidently. 'Lots of bright colours, that kind of thing. He's working on a really big canvas at the moment, some New York gallery's commissioned it.'

'Commissioned? You mean, he's actually making money out of this?'

'A fortune! You wouldn't believe the prices people in the Valley will pay for things.'

'Good Lord!' exclaimed Anthony.

'Anyway, he asked me to ask you if you would go round to the flat and sort through the paintings he left there. His agent says it's important to get some of his earlier work on the market right now.'

'Oh, yes, his earlier work. I'm not sure if he was into his "abstract primitive" period then, but I'll have a rummage through and see what there is. But look, it's going to cost a fortune to send them over to the States. I can't possibly afford it.'

'Don't worry. Chay's agent is going to arrange for one of the London galleries to ship them across, if you'll just deliver them to the gallery. I'll send you the name and address in a couple of days.'

'Oh. Right.'

'So, how are you?'

'Oh, I'm fine. Look, tell Dad – Chay – that I'm very pleased for him. It sounds – it sounds like he's having a good time.'

'Well, he is. He'll call you. I have to go now. Bye.'

After he had hung up, Anthony pondered this unlikely turn of events with amusement. He had to hand it to his father – he had nerve. He felt a little better as he resumed his work, although in some way his sense of isolation had been heightened by Jocasta's bright, excited phone call from far away.

After a while, he went out for a sandwich, chatted to some friends in the common room, and then returned to chambers. Still no Michael. Once again that sense of exclusion began to descend upon him, although he tried to dispel it by concentrating on his work.

It was late in the afternoon when Leo came to Michael's room. Anthony's heart rose with pleasure at the sight of him. Suddenly the afternoon seemed fuller and brighter.

'Well,' said Leo, smiling and settling himself behind Michael's desk, 'that was a bit of an abrupt end to our soaring hopes this morning, wasn't it?' He chuckled slightly. 'Still, it's always nice to get one's brief fee before it settles. I had three cases settle last month before I got my fee. Bloody annoying.'

Anthony reflected that at least Leo had the solace of having made some money out of the protracted stand-off. He'd only recently submitted his first note of fees to solicitors, and he didn't expect to see any payment for some months.

'It was a bit disappointing, really, I thought. I mean, all that work – '

'Tchah!' said Leo dismissively. 'You may have been disappointed. I was relieved, frankly. Anyway, what's the difference? The work's got to be done in either event. It wouldn't have settled if I hadn't been instructed. Needed to get the fear up. Now, where's Michael?'

'I don't know. I haven't seen him all day.'

'Pity. I rather wanted a game of squash. I need some unwinding after all that build-up.' He yawned, running his hands over his hair, and glanced at Anthony. 'You play?'

Anthony hesitated. 'Yes,' he replied. 'My kit's in the locker at Middle.'

Leo slapped the desk lightly and rose. 'Excellent. See you downstairs in ten minutes.'

As Anthony was getting ready to leave, the telephone rang again.

'Another call for you,' Mr Slee said, 'sir. A gentleman this time. Wouldn't give his name.'

Anthony knew who it was even before he spoke. His heart sank. 'Hello, Len?'

' 'Allo, Tone?' In the background, Anthony could hear the clink of glasses and the roar of pub conversation. 'Sorry to bother you at work, an' that, but I was wondering whether you'd got me readies yet?'

'Look, Len, can you give me a couple more weeks?' He tried to sound casually apologetic, to keep any note of anxiety from his voice.

'Whassat? Sorry, Tone, there's a hell of a racket in 'ere.' Anthony could hear him cupping his hand over the mouthpiece. 'Come on, keep it down, Tel! Sorry mate,' he said, returning to Anthony, 'what was that?'

Anthony breathed deeply. 'I haven't quite got it all together yet, Len, and I wondered whether – '

'Well, fifty would do for the moment. I'm a bit desperate, Tone.'

'Len, I'm afraid I can't pay you anything right now, to be honest. I'm sorry. Give me another week or two.' He could hear Len muttering something to someone else at the other end. Then he spoke to Anthony again. He sounded sad.

'This is very bad news, Tone. I was counting on that dosh.' He paused. 'See, it wasn't strictly my money that I lent you.'

'Look, I'm just asking for a week or two.'

'Yeah, well, the thing is, my mate really wants 'is money back in a hurry. Know what I mean?' He still sounded sad, almost thoughtful.

Anthony sighed. Why had he ever borrowed that hundred? 'I know, I know. I'll try to sort something out. Just give me a couple of weeks. I'll have it. I promise.' There was another pause; Anthony could hear Phil Collins on the jukebox in the background.

'Well, I can only give you a week, Tone. My mate's not best pleased. He's talkin' about comin' round to pay you a visit at work. I said to him you wouldn't like that.'

'Oh, come on, Len!'

'Tone, I'll do my best, but 'e wants 'is money. I mean, you can understand that. I'll tell him a week. I'll give you a ring this time next Friday and we'll all get together for a drink. Howsat?' He sounded kindly, conciliatory.

'All right. One week. But for God's sake keep him away from here, Len.'

Putting the phone down, Anthony wondered how much of Len's story he believed. This 'friend' might be mythical, a device to worry Anthony. On the other hand, the thought of some mate of Len's strolling round to Caper Court and mouthing off indignantly about some money that Anthony owed him – it made his blood freeze. His own father had been bad enough, but that would probably finish his prospects for good.

His hands were sweating, he realised. Seven days was not a long time to get a hundred pounds together. He would think of something.

As he gathered his squash kit together and joined Leo, the pleasure of being in his company again temporarily obliterated thoughts of Len. Getting into Leo's sleek, blue Porsche, purring smoothly off through the evening traffic to Trafalgar Square and down Pall Mall, he felt something like happiness again.

Chapter thirteen

Halfway through their seventh game, Anthony felt exhausted. He had begun by playing cautiously, with the natural diffidence of the young. He knew that he was quite good and, aware that Leo was some twenty years his senior, wished at all costs to avoid embarrassment. But Leo was every bit as good as he was, and had the added advantages of weight and a ferocious competitive streak. He played hard and fast, laughing when either of them hit a particularly good shot, swearing under his breath at any shot he fluffed. Anthony, however, was faster round the court, and as the games progressed it became apparent that they were evenly matched, neither able to gain a clear advantage.

'All right!' panted Leo at last, leaning against the back wall of the court. 'I've had enough!' He laughed and wiped his brow. Anthony laughed, too, and moved with relief towards the door.

'I'm glad you said that. I was about to collapse.'

'Damn!' said Leo, slapping him on the back. 'Maybe we should have carried on. I was probably just getting into my stride.'

They made their way to the changing rooms and the showers. Leo watched as Anthony kicked off his clothes and turned on the shower. Steam filled the air and spray hissed. Leo showered as well, talking above the noise. He let the hot water stream soothingly over his body as he watched Anthony towelling himself dry. His body was slender, yet hard and muscular, his skin still pale and soft like that of a child. Leo watched as Anthony unselfconsciously thrust his slender, sinewy arms into his shirt-sleeves, pulled on his underpants and trousers, stuffed his kit into his bag. He was chatting away with the innocent good nature of any young man, unaware that at every move he made Leo felt his throat tighten and the muscles of his stomach contract.

He heard Anthony ask if he wanted a drink, and turned away from the vision, closing his eyes for a few seconds.

'Yes,' he said, after a pause, opening his eyes and gazing briefly at the wall of the changing room. Then he turned and smiled his brilliant smile. 'I'll buy you dinner afterwards, if you like. Make up for this morning's lack of excitement.'

They had a drink first in the bar of Leo's club. It was a masculine place, heavy and warmly lit, with deep leather armchairs. Anthony nursed his Scotch in its tumbler, feeling the alcohol taking delicious possession of his body, relaxed now after its exertion. Leo was less voluble than before, tired after their game. Anthony glanced at him across the table, feeling a sway of affection as Leo leaned back and closed his eyes briefly.

'Why did you become a lawyer?' he asked Leo. He was genuinely curious. He wanted to know if any further affinities bound him to this man, as though to solve the puzzle of Leo's attraction. Leo smiled and tucked his chin down. He took a moment before answering.

'Like you, I suppose, I wanted to escape.' Anthony took a quick gulp of his Scotch; it burned his throat. He wondered how much Leo knew of his own circumstances. Perhaps Michael had told him. 'I wanted to escape the petty provinciality of a Welsh village. The Bar's like another world, see? It's like nowhere else on earth. Like a great, big, special club. I wanted to belong.' He took a sip of his drink. 'You want to belong, don't you?'

Anthony laughed, embarrassed. 'Well, yes. It *is* somehow special, isn't it?'

'Exclusive, you mean? Oh, I'll say. It's surrounded itself with a mystique so strong that the people who live and work in the Temple actually begin to believe it. Some of them even live on another plane from the rest of humanity. Just look at the faces of some of those men. They're almost from another century. They've passed the whole of their lives in circumstances of such exclusive privilege that they hardly know what

145

goes on out there. They think they do, but they couldn't begin to understand ordinary lives. That's only a few, mind you.' Leo summoned the waiter over and ordered another round of drinks. 'But I'll tell you something,' he went on. 'You look closely at any barrister – even the simplest hack – and you'll find there's something strange going on. It's as though each one is slightly crippled inside, in some odd way. You can't help it. That atmosphere makes you that way. Just think of some of the oddballs you see around you in the Temple every day. You take them for granted, don't you? Just because the very peculiarity of their setting makes them seem somehow normal.'

Anthony pondered this. There were certainly some weirdos around. That Hungarian chap, with the waxed moustache and the duelling scars, who took snuff and talked nonsense, and managed to eke out a living at the criminal bar. Or the lunatic whom Anthony saw regularly in Middle Temple Bar, always smiling, carrying all his briefs around with him in an old leather suitcase, the inside pocket of his jacket stuffed with little cards on which he was playing forty or so chess games at one time with different members of the Bar. They were taken for granted, accepted as everyday features of life in the Temple. He could think of many others, less eccentric than those two, but each with his own idiosyncrasy or slight twist of the mind. They were all accepted in that microcosm of a world.

'Yes,' he conceded. 'You're right, of course. But what does that make you and I?'

'Well,' laughed Leo, reaching forward for his fresh drink, 'there are *some* fairly normal people at the Bar. You might be one of them.'

'I think I'm fairly sane,' replied Anthony seriously. Then he looked up at Leo. 'But then, I don't belong yet.'

'You're worried about Edward, aren't you?'

Anthony's second drink had removed some of his inhibitions. 'I suppose I am,' he said, and started to explain the whole thing to Leo, his fears and his hopes, his confidence in his own abilities and his doubts of the system which would probably allow a lesser man to gain the tenancy. He even touched on the sense of exclusion that he felt from time to time, the sense that he might never belong. Leo nodded.

'Let's finish this over dinner,' he said. 'I've booked a table at Le Gavroche.'

On the way to the restaurant, Anthony carried on talking.

'If I thought I wasn't good enough,' he explained, 'then I wouldn't mind. I'd have looked somewhere else. But I know I'm good. I know that commercial work suits me. Michael believes it, too.'

Leo nodded. 'He does. He thinks you should become our next member of chambers.'

But what do *you* think? Anthony wanted to ask. He couldn't; he would never know. Leo might like him, but Leo might have other ideas entirely about who was best suited for chambers. When they reached the restaurant, Anthony quickly realised that this place was rather more special than the wine bars where Leo had occasionally treated him to supper. Leo watched Anthony's face as he looked around; the waiter brought the menus, and Anthony glanced at the prices, then looked hastily away. It was amusing to Leo to watch the younger man's cautious pleasure, his curious appraisal of the other diners, some of them well-known faces. As the meal progressed, he delighted in Anthony's enthusiasm for the food, and took particular pleasure in ordering a wine that was far more expensive than was necessary. When Anthony said that he had never tasted anything so wonderful in his life, Leo knew, with a pang, that it was true, and that he had meant it. He watched Anthony's happy face, his dark eyes brilliant from the wine, his mouth moving rapidly, expressively, as he talked. The boy was an utter delight. So untouched, with so much to be shown him. His tastes, Leo reflected, were completely unformed – he was still groping, tentatively, for the mystery that was to become himself. For a moment, he almost envied Anthony the uncertainty of his future.

They finished their wine.

'No coffee, thank you. Just the bill,' said Leo to the waiter. 'I thought you might like to come back to my house for some coffee,' he said abruptly to Anthony. Anthony, happily dazzled by his evening, simply nodded in reply.

When the bill came, Anthony said anxiously to Leo, 'Look, you really shouldn't have brought me to a place like this. I wish I could split the bill with you, but – '

Leo raised a hand. 'What a ridiculous idea. You're my pupil – for the time being, anyway. The least I can do is show you how to dine expensively. The pleasure was all mine, believe me.' He flipped through the credit cards in his wallet, then glanced up at Anthony. 'You're really hard up, aren't you?'

'Well, yes,' murmured Anthony, staring at the tablecloth, and then looking up candidly at Leo. 'I am, as a matter of fact. I'm living on scholarship money.'

Leo nodded. 'I remember doing that. I'll tell you something – in my day, we had to pay our pupilmasters for the privilege of being unwaged slaves, see? You're lucky that's changed, at any rate. No, I remember how difficult it was. You could never afford a decent meal.'

'No,' said Anthony. He hesitated for a moment. The business of Len and his money was weighing on him, and he felt that he had to tell somebody. Leo seemed enough of a friend to tell. Anthony recounted his story. When he had finished, Leo smiled dismissively.

'Take out a bank loan. Or tell your mother. She won't be as upset as you think. Mothers never are. You know, you're lucky to be living at home. When I was studying at the Bar, my dear old ma was still back in the valleys. Which is where she is now, as a matter of fact.' He smiled and handed his card and the bill to the waiter. Anthony wanted to explain further to him, to make Leo understand the real difficulty of his position, but he knew that to do so would seem insufferably boring – worse, it might sound as though he were asking for Leo's help. He let the subject go, and they left.

The drive from the restaurant to Leo's mews house was short; there was little traffic in the Mayfair streets. Leo turned the car into a deserted cobbled back street, and threw Anthony a bunch of keys as they got out.

'You go on ahead while I put this in the garage,' he called. 'The white door on the left over there.'

This curiously intimate gesture made Anthony feel even happier, he did not know why. He fumbled with the key in Leo's lock, then let himself in. He found a light switch and snapped it on. A stairway was directly ahead of him, and he made his way up into a long, low-ceilinged room. It was largely in darkness, and he was feeling around for a light switch when he heard Leo on the stairs behind him. Leo brushed gently past him and clicked a switch on the far side of the room.

'I'll make some coffee,' he said with a quick smile at Anthony, and strode swiftly to the kitchen, pulling off his tie and dropping it on the sofa as he went.

Anthony looked around. The room was starkly furnished, the sofas of grey leather and the chairs and dining table of black wood and chrome. The room was lit by tall, black metallic lamps, which threw light upward in white arcs, so that the light in the lower levels of the room was ghostly and muted. Everything was immaculately tidy; even the few magazines, obscure art publications of which Anthony had never heard, were arranged exactly four-square in the corner of a low table. Some abstract sculptures stood on shelves and side tables, but even their lack of symmetry seemed somehow carefully balanced. Everything formed part of some geometric whole. It was not a room to feel particularly comfortable in, Anthony reflected. Leo's tie, lying on the sofa where he had flung it, looking almost dangerously haphazard.

Anthony stepped lightly across the grey carpet and peered through the kitchen doorway at Leo making the coffee. The kitchen, by contrast with the living room, was brilliantly lit by overhead spotlights, their light bouncing off the stark white cupboards, cooker and floor tiles. There were no dirty dishes, no toast crumbs, not a trace of human debris; somehow Leo's warm, male form, his back to the doorway and Anthony's gaze, looked like that of an animal interloper in some clinical domain.

Leo brought the coffee through in a stainless steel pot, with some little matching cups. From a low cupboard he produced a decanter of brandy and two glasses. The coffee smelt very fragrant. Anthony tried to picture Leo pushing a trolley round a supermarket, choosing the coffee, standing in the checkout queue with the fat mums and bratty kids. Somehow he couldn't.

Leo poured the coffee in silence, handed a cup to Anthony and smiled. Anthony noticed that the sugar was the little brown, rock-like crystals that you got in certain types of restaurant. He couldn't imagine that in the supermarket trolley, either. He sipped his coffee and looked across at Leo, who seemed in some way uncomfortable. Not the man himself, but something about his appearance – perhaps it was the lack of a tie and the untidy aspect of his unbuttoned shirt. His handsome face looked tired, too; the odd lighting in the room cast gaunt shadows under his cheekbones and eyes. He took some brandy when Leo offered it, although he knew that he had drunk a little too much already, and then, because Leo was still silent, he said, 'You told me why you became a barrister, but you still haven't told me why you became a lawyer.'

Leo smiled; Anthony felt a sense of relief at this, and smiled in response. 'That's very true. A fine distinction. Why did I become a lawyer?' Leo groaned in amusement and rubbed his hands across his face, covering his eyes momentarily, and then looking at Anthony. 'Because I like to win.' He leaned forward. 'Because that's all that law is about. Anybody who tells you anything else – that it's about justice, or helping the victims of society, or about seeking a higher truth – is wrong. It's a game; some of us know the rules better than others, and some of us are more likely to win. I like winning. You know, when some young sod gets off on a mugging charge on a technicality, it's no triumph for justice. The law hasn't won, right hasn't won. The lawyer who spotted the technical mistake and got him off – he's won. Some lawyers use lies like the truth.' He poured some more coffee. 'You were disappointed today because we didn't have our day in court, weren't you?' Anthony nodded and sipped his brandy, his eyes held by Leo's. 'If you look a little deeper, you'll see that you were disappointed that we didn't get the chance to win. We would have won.' He picked up his glass of brandy and sat back. 'There's no question about that. But if we had, the satisfaction wouldn't have been in the justice of it, but the success of it.'

'Doesn't justice matter at all? I mean, isn't it better if you're on the side of right? Say, if you save an innocent man from conviction? I know that's not in our line of – '

'Don't be naive, Anthony. I told you – it's a game. The law doesn't really exist, you know. It doesn't even matter unless people want it to. Look at the average business deal that falls apart and ends up in litigation. You think those people really want a court to tell them who's right, who's got justice on their side? No. They're in a fight, and they don't care if the arguments on their side are right or wrong – they just want to win. Your average litigant would just as soon slug it out in a field, if he thought he had a better chance of winning that way. But that's not the way disputes are resolved. The law says who's the winner. It's the ultimate way to win – there's nothing beyond it. The law says who gets the big prizes – money, power, freedom.' Leo leaned forward intently again and picked up a sugar crystal between finger and thumb. 'I've been in cases where I've known – in truth, mind you, not in justice, just in truth – that the other side deserved to win. But because the other side had badly prepared counsel, or a fool for a solicitor, and because I happened to see further and used the rules better – we won. Because we were cleverer, and luckier. But not because we were right.'

'Then maybe the other side didn't deserve to win, after all?' said Anthony. Leo smiled, narrowed his eyes, and crunched the sugar crystal between his teeth.

'Now you've got it. Only the winner deserves to win. That's why I won't feel sorry for you if you don't get this tenancy. Maybe Michael's right. Maybe you are the fitter man. But if you don't get it – well, then, maybe you didn't deserve to.' He sipped his brandy and looked reflectively at Anthony. Then he sighed. 'I'm tired. I'm going to change out of these things,' he said. Then he stood up and left the room.

Anthony glanced round from where he lay sprawled on the sofa. The far corners of the room were in shadow, and eventually he got up and walked around slowly, examining pictures and artefacts, trying unconsciously to plumb the depths of Leo's enigmatic being. He stopped in front of a music deck; small, expensive speakers stood on shelves at either corner of the wall. There was a record on the turntable. Playing a game with himself, Anthony pressed the 'on' switch and watched the stylus drop on to the revolving record. Some obscure jazz, or the fragmented sounds of one of the modern composers, he expected. Instead, the pastel sound of a Ravel pavane floated into the room, the delicate, single guitar notes strangely incongruous in the blank hush of this faceless setting. He went back to the leather sofa, took off his jacket, and lay back. He drank some more of his brandy, letting the delicious, sad music wash across his soul. His limbs felt languorous, and when he closed his eyes he was aware of being light-headedly drunk. He smiled to himself. The notes of music hung like crystal in the air.

When he opened his eyes, Leo stood before him, looking down at him. He was wearing a dressing-gown of supple, sea-green silk, and looked more relaxed, bright-eyed. Anthony thought he had brushed his hair.

'You looked for a moment like the dead child Ravel had in mind when he wrote this,' said Leo with a gentle smile. Anthony felt awkward. Leo was trying to give him a hint about going, obviously, by getting ready for bed. God, it must be nearly midnight. He struggled to his feet from the cushioned depths of the sofa.

'I'd better be going,' he said, picking up his jacket. 'Thanks –'

But Leo hushed him, lifting a finger to his lips. He put a hand on Anthony's arm, the one with which he held his jacket, and ran his hand down to Anthony's wrist, holding it gently but firmly. He looked into Anthony's eyes; he saw only surprise, but no fear. The young man's innocence hung like a shield between them. When Leo kissed him, he did not draw back. The sensation was dry, soft and masculine. Leo looked at him, his handsome face expressionless.

'I love you,' he said quietly. Something dissolved inside Anthony.

'I love you, too,' he heard himself say. Then he stopped the hand with which Leo was beginning, gently, to unbutton his shirt, and held it. They stood for a moment, motionless as dancers waiting for the music to begin. Anthony felt the perfection of his friendship slowly crumbling. Everything in his life seemed bound for destruction, he thought. If he had gone half an hour ago, this would not have happened. All would have been as good as before. It was almost more than he could bear to hurt this man, to deal their relationship its death blow.

'I can't,' he said at last. 'I'm sorry.' He still held Leo's hand. He was conscious that the music had come to an end. Leo lowered his head, then looked up and smiled, lifted Anthony's hand like some idle object, and dropped it. His eyes left Anthony's.

'A pity,' he said, almost carelessly. 'We could have been the perfect combination. So much I could have taught you.' It sounded like a farewell. Anthony felt cold inside. It was as though some thin wall of ice had formed between them. There was, he knew, to be no more intimacy of any nature. He felt he should apologise again, try to redress the balance, do anything to regain the easy pleasure of the past evening. But there was nothing to be done. There was an embarrassed silence.

'I'll call you a taxi,' said Leo at last, going to the telephone and stabbing gently at the buttons. While he called it, Anthony stood blankly in the middle of the room, appalled and alone. Leo put down the phone and turned to him.

'About fifteen minutes, they said. It's always rather busy on a Friday.' He paused, not meeting Anthony's eyes. 'You'll excuse me, won't you?' he murmured, and left the room.

As the minutes ticked by, Leo stood in the darkness of his bedroom, his fists clenched. There had been a time, years ago, when the loss of such a love might have broken his heart. Now he merely felt robbed of pride.

He heard the purr of the taxi in the mews outside, and went back into the living-room. Anthony was sitting on the sofa, gazing ahead of him, rubbing his temples with his hands. He jumped up when he became aware of Leo.

'Your taxi's here.'

'Thank you,' said Anthony, looking at him anxiously, miserably. But Leo could not help him. One tender word, one kind touch, and he would be lost. He should have known better. He smiled firmly at Anthony and picked his jacket up, held it for a moment, then handed it to the young man.

He followed Anthony downstairs to the door, and out into the chilly night air. As Anthony got into the cab, Leo leaned in at the front window and handed a ten-pound note to the driver. Anthony wanted to stop him, but it was too late. He pulled down the window and looked at Leo. But he was standing in the shadows and Anthony could not see his face.

'Thank you for dinner,' he said to the shadows.

'Not at all,' came the reply.

'Where to, mate?' asked the cabbie, eyeing him curiously in the mirror.

Lying back in the darkness of the taxi on the way to Chay's Islington squat, Anthony felt hot tears behind his eyelids. He tried to force his mind away from the events of the evening, but his thoughts kept returning to that shadowed room, and to Leo's compelling, warm touch and voice. He had never heard words of love spoken so simply and starkly before. Not even Julia had touched his heart as Leo had done. He had never felt such pure affection for another man and in that brittle moment it had been shattered. For an instant, Anthony recognised the burden that Leo had to carry. There could be no resolution of his feelings if his love were not returned in kind. If rejected, as Anthony had rejected him, that which remained unspoken between them must remain so forever, and as for those words which had been spoken, it must be as though they had never been said. All the affection and intimacy which, he now realised, he had so hopelessly misunderstood, had vanished like mist. It was he, Anthony, who had been rejected – not as a lover, as he had rejected Leo, but as a friend.

The bitter torment of his thoughts continued until at last they reached his father's flat. The taxi halted and Anthony got out, glancing at the meter. Eleven pounds thirty. He felt in his pocket and produced two pound coins, which he handed to the driver. When the driver called goodnight, Anthony said nothing; he did not hear him. He mounted the dark stairway to Chay's flat, fished out his key, unlocked the door, and went in. As he stood in the dark hallway, he suddenly wondered why he had come. There was no light, no electricity. The flat was cold, even colder than the night outside. The few pieces of furniture, rugs, lamps, and the now precious canvases, lay dumped in a cheerless heap on the floorboards, where he had left them after evacuating them from Bridget's.

Anthony groaned and leaned against the wall. The brandy and the numbing events of the past hour had given him a raging headache. His mood of aching melancholy was gradually giving way to vague nausea and genuine misery. Like a child who has received a bruising shock, he now wanted only to sleep. He deeply desired oblivion from the vivid thoughts of Leo. He waited, shivering, for his eyes to accustom themselves to the gloom, then he walked over to the mound of objects at the end of the room. He disentangled Chay's shabby futon and a duvet; it felt damp with the chill. Nevertheless, he wrapped it around himself and sat in the middle of the bed, as though waiting for something, someone. He thought fleetingly of Leo, of the green dressing-gown, of his warm grasp – fleetingly only, for his mind shied instinctively away from the memory of their kiss. To obliterate the very night, Anthony lay down and pulled the slippery edge of the duvet over his head. It smelt faintly of joss sticks, a smell that Anthony had long associated with his father. For a moment the thought of him, surprisingly, gave Anthony a little stab of mournfulness. He wondered in whose gullible eyes, on the other side of the world, at 6 p.m. California time, Chay was currently re-creating himself.

It is all a search for a mirror image, he thought, this quest for love. He thought again, in spite of himself, of his confession of love to Leo. The moment had expanded itself, he remembered, as he had searched the older man's face, as though seeking a reflection of his own heart. But it had not been there. After a long time spent lying in the cold, utterly silent half-darkness, Anthony finally fell asleep, his innocence folded around him as tightly as Chay's duvet.

In Mayfair, Leo lay in his warm, quiet bedroom, wide awake, watching the green ciphers on his bedside clock, tracing in his memory the contours of Anthony's white throat, faintly pulsing, and his sleeping face as the guitar notes had trembled in the air.

*

When he awoke the next morning, a mild hangover and the desolation of his surroundings combined to make Anthony feel wretched. The sunshine outside and the happy hum of Islington on a Saturday morning exacerbated his sense of loneliness. He felt worse from having slept in his clothes. He uncrumpled himself from the folds of the duvet and wandered into the grimy little bathroom. He splashed his face with cold water, realised there was no towel, and gazed at himself in the mirror. He was vaguely surprised to see his face gazing back at him in its normal way, not haggard with despair or pale from misery. Cheered, he counted out his money and, locking the flat behind him, made his way to the nearest McDonald's for breakfast. He bought a copy of *Today* on the way, and by the time he had finished his Egg McMuffin and coffee, felt better. Seen in the broad light of day, the events of the previous evening seemed less dramatic and even faintly pathetic. Or at any rate, the perspective had shifted enough for Anthony to persuade himself to see them that way. He tried to dismiss it all from his mind, only reflecting with momentary disquiet that Leo would not, after last night, be especially keen to see Anthony stay on at Caper Court indefinitely. Still, that was just something he would have to live with.

In fact, as he shaved that morning after a particularly bad night's sleep – eating out late in expensive restaurants was beginning to disagree with his digestion – Leo was reflecting that, as things had turned out, he would not have to make any particular endeavour to ensure that Edward became the next tenant. Had events been otherwise, it would naturally not have done for his lover to occupy the same set of chambers as himself. As it was, let Anthony do as he deserved. He finished shaving and took some more Milk of Magnesia to ease the vague pain near his heart.

Returning to the flat, Anthony bundled up the duvet and pushed Chay's futon back into a corner. Then he draggd out the canvases stacked in a heap on the floor. He turned one over, half-expecting, after Jocasta's telephone call, the light of genius to shine forth as he gazed on it. But no – he was looking at Chay's familiar and rather depressing daubs. This one was especially unrevealing. It consisted of a series of crimson rectangles which faded in perspective into a welling pool of what looked like yellow ochre, edged with dirty white. He turned it on its side; the effect was distinctly better, he thought. Given a suitably enigmatic title, no doubt it could hang with quite as much honesty as any other piece of modern art on the walls of a New York gallery. Sighing, he examined the rest of the canvases. They were all abstracts, except for one which seemed to be a particularly ugly representation of a nude woman, whom Anthony thought he recognised as a long-gone lover. He didn't really think, surveying the picture, that any woman could possibly have breasts like that. He put it to one side. The rest he stacked gently against a wall. Then he stood back, thought for a moment, and fetched a rug from the heap of furniture and draped it carefully over the pictures. There might, he reflected, be hundreds of thousands of pounds worth of rather bad painting leaning against that wall.

Amused by his morning's doings, he locked up and went out into the morning sunshine.

Chapter fourteen

'Guess what?' he announced to his mother, on arriving home. She was sitting cross-legged on a large, moth-eaten Indian cushion, marking exercise books to the background of an Open University programme. She had grown her dark hair longer recently, Anthony noticed, and now it fell in a shining curtain over one half of her face as she bent over her work. She was wearing only a loose cotton robe, new from a Japanese shop in Kensington, and it struck Anthony that she looked rather pretty, younger than her thirty-nine years. She didn't look up when he came in.

'What? I wish you would tell me when you're going to be out all night. I still get worried, you know.' She knew better than to ask where he had been. He volunteered little information, normally, regarding his activities. He had told her, to her unspoken relief, of the demise of Bridget, and had mentioned Julia once or twice. She knew that it was unlikely that Anthony would bring Julia home to meet her.

Anthony flopped into an armchair. His hangover, although now receding, had left a hollow vibration in his nervous system; he felt jangled and tired.

'Sorry. I forgot. The fact is, I spent the night at Dad's.'

She looked up, tucking her hair behind her ears. 'Why? I thought he was in America?'

'He is,' said Anthony, and then told her about Jocasta's phone call and Chay's new-found fame as an abstract artist in the eager-to-be-pleased world of the West Coast. She laughed, as he had known she would.

'My God,' she said, shaking her head. 'He does land on his feet. I remember when I first met him he was convinced that the modern art world was a complete con. He used to say that anyone, no matter how talentless, could become famous if they knew how to market a thing properly.'

'I wonder if he still thinks that?' mused Anthony.

'I doubt it.' Judith uncrossed her legs and stood up, tightening the belt of her robe as she went into the kitchen. 'I suspect he's grown less cynical over the years. I think he always seriously thought he was a good artist. Coffee?'

Anthony followed her into the kitchen and began to rummage in the fridge for some cheese. 'No thanks.' He pulled out the remains of a lump of Cheddar, looked at it, and put it back. 'Anyway, I went over last night to see what there was at the flat – pictures, I mean. His girlfriend said now was the time to root out his stuff and jump on the bandwagon. Well,' he added, peering into the biscuit tin, 'she didn't put it quite like that. But that was the general idea. So I had a look round. I'd forgotten they'd turned his electricity off, so I slept there and had a look round this morning.'

'And?'

'And there are about six or seven canvases that look like the usual thing you see in modern art galleries. Pretty bloody, if you ask me.'

Judith smiled as she carried her coffee back into the living-room. 'Funnily enough,' she said, settling herself back on to her cushion, 'I've still got a whole collection of his drawings and things. Things he used to do when I first met him.' She sipped her coffee. 'I wonder if they're worth anything now.'

'Not in the long run, I shouldn't imagine,' replied Anthony. 'As for the present, I wouldn't say he's exactly found worldwide fame. Just a little bit of a cult following amongst the art-lovers of California, from what I can gather. I wouldn't imagine they'd be of any interest to anyone over here. Anyway,' he added, stretching, 'it's paintings they want.' He wanted to change the subject; the matter of Len's money was on his mind. Seven days had turned into six.

'I think I'll have a look through them later, at any rate,' mused Judith, resuming her marking. Anthony picked up the paper and flicked through it for a moment or two.

'Mum?' he said, 'I was wondering . . .'

'Mmm?'

'Could you let me have an advance on my scholarship money? Say, a hundred or so?'

'What for?' she asked, without looking up. This sounded hopeful to Anthony, but she added before he could reply, 'You know I can't give you that much in one go.'

'Oh. Oh, well, not to worry.'

'What did you want it for?'

'Oh, nothing. A new suit. I thought my old one was getting a bit shabby.'

'Well, if you will go around sleeping in it.' She paused. 'Are you going out tonight?'

'No – that is, I don't know. Why?' His mother went a little pink, and then bent her head over the books.

'I'm having someone over to dinner. He's a new teacher at school. Teaches art.'

'Oh.' Anthony was surprised, but pleased. 'Oh, well, in that case I probably am.' She looked up, and they smiled at one another. No wonder she's looking rather nice these days, he thought. 'You can show him Chay's drawings and get a professional opinion, then, can't you?'

After a dreary weekend, one in which only his severe lack of money prevented him from ringing Julia, Anthony arrived at chambers on Monday morning to find some mail waiting on his desk. This was unprecedented. It was a magazine, sent airmail from the States. He undid the wrapper and stared at it. It was called *Metropolis*, and apparently cost $4.80. Bemused, he gazed at the cover picture of a steel spiral, and then the words 'Chay Cross –The Primal Moment Arrives' caught his eye. He laughed out loud and flipped through the pages until he came to the article on his father. It was long and extremely difficult to read, due largely to the impenetrability of the language, but Anthony gathered that its tone was complimentary.

'Chay Cross has questioned and deconstructed styles from past art, in the process making art which is the indispensable coda to a modern art collection. His work, utilizing shimmering, seductive presences whose brilliant blues, yellows and reds

enhance a ripe and often erotic allure, has a disembodying effect,
plain statement giving way to conundrum and material
certainty replaced by an awareness of the unknown. Of his own
art, and of the neo-Modernist movement which he espouses,
Cross says that it is 'the product of a tradition that seems to
demand, paradoxically, its own rejection or denial.' This début
show from the London-based artist betrays profound religious
influences, as expressed in the meditative use of muted color,
contrasted with the primordial force of rich splashes of forms
reminiscent of fruit, breasts, and mountains. The effect is one of
skill beyond craft, of the subject as a self-discovered, self-
manifesting entity. Best expressed in Cross' own words, the
intention is 'to arrive at a state where the painting just is. *The*
best works are the ones that leave me out, so that there's more
space for the viewer to respond.' This is a startling first showing
from an artist whose works offer an impregnable solidity giving
way to an ethereal alternative, and who could develop into an
outstanding severe and refined abstract painter.'

There was more, much more, on these lines. Turning the page,
Anthony was confronted by colour reproductions of Chay's
work. They all looked largely like the ones at the squat,
although cleaner and more colourful. Beneath the pictures
were little one-line legends: 'Combines subversive wit with
melancholy power'; 'A wonderfully adroit manipulation of
enticing images'. Anthony stared at them, read the lines over,
and wondered whether he lacked the insight of these critics.
Then he sighed, gave up, and turned back to the text. Its tone
was unquestionably one of excited awe. He flipped through
the pages, wondering whether Jocasta had sent a note with the
magazine about the London gallery. Then he realised that this
must have been mailed before she had spoken to him. Smiling,
he tucked the magazine into his briefcase, intending to show it
to his mother that evening.

As he did so, he heard voices on the landing outside. The
door opened, and Michael came in with Leo. Anthony felt his
pulse surge. Leo glanced calmly, almost unseeingly, at
Anthony as he carried on talking to Michael. It seemed to
Anthony as though some sudden force had whirled into the

calm of his mind. He closed his briefcase with shaking hands, and glanced quickly up as though to drink in, in one swift draught, the vivid charm of Leo's form and face, the masculine grace of his hands as he set some papers down on Michael's desk, the loose ease with which he settled into a chair as he talked. His very presence seemed to charge the air. Anthony was reminded suddenly of his emotions at seeing Julia for the first time in a long time, that evening that they had first gone out together. Then, as now, the air surrounding the beloved object seemed to possess some special luminosity. This, in no more than the merest brush of a glance. He pulled some papers from the drawer of his desk, murmuring an apparently abstracted 'Good morning' to both men, then gazed down unseeingly at the printed page before him. His heart beat heavily, as though it must be heard. Blindly, Anthony contemplated the confusion of his own emotions. He had thought, on Saturday morning, in the chill and fret of the desolate squat and his own hangover, that there would be no more intensity of feeling – that the thread, which had been vibrating unseen between them, had snapped, the tension lost. He had buried whatever emotion he had felt beneath the grey domesticity of the weekend, setting Leo and Friday evening away from himself, refusing to contemplate either. It had been false, he knew, damnably false. He realised, with appalled certainty, that whatever painful, powerful attraction had grown within him for this man was there still. By his own hand, he had sought, on Friday night, to wrench it out of existence, deny it life. He had only succeeded, he saw, in destroying the green, living part, while the root remained. He longed to – but could not – look at Leo again. He stared instead at his work, mechanically turning one unread page after the other.

Things were little better for Leo, despite his demeanour. He had caught up with Michael on his way from the car park, had idly engaged him in some spurious conversation concerning a case they had between them, hoping to prolong it as far as Michael's room, where he knew Anthony would probably already be. He had felt, in spite of himself, a mounting sense of hope and faint excitement as they had climbed the stairs. His mouth was a little dry as they entered the room. He could do no more than cast the briefest, most aloof of glances at Anthony, feeling as he did so, scanning the dark, familiar features for the clearest of seconds, a sharp stab of love. So he was lost, after all. There was to be no mastery, no ability, with maturity, to set his heart aside and ignore his love.

Neither looked at the other for the rest of the time that Leo spent talking to Michael. There was no need. For both men the tension and the vivid awareness of the other was electric. Anthony found it almost unbearable, particularly because he longed, with all of his heart, for the feeling to vanish, never to have been. After a time he looked up, conscious of his heart tightening as he looked at Leo, who was talking with idle amusement of some mutual acquaintance. When he stood up to leave, tapping his thigh lightly with his newspaper, he glanced over at Anthony for a second or two. His eyes as they met Anthony's were cool, detached.

'You know, don't you,' he remarked to Michael, his eyes still on Anthony, 'about our great affair – Anthony's and mine, that is – collapsing into a pile of dust on Friday?'

For a second, Anthony's mind felt paralysed. But Michael merely replied, 'The stevedore case? Settled, did it? Well, it's just astonishing that the thing dragged on for as long as it did. Still, more money in the bank.' Leo smiled lightly, and tapped Anthony's desk with his newspaper.

'I hope Anthony didn't find his time entirely wasted.'

'No,' replied Anthony, looking up briefly, 'it was fascinating. I'm almost sorry it's finished.' He found himself speaking in spite of himself, abhorred the innuendo, didn't want this conversation to continue.

'Maybe Leo will find something else for you once we've finished with this hearing,' said Michael. 'His work always seems a good deal more exciting than mine.'

'I shouldn't think I would have anything that would interest him much,' said Leo, opening the door. 'Though we can always see.'

As he went downstairs to his room, he clenched the newspaper tightly in his fist. God, why had he done that? Why had he let this whole business get the better of him? He should just have left well alone. The boy had made it clear enough on Friday night that he wasn't interested. That ludicrous conversation. Those absurd *double entendres* . . . It was always the way, he knew. Distance from the object of one's passion lent a certain detachment; one could resolve, coldly, not to allow oneself to be manipulated by useless feelings. But then one was in the presence of that person again, and one was borne hopelessly along. He had been so near, within touching distance. He sat in his chair, surveying sightlessly the spotless calm of his room. This must stop. There was, there could be, no point.

At his desk, Anthony was endeavouring to read and comprehend the work before him. He had dwelt too long on Leo's last look as he left the room; had sought, in spite of himself, for some meaning. But the blue eyes had been cold, almost mocking, and that little game of words had been played merely to vanquish any trace of conceit that Leo thought Anthony might have had after Friday night. He wished that events had never happened, that he could still enjoy being with Leo as he had done only a few days ago. But he knew that the game had moved on; the rules were altered, and it was now one that he did not think he could possibly play.

On Wednesday morning Anthony received a brief letter from his father, giving him the name of the gallery in New Bond Street, where he was to take the paintings.

Dear Anthony,

I have found in my contemplation here a renewed vigour and light in my painting. Jocasta has told you of the material success that has followed. This is secondary, but for the sake of others I must make of it what I can. There is a woman called Betty Marks at the Marks-Schlomm Gallery in New Bond St, who knows you will be bringing the paintings from Islington. Why don't you call her and introduce yourself.

The other thing is, I rang Graham and am sending him the bail money. I think if this thing takes off in a big way I may have to come back and face things. I have to legitimise myself. There is a lawyer here who spoke to a lawyer there who says it may only

be a fine, although jumping bail might be a bit tricky. Anyway,
you know about that kind of thing, I presume. I will let you know
what I decide.

Maybe you should come here for a time. The people can be
weird —the gallery people, I mean — but the place heals the soul.

Peace. Chay.

I need some soul-healing, thought Anthony, folding the letter
up. He went down to the clerks' room and looked the gallery
up in the telephone book. He rang and spoke to Mrs Marks,
who had a rasping, cool voice, and who seemed elegantly
enthusiastic when Anthony told her about the paintings at the
flat.

'How wonderful. His work is receiving the most fabulous
write-ups. *Very* thrilling for your family.'

'Yes, I read something in an American magazine that my
father sent me. It seems to be going down well. I thought
perhaps if you sent a taxi over to Islington at six o'clock this
evening to collect the paintings?' This had struck Anthony as
the best financial solution; he knew the chances of recouping a
taxi fare from Chay were long and slender.

'A very good idea. I shall arrange that. Why don't you bring
yourself along with the paintings? I should so like to meet
Chay Cross' son.'

Anthony hesitated. Why not? Fill up another blank hour or
two. 'Yes, all right. Thank you.' And he gave her the address.

At ten to six that evening, Anthony stood in the barren
disorder of the Islington living-room, watching the street
below from the window. Although the late April air outside
was invitingly warm, the atmosphere in the flat was still chilly
and bleak. The paintings stood ranged against the wall, their
awkward blooms of colour gaping at the room. Anthony
watched a couple walking slowly under the spring trees. The
girl lifted her head and laughed soundlessly and moved like a
slow dancer into the man's embracing arm. Anthony thought
of Julia; he hadn't seen her for weeks. He hadn't even
unconsciously scanned the distant faces in the human traffic of
the Temple for her features. He did not want to remember. The

thought of her mouth, of her warm, slender body filled him with unbearable need and a sense of loss. He leaned his head against the naked window-frame. How could he possibly feel such longing for her and still be prey to some inchoate attraction for another man? It was different – was it different? Was the mesmeric quality of Leo's voice and look, the charm of his attitudes and restless movements, on some other plane, set apart from the petulant, arresting loveliness of Julia? He tried, for the first time, to resolve and understand his attraction to Leo. He took it apart in his mind and examined each aspect. It was not sexual, but it was more than platonic. It was hunger for – what? What could he possibly want from Leo? He knew he wanted to be with him, to listen to and watch him, to be able to enjoy the pleasure of his face and feelings. But what more? The truth was, he did not know what more there could be. He had never been there, never tasted the absolute possession of another man's attention, devotion. He wanted to matter, to be of the utmost importance, that much he knew. But, as he remembered Leo's look on Monday morning, he thought that that was now impossible.

As he watched and pondered, he saw a black cab pull up in the street below. With a sigh, he pulled himself away from the window and bounced down the shabby staircase into the street. With the help of the driver, the canvases were loaded into the taxi, and they set off through the London evening traffic.

When the paintings were unloaded at the other end, Anthony discovered in himself a faint anxiety. He hoped they were not going to disappoint Mrs Marks. But Mrs Marks, who was younger and less elegant than Anthony had imagined, seemed delighted. She picked up one of the smaller ones and brought it over to the light.

'Mmm,' she murmured appreciatively, 'clearly in his formative period, but *very* much with that primitive clarity.'

Anthony murmured in agreement, trying to see beyond the unevenly textured series of mango-shaped splashes that glowed against a navy blue background. Mrs Marks put her neatly cropped dark head on one side and smiled at Anthony, then laid the painting carefully back with the others.

'Do you paint – Anthony, is it?'

'No,' said Anthony, 'I'm a barrister.'

'How exciting!' replied Mrs Marks, with the vague, practised thrill of one who customarily said this in reply to any revelation. 'Will you have a drink?' She brought out a bottle of Beefeater gin and another of vermouth from a cupboard next to the smart, oval reception desk. 'We have a new exhibition opening here tomorrow – Vernon Dunn. Such exciting work. Sculptures. Do you like sculpture, Anthony?'

She was leading him, by gesture, towards some aggressive abstract pieces balanced beautifully on long, white, slender columns. He stood and looked at them while she went back and began expertly to mix two cocktails. They all seemed to Anthony to be variations on the same theme, though he was uncertain what that was. There were more further down the room, beautifully lit, the larger ones resting on low, squat plinths. Leo would like these, thought Anthony. Mrs Marks handed him his drink. He took a sip, and instantly felt the delightful, numbing effect of almost neat gin.

'Delicious,' he said, with surprise.

'I learnt how to make a proper martini when I was living in New York as a girl. So much better than our boring gin and tonic, don't you think?' She gave a laugh. 'Of course, that was a long time ago.'

'Surely not,' replied Anthony gallantly. He glanced at her speculatively. About his mother's age, probably; small, spare, with very square features. Her mustard-coloured dress was well cut and close fitting. She smiled a lot, probably from practice.

'Well,' and she laughed again, looking up at Anthony from under her eyelashes as she sipped her drink, 'not *that* long ago, perhaps.' She eyed him as he looked blankly at the sculptures. A *very* attractive boy, she thought – how lovely when they still had that half-formed, childish strength. *Such* dark eyes. Beautiful hands. Her small tongue darted unconsciously over her lips. So young. Would he . . . ? she wondered. He finished his drink, suddenly aware that it had gone to his head somewhat. He hadn't eaten much at lunchtime.

'When will you be sending the paintings to America?' he

asked, for something to say. She stood smiling and looking at him, her head on one side.

'We might keep them here. Our New York gallery is incredibly busy this year. I was thinking that it really might be a good idea to introduce his talent over here now. A small summer exhibition, I thought. Perhaps we could use these and some of his more recent work. It would be wonderful if we could entice him back here, don't you think?'

Anthony thought briefly of Islington Magistrates' Court. 'Wonderful,' he said. 'Yes, I'm sure that would be a good idea.'

He put his empty glass down and ran his fingers through his hair, unaware of the stir this caused in Mrs Marks' well-worn heart. She saw that he was about to go, and said quickly, 'Won't you have another drink? You haven't looked at the rest of the exhibition yet.' And she splashed some more gin into his glass and a hasty dash of vermouth. Anthony opened his mouth to refuse, saw that it was too late, and said nothing. He wished he could think of some intelligent conversation to offer this woman. He thanked her when she gave him his second drink, and then set off uncertainly up the room. She followed a little way behind, cat-like. Just when he was trying to work out what one of the sculptures reminded him of – a fir cone? the thing at the end of a lavatory chain? – he felt, to his surprise, a hand on the back of his thigh.

'You are *such* a charming young man, my dear,' Mrs Marks was saying, somewhat breathily. 'Don't you think we should carry on our little conversation somewhere more comfortable? My flat isn't very far away.' She slid round in front of him, her hand still on his leg, and looked up at him winsomely.

'Ah, no – not really,' said Anthony, bemused. What on earth was going on? He hardly knew this woman, and she was fondling his bum.

'Oh, come on,' she persisted, quite blatant now, using her most seductive rasp, and rubbing her hand on his crotch. He stepped back in alarm, and then laughed.

'Listen, thanks for the drink, but I must go.' And he headed for the door, his footsteps rapid and clear on the polished floor of the gallery. She scuttled up behind him as he reached the door.

'There could even be a little . . . present for you. You look as though you could do with some extra money. For a new suit, perhaps.' He was struggling with the catch of the locked door. What an appalling situation, he thought.

'No, honestly, thanks very much,' he gasped politely. At last she opened the door for him, smiling slyly.

'Don't forget,' she cooed, as he fled into the night, 'I'm always here.' She watched his figure retreating down the pavement. '*What* a darling,' she murmured to herself. 'What a pity.'

Anthony walked fairly fast until he reached Albemarle Street, then slowed down and began to laugh. She hadn't wasted any time, you had to give her that. Offering him money, too. Nice work if you could get it. He wondered, idly, how much his twenty-two-year-old body was worth. A fortune, to the right person, he supposed. He glanced in the windows of the expensive shops and galleries as he made his way towards Piccadilly, coveting the cashmere sweaters and handmade shoes, the badger-bristle shaving brushes and other expensive trinkets that the rich seemed to amuse themselves with. He cut down into Jermyn Street and admired the ties and expensive shirts, the immaculately thick, creamy cotton, the rough, colour-splashed silk. Oh, he sighed. One day, when he was a tenant at Caper Court – a QC, even – he would be able to fritter away his money on silk dressing-gowns and expensive rubbish. He'd even be able to afford one of those sculptures in Mrs Marks' gallery. He would be able to give it to Leo. At this point, his fantasies stopped. Leo. And money. Or rather, the lack of it. In only two days Len would doubtless be ringing him up again, demanding his friend's money. And where the hell was he going to get it? Maybe he should go back to New Bond Street and knock on Mrs Marks' door again, he thought ruefully. The weight of his debt to Len pressed on him, blotting his mind to all other thoughts, as he made his way home.

By the time Friday came, Anthony had exhausted all possibilities. He had asked Barry, knowing that it was hopeless, and had been met with a guffaw of incredulity. He thought of pressing the matter with his mother, then thought again. He even considered approaching Michael, but could not bring himself to this. Once or twice he had been on the verge of phoning Len to ask him to put the thing off until his next scholarship cheque came through, but he weighed this against the possibility that Len didn't need the money as badly as he had said, and might not even ring for a bit. He decided to take the chance that Len might forget the matter, for the moment.

Friday morning passed without incident, although on the two occasions when the telephone had rung, he had felt the palms of his hands sweating and his heart contracting with dread. But as he came back into chambers from lunch, passing the clerks' room, Mr Slee called out to him.

'Gentleman called when you was out at lunch, Mr Cross. Said he'd call back again.'

'When was that?' Anthony could think of no one, except Len, who might call on him and whom Mr Slee would not recognise.

'Oh, ten minutes or so ago.'

Anthony took the stairs two at a time and went into his room. Michael was still out. Anthony went over and stood at the window, watching the people passing from the car park to the courtyard, coming and going up and down King's Bench Walk, in the spring sunshine. He watched for some fifteen minutes. And then he saw, distinctive in its sauntering lack of purpose from the other businesslike figures, a man dressed in working clothes making his way towards Caper Court. It wasn't Len, but something told Anthony that this was something to do with him. As he watched, with dread, the man approaching the steps of chambers, he saw Leo following in his wake, head down, the sun glinting on his thick silver hair.

Without waiting for the phone to ring, Anthony hurried down, his footsteps hollow on the wooden stairs, and as he reached the bottom the man in working clothes was turning towards him and Mr Slee was saying, 'Yes, Mr Cross is back now. Oh, here he is.'

The man smiled slowly and unpleasantly as he looked at Anthony, and said, 'I'm a friend of Len's. Paul.' Over his shoulder, Anthony could see Sir Basil and Cameron Renshaw, both in shirt-sleeves, standing in the clerks' room by the telex machine, talking. Oh, Christ.

'I thought I'd pop over about my money,' Paul was saying in a casual, low voice. 'Len told me where you worked. Said sorry he didn't ring.'

'Look, can we go outside and talk about this?' asked Anthony softly, desperately hoping that the man would agree. But he shook his head regretfully, slowly.

'Sorry. Nothing to talk about. Just give me the dosh and I'll be on my way.'

'The thing is – ' Anthony hesitated. He knew that as soon as it became evident that he was not going to give Paul any money, the trouble would begin. He started again. 'I'll have to go to the bank. It's just up on the Strand, if you want to – ' Paul smiled and shook his head again. He looked round at the bustling clerks' room. Sir Basil had already glanced over once or twice at Anthony and his incongruously dressed acquaintance.

'Look, Anthony,' he said, still talking quietly, laying unpleasant stress on Anthony's name, 'Len was more than generous with you, giving you all that money. But unfortunately, that money wasn't strictly his. Now, I don't like to get unpleasant with Len, 'cause he's my mate. But I don't mind getting unpleasant with you, *see*?' He said the last word suddenly loudly, jabbing Anthony in the chest with his finger. 'And I don't mind getting very fucking noisy, either!' He was almost shouting, and both Sir Basil and Cameron Renshaw looked up, startled. Anthony closed his eyes, praying for words that would stem the flow of Paul's eloquence. He opened them and saw from Paul's angry face that he was about to continue, when suddenly the cold, low sound of Leo's voice cut in.

'Now,' he said softly, the Welsh accent very clear. 'One more word – ' Paul opened his mouth, but Leo was faster. '– and we don't get our money.' The words were barely audible. Leo pulled his wallet swiftly, discreetly from his pocket and Paul glanced at it. Leo's slender fingers pulled out five twenty-pound notes and whipped them into Paul's hand so quickly that the thing was barely seen. Paul pocketed the money and turned as if to say something else to Anthony.

'Give our regards to Len,' said Leo quickly, and motioned Anthony to the stairs. 'Go on, upstairs!' he hissed at him. Anthony moved off uncertainly, glancing over his shoulder with relief at Paul's figure as he made his way out of the building.

He went weakly into Michael's room, and heard Leo come in behind him and close the door.

'Thank you,' said Anthony with difficulty, turning round to look at him. 'If he'd carried on as he started, Sir Basil and Cameron would have heard him bawling the building down. Christ.' He put his hands over his eyes. 'That would have finished me for good.'

'I agree,' said Leo evenly. 'That wouldn't have been too clever. He sounded like he knew an awful lot of very nasty words.' He sat down in Michael's chair and looked at Anthony. There was nothing in his face. 'Why the hell didn't you get a bank loan? I told you to the other night.' There. It had been mentioned, and he had intended never to refer to it again. The other night. Each looked away from the other. Anthony said nothing. Leo sighed and looked out of the window at the crisp blue of the April sky. He felt tired, even a little old. Sick of love and its pointlessness. 'Look,' he said, 'I told you, remember? There's something a little crippled inside all of us. Put that whole damned evening out of your head. Forget it.'

'I don't think you're crippled,' replied Anthony. His voice was unbearably gentle. Please don't make me hope, thought Leo, turning his eyes slowly to Anthony.

At that moment the door opened and Michael entered. Anthony was startled, but Leo merely looked up and smiled mildly.

'The wanderer returns,' he said pleasantly. 'I thought I'd come and ask you where our very valuable copy of Russell on Arbitration has got to. I've been all over chambers looking for the thing.'

'Sorry. Can't help you,' replied Michael. 'Go and ask Jeremy. He seems to like books.'

As Leo reached the door, Anthony said, 'I'll get that back to you as soon as I can.' Leo paused, smiled, and nodded, then left without a word.

Chapter fifteen

Nowhere is the overly ornate dignity and splendour with which the Victorians in their era invested the institution of law more faithfully reflected than in the Royal Courts of Justice in the Strand, London. The very building's labyrinthine qualities evoke the tortuous, meandering dimness of the complexities of the law itself. No mere layman could hope to find his way through this maze of grim splendour. Cross the road through the bustling traffic in the hopeful light of day, and your eye will be struck by the arcane, over-turreted, over-buttressed, over-built grandeur of its façade. Once inside the unassuming wooden entrance doors, through which solicitors and barristers hurry with the rapid nonchalance that scarcely conceals their conceit in the mysteries of their profession, you find yourself in an enormous, vaulted hallway, with mullioned windows, high, high as a cathedral, a very monument to the holiness of the law. On the walls are vast oil paintings of long-dead, long-forgotten judges, chancellors and masters. They look down with all their pomp and coldness at the small workings of the world below. Beneath their grey gaze the heart shrivels and the real world recedes in the face of the law's mighty importance. Pass through one of the low stone archways that lead from this cathedral, pass up the worn, winding stone steps that lead into a deeper mystery, and find yourself in a long corridor, one of many long corridors. The traffic and the Strand and the bright light of day are already far away. Off this corridor – or any one of the identical corridors – are set the courtrooms. They have not changed, in essence, in over a hundred years. Peep in through the door – you may, this is a public place – creep into one of the creaking wooden pews, and you may watch the murmurous proceedings. Voices rise and fall with the figures of counsel, solicitors lean and whisper, judges write and nod, witnesses sigh and shift, papers rustle, clerks fold their hands and settle their gowns – every day, in and out, through the seasons of a hundred years, the workings of the law have ground on in this way, in this place.

Leave the courtroom – for you don't, and never could, understand what is going on – and follow the maze of passageways and galleries in circle after circle. Lawyers pass like ghosts, the spectres of all the other lawyers, long dead, who have come and gone about their business here down the years. They do not see you. They are in their temple and busy at their devotions. Walk as long and as far as you like, until your eyes are weary with the interminable splendour of these corridors, and you will never learn your way. Only lawyers are privileged to understand the mysteries of this place.

One day in May, Anthony came across the Strand through the traffic, passed through the swing doors, across the echoing flags of the great hallway and, heedless of the tourists and with the unthinking confidence of the initiate, doubled back through another doorway, ran up some stairs, back again through another doorway, up another flight of stairs, through a door, and emerged into a cheerful, ornate antechamber, full of the hum of lawyers' voices, a sudden contrast to the austere quiet of the court corridors. Nicknamed the Bear Garden, this was where lawyers and litigants congregated daily to do urgent business, to make last-minute applications, seek hasty injunctions, and to wait around for nail-biting half-hours for audiences with the Masters and judges whose chambers led off from the Bear Garden itself. Although an altogether brighter place than the rest of the Law Courts, faster and livelier, reflecting the day-to-day, businesslike face of the law, it was still grand. The ceilings were high, and the long, dark wooden tables at which lawyers sat to scribble their last-minute amendments and check the correctness of their applications were burnished with the polishings of thousands of elbows over many years.

Anthony leaned against one of the stone pillars, waiting for his solicitor to come hurrying up with the papers for their hearing before the Master. Late, he supposed. Idly he watched the anxious litigants fidget and stare around at their unfamiliar surroundings with curious eyes, wondering how they were ever to find their way out again. He nodded and smiled at a few acquaintances, exchanged a few words with another. Then he leaned back and waited. Suddenly, coming through the door, he saw the unmistakable figure of Julia, her blonde head bent in conversation with a male companion, hugging some papers to her chest. It had been over six weeks since he had last seen her. He felt as though his stomach had caved in. He did not move, and as she passed him she suddenly looked up and saw him. She stopped, then smiled her wonderful smile at him, and turned to her companion.

'You go on. I'll be with you in a minute.'

The man nodded and moved off. Julia stood looking up at Anthony, who smiled back feebly. She was the most wonderful sight he had seen in weeks. How could he have let her go? How could he have been such a fool?

'Hello,' she said. 'What are you doing here?'

'Oh,' he replied, pushing himself off the pillar in what he hoped was a casual way and running his fingers through his hair in unmistakable agitation, 'just a quick interlocutory. You?'

'Assessment of damages.' There was a long pause. They looked at each other, discomfort fading as they absorbed one another's features. Anthony wondered what would happen if you suddenly grabbed a lady counsel in the middle of the Bear Garden and kissed her until she couldn't breathe.

'Have you been busy?' he asked instead. She smiled and shrugged. She was wearing, underneath her black suit jacket, a white cotton shirt with a high, ruffled collar fastened with a little gold pin; her face, framed by its short blonde hair, looked to him like some tender flower. He wanted to stroke her cheek, unfasten the little gold pin, unbutton her collar and kiss her white throat. Then he thought of all the other things he wanted to do, had done, and wanted to do again. Longing overwhelmed him.

'Can I see you?' he said faintly.

'Why?' Her voice sounded sad and a little cold.

'Because.' He could think of nothing else. Out of the corner of his eye he could see Malcolm, his solicitor, hurrying through the doorway. 'Can I?' he asked again.

'All right,' she said at last, reluctantly.

'Right,' he said quickly, as Malcolm headed towards him. 'Friday. Friday at six. In the bar.' She nodded, and walked off. Anthony watched as she went; he wondered if she would show up. She had every reason not to. He let out a deep breath as Malcolm greeted him, and they began to discuss the business of the day.

It had seemed to him as though Friday would never come. And now it was here, it was a quarter past six, and there was no sign of Julia. Anthony sat in the bar near to the open french windows. Down on the lawn below the rose garden, people sat scattered on the grass in the May sunshine. Anthony stared at the chess game that his friend, Simon, was playing with someone else, trying to fasten his mind on the moves. But his thoughts kept darting anxiously to Julia, and whether or not she would come. How long should he wait? All evening, he supposed, if necessary. Bored with the chess game, he turned his gaze idly to the figure of the large coloured man who sat, slumped asleep, in one of the high-backed chairs at the end of the room. He had a silver foil pie dish on his head, and in his arms he cradled a bottle of Johnnie Walker Black Label whisky. His enormous head nodded drunkenly. No one paid him the slightest heed; he was a familiar sight, another one of the Bar's freaks. No doubt one of the porters would throw him out soon. Gazing at him, Anthony thought of what Leo had said about the eccentric inhabitants of the tiny world of the Bar. He was right. Nowhere else, not even in a Northern Line tube station, would such a thing be tolerated, let alone mildly accepted.

He looked at his watch. Twenty-five past, and he couldn't even afford to buy himself another drink. He only had enough money left to buy Julia one – if she showed up, that was. He picked up a copy of the *Sun* and read abstractedly. If she's not here by half-past, he was thinking – But when he looked up again, she was coming through the doorway, trying to look collected and unconcerned. She saw him, gave a little wave

176

and, out of habit, turned to the bar to get herself a drink. He stood up quickly and went over to her.

'Here, I'll get that,' he said.

'That's all right,' she replied, and was already scooping up her change and tucking her bag under her arm as she reached for her drink. She took a sip and walked back with him to the table by the window.

She smiled at him in a kind, cool fashion as they sat down. Anthony did not know that she had spent ten anxious minutes in the ladies' cloakroom, fiddling with her skirt and scrutinising her make-up, trying to suppress her faint nervousness. Several weeks of not seeing Anthony – Anthony, the only man who had ever unnerved her by giving her up – had had the cumulative effect of making the prospect of spending an evening with him quite daunting. She was determined, after their last parting, to remain impassive, nonchalant. But she could not ignore the fact that her stomach tightened as she caught sight of him sitting by the window lost in his newspaper, and that she felt distinctly nervous when he looked at her.

He took a sip at what remained of his drink. 'Good day?' he asked.

'Not bad,' she replied, glancing down at the table top. 'We've just finished three weeks of the most almighty Treasury case. When I wasn't half asleep, I hadn't a clue what was going on.'

'The judge probably hadn't, either,' said Anthony. She smiled, and there was a pause. Anthony felt awkward. He wasn't at all sure what he had wanted to happen this evening, or even why he had suggested meeting at all. Nothing had changed; he still hadn't a bean, and the debt was still there, just shifted from one creditor to another. He looked up at Julia, and she glanced away. They said nothing for a moment or two.

'Look,' said Anthony with a sigh, 'this is bloody silly. I don't know why we're doing this. I can't take you out, I *still* don't have any money. It was a stupid idea. We can just finish our drinks and you go off, if you want to.'

A little wave of panic rose in her. 'No,' she said quickly, and then tried to adjust her voice to a level of nonchalance. 'I don't mind sitting and talking, really.'

Anthony leaned back in his chair and looked at her speculatively. He longed to ask her if she had been seeing Piers, but knew this was probably not a clever idea. He remembered all the reasons why he had stopped seeing her, but, as he looked at her, they seemed quite inconsequential now.

'All right,' he said. 'Let's go outside.' He picked up her drink and they both rose and went down the curving stone steps to the garden below. They walked in silence along one of the gravel paths and sat on an empty bench against the wall. The light evening breeze lifted tendrils of her blonde hair as she looked out across the lawn and past the railings to where people were hurrying towards Temple station.

'I've had the most bloody six weeks without you,' he said, gazing at her profile. The faintest of summer scents drifted from the rose garden.

'Seven,' she replied, without looking at him. She leaned back against the bench, closing her eyes, the sun on her face, as though exhausted in spirit. He looked at her, then kissed her. She did not move. He kissed her again, turning her body towards his own, until at last she responded, her arms around his neck. He suddenly realised, through their kiss, that her face was wet with tears. She pulled away and tried to laugh, a little laugh of embarrassment, through her crying.

'I'm sorry,' she said, wiping at her eyes with her sleeve, inwardly cursing herself for her weakness. It was the culmination of weeks of loneliness. Piers had been nowhere; Anthony had thrown her over; she had felt entirely abandoned. Added to which, this Treasury case had been intensely demanding, and she now felt weary in mind and spirit. Everything overflowed suddenly in tears. Anthony stroked her hair and muttered some soothing nonsense. She looked at him. She had lost whatever resolve she might have had to remain aloof and self-possessed. She needed too badly to be loved.

'Please,' she said, 'can we go home?' She kissed him, a quick, urgent kiss, damp with tears. 'I want you so badly,' she whispered, twisting her fingers in the lapels of his jacket.

'Oh, God,' he murmured, feeling as though he were falling into some deep, blue void of longing. 'So do I.'

And so it begins again, thought Anthony. He was sitting slumped on the underground, groggy with love and lack of sleep, his unfocused eyes staring at a traffic warden recruitment advertisement. He knew that he should feel happier than he did, but he didn't. Last night had been as blissful as any such reconciliation possibly could be. It had been as good as the first time they had made love. Better. He had felt ardent, powerful, wanting to overwhelm her entirely with love. That was what seven weeks of abstention did to you, he supposed. He rubbed his eyes with the flats of his hands. He wished he'd bought a newspaper. Anything not to have to think. Already the problem of tonight was looming. Well, maybe it wouldn't be *that* much of a problem. The novelty wouldn't quite have worn off, and Julia would probably be content with home-made spaghetti bolognese, a bottle of wine, and more and more love. Then what? Then there was next weekend, and the weekend after that, and all the odd, spur-of-the-moment decisions to go to Mario and Franco's, or to some wine bar, in the middle of the week.

He yawned and discreetly examined the couple who sat opposite him, swaying together like unconscious reeds as the train racketed towards Embankment, their eyes glazed as they stared up at the advertisements. They had blonde hair, and rucksacks, and looked tired. Swedes, thought Anthony. Or maybe Norwegians. The woman's hand clasped that of the man. They gave the impression, with their identically expressionless faces and linked hands, of two beings travelling dumbly towards eternity, unified, silent. Anthony wondered what it would be like to be married, to be sealed to someone in that fateful way. He stopped looking at them. They depressed him. When he had money, he wouldn't take the love of his life hitch-hiking through Europe. Or maybe that was what you did when you had no money.

He got out at Embankment and walked up to Charing Cross station, feeling vaguely un-Saturday-like in his crumpled suit. He had not, quite naturally, had time to hang it up last night. He reflected that his scholarship cheque was due to arrive next week, which normally would have helped. But his Barclaycard statement was imminent, and he now owed Leo a hundred pounds on top of that. He didn't suppose that Leo was feeling particularly hard up because of it, but the idea of being in debt to him made Anthony peculiarly uncomfortable. In fact, after last night, he decided that it would be a good idea if he didn't think about Leo at all, and stayed out of his way in chambers as much as possible. It shouldn't be difficult.

It was not, in fact, at all difficult, since Leo had gone, with Roderick Hayter, to a conference of lawyers in Japan for two weeks, as Anthony discovered that Monday morning.

'Leo's got some work for you,' Michael remarked to Anthony when he arrived. Anthony, in spite of his resolution, felt a little surge of surprise and pleasure. Maybe everything was going to return to normal, and all would be as it had been before. He was about to dump his things and go off to Leo's room, when Michael threw some papers, neatly tied up with red tape, across to him.

'He's gone off for a couple of weeks to some conference. Said he thought you could probably make a good job of this while he's away.' Michael smiled encouragingly at Anthony, who stood motionless, acutely aware of his own disappointment. 'A good sign, don't you think? Leo seems to think there isn't much you can't handle on your own. Bodes well, I'd say.'

'That's true,' replied Anthony, and returned the smile. He sat down and untied the papers, scanning them. It was something, after all, to be doing Leo's work. It made him somehow closer. Anthony was scarcely conscious that these thoughts flowed through his mind.

The case was complex, but interesting, involving bills of exchange and letters of credit. Anthony worked on it through the morning, and, as Michael had a conference in his room that afternoon, took the papers off to the library after lunch to continue his work there. He found a vacant table in the gallery, tucked away between the shelves of Canadian Law Reports, where no one was likely to disturb him. He slid the papers along the dark polished table to the window and sat down. As he sorted through the documents, there fell from between the sheaf of case notes that Leo had jotted down, a piece of paper.

It was heavy, cream-coloured paper, the kind one wrote letters on, and covered with a few lines of writing in Leo's neat, dashing hand. Anthony picked it up and looked at it. It was a poem. He read:

> That you were once unkind befriends me now,
> And for that sorrow, which I then did feel,
> Needs must I under my transgression bow,
> Unless my nerves were brass or hammer'd steel.

That was all. Anthony turned the paper over. There was nothing on the other side. He looked at the verse again, without comprehension. 'That you were once unkind befriends me now.' He liked that. It struck him that this was part of a poem, although not one he recognised. It was with a small thrill of surprise that it suddenly occurred to him that the poem was perhaps meant for him. He felt himself flush, even in the cool, calm silence of the library, and folded the paper quickly and put it in his pocket.

It was not until a few nights later that he remembered it. He and Julia had spent much of the evening in the bar with Edward in some hilarity, Anthony conscious that he was allowing himself to drift back into the same pattern as before, spending more than he had, seeing people that he only half-liked, idling away his time, but happy that he was with Julia. They had gone back to her flat, and he was lying on the sofa, a little drunk, his tie and jacket off, watching the news with Julia and drinking coffee. He glanced across at his jacket and was thinking that he really should hang it up, when he thought of the piece of paper. He got up and felt in the pockets for it. He found it and pulled it out, and went back to the sofa with it.

'What's that?' asked Julia, as he unfolded it.

'I don't really know,' replied Anthony. 'It's just something I found. I think it's part of a poem, but I'm not sure.'

'Here, let's have a look,' said Julia with interest, taking the paper from him. She rather prided herself on being well read. She read the lines over to herself. 'It sounds Shakespearian. Or Elizabethan, at any rate.' She got up and went over to the tall bookcases. 'There must be some Shakespeare sonnets amongst this lot,' she said, scanning the rows of books.

'Poetry. Yes, here we are.' And she pulled out a volume and brought it back to where Anthony was trying to watch the weather forecast with one eye shut. 'I shouldn't think this has been opened much,' she remarked, flipping through the pages. 'Here we go. Index of first lines. "That you were once unkind . . ." ' She riffled again through the pages. 'There. Told you it was Shakespeare.' She handed the book to Anthony with a pleased little smile, then picked up the coffee cups and took them out to the kitchen.

> That you were once unkind befriends me now,
> And for that sorrow, which I then did feel,
> Needs must I under my transgression bow,
> Unless my nerves were brass or hammer'd steel.
> For if you were by my unkindness shaken,
> As I by yours, you've pass'd a hell of time,
> Unless my nerves were brass or hammer'd steel.
> And I, a tyrant, have no leisure taken
> To weigh how once I suffer'd in your crime.
> O, that our night of woe might have remember'd
> My deepest sense, now hard true sorrow hits,
> And soon to you, as you to me, then tender'd
> The humble salve which wounded bosoms fits!
>   But that your trespass now becomes a fee,
>   Mine ransoms yours, and yours must ransom me.

Anthony felt his heart lurch painfully as he read, knowing without a doubt that Leo had meant this for him. He felt himself redden, and closed his eyes. Without fully under-standing that which he read, he was aware that this was, without question, a letter of love. The words were more beautiful, in their half-hidden sense, than anything more direct that Leo might have said to him. More poignant still, it came as though in secret, cloaked in verse. He opened his eyes and read it again, devouring it, pulling the meaning of each lovely phrase close to himself, seeking some meaning in the lines that could only be for him, for them alone. As Julia returned, he looked up, mildly shocked and ashamed.

'Well?' she said, sitting down beside him, her arm round his neck, peering at the book over his shoulder.

'I still don't understand it,' he said, closing the book.

'Here, let me read it,' she said, pulling the book from his hands. She found the page and read out loud, slowly and well. He listened with his head thrown back and his eyes closed. 'It's very beautiful,' she said when she had finished, scanning the lines again. 'I think he means that the other person – I mean, the woman, or whoever it's written for – is indebted to him just as much as he is to her, because they've hurt each other in some way. It binds them.' She yawned. 'I think that's what it's about, anyway.'

She tossed the book to one side, kissed Anthony briefly and smiled at him. He looked back at her sweet face, trying to unlock his mind. He shook his head rapidly, as though to clear it.

'I can't take these sessions in the bar,' he said rubbing his face. 'I'm going to feel rather the worse for wear tomorrow.'

'Well, come to bed,' Julia said, pulling at his hands. 'I want you – ' She paused and laughed, trying to read his face. ' – to tell me what I should wear to the May Ball.'

'The May Ball?'

'The May Ball. The one that's being held in Inner Temple Gardens. It's going to be fantastic. There's going to be an enormous marquee, and a really good band. Lots of champagne. Someone said the Queen Mother's coming.'

'Well, well,' said Anthony, 'that's a big draw. But I can't afford that! The tickets will cost a fortune!' His mind had come back to earth.

'Oh, Anthony, come on! *Everyone*'s going. You can't not go. Please!' He said nothing, but he knew that he would have to go; he would never hear the end of it if he didn't. He felt too sleepy to argue.

It was only some hours later, when he woke without reason in the night, that he realised the words of the poem were still coursing through his brain.

' "Mine ransoms yours, and yours must ransom me",' he repeated softly to himself in the darkness. He glanced across at Julia's sleeping form, just discernible. He touched her hair lightly and squeezed his eyes tight shut, as though to rid himself of some other vision.

Chapter sixteen

Anthony sat in chambers surveying the wreckage of his finances. On one side of a sheet of paper he had set out his income – this consisted of his scholarship money and a £200 figure with a question mark beside it – and on the other he had listed his outgoings. He sighed as he contemplated these. They could be summed up, he reflected, in a single word. Julia. There was, of course, his debt to Leo; he knew that he could probably safely leave it out of account for the present, but it still made him uneasy. And the May Ball was eating a bigger hole in his purse than he had anticipated. On top of the thirty pounds for the ticket, there was evening dress to hire, and there would be the expenses of the evening, of course. He did not see how he was possibly going to manage all this without extra financial help from somewhere, and so, as he had done so often in the past, he had been casting around to find out what grants and prizes were going at the moment. He had discovered that the Benchers of Middle Temple had set an essay competition, the compelling title of which was 'Aspects of the Administrative Jurisdiction of the Divisional Court'. Anthony fancied that there were not likely to be many entrants. It carried a prize of two hundred pounds – hence its tentative place in the list of his finances – and Anthony, who had become well accustomed over the years to supplementing his income by entering for any and all such prizes, saw no reason why he should not win it. Experience had taught him much; he was adept at judging the proportions of originality to academic merit required by the judges of such things.

He got up and walked over to the window, staring down at the figures coming and going across the courtyard. He glanced over at the car park, and was suddenly aware that his eyes were seeking, and not finding, the dark, familiar shape of

Leo's Porsche. He realised that he had, without admitting it to himself, customarily wandered over to the window every morning at ten, which was when Leo usually arrived, and watched for the silver-haired figure to stride briskly across the courtyard towards chambers. He was forced to acknowledge that the days of Leo's absence had seemed long and empty ones, despite the fact of Julia. He realised now how, over the months, his ear had learned to half-listen for the sound of Leo's voice, his footstep on the stair, and that he had lived, in a small way, for Leo's fleeting visits to Michael's room, when the air would come alive and all the other moments of the day would seem to find their focus. He acknowledged this now, as he stood by the window. Something in him was waiting for Leo to return, though to what end he could not imagine.

He stood for a moment, then returned to his desk and to his calculations. He stared at the piece of paper for a moment, groaned, and laid his head on his desk. At that moment Michael came in and, glancing down at the dark head, remarked, 'Forgive me for saying so, but don't you think you need a haircut?' He hung up his coat and then went back outside to get himself a cup of coffee, and reappeared. Anthony sighed and looked up.

'You're right,' he replied. 'I'll get one at lunchtime.' Then he picked up the scrap of paper containing the details of the essay competition, and handed it to Michael, who took it and read it. 'Where can I find out everything there is to know about the functions of the Divisional Court?' asked Anthony.

'Good God,' said Michael with a smile, 'times must be hard.' He took a sip of his coffee and laughed, rather unnecessarily, Anthony thought. 'Tell you what,' he said after a moment or two, 'Cameron gave a paper a year or so ago that had something in it about the Divisional Court. Why don't you go and ask him if you can have a look at it? He's always got an original turn of mind. He came in with me – go and catch him before he starts work.'

Anthony went off to seek out Cameron Renshaw, who inhabited one of the larger, darker rooms at the top of the building, opposite Roderick Hayter's. Although Cameron was a popular figure in chambers, Anthony found him somewhat intimidating. He was a tall, bulky, glowering man with a roaring voice and a powerful, but unpredictable mind. It was Anthony's policy to steer clear of him, although Edward appeared not to be in the least bit in awe of him, despite Cameron's obvious contempt for Edward's intellectual short-comings. Anthony found him staring at his bookshelves, muttering under his breath. He was rather impressed by the state of Cameron's room, which was in stark contrast to Leo's. Untidy dark shelves and assorted small tables overflowed with papers, folders and files stood in jumbled heaps on the floor, their frail cardboard corners bulging with documents, and briefs lined the windowsill in jostling array. Anthony won-dered how any lawyer could possibly work in such confusion. Two old wig tins, a battered wooden collar-box, and Cameron's shabby silk gown lay in a heap behind the door. The air held the powdery, mouldering smell of old paper, ink, and cigars. It reminded Anthony of the room of a certain jurisprudence professor at university.

'Excuse me,' said Anthony gently, when Cameron failed to notice him.

'What? Yes?' Cameron wheeled round, examining the space where Anthony stood.

'I'm sorry to disturb you,' said Anthony, 'but I'm doing some work concerning the Divisional Court, and Michael said that you did a paper on it a while ago. I wondered – '

'A paper! A paper?' Cameron stared at him. Then after a pause, 'Yes! Yes, quite right. I remember now. It was to the Minneapolis Bar Association. Piece of nonsense. Excellent paper, utterly wasted on those tuppenny-ha'penny Americans. Come in, come in.' Anthony came in and closed the door behind him, and stepped over a small pile of books. 'Cross, isn't it? Yes, yes.'

He scratched his head, hitched his braces, and began to pull a series of loose-leaf folders off the shelves and thumb through them. He talked continually as he did so.

'Now, let's see . . . Air Space Treaties . . . You were at Bristol, weren't you? Knew someone who lectured there – Leslie Morris. Know him? Bit before your time, maybe . . . You got a first, didn't you? Yes, I remember that. Very creditable.

Let's see . . . ''Judgments in a Foreign Currency: a Commentary''. No, not what you're after. Rather good, that, though. Went down very well.' He thumbed through some sheets, chuckling. 'Rather good.'

It struck Anthony that this search might prove well-nigh impossible, as he gazed around at the chaos. Cameron put the last folder back with a sigh. 'No. That's where I usually keep 'em. Can't understand why it's not there. Tell you what. Why don't you run down and see if one of the girls has it on their word processor? It's called ''Functions of the Courts of England and Wales''. Something like that.'

It seemed to Anthony unlikely that something from a year ago would have been kept, but he trotted downstairs to enquire. Violet, who usually did Michael's work and whom Anthony knew best, looked blank when he made his request.

'Ooh, I haven't a clue, dear. Ask Sandra – she usually does for Mr Renshaw. Sandra!' she called across to a thin, middle-aged woman who was working at a keyboard with what seemed to Anthony to be quite extraordinary rapidity. 'Sandra, do you remember a paper of Mr Renshaw's of a year ago? Something about court functions.' She turned to Anthony. 'You tell her what it was, dear.' She called across to Sandra again. 'Mr Cross'll tell you what it was called, Sandra.'

Anthony made his way over to Sandra's desk and told her the name of the paper. She did not look up, but gazed at the screen in front of her, her fingers still flying across the keyboard. She pulled her earphones off and asked Anthony to repeat it, sat for a moment, and then nodded. When she spoke, it was not to Anthony, but back to Violet.

'Yes, I remember that now, Vi – that big long thing, remember? that he kept coming down and changing. Got on my bloody nerves, that thing did.' Then she looked at Anthony. 'That's going back a while, mind. But you might be lucky. I try not to throw any of his long things away. Goes bloody mad if I do. Let's have a look.'

She pulled a box of computer discs from a drawer and riffled through them. Then she pulled out another and tried that. From that she took a disc, looked at it speculatively, and slotted it into her machine. Anthony gazed at the magic screen as the list of contents flashed up in green letters. Sandra ran through them, then stopped. 'There you are. Told you I never throw his long stuff out. You want this now?

'If you don't mind,' said Anthony, with charming diffidence. Sandra glanced at him wryly. She liked young Mr Cross; she always liked a good-looking man. Her weakness, really.

'All right, then. I should strictly be finishing this affidavit for Mr Hayter, but seeing as it's you . . .' Anthony smiled at her.

'That's really very kind of you,' he said, winning her heart completely. Sandra sat and Anthony watched as the machine poured forth words on to paper, sheet after sheet. When it was complete, she handed it to Anthony, and he thanked her again.

'He's a lovely boy, that,' she remarked to Violet after Anthony had left. 'They say he's very bright, too.'

'He may be lovely and bright,' replied Violet, who was less susceptible to young masculine charms and had a more jaundiced view of the world, 'but he's not Sir Basil's nephew, is he?' She looked meaningfully at Sandra, who sighed and said again that he was a lovely boy, and that it was a pity, really.

Anthony returned to Cameron's room with the copy of the paper, and handed it to him.

'Ah! Still had it, did they? Knew they would.' He rose from his chair, hitching his braces with one hand, and took the sheaf of papers over to the window. 'Let's see. Here's the bit you want.' He read for a moment, then shook his head. 'Good stuff, this.' Cameron was a great admirer of his own work. He read out loud, ' "General principles governing prerogative remedies". Hmm. Can't think what the Minneapolis Bar Association made of that. Still.' He handed the few relevant sheets to Anthony, eyeing him with curiosity. 'What d'you want this for, anyway? What does Michael want with stuff on the Divisional Court?'

'Oh, it's not for Michael,' replied Anthony. 'It's for an essay I'm doing. Something the Benchers have set. I thought I might have a shot at it.'

'An essay? Good God, you're not doing it for the fun of it, are you? I mean, you're not one of those, are you?' exclaimed Cameron. Anthony smiled.

'Well, I hope not. It's just that – there's a two-hundred-pound prize, and I need the money.' Cameron said nothing, but stared at him. What hell it was, he thought, being a student. Two hundred pounds. The price of a couple of decent bottles of claret.

'Well, good luck,' he said,

'Thank you,' replied Anthony. 'And thank you for this.' He held up the sheets of paper. 'I'm very grateful.'

'Not at all,' said Cameron. 'Hope it's not too out of date. Glad to be of help.'

He sat for a moment after Anthony had gone. Nice chap, Cross. Seemed a good deal brighter than that poultice, Choke. Not an Oxbridge man, though. Shame. Bad luck, too, coming to chambers in the same year as Sir Basil's nephew. Unfortunate timing, really. Still, a bright lad like that would probably do well anywhere. With that thought, Cameron turned to the jumble of work that lay spread out on his desk.

Anthony was looking forward to the May Ball with mixed feelings. He knew the nature of such things from his university days, and they were not entirely to his taste. He sometimes wished that he could behave with the lack of restraint that he saw in others, who enjoyed such things with high-spirited and unselfconscious abandon. On the other hand, it made something of a welcome break from his essay on the Divisional Court and the long hours that both he and Michael were presently putting in on an appeal from an arbitration award; the past four days had been spent in court.

On Tuesday, the day before the Ball, people passing through stopped to watch the enormous marquee being erected in Inner Temple Gardens. The air was thick with summer heat, as often happens in late May, and a general sense of carelessness and excitement infected the more junior reaches of the Bar. Julia had already tried on her new dress several times, delighted with the peacock shimmer of its taffeta folds and strapless bodice. On the first of these occasions, Anthony had eyed her for a long moment before gently unzipping her.

'Isn't it beautiful?' she said to her reflection, as the gown slipped rustling to her knees. 'Mummy is perfectly wonderful, sometimes. It cost an absolute fortune.'

'Beautiful. But I think I prefer you without it. Can't you go to the Ball like this?' murmured Anthony, his lips on her bare shoulders, his hands over her small, naked breasts. At times like these, he thought, he didn't care if he had to starve for months, just so long as he could have her. It was only at other times, away from her pliant, desirable body and lovely face, that a whisper of doubt would creep into his mind.

It was there that Tuesday, as he sat in court with Michael, listening to the drone of argument from their opposing counsel, the portly Mr Farrant. They had lost the case, in the face of a particularly unsympathetic judge, and Michael had spent Tuesday morning putting forward arguments as to why they should be given leave to appeal the judgment in the Court of Appeal. Now Mr Farrant was endeavouring, at what seemed to be interminable length, to persuade the judge to the contrary.

'. . . your Lordship has had the opportunity of hearing wide-ranging argument, and I think both my learned friend and I are grateful for the attention paid to it by your Lordship in your Lordship's judgment. That being the case, it is often said that the matter should rest with the Commercial Court judge, and I would so submit. Our third point is this . . .'

Mr Justice Cox nodded mournfully and Anthony's attention strayed, returning to Julia and the eternal problem of how – or rather, whether – he could afford to go on seeing her. He had been through all this once before, and now here he was, right back where he had started, or rather, where he had finished. It was simply that, every time he saw her, he wanted to take her to bed. It was a difficult habit to break. The problem of money seemed to be getting worse now that summer was looming. She had talked of Henley, taking it for granted that he would want to go, and of tickets for Wimbledon, of a trip to France that Piers was arranging. She smiled and chattered and smiled and cajoled . . . Anthony couldn't see where it was going to stop. As he had predicted to himself, now that the days were long and warm she was no longer content to curl up with Anthony and a bottle of wine. She wanted to sit in the gardens of riverside pubs and listen to amusing conversation, or to have supper at smart little restaurants where the music was cool and the windows were open to the summer air.

'And therefore I do submit strongly, my Lord,' Farrant was saying, well into his stride now, 'that the fact that your Lordship may be persuaded to grant a certificate does not necessarily mean that your Lordship should grant leave. And that must be the case, because subsection 7(a) contemplates that division; and that is why I would urge on your Lordship . . .'

Even Michael was yawning discreetly, and the judge thumbed absently through the documents before him. A fly had found its way into the court and buzzed dazedly about; the clerk flapped at it in a muted manner, frowning, whenever it came near her.

It wasn't as though he could come to some sort of arrangement with her, seeing her only every other weekend, and not at all during the week. It simply wouldn't work. He'd asked her, in an offhand way, if she had seen Piers at all during the time that they had been apart, and she had replied, equally offhandedly, 'Now and again'. It gave Anthony no clue as to what, if anything, might have happened. It wasn't his business, he supposed; she had been free to do what she liked. But he found the thought of Piers particularly detestable. The fact was that while he, Anthony, was around, Julia did not see Piers. Not so far as he knew, at any rate. A change in voices brought Anthony back to the present.

'Mmm. I have always wondered whether that was the right approach. Yes,' Mr Justice Cox was murmuring. Encouraged, Mr Farrant pressed on.

'Indeed, my Lord, one speculates about the costs to date in this case and in the future. But I would respectfully submit that finality does demand that a time has come . . .'

She couldn't, could she? She couldn't be seeing Piers as well . . . It was possible. With Julia, anything was possible, he was beginning to realise. He closed his eyes. But she wouldn't *sleep* with two people at once, would she? If he thought that she and Piers – that would be the end of it. Still, that didn't seem possible. Very unlike Julia. Reflecting on the physical aspect of things, it was beginning to occur to Anthony that, out of bed, they perhaps had less in common than he had at first supposed. The conversation of her friends – friends whom he had once cultivated for the sake of being with her – had begun to bore him. It was gossip, mainly, not a thing he cared for, especially when it concerned people whose lives and doings did not interest him.

He glanced across at Farrant's pupil, Colin Potterton. Boiler Potterton. What a twit. He was one of Julia's charmed circle. Looking across at him as he murmured self-importantly over his shoulder to the instructing solicitor, nodding very fast in that pursed-lip, frowning way that he had picked up from Farrant, Anthony realised that he was one of a type that he had done his best to avoid at university. So why did he now spend so much time with Potterton and his like, and so little with Geoffrey and Simon, his friends from university? Because of Julia. And because of his own spinelessness.

'In individual terms,' Mr Farrant said, in tones of great dismissiveness, 'fifty thousand dollars may be a large sum, but in my respectful submission – '

'That has not prevented many cases from going so far as the House of Lords, has it?' interrupted the judge, dashing Mr Farrant slightly.

'Well, my Lord, I see that. But I always think that the cases that go that far are very often the cases where there is a very small amount involved indeed. One wonders whether that is the right approach, especially after the 1979 Act.'

Anthony scratched his head beneath his wig. The air in the courtroom was stale and warm. One of the overhead fluorescent lights had begun to fail, and was now flickering imperceptibly. The judge and the court clerk both glanced up at it.

From thinking about Julia, he fell to thinking about Leo, and the hours they had spent together in conversation, amusing and delightful hours. They had talked, talked properly. With

192

Julia, her glance would eternally wander to other tables, other people. She had an irritating habit, he had recently realised, of interrupting one in mid-sentence with some observation utterly unrelated to what one had said. She had a butterfly quality that was initially endearing and ultimately infuriating. Maybe all women were like that, he pondered; maybe only with other men did one achieve any strength of understanding, some proper exchange of ideas. He tried to concentrate on the case again as Farrant drew his arguments to their conclusion.

'. . . and that being the case, I would submit that there is no basis whatsoever for granting any certificate at all in relation to those last two points, nor, even less, in granting leave to appeal. Unless I can assist your Lordship further, those are my submissions.' Mr Farrant sat down with plump satisfaction. Anthony looked at him speculatively, wondering what it was about the Bar that made a man of thirty-eight adopt the manner of a man of fifty. Boiler Potterton was just as bad, he thought, watching him mutter importantly to Farrant as he arranged his papers with a sharp edgewise tap. Michael cleared his throat and rose slowly. His voice was gentle and reedy by contrast with Farrant's round, polished tones.

'My Lord, might I then deal, first of all, with the "unsafe port" point. Nothing that my friend has said can, in my submission – '

Mr Justice Cox interrupted brusquely with an impatient shake of his head. 'No, you need not trouble me about that point, in either aspect.'

Michael had expected no more nor less than this.

'My Lord, I am grateful for that indication,' he replied serenely, glancing down at his notes and turning a page with spidery fingers. 'May I then turn to make my submissions on the other two points and deal, first of all . . .'

Anthony hitched his gown a little and sat forward, trying to concentrate. Mr Justice Cox poured a glass of water from the flask before him, carefully replacing the little cloth weighted with beads that covered its mouth, took a drink, and glanced at the clock. Then he sat back, put the tips of his fingers together and sighed, listening patiently to Michael and looking exactly as a judge should look. From reflecting on Michael's habitual nervousness, and on whether all Wykehamists were similarly afflicted, Anthony found himself wondering whether he was so drawn to Leo by the very fact that he was not an ex-public schoolboy, that he was not cluttered with the affectations and ponderous affability of the old Marlburian, or the breezy raffishness of a Salopian, or the arrogant cut of an old Etonian. He had noticed at Bar school how so many of these types seemed to be clearly marked, like birds clucking on a lawn. Leo was none of those. Leo's charm and grace were utterly, wonderfully unique.

Mr Justice Cox leaned forward, pulling his robe around him. 'If you have leave to appeal on the second point,' he was saying, 'I do not think it is actually going to hold you up in terms of time.'

'Well, my Lord, it might have that result,' replied Michael in his well-modulated tones. He sounded almost propitiating. 'The lists of the Court of Appeal are well known to be very congested – '

'Yes.' The judge nodded.

' – and appeals do have difficulty in coming on.'

But Leo, Anthony had to acknowledge to himself, was evidently homosexual – wasn't he? – and Anthony, so far as he knew, was not. Something in him – it was not any sense of revulsion – refused to accept this idea. He could not imagine Leo in love with another man. In love. The words struck him. What else could have been meant by his words, his touch? Suddenly the recollection of the events of that evening made his pulse beat faster. His cheeks burned. He looked up at Michael's gaunt figure, trying to clear a space in his mind where he could focus on what was being said.

'My Lord, there is perhaps one further matter. If your Lordship is minded to order a variation of the Award – '

'Yes?' said Mr Justice Cox, glancing up at Michael and then glancing down again.

' – might I ask your Lordship to stay that order varying the Award, pending the progress of the appeal?'

Mr Farrant rose, flashing a quick smile at Michael. 'I was waiting for my learned friend to tell your Lordship the reason for that. I can see no reason for it whatsoever, and if my friend can tell either your Lordship or myself, I will listen with interest.'

Boiler Potterton smirked with complicit satisfaction at Anthony. Michael, however, carried smoothly on, without looking at his learned friend, who kept darting him satisfied smiles and pulling his robe happily round his large bottom.

'My Lord, the reason is simply this; that the Award, as varied, will give my friend an entitlement for costs which he may seek to enforce straight away, and we would submit that it is appropriate that that be held in abeyance pending the decision of the Court of Appeal.'

Mr Farrant now positively sprang up, and said with stiff good humour, 'My Lord, I have never heard a better reason for your Lordship amending the Award.'

Anthony wondered if Leo would be back when they returned to chambers. He would know by glancing at the car park. He remembered, with pleasure, the piece of work that Leo had left him, and over which he had taken such pains. At least he had an excuse to go and see him. But what was the point of all this speculation, this hope?

'No,' Mr Justice Cox was saying, gathering his papers together and uncapping his fountain pen to write, 'I make the usual order. I will give Mr Farrant his costs of the appeal.'

Mr Farrant bobbed up. 'I am obliged, my Lord.'

Maybe they could put that evening behind them, as though it had not happened, and start again. Leo had himself told him to forget it. Perhaps it didn't matter.

'As to the terms of the certificate,' continued the judge, finishing what he was writing and glancing up at Michael, 'it will have to reach me in the course of post, I think, because you will need my initial to it, will you not?'

'My Lord, yes,' said Michael. 'Will your Lordship be available tomorrow?'

But that poem, the sense of it. Whatever Leo envisaged between them, it was not mere friendship, or the occasional game of squash.

'No, I will not,' Mr Justice Cox was saying, again glancing at the clock. Boiler Potterton was stuffing papers into a folder in preparation to leave. 'I think it will have to reach me in the post, I'm afraid.'

'I will put it in hand straight away,' replied Michael, and sat down. The judge looked round, assembling his papers, glanced up at Michael and Mr Farrant and smiled politely.

'Yes. Well, thank you both very much.' And he rose and left through a side door. Michael and Anthony began to collect their belongings, Anthony hoping that the blue Porsche would be in its place in the car park.

Chapter seventeen

Anthony changed into his evening dress in Michael's room the following evening. He could only judge his appearance by the small mirror above the wash-hand basin in the lavatory, but he knew from the fitting at the shop that his suit hung tolerably well on him, and he rather liked the dashing effect of his bow tie and dress shirt. He combed his hair carefully and gazed at himself blankly for a few seconds, wondering if he should have brought a razor. Humming, he wandered back into Michael's room. It was a quarter to seven, and he had arranged to meet Edward and David and Julia for sherry in the minstrels' gallery in Middle Temple Hall at seven.

Idly, he wandered to the window and looked out. Most people had already made their way home or were getting ready for the Ball, and the courtyard was empty. He pulled up the sash window and leaned out into the warm evening air. There was no breeze, and the new leaves on the tree below hung motionless. He could hear from far away the hum of traffic on the Embankment. Then he heard footsteps, and a figure came into the courtyard. Anthony recognised it with a sudden thrill of surprise that seemed to electrify his body. Since his car had not been in the car park that afternoon, Anthony had assumed that Leo had not yet returned.

He drew his head quickly in from the window, bumping it on the sash; Leo did not look up as he made his way towards chambers. He was not dressed with his usual dark formality, but was wearing green corduroy trousers and a light shirt, the sleeves rolled up. Anthony had never seen him dressed informally before, and the sight made a curiously tender impression upon him. Leo's figure disappeared from sight as he entered the chambers. Anthony heard his key in the lock, then his footsteps on the wooden stairs. He was whistling.

Anthony stood motionless, gazing at the sundial on the wall of the building opposite, waiting and willing the footsteps to stop outside Michael's door. But they passed on up the stairs. After a moment he heard voices, those of Leo and Stephen, faint and far away. Then the footsteps came downstairs again, passing Michael's door without pause, down, out and away. Anthony's heart was thumping with disappointment and longing. He sat down at Michael's desk and buried his face in his hands, willing his heart to stop.

'Anthony, you're late! Where have you been?' exclaimed Julia, as he hurried up the little wooden staircase to the minstrels' gallery. Her voice sounded bright and rapid with excitement.

'Sorry,' said Anthony, 'I had some last-minute work to finish off. Thanks.' He took the small glass of sherry that David passed to him, sipped and said appreciatively to Julia, 'You look quite stunning!'

Julia's smile sparkled with pleasure; in truth, Anthony felt that he was looking at her from far away. He saw her expensive gown, from which her soft shoulders and slender arms emerged with a peach-like freshness, saw her soft blonde hair framing her happy face, her expensive little trinkets of jewellery, and felt as though he were trying to bring her into focus from some other plane. The thought of Leo was blazing in his mind like some light that would not be turned off. He greeted Edward's cousin, Anthea, who stood looking serene and willowy next to a proud and animated David, and Hermione, who was Edward's latest girlfriend and who looked to Anthony very much like the last one.

'God, this is disgusting,' he remarked of the sherry to Edward, in an attempt to bring himself back to reality.

'Yes, well, you've got the sweet stuff. They ran out of fino before you got here.'

The crush was enormous, as people foregathered for the Ball, the air stifling and heady with different perfumes, voices growing louder and louder. Gradually, with conversation, the thought, or feeling, of Leo faded.

'It's bloody hot in here,' said Edward, as Julia was bumped towards him by someone shouldering past. He steadied her.

'Why don't we make our way over to the gardens? I don't want to drink any more of this stuff, anyway.'

The others murmured in agreement, and began to make their way slowly towards the top of the staircase. They were met by the tall, easy figure of Piers as he mounted the staircase. He paused when he saw them.

'Hullo, boys and girls,' he said languidly, as they all, except Anthony, greeted him enthusiastically. He and Piers had not met since the weekend at Edward's, although they had glimpsed one another occasionally at their business around the courts. Now Piers glanced at him, reached out a large arm, and slapped him slowly and heavily on the back. 'Haven't seen you about for a bit. Jolly good, Tony.' He sounded bored.

'We're getting out of here,' Julia said to Piers. 'It's far too hot.' She pulled at his sleeve. 'Watch out, you're in everyone's way.' People on the narrow staircase were peering around Piers' large thighs, trying to get past.

'Oops, sorry,' said Piers casually and without apology, moving a couple of inches so that a stocky, red-faced young man still had to squeeze past, glaring at Piers. Piers' eyes followed his annoyed figure with lazy amusement. 'Little shit,' he murmured, then said, 'Well, love to join you, but I've got to meet my – ah – companion for the evening.' And he prepared to move on.

'Who's that?' asked Julia.

'No one you know, precious,' said Piers, stroking her lightly under the chin with a dismissive forefinger.

Julia jerked her chin up in annoyance and pulled away crossly, following Edward and David down the stairs. Anthony glanced after Piers, his tall figure making its assured way through the crowd. He bet Piers didn't have to hire his dinner jacket. Bastard.

In the gardens, women in long dresses and men in evening suits were milling about on the lawn, sipping at glasses of champagne. Assured, cultivated voices carried clearly in the soft evening air. Anthony and his friends made their way to the marquee; the little pennants that ornamented its top drifted in the faint breeze that was picking up. Maids stood at the entrance with large silver salvers of champagne in glasses.

Edward popped inside the tent for a moment to look at the seating plan, then re-emerged.

'Good stuff,' he said. 'Piers is on our table.'

'Oh,' said Anthony, 'wonderful.' Julia glanced at him.

'Anthony!' she murmured warningly. He moved away with her from the others.

'Well, I can't stand the sight of the man. He's a shit.'

'You're still jealous!'

Anthony laughed. 'Tell me what I've got to be jealous of, then. You still haven't exactly enlightened me as to how you spent your time when you weren't seeing me.' Some malevolent demon seemed to have possessed him; he felt quarrelsome and impatient.

'I don't believe you!' exclaimed Julia. 'You – you suddenly announce that we're not going out together any more, and then you expect me to account for my behaviour while I'm not seeing you! That's a bit thick!' She glared at him. 'Look, I want to enjoy this evening. I don't want to hear you carping on about Piers any more. Right? Now, if you can't behave cheerfully, don't talk to me!' She stalked off to fetch herself another glass of champagne. Anthony stared at the grass for a moment. It wasn't that he was jealous of Piers at all, he thought. He frankly didn't care.

They wandered about the lawn, making conversation with various people. Anthony found himself buttonholed by Earnest Slattery, who remembered him from the case in the House of Lords; his kind, enthusiastic conversation did something to restore Anthony's spirits.

'I don't think you've met my wife, have you?' He turned his thin, stooping figure to address her. 'Margaret, this is Anthony Cross.' He pronounced it 'Crawss'. 'He's a very bright young man indeed, or so I'm given to understand.' Anthony smiled and shook hands with Mrs Slattery. He wondered what she was knitting now. 'Very interesting case, the *Lindos*, don't you think?' remarked Slattery conversationally.

Anthony murmured in agreement, hoping that he wasn't going to be required to dredge up too much by way of specific recollection.

'Now, I don't think we really deserved to win that one,' said Earnest Slattery thoughtfully. 'You were there for that one, dear, I think?' he asked his wife. Mrs Slattery said she thought that she recollected it, but couldn't be sure.

'I go to quite a few,' she confided to Anthony. 'Quite keeps my mind alert, you know.' She nodded, smiling. Earnest Slattery nodded, too.

'I thought it was jolly bad luck that you lost. Of course, Buckhurst was against you right from the start. That was your problem . . .'

They chatted for some minutes, and then the Slatterys excused themselves and drifted off. Anthony thought he heard Mrs Slattery say, '. . . nice young man,' as she walked away. He looked around for Julia, and caught sight of her talking to one of the Commercial Court judges, Mr Justice Coker, from whom he had recently earned a rebuke during an interlocutory application for bringing the wrong document. He didn't feel like talking to him. He turned around quickly, and his heart jumped. Leo was walking across the grass towards him. He looked particularly well in evening dress, elegant and at ease. Anthony noticed that he was smoking a small cigar. He smiled at Anthony, his face a mask of social amiability.

'Hello, Anthony,' he said. 'How's life?'

'Fine,' replied Anthony, trying to collect himself. His eyes traced every one of Leo's features, the blue, amused eyes, the prominent lines of his cheekbones, the square jaw and smiling mouth. Leo took a small puff of his cigar and blew a little smoke into the air above Anthony's head. Anthony found the gesture a little ridiculous, touching. Over Leo's shoulder, he noticed the pink edge of evening beginning to creep across the sky. He felt himself grow calmer, and smiled at Leo, happy to be with him again.

'How was your trip?' he asked.

'Very good,' replied Leo, taking another little puff of his cigar and glancing at it. 'I'd never been to Japan before. It's a fascinating place.' He talked to Anthony about Japan for a minute or two, apparently with his mind on the subject, but his eyes intently absorbed the features of the face that he had

201

tried so often to summon to mind while away. Memory could not possibly hope to reproduce such vivid charm, he now realised. He stopped talking, the better to enjoy the delight of Anthony's presence.

'I finished that piece of work you left me,' remarked Anthony, to fill the little pause between them.

'Good, good,' said Leo vaguely. He couldn't even remember what it was. Against his better judgment, Anthony added, 'I found the piece of paper you left me.'

Leo looked at him. 'Piece of paper?'

Anthony knew it was too late to retrace the step. 'The poem,' he said uncertainly, his voice low. Leo frowned at him; then his face grew suddenly cold.

'I don't know what on earth you're talking about.' Anthony felt himself flush, and looked away. There was a frigid pause. 'Excuse me,' said Leo. He chucked his cigar into the grass and strolled away. He knew very well what Anthony was talking about, but it had come as a shock. He remembered jotting the lines down as he sat at home, thinking of Anthony, putting the papers in order for him before his trip. He had forgotten about it entirely, and Anthony must have found it mixed up with the documents. He was filled with a cold fury at himself, at allowing this charade to begin again. And so must follow, he thought savagely, more indiscretions, more humiliations, more deceit, and all the indignities that his position must entail. If he allowed it. If he allowed it. I shall not, he told himself as he strode across the grass, allow it. I shall not.

Anthony stood for a moment, uncertain, filled with a sudden flaring of humiliation. Why had he mentioned it? What a ludicrous thing to have done! What had he expected Leo to say? Yes, it was for you, because I adore you? God, what a thing to have done. He stood for an unhappy few seconds, staring at the glass in his hand. Maybe he had been mistaken, the poem a misplaced irrelevance.

He recovered himself at the sound of the voice of his head of chambers.

'Anthony! Good evening,' said Sir Basil. Anthony managed a feeble smile. This was all he needed.

'Good evening, sir.'

Sir Basil was feeling silkily happy, still glowing with the warmth of the little private sherry party given by the Benchers earlier. He smiled benevolently at Anthony.

'I don't think we've really had much of an opportunity for conversation since you joined us, have we?' Anthony wondered if this was always going to be his opening line.

'No,' he replied, keeping his smile fixed. 'Not since Christmas, or thereabouts.' He added the last two words to make it sound less challenging. He felt wretched and on edge.

'Ah, yes,' said Sir Basil, rosy with recollection. He had entirely forgotten Anthony's father. 'Oh, yes, thank you,' he murmured to a passing maid, who replenished his glass and Anthony's, then passed on. 'Yes, Christmas. I think we had a little chat about your future plans, didn't we? I think I mentioned something about Dover Court, if I recall.' He frowned. 'Mmm. Time is pressing on. You'll have to start thinking seriously about where you're going next. You have considerable talent, I understand,' he said gravely, shaking his head, 'and we mustn't let you waste it.'

'Oh, I shan't waste it,' said Anthony.

'No, indeed you mustn't. Michael tells me you have great ability. I hope you feel that your time with us has been valuably spent?'

'Michael has given me every encouragement,' replied Anthony. 'He has persuaded me that I have every chance of – of becoming the next tenant.' It occurred to Anthony that it might have been better not to have said that. But listening to that pompous old windbag, full of sherry and his own unquestionable ability to dictate everyone else's lives for them, had become too much. Full of sherry he might be, but Sir Basil was too fast on his feet to be wrong-footed by anyone. He smiled sagely at Anthony.

'Just so, young man,' he replied, and raised his glass a little. 'It is important, of course, that you should continue to think so. My every good wish for your endeavours.' He took a sip, nodded at Anthony, and moved away.

It was with relief that Anthony heard dinner being announced and saw Julia shimmering towards him, her humour improved by the success of her appearance and the gratifying masculine attention she was commanding.

'Come on,' she said in a friendly way, 'I was wondering where you'd got to.' She kissed his cheek lightly. For some reason, the gesture irritated him. What a sod I am, he thought. 'Wasn't that your head of chambers?' she asked, as they made their way into the marquee. 'I thought he looked a perfect sweetie.'

The words sounded to him absurd. 'Perfect sweetie', he thought. Babble, babble, babble.

They found their table and sat down with Edward and Hermione. David and Anthea joined them, and then William with a young woman he introduced as Linda. Anthony thought he had seen her several times in and around the Commercial Court, and said so.

They chatted for a few minutes as the marquee filled up and people took their places. And then William said, 'Who else is on our table, David?'

'Piers Hunt-Thompson,' replied David, 'and someone called – ' He leaned over and squinted at the place card. ' – Lady Juliet Fry.'

'I say,' said Edward mildly. 'What about the other two places?'

'It's Leo and some woman,' said David. 'I looked on the way in.' Anthony felt that this was not going to be a comfortable evening for him.

At that moment Piers and his guest arrived at the table. Anthony saw Julia glance up coldly as Piers introduced her, then look away as though uninterested. Anthony suspected the little snobberies raging in her heart. It didn't help, he thought, that Lady Juliet was very beautiful, in ways quite different from Julia. She was dark, with a classically lovely face, her hair swept up on top of her head; her dress was a simple black affair, beautifully cut, a length of black silk caught up and falling over one shoulder, leaving the other pearly and bare. She had a long, swan-like throat, and the little jewellery that she wore looked costly. Piers looked justifiably smug. David was enraptured, and in imminent danger of losing his heart yet again. He might have been inclined to take it out of

Anthea's keeping altogether, had he known that she and Piers Hunt-Thompson had been seeing a good deal of each other lately, on and off, on the weekends when he had been down to visit his parents in Surrey. Anthea smiled and murmured to Lady Juliet, flicking her blonde hair back from her shoulders, murderous with jealousy. Piers sat back in his chair and thrust his long legs under the table, glancing idly across at Anthea for a long moment. He was rather enjoying himself.

Leo was the last to arrive. Anthony was aware that he was there, but only looked up when he was introduced to Leo's companion. He looked at her, and not at Leo.

'. . . and this, Alice, is Anthony, who is a pupil at 5 Caper Court.' He looked at Anthony's strained face as he spoke, and knew that Anthony had been badly wounded by his words earlier. He felt a stab of remorse, and then an inevitable counter-surge of pitilessness.

Anthony smiled and shook hands with Alice. She was an attractive, intelligent-looking woman, older than his mother, he thought, with short, ash-blonde hair and perfect make-up. She was elegantly dressed, and her earrings, for some absurd reason, reminded Anthony of the sculptures he had seen at Leo's house – angular, clinical. She seemed to be of a piece with Leo's life, as remote and set apart as all other aspects of it. He wondered if she was more than a friend to Leo, but realised after a few moments that she was not. The fact was betrayed in the uncharged kindness of their smiles to one another and their good-humoured banter. Anthony knew that, with Leo, there would otherwise have been some emotional current that he could not have failed to detect.

Leo and Piers had not met before, and after they were introduced Anthony was quietly pleased to see that Leo watched Piers for a few cold seconds as he chatted in his loud, arrogant voice to David, and then looked away.

It had been Piers' assumption that, as usual, he would be the glory and focus of attention at this table. It would listen to his loud voice and laugh at his stories, and he would rule with the caprice and condescension of a king. But he had bargained without Leo, the force of his personality, his natural authority and wit. He overshadowed Piers, was amusing and spellbinding, and Piers, to whom he paid scant attention, was forced to retreat into the background. As the dinner progressed, his voice could be heard rising from the other end of the table, where he and Edward were drinking wine at a furious rate.

Leo's brilliance shone on everyone – on everyone, that is, except Anthony. In his determination, in his self-detestation, in his love, Leo was bent upon inflicting little miseries on Anthony. He did not look at him, addressed no remarks to him, did not appear to acknowledge his existence. All this was scarcely evident to anyone except Anthony himself, who knew the real worth between them of these small slights.

As the maids cleared the plates away before coffee, Julia sat back and turned to Anthony. He had noticed, with something sadder than amusement, that she had latterly been leaning forward and gazing at Leo, trying to compel him with her chatter and sparkle. She was a little drunk.

'What a divine man!' she said under her breath. 'You're lucky to have someone like that in chambers. When I think of our dreary lot.' He poured her another glass of wine, listening idly. 'I've never heard you talk about him,' she added.

'No,' said Anthony, without looking at her, 'I don't have a great deal to do with him.'

Music started and couples drifted, slowly and rather self-consciously at first, on to the dance floor. Anthony watched as Mr Justice Coker and his tall wife whirled effortlessly and magnificently past, their faces as calm and serious as professional ballroom dancers. After a while, he roused himself and danced with Julia, holding her close and seeking some comfort in her sensual little body and familiar perfume. As they danced, he closed his eyes and kissed, for a moment, the warm skin between her shoulder and neck, and felt her shiver with pleasure. When he opened his eyes, they were looking straight into those of Leo, who held his gaze for a fierce second before looking abruptly away. Anthony felt his heart beat painfully. He wished the man would vanish from the face of the earth.

When they sat down, the other members of their table, except Leo and Alice, were dancing. Julia commenced her bewitching assault upon Leo, who succumbed, smiled, and asked her to dance. So Anthony danced with Alice, making polite conversation, his eyes on Leo and Julia, on her small hand in his, on the other embracing his back; her head was tilted back, and her pretty mouth smiled and smiled as she talked.

The night wore on. Anthony lost track of time. They danced some more, then moved to another table to talk with friends and stayed there, drinking brandy. It was a relief to Anthony to be out of Leo's company, although Julia's gaze wandered constantly back to where Leo was sitting, smoking, chatting to Alice and Lady Juliet. Piers was now becoming rowdy on the dance floor with Hermione.

When they went back to the table, Leo and Alice were getting up to go.

'Oh, you're not going?' exclaimed Julia, her disappointment rather too obvious.

'Just me,' replied Alice with a smile. 'I'm afraid I've got an early start tomorrow. Leo is going to find me a taxi.'

Alice said her farewells, and Julia watched as they left the marquee. She turned to Anthony. 'I'm just going to the ladies'. Shan't be long.' And she left him.

Leo walked with Alice to the Embankment, and found her a taxi. He said goodnight to her and walked back round to the gardens. The air was cooler now, and through the darkness he could hear that the music had grown livelier, as the older guests departed and the younger element took over. He stood at the top of the short flight of stone steps that led down to the gardens. He should go home, too, he thought. He had sufficiently sickened himself for one evening. He was about to turn and leave, when he noticed Julia coming slowly along the gravel walk.

'Hello,' she said brightly, stopping and smiling up at him. 'I got rather tired of the noise. Thought I'd get a little fresh air.' She shivered and hugged herself momentarily, preparing to walk on.

'I'll walk with you, if I may,' said Leo indolently, coming down the steps and falling in beside her. Julia smiled into the darkness in delight. She never doubted her powers of seduction, and had spent most of the evening determining to work her charms on this most fascinating and desirable of men. With the selfishness of all true hedonists, she cared for nothing but the moment and the game. Anthony was all but forgotten.

They walked slowly across the grass and under the dark trees. This was not a thing he should be doing, Leo knew. He glanced at Julia from time to time, amused by the transparency of her intentions. What a conceited little flirt, he thought. She was very pretty, he knew. Most men would find her completely desirable. He reflected that she must have kissed the mouth he hungered for a hundred times. She would know every muscle of Anthony's young body. She knew nothing of anything.

When she lifted up her face to be kissed, it was half in Leo's mind to take her by the hand and walk her firmly back to the marquee. But in that instant he saw Anthony's figure as he approached them under the trees. He saw him stop. Without thought or desire, Leo pulled Julia to him and kissed her fiercely and thoroughly, wanting Anthony to watch and care.

Anthony stood for a few seconds. He saw Leo's arms around Julia as she gave herself up to his kiss, and his heart sickened. He turned quietly away, wretched with jealousy – of whom, he could not, in that moment, comprehend. And Julia had, for a few seconds, her empty heart's desire.

Chapter eighteen

The following morning, Edward came and groaned theatrically at Anthony. He had, as usual, drunk far too much and said he didn't think Hermione would ever speak to him again.

'Why?' asked Anthony, smiling at Edward's condition in spite of himself.

'Oh, I don't know. I tore her dress, or something. Stepped on it. Christ, d'you have any Alka-Seltzer? I think my head's going to fall off.' Sitting opposite Anthony, Edward laid his arms on the desk and rested his chin on them, gazing as Anthony resumed writing. 'How on earth can you bear to work?' he moaned.

'Takes my mind off things,' replied Anthony, not looking up. Fortunately, Edward did not ask him what the 'things' were, but gazed vacantly at the shelves behind Anthony.

'I don't think I can stand this lark,' he said after a moment or two, his eyes still scanning the shelves unseeingly. He groaned and put his head on his arms.

'What d'you mean?' asked Anthony. Edward looked up and ran his fingers through his thick, blond hair.

'Law. I don't think I'm cut out for it.' He mused for a moment, Anthony's eyes on his face. 'Don't tell my flaming uncle that, mind. He'd have a fit.'

Anthony felt, with surprise, that that which would have come as welcome news months ago did not even move him now. It was as though he were incapable of feeling any more. The events of last night had been more bruising and confusing than he had thought possible. He welcomed work, and even Edward's hungover company, as diversions from thinking.

Edward's bleary eyes shifted from the bookshelves to Anthony's face.

'Where did you get to last night, anyway? You just

disappeared. Julia was looking for you everywhere. She was trying not to look upset, but she was.' He sat up and leaned back.

'Was she?' asked Anthony without interest. 'I got fed up and went home.'

'You're a funny bugger, Tony,' said Edward kindly, folding a piece of paper carefully into a dart.

'Thanks,' said Anthony.

'Well, you could have taken her home. I mean, not quite the thing, is it?'

Anthony sighed and leaned back. 'No, you're right. But it's impossible to explain . . .' He thought briefly, painfully of Julia, lovely, amoral Julia. Maybe it shouldn't be any wonder to him that Leo should find her as desirable as other men did. He did not, he realised, understand anything. 'Just don't worry about it,' he added at last to Edward.

'Okay,' said Edward, launching his dart across the room. 'Concorde!' Michael's footsteps sounded on the stair. 'See you at lunchtime,' said Edward and left, greeting Michael airily as he went.

Leo sat in an unexpected traffic jam on Westminster Bridge and cursed, eyeing Big Ben from time to time. He had cut his neck shaving that morning, bled on the collar of his only freshly ironed shirt, and was now late for his conference at ten o'clock. Why couldn't that bloody woman iron more than two shirts when she came? And what was it that she did to them in the washing machine that made the collar of a new Turnbull & Asser shirt fray after three months? The traffic moved forward a yard or two.

He should have gone home when Alice had, he told himself for the thousandth time. Or he shouldn't have taken a stroll with that wretched little tart. His car radio told him brightly of a hold-up on Westminster Bridge, and he thanked it and switched it off. God, the things your emotions got you into. He had not handled it well. But then, he did not handle women well.

He recalled Julia's face in the half-darkness as he had said unkindly, 'I think we'd better get you back to your boyfriend. I'm afraid he just saw that.'

'I don't care,' she had said, wanting Leo to kiss her again.

'I think you should,' he had replied. 'Because I do not care in the least for you. I think you are a particularly vain and silly girl. And I do not enjoy kissing you.'

No, that had not been necessary, such unkindness. He watched as the lights changed up ahead from red to green. 'Come on, come on,' he muttered, as the traffic moved at a crawl over the bridge. The lights changed back again. It was impossible that he, at forty-two, should be behaving in such a fashion, besotted with some near-schoolboy, wasting his emotions on someone who could not begin to understand or appreciate them. He would not behave as though he were helpless. To do so would be to allow every conceivable humiliation and hurt to plague him. Too much expense of spirit. The determination he had formed last night as he had walked away from Anthony across the grass had hardened now. He must guard against his susceptibilities when he saw him, and make sure that he saw as little of him as possible. Had he not learned that there was to be no return of his love? Love! He felt something like contempt for himself, for his weakness. Perhaps it would be best, after all, if Anthony looked for a tenancy somewhere else. Even as he thought this, it was with a pang. Yes, he resolved savagely, pushing the car into gear as the traffic ahead of him began to pick up, the thing must stop. Let Edward Choke plant his useless backside at 5 Caper Court for the next forty years.

Julia sat in chambers, trying to attend to her work, her mind veering between rage, misery and anxiety. Several times she had been about to pick up the telephone and call Anthony, but each time fear bit at her. Her humiliation at the hands of Leo had left her hurt and vulnerable. She wanted Anthony and his comfort. She detested that bastard Leo. No one, no one, had ever spoken to her like that before! She could not, in truth, bear the idea that any man should kiss her without wanting to and without liking it. It was too demeaning. And then to speak to her as he had done. A rage of hurt came over her again. She told herself that she had found him detestable, refusing to acknowledge that kissing him had been in any way delightful. That was the worst of it, to have liked it. Not, she told herself, that she had. He was a bastard, and he had tasted of cigars and stale coffee.

When she had worked up a sufficient hatred for Leo and for herself, Julia fell to the business of hating men generally. There was 'Piers. He had behaved like a creep ever since that time when she and Anthony had broken up. He'd never been around at the weekends (here she was forced to recall the ignominy of telephoning him several times, after he had failed to get in touch with her), and he barely gave her more than two minutes' worth of conversation when she did see him. So much for his protestations of adoration and devotion. Not that she cared for him, but she had become used to basking in the pleasant warmth of his admiration. Another rotten bastard.

And Anthony. He could be pretty unbearable, too. Sometimes. The money thing was still a problem, of course. Well, she *tried* not to want to go out in the evenings, but it was jolly difficult when all your friends were going to smart restaurants and seeing new films. It was a bore, his never having any money. She tried to feel sorry for him, but half the time she didn't really see what he was going on about. But, no – he was impossible to hate. He loved her. Or rather, she reflected miserably, he had before he'd seen her with Leo last night. Anxiety returned to eat at her. That would probably be the last straw for him. Piers was one thing – and anyway, Anthony had believed her that time when she said she was a bit drunk – but an older member of his chambers whom she'd just met for the first time that evening? Well, that was something else. But what if he hadn't seen them? She had only Leo's word for it – she hadn't seen Anthony anywhere near. Maybe Leo had just said it as an excuse to stop kissing her. (It was unpleasant for Julia even to contemplate this possibility, but she was forced to.) But then, Anthony hadn't been there when she'd got back to the marquee, after she had watched in astonishment as Leo walked away from her across the lawn. He *must* have seen them. Why else would he have gone off without a word? She should ring him, try to explain it to him. What on earth was she going to tell him? It wouldn't be easy, but Julia had great faith in her powers of appeasement. Her hand hovered uncertainly over the phone, her stomach churning with nervousness.

'I thought you had a summons before the Master at ten-thirty?' said her pupilmaster, suddenly glancing up from his work.

'Gosh, you're right!' she exclaimed, and gathered up her papers and fled in relief.

When Julia rang Anthony after lunch, he was uncertain whether or not to take the call. Better to take it, he decided, glad that Michael was in the room. That might make it easier, in a way.

'Hello, Anthony?' Her voice sounded nervous, without any affectation of casualness.

'Yes?' he said shortly. There was a pause. She had worked out beforehand what she was going to say, but it was still a bit difficult.

'I wondered where you'd got to last night. At the Ball, I mean.'

'Oh?'

'Well . . . I thought maybe it was because of me and Leo.' There, better to get it out and over with. She waited for him to say something, but he remained silent. He picked up his pen and started writing. She carried on. 'I mean, it must have looked a bit bad, but I wish you'd waited and let me explain.'

'Go on, then.'

'Well, it was awful, really. I met him outside after I'd been to the loo, you know, and he said he wanted a bit of air and would I go for a walk with him. So I said all right.' Her voice had become hurried but casual, as though she were recounting some silly story of no importance. 'And we were just chatting away quite innocently, as I thought, when he suddenly just, you know, *grabbed* me. It was awful, really. And I suppose that's when you saw us,' she finished lamely, waiting for his response.

'Yes,' replied Anthony, the word devoid of any meaning. I don't believe it, he thought suddenly, remembering Leo in the grey light of his flat, the touch of his hand upon Anthony's wrist, the look in his eyes. But anything was possible, he supposed. What did he know, after all?

'Look, are you *very* cross?' Julia was saying. 'Please don't be. It wasn't my fault, really. I didn't know you were there.' She paused and then recovered herself rapidly. 'What I mean is – I think maybe he just did it to make you jealous. I mean, I don't see why he should want to *do* that – ' She became confused, annoyed at Anthony's laconic responses.

'Neither do I,' said Anthony, still writing. And then it occurred to him, so vividly that it almost flashed upon his brain, that he did see why. Leo had wanted to make Anthony jealous, but not in the way that Julia meant. He had wanted to hurt him and spite him, so that Anthony would see and know the wretchedness of his heart's condition. He had said: see, I am kissing someone, and it is not you. He heard Julia's voice chattering and wheedling on, but her words did not register. Seeing all as he did, Anthony suddenly felt an intolerable wave of love and pity for Leo. God, what a hideous, hopeless situation. How had he ever got into this? Well, it must stop. It was getting too intense and complex. Please, thought Anthony, let everything be sane and straightforward. He tried to listen to what Julia was saying.

'. . . and I know it looked bad, but it was just a kiss, after all, and that sort of thing happens all the time at Balls, doesn't it? I mean, everyone has a bit too much to drink and things get out of hand . . .'

'Yes, they do,' said Anthony, and sighed. He felt tired and confused. She thought she heard his voice relent.

'So *please* don't be angry. I felt awful when I got back and you weren't there. I positively *ran* back, I can tell you. It's not particularly pleasant being mauled about by someone twice your age, you know.' Oh, no? thought Anthony. She paused, testing. 'You're not saying a lot. Is Michael there?'

'Yes.'

'Do you forgive me?' She tried not to make her voice sound too small.

Anthony said nothing. I don't want to arouse that kind of feeling in any man, he thought. I'm me, Anthony, an ordinary heterosexual male with a girlfriend and an uncomplicated life. I don't want to know about some old bloke who's got a crush on me. He drummed it into himself, lie upon lie. He was tired of excessive thought and feeling. The kind of emotional responses that Leo had provoked in him over the past twenty-four hours had proved extremely wearing.

'I've said I'm sorry,' said Julia petulantly, feeling that she really had apologised sufficiently.

'All right,' said Anthony thoughtfully. 'It's all right.'

Julia felt relief slip into her heart. She did not think that her vanity could have borne another rejection. And she did not want to lose Anthony – not someone so clever and beautiful and lovely in bed. She really must be a little more careful. Happily she said, 'I knew you'd understand.' When he said nothing, she added, 'Look, I can't see you tonight, but what about tomorrow? We don't have to go out. We could just stay in, the two of us. What do you say?'

That, thought Anthony, sounded nice and normal. He was going to *be* nice and normal, and remain that way. He did not want any more flashes of emotional lightning zigzagging across his sky. Leo was simply a man that he had liked very much – perhaps too much – and the thing had got a little beyond itself. Well, no more.

'That sounds okay,' he said. 'I'll call you tomorrow.'

Standing at the bus stop that evening, Anthony pulled from his pocket the piece of paper on which he had copied out the sonnet. He crumpled it into a ball and threw it into the nearest bin without reading it again. He did not have to read it. He knew it by heart.

Anthony got back that evening to find his mother and Barry sitting at the kitchen table with a folder of drawings and sketches spread out in front of them.

'Get a load of these,' said Barry, turning as Anthony came in. 'The great man's early work.' Anthony came closer to look.

'Well, I wouldn't say great,' murmured Judith into the fist upon which her chin was resting.

'Mum dug them out from the attic,' said Barry, getting up and going to root in the fridge. 'Have we got any tomatoes, Mum?'

'In the brown bag,' said Judith. 'These are the ones I told you about,' she said to Anthony, as he sat down in Barry's chair

215

and pulled some of the drawings towards him. They reminded him of the drawings in *A Spaniard in the Works*. Cross out of Lennon out of Milligan out of Lear. There were some cartoons, some sketches of Judith, and what looked to him like very bad still-life drawings. Anthony picked up a drawing of Judith, much younger, with long, dark hair parted in the middle, sitting on a chair.

'Crap, isn't it?' said Barry over his shoulder.

'Do you know,' said Anthony, staring at it briefly and then picking up another of Judith wearing nothing except what appeared to be a thermal vest, 'I wouldn't say they were *good* exactly, but at least you can tell what they're meant to be about.'

'Our mother in her knickers. Anyway, that's probably not a good thing, is it?' said Barry, returning to the table with three tomatoes on a plate and a piece of cheese. 'That's my chair.'

Anthony got up and went to put on the kettle. 'I mean,' continued Barry, sitting down, 'it's obviously only his inscrutable stuff that people feel they have to like. People may suspect it's junk, but they can't prove it. They can look at this and say, "Oh, that's not a very good drawing, is it? Her arm's all wrong." ' He bit into his cheese.

'You have a point there,' remarked Anthony, taking off his jacket as he waited for the kettle to boil.

'I remember when he did this one,' said Judith without any particular expression in her voice, picking up a small comic drawing of someone in an Afghan coat with long hair and flared trousers. She paused and then said, glancing up at Anthony as if slightly embarrassed, 'I was wondering if it might be worth anything.' Barry guffawed unattractively, his mouth full of tomato. 'I mean, now that he seems to be actually making a commercial sucess of it. Barry, do you *have* to eat like that? Cut them up, or something.' She gazed at the pieces of paper spread out before her and added, a little more distantly, 'It was just a thought. You know, if he becomes really rich, we're never likely to see a penny of it. I was thinking, if we could sell these . . .'

'Why don't you hang on to them?' said Anthony, bringing his mug of tea and a third chair over to the table. 'They might be worth even more in ten years or so.' He sipped his tea and glanced through them. Judith smiled a little sideways smile.

'I doubt it. These things never last. We might hold on to them and find they're completely worthless in a few years' time. But they must be worth something now.'

'They're completely worthless now, if you ask me,' said Barry. Judith ignored him.

'God knows, we deserve to make something out of it. He hasn't paid any maintenance for years.'

'You mean you don't want to keep them for sentimental reasons?' said Barry, grinning. She made as if to swipe at him.

'You met that woman at the art gallery when you took the paintings over,' said Judith. 'Why don't you take these to her and ask her what they'd fetch?' She got up and took her mug to the sink and rinsed it out. Anthony thought of Mrs Marks and winced. 'I'm sure she'd be interested to see them, at any rate.' She dried her hands, looking at Anthony.

Maybe, thought Anthony, he could take them over when there were lots of people about. Yes, that would be the safest thing.

'Okay,' he said. 'I'll pop over at lunchtime tomorrow.'

There were not, unfortunately, lots of people about when Anthony arrived at the gallery. Mrs Marks was standing at the curved white reception desk, talking to a very elegant, beautifully dressed young woman who was seated behind it, and going through a sheaf of price lists. She smiled with surprise when she saw Anthony.

'Anthony!' she said. 'What a delightful surprise. Moira,' she said, pronouncing it 'Mwara', 'this is Anthony Cross, the son of Chay Cross, you know, whose exhibition is coming up soon. Moira, my assistant.' Moira gave Anthony a chilly little smile. 'How are you, my dear?' Mrs Marks asked Anthony, with genuine interest, handing the sheaf of papers to Moira. She seemed utterly at ease, quite unembarrassed by any recollection of their previous encounter.

Anthony said that he was very well, and glanced apprehensively as Moira slid into her jacket, murmured that she was going to lunch, and left.

'Come this way,' said Mrs Marks in her low voice, leading Anthony up the gallery. 'Vincent Stammels,' she murmured, indicating a large blue and white abstract that they happened to be passing. 'Very compelling. Do you know his work?' They reached a door and Mrs Marks opened it, ushering the hapless Anthony through ahead of her. They were in a small office, painted white like the gallery, with a large, low window covered by a white micro-blind. Apart from a desk and a few chairs, the only other objects in the room were some large green plants.

'Drink?' asked Mrs Marks, glancing enquiringly at Anthony. She saw the faint apprehension on his face, and laughed suddenly. 'Oh, darling!' she exclaimed. Anthony began to feel worried. 'Don't look so *terrified*!'

'Do I?' asked Anthony in surprise. She laughed again and was hauling out the gin and vermouth bottles in her merriment. Anthony wondered if he should go.

'Dearest, don't even *think* about the silliness last time you came here! That was just a test run, so to speak. Call it an old woman's folly.' She handed a very full glass to him. 'You're perfectly safe,' she added in a soft, sweet voice, like someone calming a frightened child. Anthony smiled, still doubtful. She looked at him, her head on one side. 'Was it too awful?' she cajoled.

'Well, actually,' said Anthony uncertainly, 'I was a bit – thrown, if you know what I mean.'

'I know just what you mean,' she said. 'Now, sit down and tell me to what I owe this charming visit.' Feeling a little better, Anthony sat down in a chair by the window. He took a sip of his drink, remembered his last visit, and laid it gently on the windowsill, determined not to touch it again. He untied the piece of ribbon that held the folder together and cleared his throat.

'My mother found these in our house,' he said, pulling out one or two of the drawings. Mrs Marks was looking at him with kind, expectant interest. He laid the folder on the windowsill beside his drink, and got up and carried the drawings over to where she was sitting at her desk. 'They're some things my father did when he first knew my mother. I wondered if they'd be of any interest to you.'

Mrs Marks spread the drawings out on her desk and looked at them critically, saying nothing for a long time. 'My dear,' she said eventually, 'some of these are *very* interesting. They could be extremely exciting. You know how acclaimed your father is at present?'

Anthony said, diffidently, that he didn't know, really.

'Perhaps he's not so well known in this country yet,' continued Mrs Marks, picking up a picture of Judith and running her eye over it, 'but that's just a matter of time. He's a complete runaway success in the States.' She paused. 'We'd have to sort them out, but these could be worth two or three thousand each on the Californian market.'

Anthony nodded, dazed, and took a large gulp of his drink. The gin buzzed in his veins. Thousands! It was extraordinary. People must be mad. Suddenly he thought of the painting, the nude, that he had discarded and left at Chay's flat. Why should his father have it all? Why shouldn't his mother have something out of it as well? She'd had a hard enough life, without any help from Chay.

'I have another painting,' he said suddenly to Mrs Marks. She looked up from the drawings. 'It's mine – something he left me when he went to America. I'd like to sell that, too.'

'Another painting!' Mrs Marks was visibly, but collectedly excited. 'My dear! When can I see it?

'I'll bring it over tomorrow,' said Anthony with decision. Chay could argue about the ownership of it later, if he wanted to, but by that time it would be well and truly sold. Mrs Marks was gazing at him. He finished his drink and then remembered that he hadn't meant to. He had eaten nothing and felt quite light-headed. Thousands. Thousands!

'Mrs Marks,' he said suddenly, looking at her so intently that she felt a little unnerved. Such a lovely boy.

'Yes, my dear?' She was carefully putting the drawings into their folder.

He wondered whether he should ask her about this, whether it was even a question worth asking. But he couldn't think of anyone else to ask – she seemed sympathetic, and, somehow, the right kind of person.

'Mrs Marks, do you think that I'm attractive to – men?'

She looked up in astonishment, her eyes meeting his, and laughed. 'Oh, my dear! What a question!'

*

He took the call from Mrs Marks two weeks later, in the third week of June, the second week of Trinity Term. Anthony and Michael were working in their shirt-sleeves, the window wide open. Work was going on down below on some of the Caper Court telephone lines, and the sound of machinery and workmen's voices floated up through the summer air.

'Anthony, I have some *excellent* news for you,' said Mrs Marks. 'We've found a buyer in New York for that nude study. Very exciting – such a *different* work, you know. Rather reminiscent of Lucien Freud. It's the Blake Gallery. They're prepared to offer fifty thousand dollars for it.'

Anthony took a sip of his cooling tea to steady himself. 'Fifty thousand?'

'That's right, dear. So that makes, with the drawings we've sold in the States so far, nearly sixty-eight thousand. Not bad, really!'

Not bad at all, thought Anthony. He wanted very much to tell his mother straight away, but knew that it would be difficult to reach her at school. It would have to wait until this evening. He didn't think he could wait; the anticipation of her pleasure was too great. Who were these madmen that paid all this money for mediocre paintings and adolescent scribbles?

It was a week later that Leo, coming into his room in the morning, found a small brown envelope lying in the middle of his desk. He opened it without interest. Inside was a cheque for a hundred pounds. It was signed 'A. C. Cross'. Leo gazed for a while at the signature, at the clear, decisive writing, as if to learn something hidden there. There was a note as well. He paused before unfolding it, all too well aware of his quickened pulse and the trembling of hope in his mind. He closed his eyes and willed himself to stop, to bring a clinical regard to the matter. He opened the note quickly. It read, 'With many thanks, Anthony.' What else had he expected it to say? He took his wallet from his breast pocket and opened it, slipping the cheque inside. Then he picked up the note, looked at it, folded it, hesitated, and flicked it neatly into the empty waste-paper basket by his desk. He looked up.

'Think nothing of it,' he said to the empty room.

Chapter nineteen

There had been trouble with his mother over the painting and the fifty thousand dollars that he had received for it.

'But you can't sell it!' his mother had exclaimed. 'It wasn't ours to sell! You of all people should know that.'

'I don't care,' Anthony had said. 'Anyway, I doubt if he's going to make a big thing of it.'

But at last he agreed to compromise. The fifty thousand dollars was put into a deposit account for the time being. Of the remaining eighteen thousand, Judith insisted on giving the boys six thousand each.

Anthony had never had so much money in his life. It came out at just under four thousand pounds, enough to make a significant difference to his life until the fee notes began to trickle through.

The first difference it made was with Julia. It was impossible for him to throw off his natural prudence where money was concerned, but for the first time he was free of the business of worrying about it. The prospect of the week's expenditure ceased to daunt, and Julia's pleasure in being with Anthony was no longer soured by the eternal question of whether or not he could afford things. Anthony felt less adrift from her and her friends, and began to realise what life could be like if one could always afford its more modest pleasures, like a decent bottle of wine, or an evening in a good restaurant, without having to worry about whether there would be enough left for the bus home. Life became altogether sweeter. Although things between Anthony and Julia were now pleasanter, however, he began to detect an element of sameness about the times they spent together. Julia was easily bored, and occasionally felt vague longings for some new stimulus in her life. If he saw this, Anthony did not acknowledge it.

As regarded Leo, Anthony avoided tea in the common room whenever he could, and was careful not to run into him in chambers. Leo still came to Michael's room from time to time, but they were no more than polite and friendly to one another, and Anthony told himself that the stomach-tightening nervousness that he still felt whenever he encountered the man would gradually pass. After all, he had been forced to lose a friendship more pleasant and valuable than any he had ever had with any man. That was no small emotional wrench. But it had been a necessary excision. Leo told himself the same thing, and was relieved to find that the affair seemed to matter less as the days passed. Anthony was just another young man, after all.

In their encounters, their eyes never quite met, as though each was afraid to see past the polite indifference of the other's gaze.

Anthony was also conscious that the time was fast approaching when a decision would have to be taken in chambers as to who would become the next tenant. On some days he felt gloomily that the matter must surely be a foregone conclusion. On others, particularly those when Edward came to him with a perplexed face and some query regarding the work he was supposed to be doing, he felt more optimistic. The matter began to prey on his mind to such an extent that he was forced to mention it to Michael.

'Yes. I think we're having a meeting about that at the beginning of next week.' He looked over at Anthony, who was sitting at his desk, staring dismally at the window. 'Don't worry. You've done your best. What more can you do? I give you a better than even chance.'

Anthony sighed. 'It's not really the kind of thing that should require much discussion amongst members of chambers, is it?'

'Not normally, no,' said Michael. He hesitated. 'But in this case I think it's a little different. Some of us feel quite strongly about it. A lot of people think very highly of you, you know.'

'Don't tell me,' groaned Anthony. A lot of people thought even more highly of Sir Basil, and Sir Basil's wishes, Anthony knew.

On the next weekend, the second in July, the first of the chambers cricket matches was due to take place.

'We're playing 4 Sussex Court,' Edward told Anthony at lunchtime that day.

'That's Piers' set, isn't it?' said Anthony. 'God, what fun. I can't stand that man.'

'Why ever not?' asked Edward. 'He's a great chap. Anyway, I don't think he's after Julia any more, if that's what's worrying you. Wait till they get a taste of my outswinger.' Edward took a little run and bowled at some imaginary stumps.

Anthony had to admit that this was true, but he still did not relish the prospect of having to spend several hours in Piers' company at a cricket match.

The match was to take place in the village where Roderick Hayter had his home, at the Great Salingham cricket club. Members of chambers were making their way down to Great Salingham by car on Saturday morning, in time for lunch at Roderick's, and the clerks, who made up the numbers, were to join them at the cricket club. No one, least of all the clerks, thought anything of this social division. They would much prefer to spend a couple of hours in the pub nearest the cricket ground than in the uneasy formality of Roderick Hayter's splendid home.

Anthony was told to bring Julia, if he wished. 'I can give you both a lift,' said Michael. 'Elizabeth is coming as well.'

Julia's reaction, when Anthony mentioned it to her, was mixed. The prospect of cricket was not enlivening – on the other hand, there might be an opportunity to score a little off that arrogant man, Leo Davies. She hesitated.

'We're playing Piers' chambers,' Anthony added. At that, Julia said she would go. She thought that Piers had rather been avoiding her of late, which was both galling and puzzling. She wondered if he was still seeing Lady Juliet. She recalled his lazy protestations of undying love just a few months ago, the ones which she had affected to find tiresome, but which she really rather cherished. She missed his amusing, wicked conversation, too. How could she possibly have ceased to be attractive to him? The prospect of re-exercising her fascination over Piers made the idea of the cricket match much more interesting. All foolish little emotional games, especially ones that she could dress up for, were irresistible to Julia.

The day of the cricket match was a particularly hot one, with only a slight breeze and a few cotton-wool clouds drifting in the sky. In the garden of Roderick Hayter's Gloucestershire home, the silence was deep and green and lovely, broken only by faint birdsong, the occasional chirrup of a cricket hidden in the sunny grass, and the murmur of educated voices making conversation over pre-luncheon drinks. Anthony strolled around with Julia and Edward, awestruck by the magnificence of the grounds and the beauty of the house. It would take a lifetime of understanding, he reflected, a lifetime that he had not even begun, to bring together such loveliness. Even Julia was impressed. She had taken care to look especially attractive, Anthony thought; he reflected that this might, in some obscure way, be for Leo's benefit, but he scarcely cared about that. For their separate reasons, both Anthony and Julia avoided any group that contained Leo. He was placed at the other end of the long table at luncheon, so that only drifts of amusement at his conversation reached them from time to time. Each wished vaguely that they could hear what he was saying.

After lunch they made their way to the cricket ground. Piers and his fellow members of chambers were already there, busily changing. Anthony and Michael left Julia and Elizabeth and made their way into the familiar, musty woodenness that is every cricket pavilion. They found the changing rooms and dumped their kit. When Anthony emerged, clumping with the unaccustomed slight extra weight of his cricket boots across the verandah to where Julia stood, he saw that she was talking to Piers. He looked, leaning against one of the pillars of the verandah in his cricket whites, even larger than usual. His trousers were old and off-white, but obviously very good, and were held up by a frayed, knotted Harrow tie. He greeted Anthony lazily, arms folded.

'Hello, Tony. Going to get a lot of runs?' He chuckled slightly and gazed out across the pitch. 'Bit of a dry wicket, I'd say.' Edward joined them, looking faintly annoyed.

'I've had to borrow these from Stephen,' he said, looking

down at his trousers, which fell some three inches above the tops of his boots. He hitched at the waistband. 'Mine've got a great bloody rip in them from last year. I'd just put them away and forgotten about it. Do I look a complete prat?' he asked Julia.

'No,' she laughed. 'No more than usual.'

'Oh, thanks. Thanks very much.' He turned to Piers. 'Who's your captain?'

'Jefferies, of course,' replied Piers, referring to his head of chambers. 'Who's yours?'

'Well, Uncle Basil's a bit past it,' said Edward. 'He's going to umpire. Leo Davies is our captain.'

'Is he especially good?' asked Julia, with only faint interest.

'Natural authority,' replied Anthony shortly. At that moment, the clerks arrived from the pub, where they seemed to have enjoyed a particularly good lunch.

'Oh, God,' said Edward, watching the clerks as they made their chortling way to the changing rooms, 'look at Robert.'

'One of your clerks, is he?' enquired Piers. 'Looks a little the worse for wear.'

'I know,' said Edward despondently. 'He's meant to be one of our best players.'

'That's the trouble with clerks,' said Piers. 'At least we don't have to rely on ours to do anything more than make up the numbers.' He heaved himself off the pillar, flexed his thighs, and glanced at Julia's low-cut, yellow cotton dress. It clung prettily to her slender figure. 'You're looking very well these days,' he remarked, with indolent appreciation. 'I could almost fall in love with you again.'

She flushed slightly and lifted her chin.

By now the clerks had changed and everyone was ready. Anthony's chambers won the toss and went in to bat. Leo came across to where Anthony was sitting under the trees with Julia.

'I've put you in at number nine. Okay?' Anthony barely glanced at him, but smiled and nodded.

'Fine, thanks.' His eyes rested for a long moment on the sinewy brown curve of Leo's forearms against the crumpled whiteness of his rolled-up shirt-sleeves. Leo paused and glanced down at Julia. 'How nice to see you again, Julia.'

225

She said nothing, but gave him a cool little smile.

Jeremy Vine opened the batting. A reliable, unflamboyant player, he notched up a competent twenty before being bowled, and was followed by Stephen Bishop who, after a plodding fashion, brought the score up to thirty-three before being caught out. William followed, and then David. The afternoon grew hotter as it wore on.

Julia, having taken an initial token interest in the game, began to feel bored and restless. Much as she liked Michael's wife, Elizabeth, she didn't really have much in common with someone so much older than herself. There were no other girls of her age there. She supposed she should be glad that Piers hadn't brought the awesome Lady Juliet along. She looked out to where Piers' large figure was fielding at cover. He was standing with his arms folded, watching play with languid intentness. He looked very attractive in his cricket whites, thought Julia – Piers always managed to look so *right*, so thoroughly in his element. She thought of his remark earlier, and felt a faint glow of pleasure. She glanced idly at Anthony, whose eyes were fixed on the game.

'Oh, good shot!' he called, along with the others, as David knocked a clean, high ball over to the boundary, where the pitch met the line of summer trees. The ragged clapping died away. The sun was fierce now, and Julia put her hat on, wishing she'd brought that Jilly Cooper novel, instead of Anita Brookner.

'This is their really good man,' Anthony said suddenly to Julia. She looked up from her book to see a slight, dark man with thinning hair strolling across the pitch, rubbing the ball on his thigh. 'He's a Cambridge blue. Adrian Sutton.' Julia smiled faintly at the earnestness in Anthony's voice. It was sweet, she thought, how seriously he took everything, even a game of cricket. Sometimes she felt, though, that he could do with a touch of Piers' detachment. It somehow made a man more interesting, less predictable. She fanned herself lightly with her book.

David was still batting, with Cameron at the other end, a large, restless figure with his shirt hanging over his trousers. The score stood at eighty-four for three. David had batted exceptionally well. Sutton's bowling began to slow him up, however, and he grew impatient. He knocked a slow ball in the direction of cover and began to run. Cameron at his end hesitated, glancing out, and shouted 'No!' David stopped in mid-run, clumsily, and slipped as he tried to scramble back to the wicket. But Piers had already run from cover and scooped the ball up, and had thrown the stumps down before David could recover his ground. Sir Basil raised a finger, and David began to walk towards the pavilion, taking off his gloves.

'Typical,' said Anthony, to no one in particular.

'What's wrong with that?' asked Julia. 'He got him out, didn't he?'

'Anyone else,' replied Anthony dryly, 'would have thrown it to the wicket-keeper.'

'You really can't find a single good thing to say about Piers, can you?' she asked mildly, looking at Anthony. Then she glanced across to where Piers was walking back to cover. 'I thought he was very good, actually.'

The game continued, Roderick batting, then Leo, then Robert. Still somewhat affected by his lunchtime libations at the Great Salingham Arms, Robert's batting was, at first, a little erratic, but he was a strong, swift young man, and a naturally stylish cricketer. Anthony went in to bat, giving Robert a nod and a smile as he stepped up to the crease and took guard.

'Middle and leg,' he said, making a furrow in the dusty ground with his bat. From the verandah, Leo watched. The July breeze fluttered Anthony's shirt lightly where it had come loose from his waistband, and he watched as the boy unconsciously tucked it back in, waiting for the first ball. A clerk from the other side's chambers was bowling, a big, beefy, quick man. Anthony hit a steady series of sharp singles, pushed to cover. He and Robert ran well. Leo, his mind absorbed in the game, which he very much wanted them to win, watched Anthony's lithe figure with subconscious pleasure as he took his runs. He felt a little plunge of disappointment when Anthony mistimed a drive and was caught neatly at mid-wicket.

Anthony tucked his bat under his arm and walked back over

the to where Julia sat, smiling. Leo turned away. It was a quarter to five, teatime, and they were a hundred and eighty-five for eight. Not bad, so far.

At tea, Anthony was standing talking to Stephen Bishop in the pavilion when Leo came over.

'Good innings, Stephen,' said Leo. Stephen shook his head. 'Too much weight. I can't run the way I used to. No puff.' He glanced over to where William was talking to someone from the other chambers. 'There's Preston. I've been trying to catch him all afternoon to find out what he means by serving that Civil Evidence Act notice. Excuse me, won't you?' He bustled off with his teacup. Anthony and Leo were left standing together. They had not been alone since the evening of the May Ball. Anthony could think of nothing to say, and glanced at Leo, who was smiling at him, and burst out laughing. Leo laughed, too.

'It is bloody absurd,' he agreed. The sound of his cool, Welsh voice lifted Anthony's heart. He shook his head and began to say something, but Leo stopped him by laying a hand on his arm. 'Come on,' he said. 'We'll have to start again in a minute.' They walked out together into the sunshine. Julia glanced over at the two men as they emerged from the pavilion. She didn't feel quite brave enough to join them, and sat down with Anita Brookner at the end of a row of chairs. She felt more than a little pleased when Piers threw his large frame into the chair next to hers, and began to buckle on his pads.

'You fielded very well,' she remarked. Piers laughed and straightened up.

'Since when did you care anything about cricket?' He folded his arms and watched the fielders take their places. Leo had placed Anthony at mid-on, and stood himself in the slips, near to where a nervous Edward stood as wicket-keeper. 'You're only here because of darling Anthony,' he continued, shading his eyes with his hand. He did not look at Julia. 'What keeps you two going, anyway? I thought he didn't have any money?'

'He has other – qualities,' replied Julia, with a little smile. He shifted a little closer to her so that he could murmur into her ear, 'Oh, don't be so coy, Julia, darling. I think we can all guess what those qualities are. Time you gave someone else a try.'

His voice was cool and bored, but his smile never wavered. With his body so close to hers, Julia could smell a faint, and not unpleasant, tang of sweat. She looked up into his face.

'By which you mean – you?' Her voice was light and mocking.

Piers settled his body further down into the chair, so that his shoulder was level with hers. His long legs were stretched out under the empty chair in front of him. His voice was no more than a murmur, his eyes narrow with calculation.

'You're just dying to, aren't you?' he said with a caressing drawl, and at the same time slid his hand under her dress and along the inside of her thigh. With a small, swift movement, she pushed his hand away and crossed her legs.

'Not here,' she muttered. He picked this up as though it were a cue.

'Where, then?' he asked slowly, turning his eyes to hers. She glanced at him and said nothing, then looked back at the game. Piers laughed with lazy confidence and said softly, 'You want to as much as I do, don't you?' He slid his tongue between his teeth, still looking at her. Still she said nothing, her gaze turned to where Anthony was fielding. She felt hot between her thighs.

Someone had been caught, and Piers pulled himself out of his chair and picked up his bat. Julia watched his tall, ambling figure as he walked out across the grass.

Anthony stood with a daisy in his mouth, watching Piers as he took guard. Leo was bowling, and the score stood at eighty-two for three.

'Two,' said Piers. Even on a cricket pitch, thought Anthony, he was loud. He noticed that Piers wasn't wearing the usual cricket boots, but a softer, trainer-like shoe of the kind that professional cricketers wore. It was on a par with Piers talking loudly at teatime about the Eton–Harrow match. I hope you get hit on the toe, you great twat, thought Anthony, watching Leo run in to bowl. The ball struck Piers' pad plumb in front of the stumps, and with elation Anthony looked expectantly at Sir Basil.

'It hit my bat,' said Piers quickly. There was a pause, and Sir Basil put his hands back into his pockets.

Piers blocked the next two balls. Anthony was now longing for him to be out. Leo prepared to bowl the last ball of the over, and Anthony watched him as he walked back to his mark, tossing the ball, the fingers of his other hand smoothing back stray locks of hair. Leo had placed Robert, who was considerably more sober now, at silly mid-on, some four yards away from Piers. Leo bowled and Piers pushed forward, the ball striking his bat and then his pad, then popping up over Robert's head. Robert turned swiftly and dived backwards, scooping the ball in a cloud of dust from the dry pitch just as it came down. From where Sir Basil stood the dust made the view difficult, but he nonetheless raised a majestic finger. But instead of walking, Piers turned to the square leg umpire, who happened to be his own head clerk.

'Are you sure that carried?' he asked loudly. The square leg umpire scratched his chin.

'I couldn't see,' he replied, indicating Jeremy. Piers glanced at Anthony, his hand on his hip. At short mid-on, he knew that Anthony must have had as good a view as anyone. But Anthony chose to say nothing, exchanging only the briefest of glances with Robert as Piers made his ungracious way back to the pavilion.

His labours over for the afternoon, Piers fetched himself a beer from the bar and took a large Pimms down to Julia. Neither said a word as he sat down beside her.

Robert was bowling now, and had found his length and pace. Four wickets fell. Michael bowled, and then David. One by one, the opposition team was bowled out, and by seven o'clock they were all out for a hundred and ten.

The players drifted from the pitch, broken clapping died upon the warm air, and people made their way into the pavilion.

Anthony was elated by the afternoon's success. He stood talking over the game with David and William and a couple of men from the other chambers. After a while, he looked round for Julia. He'd probably better buy her a drink. He found her chatting to Edward out on the verandah.

'Sorry, I got caught up in there. Drink?'

She smiled at him. 'I've already had several more than I should, but I suppose another won't hurt. G-and-t, please.'

230

'Mine's a pint!' called Edward, as Anthony made his way back to the bar.

As he was coming out on to the verandah with the drinks, Piers stopped him in the doorway.

'Good match,' he said idly. 'What about that catch, though? Can't possibly have been good.' He took a sip of his drink and looked lazily at Anthony. 'What did you think? You had the best view.'

'I really couldn't say, you know,' replied Anthony.

'Well, that's the trouble with letting clerks play, I suppose,' said Piers, lifting his glass. Anthony paused for a second.

'Piers,' he said. Piers looked at him enquiringly. 'As we say in East Dulwich, Piers,' continued Anthony in a quiet, conversational tone, 'why don't you fuck off?' He made his way out into the evening sunlight.

There was a light supper, and more drinking, and by the time the heat of day had softened into late evening, and the shadows stretched long upon the grass, Anthony felt tired and happy. He had spent half an hour talking with Leo and Michael and David, and was pleased simply to be able to look at and listen to Leo, to be smiled at by him, and occasionally to feel his arm brushing his.

Piers had spent the same half-hour talking quietly to Julia alone on the verandah. He had made sure that her glass was never empty. They stood close together in the rosy evening light, their voices never rising above a murmur. Eventually they moved off down the steps together, out of sight of the others, and strolled slowly into the shadows under the trees. Piers turned once to glance over his shoulder.

Back in the pavilion, Michael said, 'Right, we'd better collect these glasses up and make a move.'

David glanced at his watch. 'Good God, is that the time? I'll have to be getting back. Here, I must find Roderick . . .' He drifted off, and Michael began to pick up glasses and put them on the bar.

'I'll fetch the ones from outside,' said Leo. Anthony followed him out and they made their way down the wooden steps together.

'What a glorious evening,' said Leo, pausing to gaze across

the darkening line of far off trees against a gathering haze of coral cloud. The sky above them was a deep, fading blue and the first faint stars were beginning to appear. After London, the air smelt full and sweet. Together they picked up the few glasses scattered amongst the chairs, stacking them in their arms. Anthony walked past the end of the rows of chairs towards the trees, to where he saw a glass glinting further off. He stooped to pick it up. As he straightened, he heard the murmur of voices, and then a faint moan. Not more than five yards away, he could make out the unmistakable, large figure of Piers, locked in a close embrace with a girl who was leaning with her back against a tree, the yellow skirt of her dress around her waist, the pale curve of her thigh gleaming in the blue shadows.

He was standing there when Leo came up beside him, saying, 'I think that's the lot . . .' He stopped and followed Anthony's gaze, then put his hand around Anthony's arm and pulled him away. The lovers under the trees were oblivious. Leo and Anthony walked back together. Leo could see Anthony's face was set and white; he could think of nothing to say to him.

When they got back to the pavilion, Anthony went without a word to the changing rooms and fetched his kit. Michael met him as he came out.

'Ah, there you are. We're just off. You and Julia want a lift back?'

'It's all right,' said Leo to Michael with a smile. 'I think Julia's already left. Bit tired. Anthony's taking a lift with me.'

They drove for some twenty minutes in complete silence. Anthony watched the dark shapes of summer trees and hedgerows slip by, the lights of other cars flash past. Leo put a tape into the cassette player. As the soothing, majestic sounds of a Mozart violin concerto filled the car, Anthony felt his mind drift loose on the current of music, like some lost thing about to be washed into the night. He closed his eyes and laid his head back. At last he spoke.

'That was the third bloody time, you know,' he said quietly.

'What?' asked Leo, turning the music down.

'The third time,' Anthony said again. 'The first time was when I found him kissing her at a party, the second time was with you, and then – tonight.' He stared ahead. Leo was about to say something about the time that he had kissed Julia, but decided against it. There was silence for a few moments.

'Do you love her very much?' asked Leo. The question was a fragile one; he almost wished he hadn't asked it, afraid of the answer.

'I don't know. No, I don't think I can, now,' said Anthony, after a while. 'I've never known anyone like her before. She was from quite another world.' There was silence for a moment. Leo drove. 'I did think she loved me, after a fashion. Which just goes to show.' He laughed, sighed, and leaned his head back again. Then he glanced at one of the road signs that flashed past. 'Where are we going?'

'To my house.' Leo glanced at him. 'My own house. Not the place in London. Is that all right?'

Anthony stared ahead, then nodded. He was trying not to think of Julia being made love to under the trees, in the half-darkness, by Piers. 'God,' he said aloud, 'I hate that bastard.' He turned suddenly to Leo. 'Did you see that first ball you bowled him? It never touched his bat.'

Leo smiled in the darkness. 'I know. He cheats.'

There was silence once more, with the faint undercurrent of the music, as they drove for several miles. Then Leo heard Anthony sigh again, a slight, shuddering breath that seemed to have a sob caught in it. Quickly he pulled in to the left and brought the car to a halt. The handbrake creaked as he pulled it on. He turned to Anthony, who sat with his hand shading his eyes.

'Look,' said Leo gently, longing to take Anthony into his arms, to console him, 'do you want me to take you back to London?' Anthony said nothing for a moment, his hand still over his eyes. Then he took his hand away and looked across at Leo's face. Leo did not think he had been crying.

'No,' said Anthony. He wanted to be held, to be soothed, to find some comfort to fill the void of loss and humiliation. Both men sat looking at one another. 'No, I don't think so.' There was a pause. 'Thank you,' added Anthony. He shifted in his seat, the sound of his movements magnified in the enclosed stillness of the car. 'At least I learned one thing,' he said, with a smile. 'Not to trust women.'

Leo smiled back. 'I don't think they're naturally monogamous, you know.'

'No? I wouldn't know.'

'Not ones like Julia, at any rate. Made for love.'

'That's not love,' said Anthony. 'That's just screwing around.'

'I don't know what love is,' replied Leo, turning away to look out of the window. He let out a deep breath. 'I really don't know.' He looked back at Anthony, and Anthony returned his gaze. Leo started the car, and they drove on through the night.

It was past two when they reached Leo's house. Anthony got out and stretched his legs. The countryside around was magically still, the air only faintly chill. He gazed up at the black night, at the stars he never saw in London, filling his lungs with the pure night air. He felt adrift, sad, tired.

He heard the car door slam and the sound of Leo's footsteps on the gravel, and turned to follow him into the house. Leo switched on the light in the hallway, and Anthony looked around. It was a low-beamed hallway, softly lit, leading into a large sitting-room. Leo went ahead and switched on more lamps. It was utterly different, thought Anthony, from the flat in London. The dark floorboards were shiny and worn, with old patterned carpets scattered here and there. The furniture was haphazard and comfortable, large armchairs and high-backed sofas filled with cushions, a battered, polished table, a cushioned window-seat, a low table between the sofas. The glow of the lamps was warm and comforting. In the cold grate lay the ashes of some long-dead log fire, and on either side of the fireplace stood bookshelves, filled to the low ceiling with an incongruous array of books. The curtains were crimson, soft and faded. Leo did not pull them.

'Sit down,' he said to Anthony. Anthony fell into one of the sofas. Leo opened the creaking door of a low corner cupboard and pulled out a bottle and two glasses. Then he opened one of the windows to let the fresh night air into the room. He brought the bottle and glasses over and set them on the polished table, then poured a large measure of brandy into each. He handed a glass to Anthony.

'Thank you,' he said, and sipped.

'Are you hungry?' asked Leo. Anthony shook his head.

'Not really, thanks. I'm just a bit tired.'

'I'll get you some blankets in a moment. You can make up the bed in the spare room.' He sat down at the other end of the sofa and took a large swallow of brandy. In the silence, Anthony could feel a tension growing between them. He turned and glanced round the room.

'It's very different from your place in London,' he said. Leo took another drink and nodded.

'It's meant to be,' he replied. 'I live here. I don't call what I do there living.' There was a silence again. 'Don't think about her any more,' he said, looking at Anthony, who was gazing into his glass.

'I wasn't,' said Anthony. 'I was thinking about you.' Leo felt his heart miss a beat. He looked down at his drink.

'Don't think about me, either,' he said firmly, quietly. Anthony looked up at him.

'Why not?'

Leo sighed and stood up, looking down at Anthony. He said nothing. He did not know what he was thinking, except that he could not bear to see those dark, sad, lovely eyes looking up at him. He turned to go and fetch the blankets for the spare bed, when Anthony reached up and took his hand. Leo stood there for a moment, held. Then he sat down next to Anthony, put his glass gently on the floorboards at his feet, and looked at him. Anthony dropped his hand and leaned his head back, closing his eyes.

'I'm so lost,' he said eventually, his voice uneven. 'I'm so confused and lost that I don't know . . .' The words trailed away. Leo lifted his hand, hesitated, and then stroked the curve of Anthony's throat just where the pulse beat.

'You don't have to worry,' he said, then bent to kiss Anthony's cheek. Anthony turned his head and returned the kiss, gently, and Leo put his arms around him. He smelt masculine, strong, comforting. Leo held him for a moment and then pulled slowly away. He gazed directly at Anthony, his blue eyes very intent.

'You know,' he said quietly, 'that if you become my lover – ' It seemed to Anthony that the word almost took shape in the air between them. ' – you cannot stay in chambers. And that if you do, there can be nothing – nothing – between us.'

Lover, thought Anthony. I don't even know what it means, or what I want. He looked back at Leo.

'There's a good chance I won't be staying, anyway,' he replied with a smile, his voice low. 'Maybe you should just let fate dispose of that.'

'Perhaps,' said Leo, never taking his eyes from Anthony's, 'but if you do – '

If I do, thought Anthony. If I do what? He rubbed his hands over his eyes and rose slowly, walking over to the open window. Then he turned and looked back at Leo, who was leaning back against the sofa, his face a little grim. You are so young, he was thinking, staring at Anthony. So young and so powerful.

'It's very precious to me,' said Anthony, 'that tenancy.' Leo nodded slowly, still looking at him. 'You could do quite a lot to prevent my getting it.' Leo nodded again. 'If you had to.'

'If I had to,' said Leo. They looked at one another for a long, long moment. Sudden, single notes of birdsong rose from the dark garden. It was the blurred hour of night just before dawn. Anthony was so tired he felt far away.

'You don't know what you want,' said Leo to Anthony, still looking directly at him. 'Do you?'

Anthony looked back at Leo, at the weary, familiar lines of his face and body.

'I just want to be loved,' he replied.

Anthony woke after two hours of uneasy sleep. It took a moment for him to recall where he was. His eyes felt hot and gritty with lack of sleep, his mind brittle. He rose and dressed, then padded out to the landing, his shoes in his hand. The light outside was still milky and new; it could only be about six o'clock, he guessed. He went downstairs quietly, anxious not to wake Leo, sat down on the sofa where he and Leo had talked a few hours before, and put on his shoes. The empty brandy glasses and the bottle were still standing mutely on the table. Picking up his jacket, he looked around for a moment at the place where Leo lived, then quietly let himself out. The morning was very still, bright with the beautiful promise of July, the air only just touched with new sun. Anthony crossed the gravel to the car. It was locked. His kit would just have to stay there until Monday, he supposed. Checking the money in his pocket, Anthony set off in the direction of the nearest village, whose rooftops he could see some fields away. He wondered how far it was to the nearest station, and how often the trains ran on Sundays.

Chapter twenty

It was lunchtime when Anthony arrived home. His mother was spooning chicken casserole on to plates in the kitchen, and the sound of music came from Barry's room.

'Just in time,' said his mother, glancing up as he came in. 'Can you get some knives and forks out?' She put a mat and a dish of potatoes on the table and went into the hall to call upstairs to Barry. When she returned, Anthony was putting the cutlery on the table.

'How was your cricket match?' she asked. 'I thought you said you'd be back last night?'

'Oh, things went on for a bit. Someone from chambers gave me a bed for the night.' He sat down. 'We won,' he added, staring at the potatoes. Then he looked up and gave his mother a quick smile. He looked pale and tired, she thought.

After lunch, he washed up with Barry and then lay on the sofa with bits of the Sunday papers. After a while, he gave up and closed his eyes and thought of Leo. He had the curious sensation that his body was dropping through the sofa. Just as he was beginning to fall asleep, the telephone rang, jangling the fibres of his body. He lay with his eyes shut, waiting for someone to answer it, but he realised after a moment that Barry had gone out and that his mother must be in the garden. Stiff with tiredness, he got up and padded in his bare feet into the hall.

'Hello?' He could not keep the yawn out of his voice.

'Anthony? Hi, it's Chay.'

'Dad!' Anthony ran his fingers through his hair in surprise. 'Where are you calling from?'

'Well, I'm in a hotel at the moment.'

'A hotel where? In London?'

'Yes. Yes, it's near Marble Arch, as a matter of fact.' Chay was not the kind of man one associated with hotels, thought Anthony. 'I thought we might meet, if you'd like to come over.'

'Yes. Yes, great.' The thought of seeing his father in his new persona was rather stimulating, and Anthony felt he needed to do something to drive away thoughts of the past twenty-four hours. He took the address of the hotel, hung up, and went to put on his shoes.

He went out to the garden, where his mother was lying in a deck-chair with a book. She looked up at Anthony through her sunglasses.

'Who was that on the phone?'

'It was Dad, as a matter of fact.'

'Really?' Even Judith sounded more than usually interested.

'Yes. He's staying in a hotel near Marble Arch. I'm going over for tea, or something.'

'Tea?' Judith mused for a moment. 'Well, have fun. I think it might be a good idea if you mentioned that painting that you stole.'

'I didn't steal it. He left it.'

'Yes, well,' said Judith, returning to her book.

The hotel was in a side street off Oxford Street, a bustling, smart affair with liveried porters carrying expensive luggage in and out, sleek cars coming and going. Anthony asked at reception for his father, and was directed to a lounge where tea was being served. Anthony couldn't quite imagine his father in a tea-room. He made his way uncertainly through to a spacious lounge, elegantly decorated in lemon and grey, full of the tinkle and murmur of Sunday afternoon tea. He could hear quite a lot of American voices. Everyone he saw seemed to be expensively dressed, and he wished he'd worn something a bit better than his jeans and a rugby shirt.

He caught sight of his father at a table in the corner – or rather, his father caught sight of him. He rose and raised a hand, and Anthony made his way over. They greeted each other, and Anthony sat down in one of the little chintz-covered armchairs. He looked at his father, curiously pleased to see him. Chay looked quite different, he thought. His hair had grown, and although it was still short, it looked silvery and healthy. His skin was slightly tanned and his figure had filled out. He was wearing a white T-shirt under what looked to Anthony to be a very expensive soft leather jacket, trousers of a faded red, and Fry's boots. Very much the successful post modernist.

'You're looking well,' said Anthony.

'Thanks,' replied Chay, with a diffident smile that was very much like Anthony's. Less like a human lentil, thought Anthony.

'So,' said Anthony, 'tell me about it. What's happened about the charges, and all that stuff?'

Chay sat back, crossing his legs so that one ankle was resting on his knee. 'I thought you'd want to know about my painting.' Still a touch of the old, petulant vanity, thought Anthony.

'Well, I do, but I'm more interested, for the moment, in whether or not you're going to jail.'

Chay shook his head. At that moment, a waitress came over to their table.

'Would you care for afternoon tea, gentlemen?'

'Yes, thank you,' said Chay, glancing at Anthony, who nodded, smiling. Why should he find it so amusing to see his father ordering afternoon tea? People did it every day.

'An assortment of sandwiches and cakes?' asked the waitress.

'Thank you,' said Chay, then asked, 'Do you have any Lapsang Souchong?' She nodded, writing. 'And cream cakes, please,' he added.

'They're all fresh cream, sir. What room number, sir?' Chay gave his room number, while Anthony looked on, marvelling. The waitress whisked away.

'No,' resumed Chay, 'that's all sorted out. I had a good lawyer.' Anthony thought briefly of Chay's much-professed contempt for lawyers. 'I got a bit of a stiff fine for jumping bail, and a two-month suspended sentence for possession.'

To Anthony's surprise, Chay brought out a small packet of cigars and lit one. Anthony thought of Leo.

'I suppose the fine didn't worry you too much?' asked

Anthony. Chay looked faintly embarrassed. 'With your new-found wealth, I mean,' added Anthony, smiling. He thought of Sunday afternoons, much like this one, spent listening to Chay denounce the capitalist system, while his long fingers shredded tobacco into cigarette papers to make roll-ups. The memory was a curiously fond one.

'It's all been very strange,' said Chay in a musing voice, gazing into nowhere. Anthony suddenly realised that this was true, that his father must find the change in his fortunes very peculiar. 'Finding acceptance after spending all your life . . .' Chay continued. Just then the waitress returned with a laden tray, and set down the cups, saucers, plates, teapot, milk jug, hot water, sandwiches and cakes. Anthony was looking at his father, realising that his must have been a wretched kind of life until now, devoid of any dignity save that which he had been able to scrape from his artistic pretensions. And now they were pretensions no longer.

'Spending your life . . . ?' he prompted, when the waitress had left. Chay paused, holding the milk jug suspended over Anthony's cup.

'Getting nowhere, I suppose,' Chay said after a moment.

'And now you're the toast of Santa Barbara,' said Anthony with a smile, picking up a sandwich. Chay nodded.

'It's extraordinary.' He gazed at his tea for a while, chewing a cucumber sandwich. 'It's fantastic how much people are prepared to pay for art out there.'

'It's what the market will bear, I suppose,' replied Anthony. 'Just think of all those really wealthy people vying with one another to add the most expensive post modernist to their collection.'

'It's more than just a trend, you know,' said Chay, with a touch of dignified resentment. 'It's a movement.'

'Is it?' asked Anthony. 'I'm not really up on these things. Do you think you'll go on selling?' What he wanted to ask was whether his father really believed in his work, in its value. For some reason, he could not put the question directly.

Chay shook his head. 'I don't know. God knows.'

Anthony wondered whether he meant this figuratively or literally. With Chay, one never knew.

'So, what are you going to do?' he asked. 'What are you doing now?'

'I had to to come back. Green card, all that stuff.' Chay carefully selected a cream horn with a little dusting of icing sugar on the top. Anthony had never seen his father eat a cream cake before. Cream cakes would fall into the range of things that were despicably bourgeois. He supposed that his father, long ago, must have been taken to afternoon tea by his parents. He tried to imagine this. 'It's a nice hotel, this, don't you think?' Chay said glancing up at Anthony, and then around the room.

'Yes,' said Anthony, with mild surprise. Maybe there had been a normal person inside his father all the time, too terrified to come out. Here he was, taking afternoon tea in a nice hotel, paying for it with money which he had earned from doing something that other people seemed to want him to do. What could be more straightforward than that? Perhaps this wasn't just another phase, another pose, after all. Maybe this was as real as Chay could get.

'I sold one of your paintings,' said Anthony, looking straight at his father. 'It was one I didn't take round to Mrs Mark's gallery with the others, the first time. A sort of nude thing.'

'Yes, Mrs Marks. I've got to go and see her tomorrow morning. She's doing an exhibition of my work. You might like to come to the opening.'

'Yes, thanks,' said Anthony. 'You'll like Mrs Marks,' he added, and then wondered if Chay would. 'She's a jolly sort of woman.'

'So how much did you get for it?' asked Chay, still obviously mildly amused by the amount of money that his talent could command. Then he added quickly, 'I don't really care. You can keep it. You probably need it. Or your mother does.' Anthony was surprised; Chay hardly ever referred to Judith.

'Fifty thousand,' said Anthony. 'Dollars,' he added.

Chay shook his head and smiled. 'Outrageous.'

'*You're* outrageous,' replied Anthony. Chay looked up, still smiling.

'Yes, I am outrageous.' Neither was quite sure what the other really meant.

242

'So,' said Chay, 'how's your life? How's the Bar?'

'It's good,' said Anthony, nodding at his plate. 'I'm doing just the kind of work I want to do. You know, commercial, shipping, that kind of thing.' He thought of the chambers meeting that was to take place next day, and swallowed with fear. 'I still don't know if I've got a tenancy at Caper Court or not, yet.' Chay nodded vaguely; his interest in Anthony's career was, Anthony knew, minimal.

'How are you off for money?'

Anthony laughed. It was the kind of paternal question he had occasionally asked Chay, but had never expected to hear from him in return.

'So-so,' he said. 'Much better, if you meant what you said about the painting.'

'Yes,' said Chay, finishing his tea and lighting another cigar. 'I meant it. Tell me if you need any more.'

A weight dropped from Anthony's mind; the money from the painting, even a third of it, would be more than enough to tide him over until he began earning properly, even if he had to look for another set of chambers.

They talked on for a while about California, and about Chay's work. Anthony was surprised at the enthusiasm with which his father spoke, at the confidence and self-possession which he wore like a new set of clothes. For the first time, Anthony felt that he liked his father. It was not difficult, he supposed, to be an unlikeable person, when you had no money and the life that you lived was a mere sham, a posture struck in adolescence which you were forced to maintain. All ambition a mere pretence. Add money, success and respect, and the pretence suddenly became solid, a reality, the truth.

Anthony rose after a while. 'I have to be getting back,' he said. Chay nodded and got up. They walked back through the hotel together.

'I'll call you about the opening,' Chay said. 'You can reach me here, if you need to.' He smiled, and they said farewell. Anthony watched, bemused, as his father stepped into the lift, and the doors slid smoothly shut behind him.

The chambers meeting was to take place on Monday, at four-thirty. Anthony was glad that he had to spend the afternoon with solicitors in the City and would not be back until after five. Edward had still not appeared in chambers by lunchtime.

Just after two, Anthony was scrabbling his papers together and bundling them into his briefcase. He glanced at his watch; he was going to be late. He thundered down the stairs and set off at a run, coming through Pump Court and into Middle Temple Lane, and running straight into Julia. He was too startled to say anything, but a pain grabbed at his heart.

'I was just coming round to your chambers to leave you a note,' she said. She looked hesitant.

'Oh?' said Anthony, glancing past her, thinking that this was going to make him even later. Well, what the hell. He leaned against the wall, recovering his breath a little. He looked at her. 'I can save you the trouble. You can give it to me now.' He paused. 'Or do you want to tell me?'

'Look, can't we talk?' She glanced round at the people making their way up and down the lane, her face troubled.

'No,' said Anthony, with finality. He felt he could do no more than refer obliquely to the events of Saturday. 'I'm afraid too much has happened.' It sounded wooden, but he could think of no other words. 'Look, I'm late. I've got to find a taxi.' He began to walk towards the Strand, and she walked with him. They said nothing until they had passed through the gate, and then he stopped and turned to her.

'We can't see each other any more. You know that. It should never have started again. There's Piers – '

'Yes,' she said, and looked down.

' – and a whole lot of other things.'

'That's really what my note was about.'

Anthony saw the yellow light of an empty cab coming through the traffic. Julia was holding out her note to him. He lifted his arm and the cab swung in to the kerb towards them.

'No, I don't want it,' he said, and glanced briefly at her, thinking how pretty she looked, standing with her sweet, troubled face in the middle of the Strand, getting in everyone's way. He got into the taxi without looking back.

The meeting was, like all chambers meetings, to take place in Sir Basil's room. When Michael arrived just after four-thirty,

Sir Basil was not there. David and William followed him into the empty room, and then Cameron's heavy footstep sounded on the stair.

'Basil's downstairs. He'll be a few minutes,' said Cameron, as they all sat down. 'Why the devil are we having this meeting, anyway?' he said tetchily. 'I thought it was understood that Basil's nephew was staying on.'

Roderick Hayter came in with Jeremy, and then Stephen puffed in, pulling on his jacket. They found chairs and sat down.

'Well, some of us feel he may not be the right choice,' said Michael mildly, feeling in his pocket for a handkerchief; he had a summer cold.

'Your boy Anthony may be very bright,' said Cameron crossly, 'but I cannot see why it is of such importance that a question need arise. We don't normally disagree about these things.' He was in a bad mood. A case that he was running in the High Court had run into evidential difficulties, and he had spent the morning with a ship's master who turned out to speak very little English.

'It may be of considerable importance,' said Roderick, to the surprise of the others. 'I've already discussed with Michael and Stephen the fact that I do not see how we can afford to take on someone whom solicitors are reluctant to instruct. We all rely on work from below.'

Michael nodded, blowing his nose.

'Come to that,' said Stephen, 'I've already pointed out to you that we can surely afford to carry someone, if that someone happens to be Sir Basil's nephew.'

'Oh, come,' said David, 'it's hardly a question of carrying him. He's not that bad. He'll get better – I'm sure he'll get plenty of work. This set has a reputation, you know.'

'Exactly,' said Roderick.

'There is something in what Roderick says,' said Jeremy suddenly. Michael looked at him; this was support from an unexpected quarter. 'I mean,' Jeremy went on heavily, 'I have watched him. He's not . . . steady.'

'Steady!' exclaimed Cameron. 'What is the relevance of that?

If he has any aptitude, and if he's the right kind of man, I don't see why we should worry about how steady he is. Am I steady?'

No one answered this. Roderick gave a sigh of exasperation. All were rather dismayed by the fact that real differences seemed to exist amongst them. This had not happened before. The whole existence of the chambers was based on a sense of common purpose and shared views. Now a certain dubious tension filled the air.

Sir Basil's footsteps sounded on the stair, and he came in hurriedly, a bundle of papers under his arm. He was in his shirt-sleeves and had his glasses on.

'I apologise for keeping everyone waiting,' he said, looking round with a smile as he made his way to his desk. 'Now,' he said, slipping on his jacket and folding his spectacles into their case. He sat down at his desk, looked down briefly, and then looked up. The smile had gone. 'We are here to discuss – Oh, are we still waiting for Leo? Well, anyway, we may as well commence. We are discussing who is to become the next tenant of these chambers. It was not a matter upon which I had anticipated holding more than the merest formality of a meeting, but,' he went on, 'I understand that there may be certain . . . feelings among some members that a doubt exists. I cannot, myself, comment upon that doubt, but must instead ask those in whose minds it exists to assist the rest of us.'

Sir Basil spoke as kindly and as mildly as he could, but his words could not but betray his displeasure at the fact that the choice of tenant which he had so clearly indicated as his preference, should in any way be disputed. He was not accustomed to dissent in chambers; it made him both unhappy and uneasy. He looked at Michael. Michael decided that the thing had best be put bluntly.

'I think we all realise,' he began in his reedy voice, wishing that he did not have this wretched cold, 'that any disagreement on a matter such as this is very unpleasant. But some of us feel that it is not perhaps in the best interests of chambers that Edward should become the next tenant.' Sir Basil lifted his chin a little, still looking at Michael, but said nothing. Roderick crossed his legs and looked up.

'I must endorse what Michael says, Basil.' There was a silence as Sir Basil glanced at Roderick in surprise. He had not realised that the most senior figure in chambers, next to himself, shared Michael's view. This was not pleasing. At that moment the door opened, and Leo came in. He smiled unhurriedly and took a seat next to Cameron.

'I apologise for being late,' he said. 'Mr Justice Robinson has been taking me to task for not having read my Scrutton thoroughly.' The others smiled, pleased that Leo's relaxing presence was now among them. Sir Basil did not smile.

'We are discussing the relative merits of our two pupils. It seems Roderick feels that perhaps Edward is not quite – '

'No,' interrupted Roderick, trying not to sound heated. 'It is not a question of that. It has nothing to do with that. Anthony Cross is an exceptionally able – even brilliant – young man. I do not feel we can overlook that. I do not feel we can afford to lose him.' That was as much as Roderick intended to say on the matter, and for Michael it was enough.

'Well,' said Sir Basil, sitting back in his chair, 'it seems that there is a stronger division of opinion than I had expected. I had believed that most of us felt that Edward was eminently suited to join us. He has, I think, performed work for some of you besides Jeremy.' Roderick did not look up; he found the business of disagreeing with Basil distressing, and would say no more. 'Leo?'

Sir Basil looked at Leo, who glanced up, flicking a speck of lint from the knee of his trousers. He paused for a long second.

'Yes,' he said. 'I can't see that any of us can have any exception to Edward joining us as the next tenant. He seems perfectly competent and is a very pleasant young man. Of course, Anthony is very talented. I'm sure he will do very well wherever he goes.'

That settled it for David. But Michael glanced at Leo with a frown. Again to Michael's surprise, Jeremy spoke up.

'Roderick has previously made the point – though not, I think, to you, Basil – that it is important for the more senior among us that any new tenant should generate a sufficiency of new work.' He paused. 'Otherwise the thing is pointless.'

'I don't think you can possibly suggest,' said Stephen,

glancing up with a smile, the light glinting on his glasses, 'that anyone's work is likely to dry up. Besides which, solicitors will always continue to instruct anyone that this set of chambers sees fit to take on as a tenant.'

Sir Basil did not like this; it was getting a little too close to the bone. He leaned forward and looked round.

'Well, it is disappointing for us to find that we are not all of one mind on any issue. However,' he went on, 'since those are the circumstances, I do not see that we have any alternative but to vote on the matter.' He smiled. He was not without confidence in the influence of his own views, and he had not needed to express these, merely to make them felt. 'I think it best that we do it by secret ballot,' he said, rummaging in one of his drawers for a counsel's notebook. 'Here we are.' He produced one, tore out a page carefully along the perforations, and folded it and tore it into ten scraps of paper, one of which he dropped into the waste-paper basket. Of the remaining nine, each member of chambers took one; they were embarrassed and vexed at having to reach a decision in this clumsy and unfriendly fashion. It was a thing that had never been done before. When there had been some borrowing of pens and folding up of paper, Sir Basil drew the little pile of papers across the desk towards him. He took out his spectacle case, unfolded his glasses, and put them on. He read out each piece of paper as he unfolded it, and laid it to one side.

'Mr Cross,' he read. 'Mr Choke. Mr Choke. Mr Cross. Mr Cross. Mr Choke. Mr Choke. Mr Cross.' He paused as he opened the last one, and glanced at Michael. 'Mr Choke.' He took off his glasses.

Michael felt heavy with disappointment for Anthony. Still, there it was. The matter was decided. From the discussion, it had been clear that he and Roderick and Jeremy were for Anthony. William must have been the other. He was surprised at Leo – but then, no one could ever predict how Leo's mind would work. He probably hadn't particularly cared about the matter one way or the other, and had simply gone with the old man.

The meeting broke up, everyone relieved that it was over and that Sir Basil's nose had not been put out of joint. They

248

could resume their usual, harmonious relationship and all would go on smoothly as before. Edward would be neither a blessing nor a curse, and young Mr Cross would make his fortune elsewhere.

Michael mounted the stairs with Roderick.

'That's a damned shame,' said Roderick, shaking his head. 'He would have been first class. Still . . .'

'Yes,' said Michael. 'Still.'

They exchanged a smile, and Michael was about to go into his room, when Leo leaned over and called down from the landing above, 'Tell Anthony I've got his cricket kit, would you, Michael? He left it in my car.'

Michael nodded and called back, 'Right, I'll tell him when he comes in.' He went into his room and sat down at his desk, when William put his head round the door.

'By the way, it won't be much consolation to Anthony, but I happened to pass the noticeboard outside the common room in Middle Temple at lunchtime, and he's won that essay prize. Maybe he already knows, but I thought I'd mention it.' William closed the door and went off.

No, thought Michael, it would not be any consolation. There was another knock at the door and, to Michael's surprise, Edward looked in.

'Hello,' said Michael, giving him a smile. 'You've heard, have you? Congratulations.'

'What?' said Edward, looking more than usually uncollected. 'No, what? But listen,' and he came in, closing the door, and sat down in a chair in front of Michael's desk. 'Can I talk to you about something?'

'Anything,' said Michael, sitting back.

'The thing is,' said Edward, 'I can't tell my uncle. I thought if I told you – '

'Told me what?' asked Michael helpfully, as Edward sat looking pained and disordered.

'Well, the thing is, I'm not going to stay on here. I've talked to my father about it. I'm not really cut out for this, y'know. I mean, I'm terrified every time anyone gives me a piece of work. Imagine what I'd be like when I had my own practice!'

There is a divine providence, thought Michael.

'What are you going to do?' he asked, gazing at Edward with gentle speculation.

'Oh, I'm going to go in for farming. I think I can handle that. Help Dad out a bit, you know.' He paused for a moment, looking happier. 'I think he's quite pleased, really. My mother went on a bit, wasting all that training, that kind of thing, but I told her it would be a useful sort of background if I ever wanted to go into politics.'

'Politics?' enquired Michael, slightly dazed.

'My grandfather was MP for round our way, you know. And his father. Sort of runs in the family. The old man isn't really into that sort of thing, but I might give it a go.'

'I see,' said Michael.

'Anyway,' resumed Edward, 'the point is,' and his face became pained again, 'I don't think my uncle is going to be very pleased.'

'It will disappoint him, I imagine,' replied Michael.

'I don't think I want to tell him. Could you – ?'

'No, I don't think that would go down very well,' said Michael. 'I think you'd better see him yourself.' He paused. 'You are very sure about all this?'

'Oh, yes,' said Edward. 'Definitely. I mean, it's been great fun working with you all, but – Anyway, Anthony's much brighter than I am. He'll get on tremendously.'

'I dare say he will.'

'I'd better get it over with,' said Edward, and got up quickly. 'Oh, God.' He stopped at the door. 'Thanks.' And he fled in anxiety.

Michael got up, blew his nose, and walked over to the window. He looked down at the clerks and barristers hurrying about their business in the courtyard below, and smiled to himself, looking forward to telling Anthony his good news. Then he remembered the bet that he had had with Leo as to who would become the next member of chambers. He must go and remind Leo that he owed him ten pounds. Leo would be amused.

If you have enjoyed *The Pupil*
here is a taste of Caro Fraser's
JUDICIAL WHISPERS

Available in Orion Paperback
ISBN: 1 85799 377 2
Price: £5.99

Chapter one

Anthony Cross woke suddenly in the grey half-light of morning and knew that he had been dreaming of Leo. He closed his eyes again quickly, trying to summon back the feeling of safe happiness, of intimacy recaptured, but already his mind was breaking the surface of his dream like a stone left by the tide. He lay nursing his sense of loss for a moment or two, then turned his head upon the pillow to look at the girl sleeping next to him, at her blonde, anonymous head, her hand upon his shoulder. He moved the hand gently away and rose, pulling on his robe, and went through to the bathroom.

There he stared briefly at himself in the mirror, at his own handsome features, slack with sleep, and wondered why he had these dreams. He passed a hand through his dark hair, yawned, and began to run his shaving water. The dreams occurred every few months, like strange, tender echoes. Although each dream left in him a small, hollow pain which he could not fathom, he welcomed them. They took him back in time as though to some forgotten country.

Anthony began to lather his face, remembering the closeness of the hours he and Leo had once spent together, working, talking, sometimes just dawdling time away. He dipped his razor into the water and watched the scum of lather and tiny black bristles float away from the blade. He wondered if Leo ever dreamt of him – and then pushed the thought away as absurd. What might have happened if the affair had not ended before it had even begun? Anthony often wondered this, often wondered what depths there might have been to their unexplored relationship. But now they worked together, side by side, barristers in the same chambers, and there was no hint that such intimacy had ever existed. They met only in the company of others now, and every encounter was hedged with a casual remoteness.

Perhaps, thought Anthony, as he rubbed his face with the towel, the dreams were a kind of compensation. Compensation for loss, the loss of Leo's company, smiles, attention, conversation. Perhaps the pain of losing such a close friendship had not died away in his heart after all; perhaps it was merely buried, so that the recollection of that which he had lost floated to the surface of his subconscious as he slept. Perhaps.

He went through to the kitchen where his flatmate, Adam, was already dressed and gulping down coffee.

'Hi,' he said. 'Want some? I'm off in a sec.'

'Yes, thanks,' said Anthony, and put a slice of bread in the toaster.

'I taped the cricket for you,' said Adam, then added, 'since you and Lizzie seemed to have gone to bed early.' He grinned at Anthony and handed him his coffee.

'Oh, thanks. Yes,' replied Anthony abstractedly, thinking with guilt and boredom of the girl still sleeping in his bed.

Adam studied his face, able to gather what was in Anthony's mind. Another one for the chop, he thought. Adam, with his sandy hair and pale, thin face, thought that if he was tall and good-looking like Anthony, and apparently able to have any girl he wanted, he'd manage to look a bit happier about it. He turned and rinsed his mug out under the tap. 'You in tonight?'

'I think so.' Anthony took his toast from the toaster, and rummaged in the fridge for the butter. 'Then again, I don't know. I never know.'

'Okay. See you later then.'

'Bye,' said Anthony.

He drank his coffee and ate his toast, then went back into his bedroom to dress. He moved about quietly, closing drawers and cupboards gently so as not to wake the girl. He was tying his tie when she woke; she simply opened her eyes and lay gazing at him sleepily. He looked wonderful, she thought, in the dim light, the raised collar of his white shirt framing his lean face, his dark eyes expressionless. He glanced at her, turned down his collar, and bent to fasten his shoelaces. His demeanour had a telling remoteness about it,

2

each movement was made with a brisk finality. But she was not sufficiently awake to read any of the signals.

As he came to the side of the bed to pick up his watch, she stretched out lazy arms to him. 'Do you have to go just yet?' she murmured, and kissed him gently.

'Lizzie,' said Anthony, a note that was almost one of pain in his voice, 'I'm going to be late.'

She merely smiled and drew him towards her again, but there was a stiffness about him, an impatient reserve, that made her drop her arms. She lay back and looked at him as he straightened up and took his jacket from its coathanger. Something in the atmosphere made her feel suddenly like an intruder.

'Will I see you tonight?' she asked. She knew the answer, but still she had to ask.

Anthony hesitated in the doorway. What should he say? 'Lizzie –' he began, then stopped. Say something final, he thought. Tell her. No, there might be tears and awfulness, and he'd be late. He glanced at his watch. 'Lizzie, look – I'm really busy for the next week or so. I don't know. I'll ring you, okay?'

She said nothing, merely lay there, feeling the space between them widen into infinity. Anthony added, 'There's some coffee left in the pot. Help yourself to breakfast.' And he went.

He clattered downstairs and out into the early September sunshine, hating himself. What did you do when the whole thing had become stale and lifeless, when there was no point in going on? Nothing, except let it peter out. Anything was better than tears and scenes. But every relationship seemed to end in this way. Perhaps it all came too easily. Perhaps it was just as well; he didn't want to become serious about anyone again, not after Julia.

In the train in took some papers from his briefcase and tried to concentrate on them, but the dream of Leo hung about him like a scent that clung to the air, imparting itself to everything, distracting him. He could not recall any detail of it, except that Leo had been there and things had been happy. The happiness of dreams, he mused, elusive and wonderful. The best kind of happiness. Am I happy now? wondered Anthony. He supposed he must be. He should be. At twenty-four, he had a new and flourishing barrister's practice in one of the best sets of commercial chambers in the Temple, he shared a decent flat in South Ken with his friend, Adam (which was a bit of an improvement on life in a tiny semi in East Dulwich with his mother and his brother), and he had a good social life, money to spend, girlfriends . . . I must be happy, he thought, and stared sightlessly at the window opposite, wondering why, in that case, he ever stopped to think about it.

The dream was still so present in his mind as he strode swiftly from the tube station through Temple Place that it came as a real shock when he bumped into Leo Davies hurrying up from the Embankment.

'Good God!' said Leo, steadying himself from the slight collison. 'Hello.'

'Hello,' stammered Anthony. 'Sorry. I'm in a bit of a hurry. Got a con at nine and a summons at half ten.'

'My bloody car broke down halfway along the Embankment,' said Leo and sighed, passing a hand over his hair. 'I had to leave it there. Must ring the AA from Chambers.' Although he was only forty-four, his hair was silver, lending his gaunt good looks a maturity they would not otherwise possess, for his smile was brilliant, boyish, and his blue eyes candid and restless. He was of Anthony's height, but more squarely built, and was expensively dressed, almost to the point of dandyism.

They fell into step together as they made their way to chambers. There was an uneasy silence between them. They were not accustomed to being alone in one another's company, these days.

Anthony muttered something inconsequential about a recent House of Lords judgment and Leo uttered some words in reply. He glanced at Anthony, feeling in his heart the faint pleasure he always felt when looking at the young man. Then he made some remark about his car and Anthony laughed. Leo loved to see him laugh. It's absurd, he thought, that we hardly ever speak to one another these days. Ridiculous. That business was all finished a long time ago. None of it mattered any more.

4

'Look,' said Leo, stopping at the foot of the steps to 5 Caper Court, 'what about a game of squash this evening? Ring up the club and see if they have a court free. Yes?'

Anthony was startled. Leo had not invited Anthony to spend time with him since the day he had got his tenancy.

'Yes.' he replied hesitantly. 'All right.' They went upstairs together. Anthony's room was on the first landing, Leo's on the second. Anthony paused at his door. 'I'll see you later, then.' And he smiled at Leo, his happiness so evident that the older man was touched, first with pleasure, then with a slight misgiving.

'Six thirty,' said Leo. 'Try to get a court around then.' And he passed on up the stairs to his room.

At six fifteen Leo was sitting at his desk itself was of pale ash, it, surface devoid of any other object save the document. All the furniture was of the same pale wood, quite unlike the old, dark, comfortable furniture favoured by most other barristers. No cosy Dickensian shades hung around Leo's room. All was austere, clinical. There was no friendly muddle of papers and briefs lining the shelves and windowsills; everything was neatly tidied away behind the doors of expensive, functionalist cupboards. Even the pictures that hung upon the wall were anodyne modern abstracts, and not the usual charcoal sketches of the law courts, framed watercolours of ships or landscapes, that hung in the rooms of other members of chambers. It all seemed of a piece with the man himself – one of them, yet set apart from them in unusual ways.

Leo was one of the most exceptional advocates in the Temple, with a mercurial personality and a ready wit, and was popular in chambers. Life always seemed to lighten up when Leo was around. He was charming, amusing, and although he moved within the well-defined codes of the Bar with deference and circumspection, there was a certain unconventionality about him; he was an elusive man, and few knew anything of his life outside work.

As he sat studying the document, all his customary energy and restless habit of movement seemed concentrated and contained. The evening light that fell through the window glinted on his hair, and the angular shadows beneath his brow and cheekbones lent his face a brooding, hawklike quality.

The document was headed 'Lord Chancellor's Department. Application for Appointment as Queen's Counsel'. Beneath the word 'Title' were five little boxes, mared 'Mr,' 'Mrs', 'Miss', 'Ms' and, slightly larger than the rest, 'Other'. Leo sighed and passed his hand over his head. 'Other'. That about sums me up, he thought.

He rubbed his hands over his eyes. At forty-four, he supposed it was about time that he did this. It was part of the plan, the next step up the golden ladder. There was almost an inevitability about taking silk which bored him. He would achieve this just as he had achieved everything else – his successful practice, his cars, his clubs, his houses in Mayfair and Oxfordshire, his polished circle of social acquaintances. All a long way from the Welsh mining village of his childhood, where he had struggled to free himself from his beginnings and to create a new identity. This would be part of that identity, part of the image which he had cultivated as assiduously as his own charm and urbanity. Leo Davies, QC. Another stitch in that tapestry of his life, the one behind which he could conceal himself from the rest of the world.

He sat flipping through the pages of the form, wondering how long it would take for his income to climb to six figures, once he had taken silk, when there was a knock at his door and Anthony came in.

'Hello,' said Leo, glancing up.

'Hi. Squash courts are all booked up, I'm afraid. They've got some competition ladder, or something, I don't know.'

'Pity,' said Leo. 'I could have done with a game. I'm right out of condition.' His voice still held an attractive Welsh cadence. He leaned back and flexed his arms above his head, studying Anthony. The young man's face was leaner now, and without any of the softness which had caused Leo to fall in love with him some eighteen months before. Nearly two years. It seemed like a lifetime ago. Well, thought Leo, that had all ended as soon as it had begun. They were friends now, colleagues, no need to let the slightest shadow of it hang between them. They never alluded now to anything in the past, and Leo had hidden away any lingering traces of his former love as easily and effectively as he hid so much from himself and others.

'What's this?' asked Anthony, coming over to the desk and squinting down at the paper. Leo was about to pull the document away and fold it up, but stopped. Why shouldn't Anthony know?

'Application to take silk,' he replied, and leaned back again. 'Have a look, if you like,' he added, and Anthony picked the paper up and flipped through it curiously.

'Listen to this,' said Anthony, smiling; he read aloud: "Have you ever had an action brought against you in respect of another matter involving you personally, or under your supervision, for professional negligence? Have you ever been subject ot the disciplinary process of the Bar without the matter having been dismissed? Have you ever been adjudged bankrupt, made a composition with your creditors, or been sued to judgment for any debt?" ' He looked up at Leo and laughed.

'Well quite,' replied Leo, dryly. 'Instead of "yes" and "no" boxes, they should put one marked "no" and the other marked "forget your application, in that case".' He took the document from Anthony, folded it up and put it into his breast pocket. 'Well, if we can't have a game of squash, a vigorous drink seems like the next best thing.'

They made their way downstairs and out into Caper Court, where a light drizzle had begun to fall; the flush of golden light at the end of the September day was beginning to be eclipsed by banks of grey cloud. They ran through the cloisters and over King's Bench Walk, out into the back alleys of Fleet Street. Leo paused in the doorway of the pub before going in and tapped his breast pocket lightly.

'I'd rather you didn't mention this to anyone. The silk thing, I mean.'

Anthony gazed at him and raised a hand to brush away the surface drops of rain from his dark hair. He nodded. 'Of course. But why did you let *me* know?'

Leo looked back at him candidly. All that ground was too well trodden. Anyway, he didn't really know himself.

Something to do with the slender thread of once-shared intimacy which he liked to feel still bound him to this young man, however loosely. He wanted Anthony to know things, wanted to share whatever hopes and disappointments there might be. But he could not acknowledge this.

'Probably,' he replied, 'because you happened to come into my room when I was reading the bloody thing. I was never a good dissembler.' No, never. At that moment someone brushed between them and went into the pub. 'Come on,' said Leo, and Anthony followed him in.

He was pleased to be alone with Leo once more. Tonight's invitation to a game of squash had seemed to him like a return to old times; perhaps the defences were coming down, and he could enjoy Leo's solitary company as he had once done. It struck him as strange and propitious that he should have dreamt of Leo that very morning. For these reasons, he was conscious of a vague disappointment when he saw Stephen Bishop, a fellow member of chambers, sitting alone at a table with a pint of beer and the *Financial Times*. He looked pleased to see Leo and Anthony, and folded up his paper.

'What will you have?' he asked them.

'Large Scotch, please, Stephen, since I happen to know you can afford it,' replied Leo, settling himself into a chair. 'William told me this afternoon about your disgustingly fat fee for that Harvey case.'

Stephen smiled and took his glasses off to polish them with a large handkerchief. 'Yes, well, you know, some of us are just born to greatness. But I have to admit it's nice to get the odd moneyspinner.' Stephen was a portly, cheerful man with an easy manner and a mild nature. His practice was steady but unremarkable, and he never let it interfere with the harmony of his life at home with his wife and four children. He was liked and respected at the Commercial Bar, but he never brought to his cases the energy and dedication that Leo did. Safe, but unexciting, was the verdict on Stephen. He put his glasses back on and turned to Anthony. 'What about you, Anthony?'

'Just a small Scotch, please,' said Anthony. 'I still have some papers to look at tonight.'

Stephen fetched the drinks and sat back down.

'So,' he said, 'how's the day been?' He glanced at Leo. 'Still plugging away at that supply contract dispute?'

Leo yawned and rubbed his jaw with his hand. 'Yes, unfortunately. But, surprise, surprise, Stott has to go off and sit on some judicial enquiry for the next four days, so it's been adjourned till next week. Since I don't have anything else in particular to occupy me, I think I'll absent myself from chambers for a few days.'

Anthony felt a little pang. It was absurd, he knew, but he liked to know that Leo was around, liked to hear him whistling on the stairs, to catch an occasional glimpse of him at tea or in the clerks' room. When Leo was away, life for Anthony, even though he was remarkably busy himself, became a little bit emptier. Leo just had that kind of personality, that was all.

'What will you do?' he asked Leo, and took a sip of his Scotch.

'Oh, go down to the country, I think, drink in the last of the summer in peace.' He thought briefly of his house in Oxfordshire, and of its present occupants. 'Relative peace,' he added thoughtfully. Without looking up he could feel Anthony's eyes on him, knew that he was wondering who would be there with him. Was he jealous? Well, thought Leo roughly, knocking back the remains of his drink in one, it didn't matter to either of them if he was. That was all water under the bridge. And why was he even thinking like this? It had been a mistake to ask him for that game of squash this evening. It just made life more complicated.

'I wish I had somewhere worth retreating to,' observed Anthony. 'I mean, somewhere like your place,' he added awkwardly. 'If ever I get anything adjourned, there's always another piece of work to plod on with.'

'Oh, what it is to be young and thrusting and ever so popular with solicitors,' laughed Leo. 'I remember being like that – don't you, Stephen? Never turning work down, working all the hours God gave, buttering up your clerk, trying to cultivate a worldly image.'

Anthony smiled, and Leo was charmed to see him colour faintly.

'Yes,' observed Stephen dryly, 'I understand that we're *particularly* popular with lady solicitors.'

'Oh, balls,' said Anthony. 'Anyway, no doubt it's all very well when you're middle-aged and established and don't have to keep chasing fee notes.'

'Less of the middle-aged,' said Leo. 'I feel quite coltish as I sit there in number five court, listening to Marcus Field enlightening us all on the official policy of the Government of Qatar towards brokerage commissions. Thank God I'm off the hook till next Monday.'

Stephen drained his glass and shook his head. 'I'm glad I'm not Anthony's age any more. Too much cut-and-thrust . . . You have to be so energetic, so determined. Exhausting, just to think of it.'

'Not thinking of retiring, are you, Stephen?' asked Leo jokingly, crushing out the butt of his cigar.

Stephen smiled. 'The fees at Marlborough won't permit it, I'm afraid. Got to keep slogging away. Anyway, see you chaps tomorrow. I'd better be making a move.' He rose and picked up his newspaper. 'Goodnight.'

When Stephen had gone, Leo sat in silence with Anthony for a few seconds, then picked up his empty glass. 'Another?' he asked Anthony.

Anthony hesitated. He felt tired. He had an interlocutory application in the morning and he hadn't even looked at the papers yet. But he wanted to stay. He glanced up and smiled. 'Yes. Okay, another, thanks.'

Leo brought the drinks and sat back down. Anthony looked on idly as Leo lit another little cigar, watching the lean, fine hands he had always found so fascinating. He enjoyed watching Leo, enjoyed his restless, elegant movements, the way he turned his head, the way the side of his mouth jerked when he made a joke. His mind strayed back to Leo's remark as they had entered the pub earlier and he asked, 'Isn't Stephen senior to you in chambers?'

'Yes. He joined two years before I did. Sixty-two.' Leo blew out a little smoke and looked at Anthony. 'Why?'

Anthony looked uncomfortable and turned his whisky glass

between finger and thumb. 'Isn't it . . . I mean, wouldn't you expect him to take silk first, or something?'

Or something. Still with that charmingly juvenile sloppiness of speech when embarrassed, thought Leo. He looked levelly at Anthony. 'In the normal course of events, yes.' He paused and leaned back. 'But one can't wait around for ever for Stephen to dither his way through life. He should have applied two years ago, if he was going to go for it.' Leo stroked the glowing edge of his cigar against the rim of the ashtray. 'Maybe he did. Maybe he was turned down. All I know is, one has to be loyal to oneself, not to the other members of chambers.'

'But don't you owe the rest something? I mean, we are all one set of chambers.'

'There is something you have to learn, Anthony,' replied Leo, and his voice was hard, the blue of his gaze quite cold. 'And that is, that you must put yourself first. Every time. Look.' He leaned forward. 'I've run every case for the past two years without a leader. And won most of them. The time is right for me. I'd be a fool to pass it up this year. I don't care what Stephen does or doesn't do.'

Anthony thought for a moment. 'But what effect will it have on Stephen's career if you're successful? Could he still take silk?'

Leo looked carelessly away. 'Probably not.' He drew on his cigar. 'Almost certainly not. If it were to happen, once could take it that the Lord Chancellor's Office had assumed that he wasn't going to apply – or that they were sending out a signal that he wouldn't get it if he did apply. Either way, the writing would be on the wall.' He did not look at Anthony as he spoke. 'Besides,' he added, 'even if he did apply next year, there wouldn't be enough work to justify another silk in chambers. There would be Sir Basil, Cameron, Roderick, Michael – and myself.'

You're so confident, thought Anthony. But of course you are. Why shouldn't you be?

He nodded and said, 'So that would be it – for Stephen, I mean?'

'Well, I suppose so,' replied Leo. 'Otherwise we'd be top-heavy. We might be, in any event. Unless Sir Basil retires.'

11

'That's not likely, is it?' asked Anthony in surprise. Sir Basil Bunting, the head of chambers, was, admittedly, in his sixties, but he seemed to be riding with magnificent serenity on top of a lucrative and immensely successful practice.

Leo smoked in silence for a few moments. This was something he had thought about. Poor old Stephen was one thing – well, he had had his chance and not taken it. Why should Leo care? Considerations of Stephen were easily dismissed. One was loyal to oneself. Sir Basil was a different kettle of fish. Leo knew that Sir Basil's practice wasn't quite as flourishing as Sir Basil liked to make it appear. Clients nowadays liked younger men – they liked people on their own wavelength. Solicitors were the same, too, and God knows they seemed to be getting younger by the minute. If Leo took silk, he was confident of mopping up a good deal of work from the juniors in chambers. Sir Basil could be squeezed out. And that, thought Leo, might be no bad thing.

Just when Anthony was beginning to think that Leo hadn't heard what he had said, Leo turned to him and flashed a wicked, attractive smile. 'You never know what pressure might be brought to bear on Sir Basil,' he murmured. 'We might just have to hope that the Lord Chancellor wants another High Court judge.'

Anthony drew in his breath and stared at Leo. Will I ever become as ruthless? he wondered. Leo glanced briefly back at him and wondered the same thing. He had detected a slight toughening in Anthony over the past year or so. That touchingly tender aspect of his character seemed to be rubbing away, as the work poured steadily in and the money increased. Or was that just a physical illusion, something to do with the fact that Anthony's face was older, less boyish, that he wore decent suits and shirts now, that he was more confident – even a little arrogant – as his practice grew more successful?

'Don't worry,' he said, and drained his glass. 'It's not as bad as it sounds. And don't feel too sorry for Stephen – he's doing very nicely. Anyway, you never know – maybe he's applying for silk this year, too.'

And we know which of you is more likely to get it, if that's the case, thought Anthony. One way or the other, Stephen was the loser, and Leo, it seemed, couldn't care less.

'Want a lift anywhere?' asked Leo as they left the pub. 'The AA seem to have remedied its little defect.'

'No, thanks,' replied Anthony. 'I'm going back to chambers. My papers are still there.'

Leo nodded, and the two men said goodnight and went their separate ways.

In the kitchen of Leo's Oxfordshire house, a young, blonde-haired woman was carefully laying sheets of pasta on the bottom of an oblong dish.

'It's not a problem for me,' she remarked over her shoulder to the boy who stood looking out of the window, arms folded, at the dusk falling on the rainy garden. 'I go back to Oxford in a month's time. It's just been another episode in my life.' She paused briefly to gaze at her handiwork before moving back to the stove to stir a white sauce. 'I like to think of my life as a series of episodes. Nothing final. Nothing static.'

The boy turned to look at her. Like her, he was blond, but taller, and his face wore a sullen, dissatisfied expression. The girl's face was airily serene as she moved about her tasks.

'Don't give me that. You love him.'

'Oh, of course I do!' she turned in smiling astonishment. 'He's divine, an utterly divine man. I love him to death. He's the most wonderful fuck, and he doesn't care in the least for me – that's why he's so attractive.' She turned back to her work, still smiling. Then she added, 'He doesn't care for either of us. We're just a – summer dalliance, you might say.'

The boy turned to look back out of the window. 'At least you've got something to go to. What have I got when it's over?'

'Oh, get a job, James.'

'That's a laugh.' He picked up a knife from the draining board and fiddled with it, running his thumb along the blade. 'Anyway, I don't want a job. I want to stay here.' His voice took on a plaintive, childish tone. 'God, Sarah, I really don't want to have to go.'

'You're just insecure,' remarked Sarah. 'Pass me that grated cheese, would you?'

'So what do I do? Go back to being a photographer's assistant? Let him drop me just where he picked me up? No thanks. He owes us something, doesn't he?'

Sarah flicked her hair back from her shoulders and licked at the finger she had just dipped in the sauce. 'Not a thing. Not me, at any rate. After all, he's paying us for being here – for being his . . .' She paused and laughed, then sighed. 'His companions. He's fun. He's amusing. This was just a holiday job – I told you. My parents think I'm working as a cook for someone.'

'Well, you are.' James's voice was sulky, bored.

'That's all they know.' She began layering mince and pasta together. 'Put it down to experience, James.'

He said nothing, and she turned to look at him. Seeing the forlorn expression on his face, she came across and put her arms gently on his shoulders. 'Come on, cheer up. We've had a good time, had a laugh, haven't we? Anyway, it's not over yet.' She gave the tip of his nose a soft, pecking kiss.

'That's not the way you kiss me when we're in bed with him,' said James, staring into her eyes.

She smiled back. 'No – but that's work, isn't it?' She watched his troubled face and her smile faded. 'Oh, James, what is it you want? Why can't you just make the most of it, and be happy?'

'Because it's different for you, Sarah! Your family have got money. You've got something to fall back on. What have I got? You'll just swan off back to Oxford and forget about all this –'

'Well, I wouldn't say that.'

He ignored the interruption. ' – while I'm just sort of – thrust aside!'

'Well, face it.' She took her arms from his shoulders and went back to the dish of lasagne. 'He doesn't need you. You can see the kind of man he is. We're just a little diversion in his life. Nothing special. He doesn't want anyone to come too close. There's nothing you can do about that. Anyway, let's change the subject. What do you want to do tonight? Pub?'

'That's just about all there is to do, isn't there?' said James angrily. 'He leaves us stuck here in this hole from one weekend to the next, expecting us to stick to his stupid rules,

14

and be all bright and cheerful and eager to please when he turns up on a Friday night! I'm fed up with it. He's not the only piece of excitement around here, whatever he thinks.' James rammed his hands into his jeans pockets. 'I met this bloke when we were in Ryecot. I'm going to ask him back.' His voice was dogged.

'Don't be a berk, James. You know what Leo said.' Sarah began to pour the cheese sauce carefully over the last layer.

'What's the point of having a place like this for the whole week if we can't share it with a friend or two? I need a bit of company.'

'Thanks. What about me?'

'Well, like you said, that's just work, isn't it?' He looked at his watch. 'I'm going to ring that bloke now.'

'Fun for me,' murmured Sarah. 'I'd better see what's on telly tonight.'

'If you're very good,' said James as he left the kitchen, 'we might let you watch.'

'Ha, ha,' said Sarah to herself, as she stared admiringly at her lasagne.

She was watching the late-night film when she heard Leo's car pull up in the driveway, the beam of its headlights brushing the curtained windows with a faint arc of light. She thought of James upstairs in bed with his friend. Leo's bed. She knew she had at least thirty seconds in which to call up to them, warn them, and that James might just, possibly, be able to get him out through an upstairs window in time. She couldn't be bothered. She heard the car door slam, then his feet on the gravel, and snuggled a little lower in her armchair. She was fed up with James, anyway. Always whining round the place. And with him out of the way, who could say how things might develop? Maybe she could make her position that little bit stronger. A man like that. Life would become divinely simple. She'd never wanted to settle down, but if it could be someone like Leo . . . Some hope, she told herself, and smiled wryly at the television screen as Leo opened the front door.

'Hello,' he said, as he came into the room.

'Hello,' she replied, and smiled winningly, briefly, at him

15

round the side of the armchair. Then she stared at the television again. Her heart was thudding a little at the thought of Leo finding James. 'A midweek surprise,' she murmured. 'Just as well I made some lasagne this afternoon. I was going to put it in the freezer for Saturday.'

'Good.' Leo rubbed his face and gazed blankly for a few seconds at the television screen. 'I need a drink. No – I think I'll go upstairs and change first.'

'That's a good idea,' said Sarah. 'I'll fix you a drink while you're up there. You'll need it,' she added under her breath.

It was difficult to concentrate on the film with doors banging and voices shouting and feet thumping on the stairs, but at last they died away. She heard the front door close. Leo came into the room.

'I've poured us both a drink,' she said. 'Yours is over there.'

Leo picked it up. 'James is packing,' he said. He crossed the room and switched off the television, then turned with a sigh to Sarah. 'I'm afraid,' he added, 'that you're next.'

She smiled the impudent, tantalizing smile that he had always liked. 'Oh, well. All goods things come to an end.' She raised her glass. 'Cheers, anyway.' She took a sip. 'Can I at least stay tonight?'

Leo pushed back a stray lock of grey hair, then tugged his tie loose. He sighed, the anger gradually dying away. That bloody boy. He had known it was a mistake to let it all go on this long. It should have ended ages ago.

Sarah put down her glass and rose, moving forward to embrace him, pressing her body gently against his. 'After all,' she said softly, 'two's company. And three *was* a bit of a crowd . . .' She kissed him, parting his lips gently with her tongue. As he put his arms round her waist she felt some drops from his glass of whisky fall on the back of her skirt. His hand was shaking. She knew that his anger at the discovery upstairs had left a little legacy of excitement. Weird old Leo.

'All right,' he replied. 'Just for tonight.' He had always preferred her to James, anyway. She was far more inventive. He would be sorry to see her go, in a way. 'You go first thing in the morning,' he added, more firmly.

'First thing,' she agreed. Probably just as well, really. She had enough saved for a couple of weeks in Cyprus with Alicia. And there was always tonight. 'First thing,' she repeated with a smile, before he closed his eyes to kiss her properly.

All Orion/Phoenix titles are available at your local bookshop or from the following address:

Littlehampton Book Services
Cash Sales Department L
14 Eldon Way, Lineside Industrial Estate
Littlehampton
West Sussex BN17 7HE
telephone 01903 721596, *facsimile* 01903 730914

Payment can either be made by credit card (Visa and Mastercard accepted) or by sending a cheque or postal order made payable to *Littlehampton Book Services*.
DO NOT SEND CASH OR CURRENCY.

Please add the following to cover postage and packing

UK and BFPO:
£1.50 for the first book, and 50P for each additional book to a maximum of £3.50

Overseas and Eire:
£2.50 for the first book plus £1.00 for the second book and 50p for each additional book ordered

----

BLOCK CAPITALS PLEASE

name of cardholder ....   *delivery address*
                      ....   *(if different from cardholder)*
address of cardholder ....
....
....
....
          postcode ....   *postcode* ....

☐ I enclose my remittance for £...........................

☐ please debit my Mastercard/Visa (delete as appropriate)

card number ☐☐☐☐☐☐☐☐☐☐☐☐☐☐☐☐

expiry date ☐☐☐☐

signature ....

prices and availability are subject to change without notice